Born in Donegal, Ireland, of a Devonshire family long settled in that part, Joyce Cary was given for first name, according to a common Anglo-Irish practice, his mother's surname of Joyce. He was educated at Clifton and Trinity, Oxford, and he also studied art in Edinburgh and Paris. Afterwards he went to the Near East for the war of 1912–13.

Subsequently he studied Irish Cooperation under Sir Horace Plunkett, and in 1913 joined the Nigerian Political Service. He fought in the Nigerian Regiment during the First World War and was wounded at Mora Mountain. On returning to political duty, as magistrate and executive officer, he was sent to Borgu, then a very remote district. His health, however, had never recovered from war service and he was advised to retire from tropical Africa. He then began to write, and his first novel, *Aissa Saved*, was published in 1932. *Herself Surprised*, the first volume of his trilogy *Triptych* (Penguin, 1985), was published in 1941, and was followed by *To be a Pilgrim* in 1942 and *The Horse's Mouth* in 1944. His other work includes *A Fearful Joy*, *Mister Johnson*, the trilogy comprising *A Prisoner of Grace*, *Except the Lord* and *Not Honour More*, *A Spring Song and Other Stories* and *A House of Children* which was awarded the James Tait Black Memorial Prize in 1942 and is partly autobiographical.

Joyce Cary died in March 1957.

JOYCE CARY

THE CAPTIVE AND
THE FREE

PENGUIN BOOKS
IN ASSOCIATION WITH
MICHAEL JOSEPH

Penguin Books Ltd, Harmondsworth, Middlesex, England
Viking Penguin Inc., 40 West 23rd Street, New York, New York 10010, U.S.A.
Penguin Books Australia Ltd, Ringwood, Victoria, Australia
Penguin Books Canada Ltd, 2801 John Street, Markham, Ontario, Canada L3R 1B4
Penguin Books (N.Z.) Ltd, 182–190 Wairau Road, Auckland 10, New Zealand

First published by Michael Joseph 1959
Published in Penguin Books 1963
Reprinted 1985

Printed and bound in Great Britain by
Cox & Wyman Ltd, Reading
Set in Monotype Plantin

INTRODUCTION

BY DAVID CECIL

I VISITED Joyce Cary regularly during the tragic and heroic days of his last illness. Every time I went he was visibly worse; his fine aquiline head showed sharper and more wasted, and the dreadful paralysis had extended itself till, towards the end, he had become nearly immobile. But his glance remained keen and concentrated; and the flame of his spirit was still burning, kept alight by his sheer will to win the race he was running against death in order to finish his book.

Here is the book. It bears the mark of the extraordinary conditions in which it was written. Though Cary managed to tell his tale to the end, we are aware that he has not succeeded in evolving the final form in which to present it. There was no time for the successive and drastic revisions involving cutting and expansion on an extensive scale, to which he liked to subject his books, and of which Mrs Davin speaks in her prefatory note. Indeed, that its form appears as finished as it does is largely due to her skilful editing, which was guided by her intimate understanding both of Cary's intentions and his method of work. But signs of incompleteness remain. Some strands in the story, the marriage of Joanna and Hooper for instance, surely need further development; and the end of the book is a little indeterminate and confused. The last chapter, in particular, fails to convey the necessary sense of finality. Threads are left hanging, we long to know more as to what the future of the main characters is likely to be. The ultimate impression is a little too much like that of a piece of music of which the theme has not been fully resolved.

Yet *The Captive and the Free* is one of Cary's most important and memorable books. Like most of his works, it is the consequence of a double inspiration. On the one hand he was stimulated to write by a general theme. He wished to tell a story which embodied his sense of some important aspect of human experience. But he was also stirred to write – more instinctively and unconsciously – by his absorbed and delighted interest in the working of human nature and especially in its extreme and eccentric manifestations. His main characters are generally oddities and outcasts, inspired it may be by some divine fire, but freakish, cranky, often shady and at odds with the conventional world: Gulley the lawless artist, Nimmo the political adventurer.

The two strains in his inspiration fuse together. He designs each freak and crank especially to illuminate the particular phase of human experience which happens to be his theme. Gully illustrates Cary's view of the artist's nature, Nimmo his view of the politician's, and so on. Their stories also convey much of his ideas on art and politics in general. In all this he resembles Browning, who also created grotesque and eccentric characters as a medium through which to express his general judgements on life. Cary, like Browning, did this partly because he enjoyed the comic spectacle of truth uttering itself through a grotesque mask; but more because such a spectacle vividly illustrated his sense of the spiritual kinship of all men. As he saw it, the rogue and the freak were just as likely to have an insight into truth as were the correct and the respectable.

All this is true of *The Captive and the Free*. Here the subject is religion. Preedy, the main character, is a faith healer who runs a shabby little tabernacle in London. The respectable churches look askance at him as a charlatan and man of bad character, who had been converted as a result of seducing a girl of fourteen with whom he still has intermittent relations. But in fact his whole life is dominated by a pure intuitional faith in God, which never fails him whatever his failures or misfortunes. Contrasted with him is Syson, an Anglican clergyman who believes Preedy to be a fraud. His efforts to expose him lead him to search into his own beliefs more deeply than ever before, with the result that he loses his orthodox faith and breaks with the Church. At the end he is left believing simply in the existence of a divine beneficent spirit which it is man's duty to worship. Both these are free spirits boldly following the call of their hearts and souls without reference to other people's opinion. So also is Alice, the girl in Preedy's life. The rest are in some degree what Cary calls captives: people who, for good or bad reasons, feel themselves compelled to accept standards and religious views inherited or imposed on them by society. But captive and free alike are conceived primarily in their relation to religious truth. Everyone, consciously or not, is represented as seeking salvation.

6

Cary presents his scene with an impersonal justice that leaves his own attitude enigmatic. There is no doubt he thinks that Preedy's religion is the real thing; but whether or not his successful miracles are explicable on rational grounds, Cary does not tell us. Syson's faith has not the pure intensity of Preedy's, and he is wrong in thinking Preedy a fraud. But he is the more virtuous and intelligent man of the two, and his own final views are stated with sympathy.

In fact – though he is vigilantly careful to give no hints of this in the book – they are close to Cary's own. Cary was a profoundly religious spirit of that intensely individual and protestant kind which cannot find fulfilment in any corporate body; he had to carve out his creed by himself and for himself. Brought up as an orthodox Anglican, he lost all religious faith in early manhood to find a new one in mature life. It was not orthodox; it was not Christian in any substantial sense. Cary did not identify God with Christ or with any kind of personal spirit. But experience had convinced him that man's apprehension of beauty and of human love was inexplicable on any purely rational or materialist terms. It was proof of some transcendental spiritual reality with which a man must relate harmoniously if he is to find satisfaction. He did not hold this as a mere pious opinion. It burned within him, an intuitive conviction as strong as that of Preedy, strengthening his spirit and directing his actions. To be often in his company was to be aware of its presence. This strong faith was what enabled him at the end against appalling odds to win his tragic race with death.

EDITORIAL NOTE

JOYCE CARY wrote this novel during the last three years of his life, but died before he had finished work on it. It was of the utmost importance to him – he had twice before attempted to write a novel with this title and this theme. When he realized that he had not more than a year to live, he said, 'It will break my heart if I don't finish this.' One day, five months before his death, I found him radiant; 'The novel's in the bag.' For two months more he worked on at it. Then his health failed so rapidly that he began to despair of completing it. In January, 1957, he decided that he would not live long enough to finish both the novel and *Art and Reality*. Knowing that there was less to be done on the latter, he turned to that. For him, as he said of Beethoven, 'every moment of existence was precious for achievement.' He continued to work until 16 March, a fortnight before his death, but with ever increasing difficulty.

After his death I undertook with diffidence to edit the novel, encouraged only by the invaluable help of his secretary, Miss Edith Millen, by my practical knowledge of his working method and by the memory of his generous confidence in me. He had asked me months before to read the novel for him when it was ready, and had discussed with me the things to look out for. I think that even he did not know how nearly finished the novel was. Since the 'emotional continuity' of a novel was of far greater importance to him than its events, in the early drafts he was not careful about factual consistency, confident that his astounding inventiveness would enable him to change details of the plot where necessary. And, as he did not work from beginning to end of a novel but developed themes or characters at any point, the parts did not always 'fit'. He has described something of his method in *The Way a Novel Gets Written*.*

'A finished book of mine starts usually perhaps ten years before as a character sketch and a bit of description; it goes on to an incident or so, it gathers subsidiary characters, and then perhaps I grow interested in it, and set out to give it form as a book. I sketch a plan; I may write the end, the middle, and the beginning, and very often just in this order. That is, I decide how and where the book shall end, which is just as important to a book as a play; and then I ask myself where are the most difficult turns in the book. Then I may write one of these

* *Harper's*, CC, February, 1950; *Adam International Review*, November, 1950.

difficult passages to see if it is viable. And if, as often happens, it does not work, I may stop there. But if it does work, then I may devise a beginning and finish the book.

'But the chief problem still remains, which is to decide what I shall express in the book. All my books suffer large cuts, even in the last draft. This is largely because they are all statements about a single reality, in which every part is related to every other part.'

I may say here that I believe that in a final revision he would have made some cuts, he would have written two more scenes where there are obvious gaps, and he would have strengthened the bond between the beginning and the end – for this novel begins where it ends.

Such tasks were beyond me and outside my brief as editor. I have interpolated in square brackets the facts the narrative demands, at the two points where the gaps I refer to remain. I have removed incongruities and altered factual inconsistencies. I have cut sections which, I concluded, when I knew the novel well, had belonged to earlier drafts. The chronology offered many difficulties, and I am aware that I have not solved them all. I ask the reader's indulgence for what I have failed to do, and for what I have done I appeal to Joyce Cary, who said in *Art and Reality*:

'When the reader, checked by some inconsistency, stops to examine it, he is usually obliged to re-read the passage, in a conscious critical spirit, in order to find out exactly what has broken the spell ... This check is felt even if the failure is not at all in the continuity of feeling but merely in some matter of fact, if the writer has made roses bloom in April or sent his hero hunting in June, or merely forgotten the colour of his heroine's eyes.'

Oxford, 1958   WINIFRED DAVIN

I

THE Rev. Mr Syson, having been sentenced to six months in jail, had his eye cut by a broken bottle as they tried to smuggle him out of court by a back way.

The crowd, mostly nice people, had been gratified to hear from Syson's counsel, in pleading for a light sentence, that the man was entirely ruined, that his wife had left him, with her children, and was suing for divorce. What had enraged them was to see his demeanour as the police brought him down the steps at the back of the court. He was smiling in the most cheerful manner. It was obvious, as one angry young woman remarked, that he didn't give a damn – and so they were enraged. And some true believer threw the bottle.

The papers gave only the smallest space to this incident. What was called the Pant's Road case was not news any more. And the public was left with the impression that the man was a bad-tempered brute full of spite and hatred; a hypocrite, a liar and a good deal of a time server too; and they were not going to forget it.

This seemed to some of his former parishioners a fearful injustice because there was something to be said for the poor devil. He had had bad luck. It must be admitted that he was, as the judge remarked, a hasty man. But he did not mean to cause trouble at Pant's Road, far from it, he was very anxious not to cause trouble.

2

Two years before this, while Syson was still the curate of St Enoch's, he had been awaiting his appointment as vicar to the very nice country parish of Shillow, at a very nice stipend, and at that time he had particularly wanted to avoid upsetting the bishop. If he did not know that both the vicar and the bishop thought him more suited for a country living than for the difficult situation at St Enoch's, he had some inkling of it, and his wife understood it very well. Syson was not a good-tempered man, but he had common sense, he was devoted to his wife and knew how hard she found life on a curate's pay, and he did not mean to lose Shillow.

He had had some small trouble already; for instance, at his first arrival, very keen and full of ideas, he had tried visiting the pubs, playing the parson of the people. But this had resulted in a rather awkward fracas with a communist. Syson had received a bloody nose and given the man a black eye. He had had much sympathy in the parish, and luckily there was no summons. But the vicar, who had advised against pubs in the first place, had been much put out. In fact, Syson was leaning over backwards to avoid more trouble in the parish – it was entirely against his will that he got drawn in again.

The first thing the parish knew about it was a paragraph in the *Morning Argus* about some marvellous cures at the Pant's Road Mission of Faith and Regeneration, which had already been operating for a year actually within two hundred yards of St Enoch's Church, under the Rev. Walter Preedy.

Preedy was not at all well known then, but he had been very successful at the Mission, and he had caused much trouble in the parish. The churchgoers did not like to see the enormous notice outside his chapel, 'Do you Believe in Almighty God or don't you? We do not Split Hairs, We give the Word that Saves.' A lot of St Enoch's people went over to Preedy. However, the vicar, a highly experienced man, advised patience and refused to take part in discussion groups by Pant's Road Mission enthusiasts.

Then the *Argus* gave Preedy this boost, and printed this note, 'The local church authorities are standing aloof from Mr Preedy's work. The Rev. Mr Syson of St Enoch's has actually forbidden parishioners to attend his services.'

This was an exaggeration – Syson, of course, was only the curate and had no power to give orders in the parish. What had happened was that he had backed up one of the parishioners in forbidding his son, an hysterical youth of sixteen, to go to the Mission, and the son had complained to Preedy. Preedy then told the *Argus* reporter that St Enoch's was banning him.

The vicar, naturally anxious to avoid a direct quarrel with the Mission on such a ground, wrote a denial which was not printed. This was not because the *Argus* was trying to cover a mistake but simply because the directors were not agreed about boosting the Mission.

The vicar was all the more annoyed. He had reason to be, for Preedy had seized his chance and was already putting up bills all over the parish inviting the public to a meeting on 'Faith Healing. Where Does the Church Stand?' Preedy was not a man to miss a chance.

3

In fact, as we know now, there was a split on the *Argus* board. The paper had been losing circulation and there had been an attempt to loose the grip of Ackroyd and Tinney, who, with Sir John Rideout till his death ten years before, and since then with his widow, old Lady Rideout, had had absolute control of the whole Rideout Press for more than forty years.

This was not the first attack on the old directors, but it was the first that had really vigorous leadership, and reached a vote on the board, a vote lost only by one voice. And the reason was only that old Lady Rideout, who was ailing, had been persuaded by a certain Hooper to give Preedy a boost.

An argument had been going on now for two years, ever since the *Daily Mirror* and *Daily Express* had taken up religion. The *Argus* board was divided. Lord Ackroyd, the chairman, had urged support for Reunion; the editor was for the Wesleyans with emphasis on a peace offensive; Lady Rideout, egged on by Hooper, had urged a special feature article on Preedy and his successful mission in East London. But the editor detested Reunion and Ackroyd had vetoed Preedy. The man, he said, would be a bad bet. He had a past, he had been in serious trouble about women, even about money. And he had proposed the next business. He had assumed, rather too confidently, that Kate Rideout would give way. She usually gave way to him on any point concerning the *Argus*. Her sphere was understood, for a long time, to be the weekly *Woman's News*, where she had a free hand and where, for some years, she had been losing money, which Ackroyd permitted so long as she did not challenge his general authority on the board.

But on this occasion, to everyone's surprise, she had argued the point, and finally demanded a vote. This had gone against her but only by one voice out of ten – and a trifling issue, whether to give some free advertisement to a crank preacher, had suddenly become critical.

Ackroyd had compromised. The *Argus* had given the short notice and photograph of Preedy, and afterwards a series of articles on religion, that is to say, of the normal safe kind – the scandal of divided Christendom, the suicidal intolerance of the sects, the obscurities of the theologians.

Hooper was that Harry Hooper who wrote a best seller about his war service in the Middle East. He had been a reporter and after his success he became a foreign correspondent. But he was pretty well forgotten when in 1954 he popped up again with some violent articles in the *Argus* about the decline of Britain, the follies of the government, etc.

These were not in the *Argus*'s usual style, but Hooper had been made foreign editor and it was known that he had got the ear of old Lady Rideout, who held much the biggest block of shares in the combine.

So that at the *Post Telegraph* party, for the election of May '55, it was noticed with a good deal of interest that he was going about with Joanna Rideout.

Joanna herself, as only surviving child of the Rideouts, was heiress apparent to a large block of Press shares, and it had suddenly appeared that she might inherit very soon. Up to this time she had been not much noticed anywhere. She was a tall rather mannish figure, with a plain, pug face. She had no charm, she seemed both shy and aloof. Nobody could say that they knew her well. Now, when there was so much curiosity about a girl who could inherit power, power of a very real and desirable kind in this modern world of pressure groups and propaganda, it turned out that nobody had any idea of her character.

As for Hooper, he was generally disliked, especially by fellow-journalists. He was a little sharp-faced man, with a reputation for being on the make and not being very scrupulous in his methods. It was suspected, for instance, that he had taken up Preedy simply to curry favour with old Lady Rideout, and that now he was in pursuit of Joanna Rideout for the sake of her Press shares. He was said to be a complete egotist in all his dealings with women; on the other hand Joanna's own reputation was doubtful. She was known to have had affairs, and at twenty-eight she showed no inclination to get married.

At the *Post* party, in sudden prominence on account of her mother's illness, she walked from group to group doing, rather obviously, her duty as the Rideout representative.

Though she wore a new and expensive Dior frock, it was put on, as usual with her clothes, as if she did not care whether it were back before. While she greeted this or that celebrity, whether it were a duchess, a leading jockey, a composer, a cabinet minister, or simply some newspaper editor, she showed the same eager attention, that respectful anxiety to be instructed, which is common form in well-brought-up girls. She would put her head a little on one side and give to her rather small green eyes the bright intensity you see in a hungry dog expecting a bone – her thick lips pouted open as if to drink the rarest kind of wine. But she had a bad habit, after the first half-minute, and while keeping the same expression in mouth and pose, of letting her gaze wander towards the next objective; and as she moved on, her party smile assumed a touch of derision. It was this expression that she directed towards Hooper when, in these intervals between duty visits, she exchanged a few words with him. He followed her all the time, and spoke to no one else. His intentions were clear, so clear as to excite both amusement and contempt. But it was impossible to tell from the girl's look what impressions he had made – the only time they were heard to speak to each other she seemed to snub him.

A suffragan bishop had asked Joanna about the Preedy article in the *Argus*. Joanna answered that she had nothing to do with the policy of the paper. 'I wouldn't be allowed to.'

'I don't think the end of that notice was very fair to the curate – what's his name.'

'Syson.'

'Ah, you did read the article.'

'Oh, yes, I read the *Argus*,' Joanna smiled as if at a joke, 'I think it's quite a good paper.'

'I was wondering,' said the bishop, 'what you thought of Preedy yourself.'

The bishop was always asking young people, especially those whom he considered representative young people, what they thought of things. He hoped in this way to keep in touch with the new generation.

'I'm sorry, but I really don't know anything about Preedy. They say he's very successful, but they always say that, don't they?'

A little man standing by, an archaeologist, interjected, 'Why have the Press, at least the tabloids, taken up religion so suddenly?'

'It's a good stunt,' said a tall dark man in horn rims, 'or they think it might be. Billy Graham has been an eye-opener.'

'It's wonderful what advertisement has done for him,' said another, a well-known judge, 'I suppose the whole world knows that name.'

'A name of power,' someone said from the back, in an ironical tone.

'Just exactly that,' said another. 'Names make news; names and pictures.'

The tall man remarked, as one giving important information, 'Actually it's been quite well known for a long time that you can hypnotize people with photographs – of course, the eyes have to look straight out at the victim.'

'Musso and Hitler taught us something there.'

'And now all the papers are giving us photographs of their columnists.'

'All the same, Billy Graham,' half a dozen other voices broke in. Billy Graham was one of the topics of interest, naturally so at a party consisting largely of what might be called still the ruling class. Almost all present, from cabinet ministers to civil servants, professors, Pressmen, and simply big business men, were deeply aware of the importance of popular ideas, popular obsessions. Almost all were concerned, one way or another, with such ideas and obsessions; either in propagating them, or battling with them. Even the mere celebrities, actors and writers, conductors and brains-trusters, were everlastingly aware of how they depended for any influence or position they had on some form of propaganda.

The bishop, who liked, if he could, to approve of all modern development, remarked that when you looked into the tabloids, they were not so bad. They might have bathing girls on the front page, but inside they were all for the home virtues. 'Unless they have a good ghost story,' said the dark man, 'or something about second sight.'

'You haven't actually seen Preedy in action then?' the bishop said to Joanna.

'Is Preedy very different from the others? I wouldn't know,' the girl said.

'You don't know because you don't want to know,' Hooper exclaimed. The girl smiled down at him. 'Isn't that rather like blackmail? Are you threatening to say that I'm afraid of Preedy?'

'That's what I do mean. Because you might have to take him seriously.' Hooper spoke with such real contempt and anger that there was an immediate silence. Everybody stared at the couple with undisguised speculation.

The girl made no answer. She continued to smile at him a moment, then turned and walked off to greet another of her mother's friends, a celebrated philosopher who also played politics, who liked to see his name in the Press, and whose name was still news. Hooper pushed through the group as if they were merely natural obstacles, a kind of human shrubbery, and marched after her. The bishop, still feeling in his stomach the impact of the man's elbow, said to the archaeologist, 'A pushful young man.'

'He seems to be pushing to some purpose,' said the archaeologist, and then everybody began to discuss old Lady Rideout's illness, and the position of the Rideout Press. The shaky condition of the *Argus*, and what its future must be if old Lady Rideout died, was another popular topic at the party.

4

Lady Rideout had been taken ill at a public meeting, the opening session of the Press Exhibition. She had been asked, as representative of the women editors, to second the opening speech, and had insisted, in spite of her doctors, on carrying out the engagement. A few months before this she had had influenza and had been vaguely ill ever since; she had sudden fits of weakness, strange pains, buzzing in her ears, etc., for which she had consulted specialists and taken various cures without apparent effect. Finally she had decided to ignore all symptoms and doctors.

But what really decided her to go to the meeting was a visit from a friend in America, who expected to find her dying. The Americans, apparently, had already written her off.

Unluckily, after the first few words of her address, she fainted, and, as she was, of course, in the front row on the platform, one of the numerous photographers present seized his chance, and got two fine shots, one of her legs, as she lay on the stage behind her overturned chair, and another of her being carried out very awkwardly, by two Press barons.

There was no reference in any British paper to this incident, and even the rumours that came to Fleet Street were doubtful. The *Argus* editor was told that she had been overcome by the heat, and he knew that she had rung him up on the very next day.

But a week later those photographs had come out in an American weekly, on sale at all chief British and Continental railway stations. And with the photographs was a paragraph headed, 'What next in British Press War?' with the caption, 'Lady Rideout chief shareholder in the Rideout Press Group, who had a stroke on the fifteenth. This will mean a big shake-up in the Rideout Press, already badly split over a new look for its chief property, the ailing *Morning Argus*. Lady Rideout was for giving the paper a religious feature, in accord with the tabloid *Mirror*; but her candidate for spell-binder has not up to now proved so acceptable to her co-directors as Billy Graham has been to other British organs.'

The *Argus* now had a paragraph to say that Lady Rideout was in excellent health; her temporary illness was due to influenza, requiring a rest cure. The general public at once concluded, according to the rule governing such diplomatic statements, that the woman was dying; but couldn't care less. It was only the Americans who made a fuss about business tycoons. Old Woman Rideout could die in peace for all it cared, and go to the devil afterwards. People said to themselves, 'What have we got to do with these newspaper rackets?' and turned the page. The whole newspaper world with its trusts, its companies, its lords, its feuds and alliances, was a mystery to them. The more the Press explained itself, the less they believed; and of what they believed, they inclined to the worst. It was a ramp; it was a lot of lies; it was a skin game for millionaires who got away with everything.

They had heard about the newspaper war, but there was

always a newspaper war; something, during the late strike, about papers going down, but papers went down every year or two. If the *Argus* was going smash, its readers supposed they would have to put up with some other rag. All the same they would be sorry, for it seemed to them that the *Argus* agreed with them better than the other rags; it had a little more sense, a little more truth, and it was sound on such matters as world peace and the atom bomb. It gave you something to hold on to in the general fog of confusion that seemed to hang over everything nowadays. Not much perhaps. The editor was obviously a sound chap, you could see it in his face. And the special columnist, he was a man you could trust; rather tough, perhaps, to judge by his jaw, but no nonsense about him. A man who knew his own mind. This Preedy too, there was obviously something in him. Wonderful eyes, he had.

That photograph of Preedy in the *Argus* had been a good deal in Joanna's mind for several weeks past. The man looked exactly what she had expected, a fanatic and a bit of a poseur; all the same, she couldn't get him out of her mind, and her smile that evening was directed actually at herself. It was truly derisive, as people thought, but Joanna laughed much more at herself than at other people.

Preedy was everything she detested, a spell-binder, an evangelist. She did not believe in anything he stood for; she was sure that if he were not a crook or a fake, then he was simply some kind of lunatic, but Hooper was pushing Preedy, he was obsessed about Preedy and demanded that she should admire him too.

What amused her at the moment was that she was tempted to humour him. She asked herself, 'Have I fallen for Harry Hooper? Or do I simply detest him? It would be just like me to fall for him because he's always so rude, and to everybody. – it's probably a policy – he thinks out everything. All the same, he is serious about Preedy – at least I'm fairly certain he's serious about Preedy.'

This was really a fundamental question to Joanna. Was Hooper honest? Did he really mean what he said – did he really *feel* what he said? For this seemed to her the only thing in the world you could depend on, sincerity, personal truth, in someone you liked. She liked it even in people who repelled her in every other way, whom she hated – so that her hatred even for Hitler had been mixed with admiration for his honesty when he had said openly that the German people were sheep to be driven.

She had been drawn strongly to Hooper by the same kind of ruthless sincerity, but she could not tell whether she really cared for the man. He had been asking her all the evening to go back to his flat on her way home and each time she had refused. She was pretty sure that he intended to make some declaration, some proposal, and she did not know what to answer. She was determined not to see him for at least a week, until she could make up her mind about him. And when, at four o'clock, she decided that it was permitted for her to go, she slipped away.

She had ordered the car for four, and it was waiting for her, a vast pre-war Rolls of 1936, and since she was in her mother's place as Rideout representative, there was a footman with it as well as the driver. He was watching for her at the car door, and opened it as soon as her foot touched the pavement. But at once, Hooper darted between, stretching out his little arms as if to stop her by force – she was obliged to stop in order not to run into him.

'You're coming with me,' he said, 'aren't you? I haven't seen you – really seen you – all the evening, and my car's just here.'

Joanna gazed down at him thoughtfully and said she must go home at once, 'You know my mother is at the hospital and there may be a message.'

'It will only take ten minutes. What's wrong with you? What have I done?' He took her arm above the elbow in a hard grip and she allowed him to lead her away. He threw over his shoulder to the Rideout footman, 'You needn't wait, I'll bring Miss Rideout home.'

Joanna was not much surprised by her own action. She thought only, 'What a wobbler I am – but what's it matter – and perhaps he really is hurt.' She did not like to hurt a friend if his feeling for her was sincere. She doubted very much if Hooper really cared for her, he was probably, she had been told often enough that he was, a go-getter on the make, and running after her only because she might soon own a large block of shares in the Rideout Press.

Not that she had any objection to go-getters; she had lived all her life in a world of go-getters, of men and groups fighting for power, thinking in terms of power, defending their power, but she did care very much whether he was sincere, whether he meant and felt what he said.

She had met him for the first time at a lunch party given for him as a new member of the board. Lord Ackroyd, the chairman, and his friend Sir Robert Tinney, the physicist, had genially condescended to the young man about his best-selling war book.

But he, speaking in a detached manner, as if the question were academic, had attacked the policy of the board. What after all, did their papers stand for, in any important issue – in politics, religion, economics? Like a polite person, who is attacking other people's opinions, but too obviously applying the formula, he put his criticism in the form of questions.

What actually, he asked, were they doing about the Church? Did they really consider that Christianity mattered? Was there any other answer to communist materialism, communist science with its scientific fifth column entrenched in every Western university? Could it be that the famous Rideout tradition of liberal toleration was merely escapism? Didn't it, in fact, dodge the fundamental issue of the terrific challenge by the communists – the appeal of class envy, of racial hatred feeding on national inferiority complexes, of personal greed, personal spite, personal vanity, the whole gamut of human meanness and cruelty now being mobilized to smash civilization in the interests of the communist power gang – a challenge all the greater since Stalin's death because the new dictators seemed to have a modicum of intelligence and a great deal better idea of how Western Europe would react to the cruder kind of propaganda.

Ackroyd had tried to brush him aside. He said briefly that the Rideout public liked the papers as they were and had strongly protested against a recent very modest change in layout.

Hooper ignored this. 'We used to be called the Nonconformists' Bible,' he said. 'We actually had a religious following – a real religious following. And a lot of influence – at least among evangelicals. But we've let it trickle away.'

Joanna, sitting opposite him, turning an interested, thoughtful face to each speaker in turn, caught his eye, and suddenly he asked her, 'What do you think? You ought to know more than we do, at your age. What do your friends think?'

Joanna, after a little pause for reflection, had answered that it was difficult to say. 'There are so many opinions.'

In fact, in that reflective pause, she had had to ask herself what Hooper was talking about. She had been listening to this kind of discussion, about Rideout policy, about ideas, all her life, she knew all the arguments.

Neither Ackroyd nor Tinney had forgotten their near defeat. They knew too that Kate Rideout had not forgotten it – she still urged Preedy upon them – that ridiculous and obscure crank was still an issue that might threaten their control. That was why Ackroyd was so short with Hooper, and why Tinney intervened.

'So you're for the prophets. Billy Graham and the rest.'

He put his bird's head on one side, his little black eyes sparkled with intelligence and malice.

He was proposing to make game of this brash young man. 'It's simply a question of what you believe,' Hooper said. 'I mean really believe. I'm not talking about talk – all these professors with their stuff about democracy and liberty, but something real, something people will go to town for. Yes, die for if you like –'

'The animals went in two by two,' said Tinney, and he gave a sudden laugh, unexpectedly loud and gay.

Hooper flushed slightly. 'It's nothing to do with fundamentalism – and religion is only a part of it. That's to say, organized religion. It's a whole angle of mind – a way of feeling.'

'Bathing girls on the front page,' Tinney said. 'But the big question there, I gather, is bikinis. Are you for bikinis?'

Hooper suddenly lost his temper, and his nice manners. He answered in a tone of contemptuous rage, 'I'm not for the wobblers – the pacifists who said the answer to Hitler was to abolish armaments.' Tinney, who had been such a pacifist before the war, smiled even more joyfully and maliciously. He never lost his temper, and loved to see others lose theirs.

He laughed, and looked round the table to see that everyone was appreciating the scene.

'Ah, Mr Hooper, how good to meet a man who knows his own mind – a man of destiny.'

But Lady Rideout intervened. She hated arguments. She asked Ackroyd if he had seen the report on juvenile delinquency. At once, in his roaring voice, the voice of a deaf man who likes to keep the talk to himself, he began to orate, yes, he'd seen it, at least, he'd seen extracts – and he considered it very hopeful – so far as it went.

Hooper, now as pale as he had been red, even paler than usual, sat silent. His face expressed still nothing but contempt, but his fingers shook as he reached for the spoon in the dish offered to him. Joanna saw those shaking fingers, and suddenly felt an answering vibration in her own nerves. In her, too, all at once something trembled with revulsion, with something that would have been resentment if it had been directed against anyone or anything.

Her attention, which had once more wandered into a vague dream, while she endured this necessary lunch-party, was suddenly concentrated on Hooper. She realized him for the first time as a person, not merely another new genius on approval by Ackroyd, her mother and Tinney, a man with ideas to sell, but one with feelings, with convictions. A man with convictions so strong that he had absolutely lost his temper with these powerful and eminent persons upon whom his career depended. The very idea of his insult to the great, the revered Tinney, was shocking, and it was disgraceful to speak as he had to Ackroyd, a man of seventy-eight. She was indignant with Hooper. But the surprise, the excitement had remained with her; the picture of the little man, red with rage, and the shaking fingers of the small, delicate hand, a woman's hand, continually recurred, unasked, to the eyes of her imagination.

Meeting Hooper again at a party, and seeing him at once making for her, she felt again that deep nervous tremor, a mixture of revulsion and curiosity.

Again he had asked her opinion. What did she really think of the Rideout policy – in an age like this. Toleration – liberal *laissez-faire* – all things to all men. Ackroyd was a grand old man, but did he understand the new age, so bewildered, so anxious to find a leader. Could a man who had left school in the nineties, and joined the Press in 1901, realize the feelings, the ideas of people like themselves.

Joanna, of course, had heard all this before. It was a commonplace among the thousands of commonplaces that bombarded her all the time, and she made the usual discreet answers. Was this age really so different? Could you really judge by the papers, or even by what people said?

Suddenly, as with Tinney, Hooper had lost his temper with her, and sneered, 'You needn't be afraid I'll give you away – I

23

know it's dangerous to own to any belief nowadays. You get laughed at. The thing is just to float along and expect the worst – like poisoned rats in a sewer.'

She had laughed at this, which made him even angrier. 'Of course, if you haven't any ideas or even feelings, if you really are a jellyfish.'

'Why poisoned?' she said, according to the rule taught in the debs' school for such a case. You pick out any word in the speaker's last sentence and put why before it. For instance, if he gets on a line about temperance, you ask suddenly, 'Why whisky?' and this throws him off his balance. He can't go on orating.

'Because they are poisoned – with slops. Old stale slops. Slops in education, slops in politics, and my God, what slops in the papers. Why, look at you, what did they spend on your education and you don't even know what you feel.'

'I feel I should like another drink,' said she, handing him her glass. But he simply disappeared. It was as though he was too furious with her to get her a drink.

But again and again he had sought her out. On half a dozen occasions now he had pinned her in some corner at a cocktail party and orated about the break-up of the West, its feeble grasp of life, its feeble policies, its education pretending to be tolerant and free and achieving only shallowness and vagueness. Sometimes he was angry, sometimes he was merely gloomy and aggrieved. When he was angry she laughed; when he was gloomy, she listened with an attentive sympathetic air as advised by the school. She took care, also according to the rules, not to criticize anybody, especially not Ackroyd or Tinney, or the management of the *Argus*. But in the very act of obeying the rules, she felt that Hooper had good reason to despise her. She was dodging his questions; she was refusing to own to any conviction, to any real feeling.

After the last evening party, where again Hooper had abused her, she had not been able to sleep. She was furious with him. But all the time his question nagged at her. Was there anything she was sure about, that she would die for?

How absurd that question sounded. Suppose she asked it of any of her friends. They would think her mad. But somehow that nasty, bad-tempered little man had made it stick in her mind, or

24

rather, in some much deeper place. It stuck there like a pain, like a poisoned bullet, which kept on irritating, which would not let itself be forgotten.

5

As Joanna crumpled up her long legs in the front seat of Hooper's small car, she said, 'I really meant ten minutes,' and Hooper answered, 'That's all right, my flat is on the way.'

The Rideouts lived in Portland Place, but Hooper continued straight along the Embankment and she asked at last, 'Where exactly do you live?'

He didn't answer this, but it was a habit of his not to answer, and she did not repeat her question. After all, what did it matter? And when they reached his flat, in a large block by the river, she remarked cheerfully that it was not really far out.

'Why were you in such a hurry,' he said irritably, 'the party's still going on, and your mother is still in hospital. She won't even know when you get home.'

'No,' and she was going to say, all the same there might be a message, when she perceived that she wasn't really expecting a message, and checked herself. If Hooper were being honest with her, she must be honest with him.

'How ill exactly is she?'

'The doctors don't even agree about that.'

'Well, of course it's a private matter, I shouldn't ask.'

'I'd tell you if I knew. Why do you always think that I want to hide things from you?'

Hooper was pouring out two stiff whiskies. He handed her a glass and remarked, coldly, 'Because you do – all the time, and you know you do. But I'm not blaming you – it's your damn silly education – never to give yourself away.'

'You *are* blaming me, you never stop.'

'Is that how it seems?' He looked at her, reflecting. 'The great lump – but I've got through. She's hurt – she's reacting.'

'That's because I like you.' He plumped himself down on the sofa beside her. 'Don't you realize I've rather fallen for you?'

Joanna, startled, said nothing to this. She forgot even the rule, to say, 'Not really – you don't mean that.'

25

'Why did you think I've been chasing you all over London?' he said, 'going to cocktail parties – my God – *cocktail* parties.'

'Did we get on so well at the cocktail parties?'

'No, because we were wasting our time – I was wasting my time, because you kept dodging. You never come clean. Why? You're not really like that. You're one of the honestest people I ever met – and the nicest to everyone. You never say a spiteful thing about anybody.'

Joanna was embarrassed. This was the declaration that she had feared and she did not know what to say to it. She answered at last, 'It's very nice of you to think such things about me, but I wonder if they're true. I don't like everybody, you know. I don't think I like your Preedy.'

'You don't believe a word I say,' and suddenly he was angry with her. 'What a poker you are – it's just what people say, you don't really care tuppence for anything or anybody, you just go floating along with the crowd, talking tripe, and thinking tripe, and not bothering if it is tripe.'

Joanna examined the description of herself with some interest; it struck her as largely true, and she was about to say that the difficulty was to know what was tripe and what wasn't tripe, when Hooper suddenly attacked her, fumbling, kissing, pulling at her clothes.

Joanna pushed him back with her strong arms and when he still tried to wrestle with her, she simply held him away. She was more amused than surprised by this attack, by the man's attempt to set his flimsy weight and soft muscles against hers. She had played tennis for her county and she rode to hounds every winter. She had a good deal of pride, though she laughed at that pride, in her strength and condition. She was not at all angry with Hooper; she was more amused to think, 'After all, he's got a silly side – and he's had a good deal of champagne.'

Hooper jerked himself out of her grip. He was pink with fury. He exclaimed, 'Cold as a fish – it's just what I thought.'

Joanna flushed darkly, up to her hair. Now she was angry. 'What nonsense – what a silly, stale trick.'

'Trick?'

'That old blackmail. As if I would care if you did call me cold.' And she added in a tone full of contempt as well as anger. 'That's not at all clever.'

26

'No, it wasn't. I was a fool – it's you who are clever. A bit too clever perhaps. Why do you think I'm putting it on? Why shouldn't I want to – well, to use a word that won't shock the British magistrates – have you? Is it modesty on your part, or simply arrogance? Do you think yourself such an extraordinary piece of flesh that a common little man like me simply couldn't dream of going to bed with you?' And he added with a slow contemptuous emphasis, 'The Rideout princess.'

He could not have chosen a better phrase to enrage Joanna. It was an American paper, in an article on modern heiresses and their fortunes – usually disastrous – that had first called her the Rideout Princess. But the name had stuck; even some of her friends, half in mockery, would call her princess. She deeply resented it; she knew that the word was used to set her apart, to separate her from the common sympathies.

'That's just spite,' she exclaimed. 'Tell me, do you believe all that stuff you talk or is it just your stock in trade?'

'What stuff have I talked?'

'About – well, about religion. About Preedy and so on.'

'Of course I believe it. I'm not a liar.'

'No, but you know it's a popular kind of stuff just now – what you call a paying line.'

'You think I'm on the make?'

'I think your kind of religion must be rather a queer one if you always behave as you've done tonight.'

'Well, I am on the make. I want to do something in this silly world – and *for* it too. Simply because I believe something. I suppose you can't understand that. Of course, you can't. How could you? You don't believe – really believe – anything.'

Joanna's temper had suddenly died and Hooper's last remark made her ashamed. She felt that he had been frank with her, and that she had been making reservations with him, she had failed in generosity. She said in a subdued tone, 'I can understand that – you've done so much already.'

Hooper made no answer, he jumped up and mixed himself another stiff drink. She could see that he was still furious with her. He said abruptly, 'What time do you want to get back?'

They drove to Portland Place in silence. He did not get out of the car and as she got out he said, 'I'm sorry I tried to rape you. It won't occur again. We stop here.'

As soon as she was on the pavement he pulled the door to behind her and sprinted away with a roar. Joanna was amused by the childish bad manners of the man, but she still felt that she had behaved very badly.

'Of course,' she thought, 'that's just what he wants me to feel; but still, I shouldn't have asked him if he really believed; I hadn't any right to doubt it.'

She felt now very tired, as well as depressed. When she found that the lift, under alteration to take a wheel-chair on her mother's return from hospital, was not yet working, she sat down on the bottom step of the stairs and said, 'Oh, forget the man. Haven't I enough worries.'

But she could not forget him; almost everything he had said was still flying through her brain, 'Your rotten education –' 'dodging –' 'never grown up –' 'a dummy – got to be careful', and especially, 'cold fish'.

This was the most obvious blackmail on his part, and yet, as she was amused to find, it had a strong effect, it made her feel mean. It was almost as if Hooper, simply because he did have convictions, he did know what he wanted, had a right to be indulged; at any rate by a girl like her who, it appeared, had no idea what she wanted.

6

Lady Rideout's faint had, in fact, not lasted more than twenty minutes. She had come to in the ambulance. She had little by little gathered her senses to find herself lying in something like a large coffin, lit by a strange blue light. When she put up her hand and touched wood close over her face, she had a moment of horror. She realized what it was to be buried alive. But she knew where she was; and her wakening impression was that of an enormous, an amazing humiliation and downfall.

It was not that she had fainted in public. It was that she was here; that she had become a kind of parcel; an inert thing that is handled, pitched about, conveyed according to routine directions. And she could not help it if she tried. She had become a helpless object.

Where was she going? What had happened to her; was she

dying? There was no one to answer a question; it did not matter what she felt or said.

She was cut off in this box; cut off from the whole world. She could hear it roaring all round her, cars, buses, voices, a mysterious burst of music, perhaps from a shop, a grind of brakes, a horn blown angrily, impatiently; and then a shout apparently from her driver. He shouted and then laughed.

She had thought herself experienced in loneliness. She had been a lonely woman when her first husband died. She had loved him and she missed him bitterly when, after two years' marriage, he was killed on the Somme in '15. She had found herself unexpectedly lonely when her second husband, old John Rideout, had died in '45. She had never loved John but she had admired him, served him faithfully, been close to him; and he had loved her. She had missed him, to her surprise, much more and much longer than the smart young soldier. And then, three years ago, her son William had died.

She knew what happened to the dead. Wasn't it a rule of the newspaper world, nothing about the dead? You laid a heavy obituary on them like a stone and forgot them. They aren't news any more; they are nothing in the world.

It appeared that for some time now people had been expecting her to die. And she had known nothing about it. Of course, one never knows such things – one is the last to hear of anything important to oneself. It is just about important things that one's dearest friends unite in telling one lies.

And the doctors were worse.

She had not expected much from the doctors. Nobody with any experience of newspaper work expects much from anybody; journalists are even more sceptical than judges about experts. But what had surprised her was the discovery that she, without medical knowledge, would have to make up her own mind about what was wrong with her and what it required; and that her most intelligent friends were not only no help, they were a nuisance.

Ackroyd wanted to send her to a Swiss surgeon, instantly; Tinney advised her to take lessons in relaxation and massage her neck muscles; Mrs Mantoffle, the Bishop's wife, urged her to try a faith cure, and live meanwhile on groats and boiled raisins.

She felt then as if she had tumbled out of her old familiar

world where words made some minimum of sense, into another where there was no meaning either in words or people; a lunatic world where old friends, even one's nearest and dearest, simply gazed at one with glassy, meaningless eyes, and uttered incomprehensible but troubling noises. What did nerves mean? Were they the white strings you saw in a dead rabbit, or were they some vague stuff like imagination, a dream? Or did the two work together; and if so, how? Her brain operated madly in an enormous vacuum upon unanswerable problems, and nothing could help.

'You see too many doctors,' Ackroyd had said. 'That's always fatal. Take a good man and stick to him.'

'But which good man, Edward?'

'Steiner is the best in Europe.'

'Cartwright says he murdered Lady Wilson.'

'There you are – why listen to Cartwright?'

'He's the biggest man on stomachs in Harley Street.'

'Come now, Kate – are we going round that way again?'

'What have you against Cartwright? You can't say he's a crook.'

And this, as Kate had intended, startled old Edward. He paused, before answering in a cautious tone, 'You don't really believe in that chap Preedy?'

Kate did not believe in him. But she was exasperated, as usual, with her old friend. He was so calm, so diplomatic, so prudent. He was always thinking about the situation, the whole situation. For him she was part of a situation, Edward's situation, that is, Edward's *Argus*, Edward's board, Edward's ideas, Edward's anxiety to hold on, at seventy-eight, to his powers and dignities, to be in the swim with Prime Ministers and Presidents.

'If the doctors don't know what to do –' Kate said.

'You don't trust 'em, Kate. You don't give 'em a chance.'

'They've had three months and several hundred pounds. Preedy doesn't charge anything, anyhow.'

And then they had quarrelled. She had succeeded in frightening the old man, and he was rude. But his rudeness, after all, was a sign of affection. She was surprised by it, and soon she made up their quarrel. She would give the doctors another chance. She didn't really believe in Preedy, not all of Preedy. He deserved support, and would be a good feature in the paper, but he hadn't the whole answer.

*

Now Edward seemed farther from her than ever, farther than her maid, or the people in the street. At least they didn't pester her with contradictory advice. Even loneliness was better than confusion.

And what was any loneliness to the awful solitude of this ambulance, of this coffin which was so much lonelier than a real coffin.

In the grave she would not know death; but here, for the first time, she felt her dying. Already the world had gone from her, already she was powerless; a thing; a piece of decaying flesh handled by strangers and carted about the streets in a municipal salvage cart.

Death had put her in his condemned cell, surrounded it with barbed wire; she could still look out, but nobody could look in.

The young doctor in charge of the emergency ward was rather flustered to have Lady Rideout brought in. He had vaguely heard of her. He guessed that her pearls and her diamond ring were real. He'd never seen a diamond that size. He sent for a senior man who agreed with him that the lady should be kept for observation. Her blood pressure was high; her reflexes were abnormal.

When they explained this to the patient, she exploded in such indignation that it seemed dangerous to keep her without some authority. Luckily her daughter at this moment rang up. And she gave them the strongest support. Lady Rideout must be kept quiet at all costs. They therefore gave the old woman an injection, on the excuse of curing her nausea. And the registrar remarked to his junior, 'That's a bad sign, that obsession about getting home. All these poor old wrecks have a fit like that in their last stages. Even if they've no idea of dying, something tells 'em they're for it. And they're mad to get home. Like animals creeping down their holes.'

7

In the morning the room was full of flowers. The nurse, knowing this difficult patient was to be cheered up, said, 'There really isn't room for them all – how nice to have such nice friends.'

Old Kate muttered and stared. The nurse, not to be discouraged, said, 'And your daughter phoned. She's coming as soon as the doctors have finished their round.'

'Is she coming to take me out of this?'

'Well, not quite yet. But if you want anything –'

Kate muttered angrily to herself. The nurse went out and closed the door softly, but with satisfaction. She was a young nurse, and she still hated wilful rudeness.

Kate had not even noticed these kind remarks. Her brain indeed recorded them, but did not cast them up until a minute after the door had closed.

'Friends,' Kate said then. And she had a picture of Mrs Mantoffle saying to her secretary, 'Oh yes, and order some flowers for Lady Rideout at the St Margaret's Hospital. About thirty shillings worth. No, a pound.'

Mrs Mantoffle was her oldest and dearest friend, except Edward Ackroyd, but lately, since Kate's illness, she had called in only about once a fortnight to say how fearfully busy she was – she hadn't a moment.

Of course, this was true. Mrs Mantoffle was president of all sorts of societies and committees – and she had lately been discovered by television. All this was important for her husband's political career. And Kate, ill, was no longer much good to her.

'I'm just a waste of time for Milly,' old Kate reflected, 'and now I've cost her a pound.'

Milly Mantoffle was a good soul. Her ambition was large but it was only a little larger than her heart. She was not ungenerous, she only hated to waste things, time or money, on inessentials.

'And I've stopped being essential – I'm just a nuisance,' the old woman reflected.

Of course, everyone was something of a nuisance to everybody, a nuisance more or less compensated by advantage. But Kate was now a nuisance without much compensation; she was almost totally a waste of time, a burden. The more really affectionate people were, the bigger the burden. Joanna was coming as soon as she could be let in. But did she really look forward to coming, did Kate expect to enjoy the visit?

And what had they told Joanna so that she would not take her home? Did she really want her at home?

Joanna was in the middle of a new excitement – this fellow Hooper. She was busy with her own life, even more so than Mrs Mantoffle. It was to Joanna that she was the biggest nuisance of all, just because she was nearest.

No one was divided from her by so enormous a barrier; a dark forest of confusion in which she could only grope her way. For though she knew Joanna, though she understood her nature and needs better than her own, she could never guess how the child would react to any given word. She could never discover exactly what piece of nonsense had taken dominion over her mind at that moment. Joanna's brain had always been a tangle of nonsense. And now some new idea had seized her – it must be an idea that made her tolerate a little cad like Harry Hooper.

If she married him she would ruin her life. For what Joanna needed above all was to respect a man. She was the last person in the world to forgive meanness of any kind.

How she loved Joanna, through and through. What agonies she had suffered over the child, over her looks, her clumsiness, her fearful obstinacy, her fits of temper, her secrecy, her nonsense, her lack of even decent pride, her vulnerability. No one could suffer like Joanna for her own follies. And no one was more helpless than her mother to save her from the least of them.

A nurse came in; there was a phone call from Lord Ackroyd. He couldn't come till the afternoon. Meanwhile was there anything she wanted? Should he bring the lawyer or would she rather put it off?

'Let him come,' Kate said, 'and bring all the lawyers he likes.'

'He only said one,' the nurse said brightly.

'Tell him what I say – all the lawyers he likes.'

Kate knew what the message meant, it was a hint about business. For all Edward knew, she was dying, but he had to get business done. Probably about the deed of trust. Almost certainly about the deed. Edward had had it on the brain, for three years now – ever since William's death – a deed to put her *Argus* shares and Joanna's into a trust. As he had pointed out then, Joanna at twenty-five was not fitted for the responsibility of such a share in the Press. She herself dreaded it. Far better hand over the voting power to trustees, selected by himself and Kate.

'Otherwise to Edward himself,' Kate reflected. 'No wonder he's fussing this morning.'

But already that spurt of anger had faded. Of course Edward was anxious to hold on to his power; of course he was in a fluster that Kate had never signed that deed. She had seen Edward's point. She had only failed to bring herself to tell Joanna about

33

it. She had feared its effect on her. She had decided to wait, she had told Edward that the girl would mature. It was too early to say that she was a flibbertigibbet.

From Edward's point of view, of course, that's just what she was. Yes, it was no wonder he was pushing that deed; that now, hearing of her collapse, and probably thinking her about to die at any moment, he proposed to bring his lawyer to her. He was too worried, too anxious, to be tactful or considerate. Too much was at stake.

Edward knew nothing of Joanna. How could he? And for his purpose, he was right. But for Kate, this creature, full of nerves and fancies that changed every day, was a mystery. And ever since her son's death, her chief treasure on earth, her obsession, her joy, her agony.

Should she tell her about the deed? Or should she, as Edward had suggested, simply sign the thing and leave it to be discovered at her death?

Would Joanna hate her for that piece of treachery? Probably not. She was fond of her and would forgive her a great deal. She would say, 'Poor Mother, she was too ill.'

She was not really afraid that Joanna would hate her for anything. But she might despise her. She might say, 'Poor Mother, she was afraid to tell me.'

After all, what did it matter either way, now. The important thing was to get home. That was obviously going to be the big problem. That was where she had to be cautious, diplomatic. For she was surrounded by cunning enemies – everyone was her enemy. Joanna perhaps the most dangerous. She loved her and so she would listen to the doctors, play their game.

Her first words to Joanna were, 'What did the doctors tell you?'

'They want you to rest for a day or two.'

'I'm less of a nuisance here, I suppose –'

Joanna said nothing to this and Kate, looking at her expressionless face, went on, 'Edward thinks I'm dying.'

'Oh Mummy, that's nonsense.'

'He's fussing about those Press shares.'

'What shares?'

'Well, if I were at home – I could show you. The papers are in my safe.'

34

'I could bring you anything you wanted.'

'You couldn't find them. No, I must be at home first. You know, if I had one of those chairs, you could just wheel me out to the car.'

Joanna again said nothing. Kate thought, 'She thinks I'm mad – the doctors have stuffed her up with all their rubbish.'

'It was Edward's idea, the deed,' she said. 'After William died, to put the shares in trust.'

'Oh, you mean the shares that were going to William – your shares?'

'Yes, those, and the shares you have already. You would have to sign, too. I wouldn't sign then, I said it was too soon. Perhaps you might like them. Of course, William wanted them. But William was a real newspaper man. And Edward thought that you were not so interested.'

There was a silence. Joanna was reflecting. 'So that's it. They don't think I'm fit. And really I'm not fit.' It was on the tip of her tongue to tell the truth, that she was not fit. But she simply could not do so. An enormous obstacle had suddenly appeared which she could not surmount.

It was just this responsibility for the *Argus*, for the Press, that had suddenly grown so alarming for her in these last ten weeks since her mother's illness. She had, of course, known for some years, ever since her brother's death, that she would probably inherit this interest. She was not sure; her mother had never told her so. But she had begun from that time to talk to her about the Press. She had made her learn the details of the management, and caused her to meet editors and even some of the reporters. She had always been urging her to realize what an important responsibility it was to have a voice in running a great paper.

But she had not greatly troubled her head about that possible inheritance. Her mother seemed so strong, so well – at sixty-four she was not old; she had the energy of a woman of fifty. And at the back of her mind, as she realized, she had been ready to leave the *Argus* in the hands of Ackroyd. After all, her mother had done so for years, why shouldn't she?

But now she felt, unexpectedly, an enormous objection to dodging that responsibility; either by leaving the work to Ackroyd or by simply letting her mother sign away her powers.

No, she could not do it. She was afraid to do it. She felt that to do it would be an admission of something disastrous – a fateful admission. She would be admitting to *herself* that she was no good.

And in a strange way, she would be letting her mother down again; she would be an even bigger failure.

Joanna felt deeply guilty before her mother. What a disappointment she had been all her life. An ugly, stupid, cross child, who hated to be shown off. An awkward rough girl. And always uncooperative. Some fate had caused her to do everything that her mother most disliked.

8

'That's what Edward thinks,' Kate said in a dreamy voice, as if the whole matter had only a casual interest for her. 'Of course you ought to see the deed – I don't remember the details.'

'They only want to keep you here for observation.'

'Is that what they told you?'

'But it's true, Mummy. They're quite right to be careful.'

'You agree with them, do you? But you know, suppose I died here. What would happen to all my papers? Nothing's been arranged –'

'But Mummy, you're not going to die.'

'How do you know – no one knows. All those doctors were wrong. Doctors don't know everything. They just follow a lot of little rules laid down for them – and hope for the best. And put on airs of omniscience. They call it giving you confidence. But it doesn't blind me. Of course hospital is depressing – it's just a cleaner kind of jail. But it does make you think. I'm longing to see what prophet Preedy means when he says that doctors really *cause* disease.'

This was a clever speech. Joanna was startled. She looked anxiously at her mother.

'After all,' said Kate. 'Preedy has cured people.'

'Neurotic people – you're not neurotic, Mummy.'

'I thought you believed in Preedy. Harry Hooper believes in him.'

Joanna coloured dully. She had not known that her mother knew anything about her meetings with Hooper. But she thought, I should have known – she has her spies everywhere – reporters, gossip columnists, and people who want to curry favour with her.

'I don't think he does,' Joanna said.

'What a pity. I wanted to show him something – a letter from Preedy. It's in my bureau.'

'Shall I bring it?'

'You couldn't find it.'

'I'll ask Miss Toner.' Kate's secretary.

'She wouldn't find it either. I didn't show it to her.'

Again there was a minute's silence. Joanna thought, 'It's all simply to persuade me to take her home. It's really quite mad. But I suppose that's part of her illness, poor darling, it's made her a little mad.'

And this letter from Preedy. If her mother was so unbalanced, Preedy could be a big danger.

She said at last, 'Did he want an appointment?'

'Who, Preedy? Oh, yes, but it's more complicated than that – it was a long letter. About everything. About his past – and what he wants to do – and his cures.'

The nurse looked in and said even more brightly, 'Oh, if you don't mind. Matron is coming.'

'I don't want to see Matron,' said Kate. 'Why must I see Matron?'

'I'm afraid – well, another five minutes.'

'What a nuisance,' Joanna said. 'Is it in the top drawer?'

'I can't remember where I put it – I didn't want anyone to see it. In case people talked. You know how they talk. No, it will have to wait till I get home. If I get home.'

'But, Mummy, of course you'll get home.'

'That's what they all say.'

'But I'm not they – I promise –'

'They promise all the time.'

Kate stared at her daughter. Her owl's face with its huge black eyes, plump cheeks, sharp little nose, had an expression of intense, desperate application – like that of an owl on the hunt.

But suddenly the eyes became dull, the lids dropped. She had realized the hopelessness of discovering anything from the girl,

37

any kind of truth. She gave a deep long sigh – it was like a dying breath.

Then she held up her arms and Joanna kissed her. It was a sudden eager passionate kiss meant to convey all the love that had not been expressed – and for a moment, the two women clung together, feeling their devotion, their tenderness.

They did not speak. There was nothing they could say which would not sound like an anti-climax, which would not, perhaps, be dangerous in its inadequacy, even create a new division.

Joanna, going out, had tears in her eyes. Her throat was sore and there was a hard pressure in her chest. Why must she fight all her mother's wishes? Why must she give so much pain to the only person in the world she had ever loved?

9

Hooper avoided Joanna after their quarrel. He was furious with the woman, with a rancorous anger that surprised himself. And when, the next week, she rang up to tell him that her mother was again in touch with Preedy, he was cold and short with her.

'Has she fallen for him?'

'I don't know – but she's made an appointment to see him.'

'You're against Preedy?'

Joanna was silent. The truth was that she did not know what to think about Preedy.

'What do you want me to do?'

'I only thought you'd like to know.'

So this was a friendly office, an approach.

'Thanks.' He rang off.

He had carefully not shown any interest in Joanna's news, nor asked for any particulars. But he was excited. If the old woman fell into Preedy's hands, the vote on the board might go against Ackroyd. He called the office at once, to know Preedy's address; and the address of the Mission to know times of service.

A woman's voice told him there were services of healing three days a week; there was one that morning at eleven. Was he bringing a patient? If so he must be responsible for accompanying the patient in and out of chapel, and also for the patient's conduct in chapel. Hooper declared himself merely a visitor.

He had not yet seen Preedy at work. He took a taxi to Pant's Road in case his new car, with its bright green body, standing outside the chapel should attract attention. He imagined Pant's Road as a slum and he did not want to be conspicuous.

But the district proved to be as far as possible from a slum, from the mid-town terraces which can and have so easily become slum tenements, as well as their back streets. It was all in little semi-detached villas, bright as new, painted dolls' houses in a toy-shop window, with gardens before and behind. The chapel stood at the corner of two immensely long streets, planted with small plane trees, equally young.

The chapel itself was fire-new, in corrugated iron sheets still glittering like silver, with a vestry and porch in red brick, and next the porch, an erection between a campanile and a chimney, about twenty feet high. It was a campanile because it had a bell, hung in an opening near the top, but it was also a chimney, because a thin smoke was rising from one side of it.

When Hooper arrived the bell was still ringing and the service had not commenced, but already in the little yard, no doubt intended for a graveyard, between the church and the road fence, there were two stretchers occupied by paralytics, and a woman in a wheeled chair. Within a minute of his arrival, three other sick persons arrived, a child carried by its mother, a man in a motor chair who was then helped out of it and sat upon a folding seat, and another on a stretcher brought out from the back of a tradesman's van.

Hooper had expected scenes of excitement, an atmosphere of emotion, but in fact the whole proceeding had a calm and even casual aspect. A grocer was making his deliveries in the side road, whistling his way from house to house; some small children were playing round the trees; two women with full shopping bags were talking at a gate. He for the moment was the only spectator of the gathering in the churchyard.

Then a nurse in a kind of uniform had appeared and was talking to the patients, who answered her in that cheerful manner obligatory in hospital. The man in the wheeled chair was obviously a known humorist. He was conversing first with one of the stretcher cases, then with a boy on crutches, and both of them began to smile even before he opened his mouth for the next remark. It was the relatives of the patients who showed

39

signs of tragic feeling. The mother of the crippled child, having sat him down on the grass, looked with a gloomy astonishment at the laughing group round the man in the wheeled chair. The two women, apparently old mother and middle-aged daughter, who had helped the old man from the motor chair, also wore grave and anxious faces.

It was now nearly eleven o'clock, and the congregation were arriving in unexpected numbers, mostly women, but including more men than Hooper had expected.

He studied the gathering with the interest of an old journalist unconsciously storing up facts and impressions. He saw at once that he would have to describe it as one coming from every variety of class; much more varied, for instance, than the Buchmanites.

He had been to a Buchmanite meeting in the days of his apprenticeship, and he had described it fairly as consisting of the county and their cooks. He remembered vividly a certain countess of his acquaintance two chairs away from him, sitting next a great red-faced woman who, if not her cook, was probably her char; and his odd sensation when a mathematician from Cambridge had described God as a solid blot of ink in the confused lines of a blotting paper; and again, when a Dutch evangelist, who strongly resembled a ball of cheese, bleached on top, had asked the whole assembly to close their eyes, empty their minds, and wait for God's voice.

Hooper had not closed his eyes. He had looked round and at the sight of rows of faces with shut eyes, resembling children in the game of hide and seek, had uttered, to his horror, a snort of laughter. His neighbours had been too polite or too resolute in the pursuit of a voice from God, to remonstrate. But afterwards, as the meeting broke up, he had received some long glances, not wholly curious. They were meant also to admonish. The cook had glared; the countess, with an absolutely expressionless countenance, had simply gazed. She relied upon the length and fixity of the gaze to stab this heretic; but Hooper, who knew the art of gazing, had disconcerted her by smiling, calling out, 'Hullo,' seizing her hand and speaking his name.

She had not melted to him, until she remembered that he had something to do with a newspaper. And Hooper had realized that this hen-brained creature had really been converted, at least

40

for the time, from bridge, racing and discreet adultery; she had even given up smoking.

As he had left the big hall, he had heard all round him the two accents, that of smart society, and that of rural Oxfordshire, 'broad as a midwife's bum'.

This congregation was not so clearly sorted. The majority were soberly dressed men and women who might have been clerks, shop assistants; there were three young men together who were students; there were two middle-aged men of a type seen any morning in Throgmorton Street, brokers, bank directors. One, bald on top, wore a pin-striped suit which, Hooper suspected, came from his own very good, very expensive tailor, and a pearl in his tie. His rosy face had the expression of a chairman of the board going into an important meeting; he glanced about him, his chin held high, as if to see who was attending and to guess at the voting.

There was a parson, an elderly man, townsman by his complexion, his tall wife, and two pretty daughters. There was a huge man in a brown and yellow checked suit who looked like a bookie in his quietest clothes.

'It's what I say,' Hooper thought, 'Faith-healing has a wider appeal than Buchmanism. It doesn't merely fill an emptiness, it offers a positive hope. And nearly everyone, if he isn't ill himself some time, has a wife, a child, a mother, some relative who is. Add to that the people who are frightened – women who think every pain is cancer – men who have had a clap or a touch of V.D. and think their brains are softening. And the impotent, the sterile – look at that young couple in new clothes. Probably straight from a honeymoon. The young man is a typical nerve case, and the girl would not help him. Elementary school class, the most ignorant, conventional and inhibited of all.'

The bell had stopped ringing. A new crowd of worshippers came hurrying and pressed towards the doors; two men, cripples in wheel-chairs, three on crutches including a boy of about six conducted by a girl not much older. The nurse was joined by two assistants in the same uniform; and finally Preedy himself, wearing his ordinary clerical dress, arrived in a large American car accompanied by two young men, a man in a black coat and striped trousers, and a very large heavy man who looked like an ex-policeman. These four men formed a kind of respectful court while he walked from patient to patient in the churchyard and spoke a few words to each.

One of them who was obviously the secretary and the sister in charge then wrote down particulars in a book and Preedy accompanied by his three assistants went into the vestry.

As each patient finished giving particulars of his case, he entered the church by a side door to which a ramp had been added to enable wheeled chairs to be pushed directly on to the floor.

Hooper waited till the last. He wanted to see all the preliminaries, as well as the members of the congregation. The result was that when he went in he found the place packed, there was no room at all at the back. At last an usher, a young woman, came to his rescue, took him to the front, and gave him a seat in the front row reserved apparently for the attendants on the sick.

Preedy entered from the vestry in surplice and bands at the same moment. He did not look at Hooper but paused a moment until he had sat down. He then made a short prayer, followed by a hymn.

This hymn caused a constriction in Hooper's throat – he dared not sing in case he should weep. But he was well accustomed to this disability, and put it down to a reflex. The sing-song of a hymn known in childhood, combined with the effect of its words, together played on his nerves, and produced sobs as certainly and mechanically as a blow in the stomach.

'Sensibility,' he thought, 'is my danger. Or perhaps it's been my salvation – in reaction.' He was pleased to find that the actual laying on of hands when Preedy prayed over each of the sick, individually, did not excite any emotion except curiosity.

There were immediate cures, but nothing dramatic. A child wheezing with asthma declared himself better; an old man said his pain had gone. Afterwards Preedy thanked God for seven cures, mentioned by name, but none of the patients' relatives or nurses made any statement.

This absence of the hysterical, the dramatic, by itself was highly satisfactory to Hooper. The whole atmosphere was that of responsibility and an established routine. He was strongly moved by a sense of discovery and conviction; he reproached himself for not coming before, for not keeping in actual touch with religion. He had always felt that in religion was the clue, the key, to a decent and, above all, stable self-respecting democracy. He had written about it often enough, but he had not for a long time exposed himself to it as an experience.

The experience had proved far more exciting, far more moving than he had expected. He waited for Preedy after the service, with a new sense of conviction, of dedication. He would back Preedy even if the board refused him; if the old gang were still obstinate, he would get publicity elsewhere. He knew half a dozen men who would put money into Preedy.

The congregation were now dispersing but not in a rapid stream, as usual after a service. It tended to form knots and groups, it hung about the gate in conversation. Obviously after one of these services of healing there was plenty to talk about; visible miracles had been performed.

Preedy himself, when, in plain clerical dress, he came out, did not linger, did not allow himself to be engaged. About a dozen persons, with three of the wheel-chair patients, had stationed themselves at the side door to intercept him. But the same four men who had been with him before the service surrounded him now, like a bodyguard, and in the midst of them he walked quickly past the waiting groups. He did not even acknowledge the salutes of some of the men, who lifted their hats. But Hooper, an old reporter, was not to be brushed aside. He planted himself in the middle of the gate and said bluntly, 'Excuse me, Mr Preedy – I'm from the *Argus*.'

Preedy, in the act of passing, stopped and turned, 'From Lady Rideout?'

'It's a Rideout paper – I think you have an appointment with Lady Rideout.'

Preedy did not rise to the bait. He merely gazed at Hooper and asked at last, 'Did you attend the service?'

'Yes, I came on purpose and I was most impressed – I had no idea of the work you're doing here.'

'The *Argus* published only a short notice. They asked for a long report but didn't publish it. Lady Rideout herself promised me a special article but that didn't appear either.'

'I shall do my best to get it published now.'

'You'd better hurry up then. I've waited six weeks and I had a *Daily Picture* man here yesterday.'

The young secretary, who carried a bundle of papers under his arm, said, 'Mr. Preedy has been very patient with the Press – this is the third time the *Argus* has let him down.'

'I can guarantee he will get publicity now.'

'Can you guarantee the *Argus*?' Preedy said shortly.

He was a small man, even shorter than Hooper, stooped in the shoulders, very thin, with a singularly long thin nose, and a small receding chin. His black eyes had a sleepy expression which was in sharp contrast with his abrupt manner of speech. He seemed to be preoccupied even as he gazed vaguely at Hooper.

'I think I can promise you.'

'That's not good enough, Mr – er. Lady Rideout gave me a promise.'

'When was that?'

He looked at Hooper with a contemptuous air, accentuated by the vague gaze, and said at last, 'The *Argus* had its chance.'

'Mr Preedy wants a paper with a good circulation,' said the secretary. 'The *Daily Picture* has three times more circulation than the *Argus*.'

'There are a good many candidates for publicity,' Hooper said dryly, 'especially among Missions of various kinds. The *Argus* is under pressure all the time.'

'Are you an editor?' Preedy asked.

'Yes, foreign editor. My name is Hooper – I'm also on the board of directors.'

'Foreign editor. What do you know about religion?'

'As I say, your service made a very strong impression.'

'Do you believe in my message?'

'I certainly believe that faith can cure disease.'

'Everyone believes that – but it's not my message. I say that God can cure all disease.'

'All without exception?'

44

'Otherwise, you don't believe it. But you think it would sell your paper.'

Hooper, now thoroughly angry, answered abruptly, 'You want publicity and I am offering to get it for you. We don't guarantee all the goods we advertise.'

The man in the striped trousers hastily intervened. Smiling at Hooper as if to say, 'You and I understand each other as men of the world,' he remarked. 'Advertisement is just what we want. That paragraph you gave us in March brought over a hundred sick people to the Mission – we had to run additional services, and many of them were cured.' He turned to Preedy, 'Perhaps if I could see Mr Hooper for a moment –'

Preedy waved his hand and walked on. The secretary and the other two men closed in on him; the effect was that of the chief, the leader, surrounded by his thugs.

'Mr Allday,' said the man in the striped trousers, holding out his hand, 'chairman of the committee.'

'He has a committee, has he – what does it do? Does it have any control?'

'An advisory committee – for finance. We wouldn't presume to lay down policy.'

'I shouldn't think it would be any good. Mr Preedy doesn't look like a man who would take suggestions well.'

Allday did not answer this, and Hooper thought, with some annoyance, 'One of your dodgers.'

For Hooper, all conversation with a stranger was a conflict; more or less secret. Sometimes he would attack openly as at the Rideout lunch, sometimes he would creep round a flank, as with Joanna, sometimes he would lie in ambush. With Allday he was specially tense, watchful; for it was obvious that, if he were going to use Preedy, his relations with the chairman of Preedy's committee might be highly important in the campaign.

'Look, Mr Allday,' he said, 'I might be able to give you a lot of help, I want to give you a lot of help, I've been greatly impressed by the service this morning, but I can't commit a paper like the *Argus* to anything definite without all available information. For instance, you say the committee deals with finance; you can't deal with finance without having a certain amount of control. Do you have control, or don't you?'

Allday was embarrassed, and cast about for an answer. Hooper cut in, sharply, 'If you want to think it over, you can let me know. You understand the position; I want to know just exactly how the Mission is run, who has the final say. Just now, I can't wait. I've got an appointment.' He walked off without any further word. He felt that Allday was the kind of man who would respond well to this kind of rough treatment; that is to say, a mild, good-natured sort of fellow, and a good Christian. As one of Preedy's committee-men, he was probably highly religious and a little bit mad. He might enjoy being trampled on.

When Hooper said he had an appointment, he meant that he had planned to see Syson also that morning. He had, in fact, allotted this day to getting a full grasp of the situation in Pant's Road and deciding finally how far he would go with it. He went straight from Allday to a telephone box and rang up the Sysons.

Mrs Syson, answering Hooper who described himself as the *Morning Argus*, said that she thought her husband was out. Then she covered the receiver with her hand and said to Syson, who was checking parish accounts at the table, 'It's some reporter and he wants to see you. You'd better be out, hadn't you?'

She spoke with impatience. Clarinda Syson had been born a Simpkins, of the celebrated scientific family. She herself had taken an excellent degree in mathematics and looked forward to a career in research. But in '44 she had fallen in love with Syson, then a night fighter pilot, and married him out of hand.

Her family had not quite cared for this. Syson was, in one sense, a good match. A civil servant, who had joined up for the war and had a good job to go back to, he belonged to the same class as the Simpkins, the public service class. He was, that's to say, not in trade, not out for himself, but a gentleman who served his country, like Sir Henry himself, head of the family, and Sir Henry's father, who had discovered an element, and in fact all the Simpkins, dons, civil servants, researchers. But not soldiers or sailors. The Simpkins allowed, theoretically, that soldiers and sailors were also gentlemen and public servants, but practically they looked askance at them, as men of blood. For though Sir Henry called himself a scientific humanist and agnostic, his father had been a Quaker and some of the family were still Quakers.

Their principal objection to Syson, however, was not the fact that he was, for the moment, a fighting man but that, like so

46

many temporary soldiers at that time, he had what seemed to them extreme views. He wanted to throw out the Churchill government and 'bring some justice and decency into the world'. He sometimes spoke almost like a communist; but if he hankered after communism, it was the Christian variety. For he was a strong churchman, and inclined to be contemptuous both of Quakers, 'those rabbits', and of agnostics, 'another name for dodgers'.

Sir Henry, good fellow, who hated strife of any kind, reacted strongly against this violent and cocksure young man, with his swagger and bounce. But unluckily Syson's very violence, like his swagger and his service exploits, seemed to increase Clarry's infatuation. She too thought that the country needed a new look; and as for religion, she had reacted already against both Sir Henry's agnosticism, and her Quaker relations. She declared privately that, 'What Daddy means by humanism is golf, food, whisky and good government grants for research.' In short, from the age of fifteen she had resolved to believe in God, and she was quite ready to marry even a strong Christian.

It was certainly a shock to her, when, after the war, Syson threw up his good job at the Ministry and went to a training college. She had not expected to find herself at thirty-two a curate's wife in the dismal Pant's Road suburb, with small pay, uncertain prospects, and an extremely shabby lodging of four rooms.

But she was not a Simpkins for nothing. She had been very angry when Syson, having decided to throw up his job, and finding her strongly against the step, offered to set her free.

'What on earth do you mean, set me free?'

'I only mean – it doesn't seem fair to you to change my job like this – it may mean a pretty hard life for a woman.'

'I didn't marry you for an easy life – and what about my promises – for better or worse? And what if you had been frightfully crippled? I took a very big chance of that.'

'In that case, too, I'd have made the same offer.'

'Would you indeed. What do you take me for? This is an eye-opener. And you talk of being a parson.'

'I'm not one yet – and it was only a suggestion.'

But Clarry had not forgiven him. She was immensely proud and here she had been ranked with creatures who fall down on their job. Eight years after that quarrel she was still apt to remark, when Tom Syson, seeing her more than usually tired in the evening, urged her to leave the washing up to him and go to bed, 'The poor little thing is not dead yet.'

She had done a magnificent job in the very tricky position of curate's wife. She had been economical without complaint, patient, tactful with parishioners. She had even won the approval of the vicar's wife, more difficult to obtain, and more important to a curate, than that of Mrs Colonel to a subaltern.

And in this stupid affair of the Pant's Road Mission, she had from the beginning taken council with the vicar. Like him, she saw danger in it. She had already warded off various callers who wanted to discuss it with Tom.

'It's easy for me to deal with 'em,' she would say, 'because they don't take me seriously – but some of those old pussies, especially the males, are just longing to put you in a corner. And then, you know, you're apt to get cross and say too much. I don't blame you, darling, but it's better if you don't get tempted.'

II

Clarinda had some reason for nervousness. For more than a month, since that paragraph in the *Argus*, Syson had been under attack from all sides: from Preedy's people, delighted to find a definite target; from Church people who were angry with him for giving them one; and from rationalists either praising him for his sensible action or jeering at him – one demanded how he could go on robbing the poor on the old God ramp if he didn't even believe in God. But the most unexpected result of that little piece of publicity in a leading morning paper, was a number of letters from people who had complaints against Preedy. They came from all over the country. A woman in Scotland accused him of being the death of her mother, a man called Rodker said Preedy had seduced his sister and caused the death of her baby, there were several who accused him of causing the death of children by persuading parents not to call in the doctor, and most of them were extremely bitter.

All the letters had a violent maniacal tone. The writers seemed obsessed with adoration of Preedy, or with violent hatred against him, fanatical faith or equally fanatical rage against any belief at all. Of course, as Clarry pointed out, it was only semi-lunatics who wrote such letters. But they upset Syson. He was upset by the charges that he, a clergyman, was, as one man wrote, 'trying to have it both ways'. He was upset above all, by a man well-known to him called Rollwright, actually living in the parish, whose wife, one of Preedy's followers, had left him because he wanted to call a doctor to their only child, a girl of eleven. She would not even let her husband see the child, because, she said, 'He breathed a bad influence on her and sucked away her faith.'

Rollwright was not a member of St Enoch's congregation but his wife had been one, and he appealed to Syson to warn Preedy off the ground. Syson had consulted the vicar, who said that he sympathized deeply with Rollwright but after all, Mrs Rollwright was no longer a member of St Enoch's, and so it was not their business to interfere. And it might be highly indiscreet. He murmured also his sympathy with Syson for 'getting in the paper like that', and promised that it would 'do him no harm'.

This very delicate reference to the Shillow promotion was not lost on Syson. But it annoyed him by the suggestion that he was being bribed. He was, it must be agreed, a touchy person. And then, when he told Rollwright the vicar's ruling, the man was rude.

Rollwright was a quiet man, not at all fanatical; all he said was that of course Syson had to think about his own skin and he supposed parsons were good for something or other, but it didn't seem much like common decency, much less Christianity.

The end of it was that Syson went to Mrs Rollwright and explained to her that if the child died there would be an inquest and she might be held responsible. He calculated that if Mrs Rollwright complained, Preedy could not do more than he had done already. But Preedy had done much more. He had got out a leaflet which was handed to the St Enoch's congregation as they came from matins, he had held more meetings, and he had put up a new notice, 'God or the Church.'

And the vicar had actually, for the first time, reprimanded Syson. He was a good chap, the vicar, he sympathized with this difficult curate of his, he understood very well that half his misfortune was simply keenness, but still this new unnecessary provocation of Preedy was simply disobedience.

Syson had not taken the reproof well. He had asked why they were so afraid of Preedy. Wouldn't it be better to take a more definite line?

'A definite line,' murmured the vicar. 'But have you a line to suggest?'

'Simply tell 'em Preedy is a crook and doesn't do these cures.'

'But he probably does do some cures – in neurotic cases certainly. And we don't know exactly the limits of neurosis. No, it's exceedingly difficult to *find* a definite line – that's the trouble.'

'Well, we'd better take one soon or we'll lose half our church members.'

'I don't think so,' the vicar said, 'my experience is that the better part of our people will always stick to us – and that Preedy will blow up in due course. They all do, you know. They all do if you give 'em time.'

Syson, as a matter of discipline, said 'Yes, sir,' in a reversion to service habits, which again slightly alarmed the vicar.

Syson had not meant to be ironical, his 'Yes, sir,' was actually next door to a reflex; it meant, 'Of course I obey, as a matter of duty.' And when Clarry now suggested that he might like to avoid Hooper, his reply was another reflex of the same sort. He did not like the idea of running away, especially as a parson, he hated the idea.

'Well,' said Clarry, cautiously feeling her way, 'we've had all this fuss already about Preedy and the *Argus*.'

'Do you want me to get under the bed because a pressman comes around?'

'Isn't that rather silly? You know what Vicar said – to leave the thing alone.'

'That's it. I can tell him what Vicar said – I mean, give him the case for the Church. It's quite time somebody did that.' He walked across the room, took the receiver out of her hand and said, 'Hello.'

'Mr. Syson?'

'Speaking. You wanted to see me? From the *Argus*, isn't it?'

'I'll be round.'

Before Hooper's arrival Syson walked up and down the small room with that jaunty air which he had brought from the Air

Force. He was looking forward to this conflict. He considered that Hooper was only a journalist and that he couldn't know so much about the matter of faith-healing as a man like himself in the profession.

He received Hooper, therefore, in a brisk and genial manner. his man to man manner, and offered him a drink. Hooper refused. He gave Clarry a nod instead of a handshake and did not sit down. Syson, irritated by this rudeness, began at once in a sharp tone, 'Why didn't the *Argus* print Mr Parsloe's letter about the Mission business? I thought the Press claimed to do the straight thing.'

'If you ask me, Mr Syson, the *Argus* is a good deal straighter than the Church.'

'Excuse me, but I wonder if you know very much about the Church.'

'Mr Syson, I didn't come here to get up a quarrel. What I was hoping was to settle this trouble with the Preedy Mission. You seem to think I'm against the Church, but I'm not; far from it. It's because I am so strong for the Church that I've come to see you today. It seems to me the Church is making the biggest mistake of its life in whiffling about this faith-healing issue. What exactly is the Church's position?'

'Simply that the matter can't be treated by slogans and mass hysteria.'

'That was what they said about Wesley and lost the whole of the Methodist movement. You'll admit that was a big disaster for the Church. Wesley put it simply and Preedy puts it simply, but I'm blessed if I can understand what the Church is after, if anything.'

'It's quite easy to know if you want to. It's all down in black and white.'

'Oh, if you mean that stuff they put out at Lambeth. I've read it. Man is a combination of body, mind and spirit, each needs appropriate treatment, and so on.'

Syson, taken aback, said, 'You mayn't like it, but it happens to be a fact.'

'The fact is, the important fact, that the Church, which is in charge and which won't deal with bodies, is dodging out. The whole statement is simply an excuse to hand over to the doctors.'

'That's just not true. All we say is that certain bodily ills need a doctor and certain spiritual ills need the Church. Of course, I suppose all that's too complicated for a stunt.'

'What do you mean, stunt? How cheap can you be?' Hooper was always enraged by the word stunt, for, like every newspaper man, he was well aware of the temptation to make stunts. 'You don't know anything about me. I might say the same of you. I might call that Lambeth Conference a stunt. Christ didn't need doctors before he healed people. The whole idea is to deny miracles and suck up to the scientists.'

'That's nonsense. The whole Church stands on the New Testament.'

'Well, why do you need a doctor's certificate before you do anything for the sick?'

'You know very well what's happened over and over again with these faith-healing quacks. People dying horribly because they haven't been properly attended to.'

'That's dodging the issue,' said Hooper. 'Preedy says that God really has power to cure the sick, to save them when they believe. He says quite plainly, "Either God has power to abolish evil or he hasn't, and if he hasn't then he isn't God, in fact there isn't any God."'

'But unluckily for Preedy it doesn't work. Most of Preedy's cures are simply neurotics who could be cured by cold potato or a mascot, anything you like, and the rest are fakes.'

'How do you know? It all turns on faith; if they don't believe, really believe, they can't be cured. It's the belief that works, that makes the contact so that the power can flow in. It's been proved again and again.'

'Who proved it? You know what Preedy is and Preedy's people are. They'd swear to anything.'

Syson felt that he was losing his temper. He had been startled by Hooper's argument and Hooper's confidence. He had not heard before this argument about the closed circuit, and it confused him, although he felt it was nonsense. He said, 'I've got evidence, you know, some pretty bad cases. Preedy's lucky to be out of jail.'

'Do you mean that?' Hooper said.

'Certainly I mean it.'

'Do you realize that you could be had up for making such a statement?'

Clarry interposed, 'All my husband means is that some of the cases at the Mission have died afterwards.'

But Hooper paid no attention to her. He was startled by Syson's manner. He had expected an easy victory over a curate and he was furious with the man. He said again, 'Do you really mean that? Would you be prepared to give the evidence?'

'Certainly I would. It's a horrible record.'

'All right, now we know where we are. But I give you fair warning, if you attempt anything against Preedy I'll advise him to take action, legal action. He'll have all the backing I can give him, and you'll find yourself in a very nasty place, very nasty indeed. Good morning,' and he went out. 'My God,' he said to himself, as he got into his car, 'if that's the sort of fool we get in the Church nowadays, it's no wonder the Church is what it is.'

Upstairs Clarry could not help remarking that it was a pity to annoy Hooper so much, 'He's obviously mad about Preedy.'

'Not a bit of it,' said Syson, who was again walking about the room, but not so confidently. 'He's just a newspaper man. To him it's a stunt. You heard that nonsense he talked about contacts and circuits, stuff he's picked up from some Preedyite. Superficial rubbish.'

'All the same,' said Clarry, 'it was the kind of argument that goes down. What is the answer?'

'Just rubbish.' Syson said, and went out of the room. The truth was that he hadn't the answer, not at the moment; it was something he'd have to look up, and he thought, with indignation, 'Why wasn't I taught to deal with a chap like that; why wasn't I given the answers?' He was so deeply disturbed and confused that he had already forgotten his anger with the brash Hooper.

12

Preedy's appointment with Lady Rideout in hospital was at four o'clock. He had asked for three o'clock on the grounds that he was accustomed to visit patients in their own homes during the late afternoon, but Lady Rideout had answered that three was impossible, she had a conference at that hour.

He decided to go just before three. He knew that he would be admitted. Lady Rideout had a private room, and a minister of

53

religion would always, if it were possible, be admitted to the sick. He presented himself, therefore, at ten minutes to three and was at once conducted to the private wing.

His purpose was simply to take the woman by surprise. This was part of his usual technique. He tried always to startle people, to 'knock them off their balance', as he put it, to crack their shell.

His common experience was that all human beings from earliest childhood set to work to build themselves a fortress, a shell, against the alarms and disappointments of the dangerous world, and they not only lived in it, if they could, for the rest of their lives, but they never exposed the least portion of their tender bodies under its edges except in completely safe conditions, in the dark, when no one was about.

His whole success depended on breaking this hard armour and getting at the terrified, quivering creature within. Only then could he put the strength where it was wanted, into the creature's mind and soul. He never doubted that the frightened mollusc existed behind the most formidable appearance; he had found it in millionaires, professors, ambassadors, the toughest crooks and the most brutal women. He had had a heavyweight boxer weeping at his knees; a Nobel prize scientist imploring him for strength only not to kill himself.

He liked to catch his quarry unprepared and he would attack from an unexpected angle, say the least-looked-for thing. As he has written in his instructions to Pant's Road Missioners, 'Do not despise modern psychiatry. It has shown us how much of man's activity is directed by subconscious forces completely beyond his control; by fear of what he can't even imagine, a lunatic terror; by hatred of what he does not know; by longing for that which he can't conceive and from which he is cut off, not only by ignorance, but by that pride which is really despair; the despair of a soldier under the last bombardment who does not move from his place because he is afraid that if he moves, he will run away and suffer a greater misery than death, the complete disintegration of his self.

It is this trembling, fearful, bewildered, creature, hiding in the dark like a wounded beast, that we have to find and persuade, support and lead into the daylight.

And do not be deceived by a bold carriage, a gay demeanour, a proud look, by the prosperous, successful persons who laugh at the very suggestion that they are not masters of their own fate, that they know the least fear of confusion. These are often the most cowed of all, the most wretched, the most dejected and despairing. It is not the brave who wear armour, or laugh at the enemy – it is not the self-respectful who swagger in arrogance. The asylums are full of fine fellows who declare that they can beat the world, that they know everything, who laugh all day and claim to be emperors, gods. For if they did not live in dreams, they would want to kill themselves. Let me tell you that I was such a lunatic – it was only by a miracle that I escaped the asylum or the grave. I myself was the bold man who feared nothing, the gay one who laughed in the face of the world, the proud one who knew better than anyone –' and then follows the celebrated passage where he describes his own conversion.

Preedy has been taken to pieces by experts. They say, 'The typical schizoid – a little Hitler. You find him everywhere – the village boy who goes from Mass to do murder is the basic type. And it works both ways. Sudden conversions are nearly all schizoid – St Augustine, St Francis, all the young men who commit every kind of crime or folly, even extreme cruelties, and then suddenly turn to religion, where they are equally violent and equally indifferent to authority, prudence or common sense.'

But what is the good of calling St Francis an egotist and an anarchist. True, he was the kind of saint that the Church might have burnt had he not, more by luck than anything else, happened to choose a policy that the Pope could approve – even if his immediate superior could not. Yet he was a saint, he sacrificed his comforts, his peace to do good as he conceived it. If he went his own way, if he sought power, then it was power for good. It's no good asking whether in doing so he made peace with his own nature, whether he had to be a devil or a saint, because no one knows what his nature was, least of all himself.

It is perfectly true, as Preedy always admitted, that as a young man, he had been a near criminal. He had escaped jail for drunkenness and violence only by good luck, and he had deserved it for seducing a girl of fourteen who had a child. His conversion followed the common pattern; a sudden complete surrender to the crudest kind of preaching. He had gone to jeer at a hell-fire evangelist at Hyde Park Corner, and had ended kneeling at his feet, the only penitent.

The conversion has been described as a 'kind of fit', very like mild epilepsy. Preedy's own description, given many times in his sermon is, 'Something broke in my brain – something enormous, dark, heavy as walls and towers – the city of despair where warriors fought for the mastery – the mastery of nothing. And light came upon me like a thunderstorm, a flash of lightning that blinded, a flash that deafened and bewildered. So that in its burning ruins I did not know where I was, or who I was; for what I had been I was not any longer, and what I was to be had not yet been decided. It was not by my own will, it was not by my own power, that I went forward that day to give myself up to God. I don't know how I moved, I don't know how I thought if I thought at all, before I found myself on my knees in the dirt, and felt within a voice that said, "Come to me – and I will give you peace." It was so little a voice in all that clangour of falling walls and screaming terrified devils, that I did not even hear it, I only felt it, I knew it only by the ears of my soul. But then the clamour fell away, and there was silence – and I heard – and I knew it for the very voice of God.'

The preacher was a man called Jackman, leader of a small evangelical sect practising faith-healing and rejecting doctors. They were also pacifists; indeed, they were anarchists of a type that perpetually recurs in religious history, since the Nazarenes and John the Baptist and probably before.

Preedy soon became Jackman's chief lieutenant and was very successful in making converts. But there had been two court cases in quick succession – one about a woman, wife of a believer, who had died of cancer, one about a child, dead of pneumonia – in which Jackman and Preedy had been severely censured by the coroner. Afterwards the Mission had split. Preedy had seceded with forty or fifty of the congregation, and founded his own mission, which had finally settled at Pant's Road in the previous year.

This was not, by any means, the first split in the Mission's history. Jackman himself had led a secession from a Methodist chapel; evangelical sects in their first inspiration and vigour invariably split. Their strength is in the faith, the only true faith, of the autonomous individual soul; their weakness is in the difficulty of persuading such souls to agree on any dogmatic statement of their faith.

As Preedy himself has written, 'The great totalitarian faiths stand like fortresses and seem to defy the utmost rage of the elements, but when at last the storm strikes, and the ancient towers fall, what have you – a heap of stones. But where the living tree is riven, the seed flies in the wind; the floods that sweep away the castle, fill every crack with fertile earth, the forests of the Lord spring far and wide, their branches cover the ruins of a thousand forgotten temples.'

Preedy, after a difficult start and some years of active poverty, had been very successful at Pant's Road, where Allday, an early disciple, had set him up financially. He had a special skill in attracting rich and well-educated converts, perhaps because he himself came from the middle-class – his father had been a parson and intended the boy for the Church. An only child, and clever, precocious in every way, but reserved, and subject to violent tempers, he demanded affection, but resented the least criticism. He took a scholarship at a public school, which delighted his parents; and then immediately, as if because of their congratulations, stopped working and set out to exasperate everybody. He was expelled at last for corrupting younger boys, for breaking bounds, for bringing drink into his study.

Meanwhile his father had died and the widow, who adored her son, kept him at home, and gave him everything he asked for. She was, in fact, terrified to refuse; if she attempted to reason with the young brute, he would threaten to kill either her or himself. He would bring his friends to the house, young hooligans, local prostitutes of the lowest class; he delighted in putting every kind of humiliation on a mother whose only fault was that she loved him to distraction. Luckily she had died before he completely ruined her.

Her death had affected him in the usual ambivalent manner; he was so overcome by grief that he broke down at the funeral and had to be taken away from the graveside; and then immediately he went on a drinking bout that sent him at last into hospital. His life followed its established pattern till he had nothing left. Then he would do casual labour, spend the proceeds on drink and live on the dole.

His first convert was one of his old school fellows, a prosperous company director; from the beginning, he had approached people of his own class. His recipe, given in his pamphlet for assistant evangelists, was 'The only difference between the starving is in their dress and their accents; their need is the same, for the simplest food in the simplest form.'

13

Kate Rideout, having demanded every hour since her first day in hospital to be sent home, having commanded Joanna to fetch her, told her secretary, Miss Toner, to order the car, complained to the matron, and finally asked Ackroyd to threaten the Ministry of Health, all at once became reasonable and obedient.

As she was brooding one night on the general mysterious evasion of her orders, on Joanna's promises to fetch her next day when the alterations were completed to the lift at Portland House – a next day that had now been put off daily for a week – on Miss Toner's news that the car was out of order, on the matron's statement that she had to wait for doctor's orders, on Edward Ackroyd's answer that the Minister would certainly not allow her to be kept against her will, it suddenly struck her that she was the victim of a conspiracy, and that she was helpless to fight it. She could not walk, at least for the moment; and so she was completely dependent on the goodwill of others. But how much goodwill had they? Joanna loved her but wouldn't it suit Joanna if she was out of the way? Joanna was far too good, too unselfish, consciously to wish her dead, but she might easily be persuaded that she ought to be retired, set aside, deprived of all authority. She was probably a burden to Joanna. She could not approve of the girl's ideas, especially of her flirtation, if it was no more than that, with young Hooper. And Joanna was a strange girl. She had been an odd child, reserved, undemonstrative; for all her dutiful air, she had gone her own way. It was impossible to know what went on behind those good-natured smiles, that affectionate good humour.

Of course, there were her friends; but who were her friends? They began to wear suddenly a quite new appearance. Mrs Mantoffle had appeared in hospital for five minutes, talked about how busy she was, and had not been seen since. Kate remembered now how often she had smiled privately at the woman's ambition, her love of the limelight. Small faults in a sterling character. But now it seemed that they were perhaps faults of serious import to their friendship. Had Mrs Mantoffle written her off as not worth the time that might be given to more profitable relations, with people still powerful, still in the news?

And Edward Ackroyd, that close ally of forty years' loyalty – he had sent flowers, fruit, called three times, arranged to hold the weekly editorial conferences in her room. But why at three o'clock? Five was the usual time. Obviously these hospital meetings were merely courtesy affairs, the real ones would be at the *Argus* office later. And he had not even asked her opinion about the last issues of the paper. Of course, he might have found it difficult to reach her in hospital – she had no telephone in her room – but for a long time before this he had not really attended to her criticisms; this sudden neglect to consult her at all was merely a failure in tact; the man could not be bothered to keep up a farce.

And was not Edward, at last, at seventy-eight, beginning to show his age? He was growing every month more deaf, more obstinate. Did he really care what happened to anybody any more? Was he not absorbed with the one thought, how much longer he could hold on to his chairmanship, his power? Would he not, at a pinch, take Joanna's part? The future belonged to Joanna, and Edward had always looked forward. It was his power of looking forward that had made their fortune; he had backed John Rideout's schemes for a popular radical paper when no one else would risk a shilling. Yes, it was very likely indeed that Edward would go in with Joanna in this scheme to relegate her, Kate Rideout, to insignificance.

The idea enraged her, but rage gave her a fright. She felt the pulses throb wildly in her head, and remembered that excitement was forbidden her; it might kill her.

'It's all nonsense,' she told herself, 'I haven't had a stroke at all – I wish I had. A stroke can be cured.'

But she lay still in horror. Perhaps it had been a stroke. Perhaps this fearful thumping would burst a blood vessel, and blind her, kill her out of hand. She must not be afraid either; fear also might kill her. She had to abolish both anger and fear.

That was why the doctors and nurses of the hospital suddenly found their patient amiable. It might, of course, be a bad sign; at a certain stage of weakness, the dying suddenly accept fate. They were watchful – but all the same, relieved. They warned the relatives to be specially careful of agitating the patient, and to relieve her as far as possible of any huge responsibility. They allowed the conferences, in fact, only after Lord Ackroyd had convinced them that they would be purely formal, that they were intended only to keep Lady Rideout in good humour, that they – Ackroyd and Tinney between them – would devise special agendas to please the old lady. On the Thursday of Preedy's visit, they were to cover long-range economics, a subject which, they agreed, could not cause any dissension, as Kate did not pretend to understand it.

She, knowing very well her deficiency, had followed her usual practice in such a case; she sent for an expert. At half past two, propped up in her best bed jacket, she received Professor Mardew and commanded him to brief her on the whole subject.

Mardew was young, keen, ambitious; he was supposed to be the coming man, but he proved to be elusive. He answered all her questions at great length, he was immensely fluent; but after twenty minutes, Kate was still unprovided with a policy. And she was very anxious to have one; she had taken a great deal of trouble to get hold of Mardew for this very purpose – she meant to show Ackroyd and Tinney that this conference, even if it had been intended merely as a courtesy, could yield results. She would take a stand. She began to be angry with Mardew, she suspected that he was stalling, that he didn't want to commit himself until he had discovered what policy Ackroyd and Tinney would follow.

At last she lost her temper, and exclaimed, 'Two minutes ago you said inflation was a good thing – now you say it's dangerous. What do you mean – do you know what you mean?'

'I'm so sorry, Lady Rideout – but the matter is really rather complicated,' and he began again to talk of the balance between production and consumption, the dead weight of the national debt, full employment, a dynamic policy.

It was at this moment that the old woman heard her name spoken and looking up saw Preedy at her bedside.

'Preedy,' he said, holding out his hand. 'Excuse me, I did knock.'

'I told you to come at four.'

'It was impossible, and rather than not come at all, I looked in.'

'I can't see you now – I told you I had a conference at three.'

She suspected some trick. No doubt the man wanted to break into the conference and push his claim for a write-up in the *Argus*.

'We have five minutes,' said Preedy, 'it's quite enough to break through.'

'Break through – what do you mean?'

'You distrust me, Lady Rideout. You've been building a wall against me from the beginning. What are you afraid of? I'm not an enemy – if you don't like what I say, you can contradict me.'

'Afraid of you,' the old woman's cheeks turned purple. 'Where did you get that idea?'

'You know, Lady Rideout, one of the great problems of the doctors – they will tell you themselves – is the patient who wants to be ill, or put it like this, who would rather go on being ill, who would rather die, than try some quite simple treatment which he doesn't want to believe in. You'd think he was mad – but it's not quite that. It's simply prejudice, habit. Lots of people die – die in agony, in misery, rather than give up a cherished prejudice.'

'Are you trying to put me in a temper – that's rather an old stale trick. As a salesman, Mr Preedy, your methods are rather crude.'

'You see, Lady Rideout, you are full of suspicion. You judge me before I've said a word. Do you really think I'm a crook and a fraud – is that why?'

'I don't know what you are. I don't know anything about you.'

'But you barred me from the *Argus* – it isn't allowed even to mention my name. Why did you change your mind so suddenly about the value of my work?'

'Will you kindly go away and let me get on with my work?'

'I have a right to an explanation, Lady Rideout. My character has been attacked. Of course, I know you're not your own mistress. You are in a difficult position, or what you think is difficult – you have to reconcile all sorts of interests which seem to you important. In fact, they are of no importance at all. If you despised them, they would simply disappear, and your position would be quite simple and immensely strengthened –'

'Will you go or must I ring for a porter?'

'Certainly ring, but I shall state my case – it's unanswerable.'

Kate Rideout was already fumbling for the bell. Preedy handed it to her and she rang.

'Good,' he said. 'Now we know where we are.'

There was a knock on the door. Ackroyd and Tinney came in, Ackroyd already talking loudly about the new wave of strikes. He had long practised the art of monologue. This was not only because of his deafness, he liked to hold the field because he was, in fact, rather bored with other people's opinions. He knew all the old ones, he had heard them a million times; and he did not want to hear new ones, they could only upset him.

'All this cackle about communists in the unions,' the old man bawled, 'and rigging the elections – it's as old as the hills. We had it in the nineties. Of course they're there. Of course there's some dirty work. But what's the alternative? Are you going to put the police on the job? That's fascism. In any democracy you've got to take some hanky-panky – it doesn't pay in the end.'

Tinney listened with a half-grin. He was bored. He had been listening to the discourse for the last ten minutes and he had heard it all before. He wondered if it would end in the argument that the golden rule of democracy, the fundamental rule, was to trust the people, because in the end they always stumbled on the right course. They might be slow to find it, and exasperatingly stupid by the way, but they always did find it.

Probably Ackroyd would have produced this statement. He did not mind repeating himself, he even seemed to enjoy throwing a cliché at his critics, as if to say, 'Take it or leave it.' But his eye fell on Preedy and he stopped.

Preedy walked up to him and offered his hand.

'Preedy – I think you know of me, Lord Ackroyd.'

'Ha.' Ackroyd, taken aback, let his mouth fall open. For a moment, he looked crazy, senile.

But Tinney was delighted by the interruption. His whole face changed. He held out his hand. 'Not *the* Preedy – the – ah – the prophet.' He shook hands with a little bend from the waist, a quick flutter.

'I have been called that – but I don't prophesy – I deal only with diseases of the present.'

'I believe you have had a good deal of success.' Tinney fixed his bird's eyes on the prophet with amused curiosity. He thought of himself as a connoisseur in human folly. He affected to despise

62

the human race. In his own words, it was a disease, a species of fungus, grown upon an insignificant star by the accident of a certain degree of damp coinciding with the presence of air and carbon at a certain temperature. It would soon die off; it could never occur again. And this was at least a consolation to intelligent forms compelled to exist within its neighbourhood.

'I can't claim any success,' Preedy said, 'thousands have been healed – but only by God's grace.'

A nurse appeared and Lady Rideout called out, 'I rang, nurse. I wanted someone to show that gentleman out.'

'My appointment was for four,' Preedy said, 'but I came early – perhaps, Lady Rideout, I can return at four.'

Before Kate could answer what seemed to her an impudent suggestion, Tinney appealed, 'But Kate, I'm sure Mr Preedy would be an acquisition. Do stay, Mr Preedy – I want to know about your methods.'

The nurse, impatient and busy, was already half-way out of the door; Tinney was drawing up a chair, 'Tell me, Mr Preedy, do you take cancer cases?'

'Certainly – and many are cured.'

'Entirely by faith. I take it you pray over them.'

'It is their faith that heals.'

'I believe there was a case of yours last year – when a patient died. And the coroner seemed to think that she could have been saved by operation.'

'It wasn't a case of mine. I don't cure anyone. As I said before, it is only God who can cure. I can only try to put the sufferer in accord with the Holy Spirit. Without faith there can be no cure. I did have a case like that some years ago – a woman died and there was an inquest. A very unhappy business, but it wasn't the Mission's fault.'

'I see, it was the woman's fault that she died.'

'Certainly.'

'And these cures of yours – I suppose there was no doubt they were suffering from cancer.'

'Specialists had diagnosed the disease.'

'Come, Bobby,' said Kate, 'we're waiting for you – and we've only an hour.'

But Tinney paid no attention. He was bored with all conferences and especially this one – a mere pretence to please a dying woman. He went on with his inquisition. Could Preedy cure a broken leg, or mental deficiency; he asked all the questions that occur to the ordinary scientific mind and received the usual answers. A broken leg would heal more quickly if the patient had faith; mental deficiency could make it impossible for a victim to believe anything; lesser degrees could often be cured, or at least, alleviated. Preedy answered easily, with confidence, and seemed as much at his ease as Tinney. Suddenly he attacked.

'You don't believe in God, Sir Robert?'

'I'm afraid not,' smiling gaily as at a joke.

'And yet you went to jail as a conscientious objector.'

'Certainly.'

'You stated that war was a great evil.'

'I think so still.'

'Why? If humanity is merely automatic machines without freedom, without responsibility, without souls?'

'Quite so, Mr Preedy. A good point. I dislike war simply because I'm made that way.'

'You can't help yourself.'

'Absolutely not. I was damned uncomfortable in jail.'

'But then you changed your mind about war. You disapproved of Hitler, I think.'

'Exactly.' Tinney laughed with pleasure. 'So I did.'

'You declared Hitler to be an evil man. Surely if you acknowledge evil in man, you admit there is good also. If there were no goodness in the world, how would you recognize evil?'

'I recognize my own comfort, Mr Preedy. Hitler frightened me. I thought, "Suppose he should win, what would happen to an old liberal like me?"'

'You claimed to be a pacifist in the first war.'

'I claim to a certain intelligent appreciation of my own comfort – and of course that is also other people's comfort. I am not unique in enjoying peace, liberty and the ordinary pleasures of life.'

'You claim to love comfort but yet you went to jail – isn't that something of a contradiction?'

'I was a different man in 1935 from what I was in 1916.'

'Not so very,' Preedy said coolly. 'You've always been a mischievous fellow. You've always loved upsetting applecarts. It's the chief motive of your existence.' At this, a faint colour appeared in Tinney's cheeks. He was irritated. He said smoothly, 'Do you mean I don't believe what I say?'

'Not exactly that, the general view is that you are rather a cold-hearted man moved chiefly by intellectual arrogance. You despise ordinary humanity and like to make it look silly. But the funny thing is that you like to be admired. You love the shop-window.'

At 'shop-window' Tinney laughed. What an absurd charge. Him to be accused of seeking popularity; the coolest brain in Europe, the destroyer of all illusions. 'Do I look so handsome? And you know, Mr Preedy, some people might say that there is a certain arrogance in your claim to know more about disease than the doctors.'

'Doctors,' said Kate suddenly, in a loud, furious voice. 'What do you know about doctors, Robert. You've never been ill in your life.'

The four men, who had completely forgotten her in the discussion, turned surprised faces towards the bed. 'Doctors don't know everything – not about real illness. They simply shoot things into you and trust to luck.'

'I see,' said Tinney, 'so you are joining Mr Preedy's denomination.'

'Why do you say that? It's perfectly true, you know, Robert, that you are the most mischievous man I ever knew. You simply love to get up arguments. No, I'm not joining Mr Preedy's church. I never even thought of it. Now perhaps we can get on with our conference, if you mean to have one at all.'

Preedy at once took leave, and Mardew began to talk about inflation.

But in his very first sentence he was interrupted by Lady Rideout. She suddenly demanded of Ackroyd why the *Argus* had not been sent to her in hospital. She had had to send out and buy a copy.

And before Ackroyd could answer, she said, fiercely, 'You think I'm finished – do you?'

'Good God, Katy –' Ackroyd was amazed.

'It's more likely the *Argus* is finished,' the old woman exclaimed, 'and whose fault is that? The trouble with you, Edward, is you won't grow up.'

Ackroyd laughed loudly and looked round him as if at a large company prepared to appreciate the joke. 'Have you gone over to the Hooper plan?' Tinney asked.

'Hooper, who's Hooper?'

'The foreign editor; he writes a column too.'

'I don't know anything about his plans.' The old woman had remembered Hooper now and his suggestions, but she wanted to cover her failure of memory by making little of him. Why, in fact, should she trouble to remember such things and such people in her situation?

'What I want to know,' she said, 'is when we're going to see the mock-up of the new front page.'

'You wouldn't like it, Kate – the complete tabloid.'

'Why didn't I see it? Why shouldn't I like it American style – at least it's something new. And it might be the only chance for the *Argus*.'

Ackroyd began to bawl. A tabloid would only lose the old *Argus* public and get no new readers in exchange. They already had their tabloids, the *Mirror*, the *Graphic*.

'That's what you always say. And meanwhile the *Argus* is dying on its feet.' She was very angry. She began to scream at Ackroyd. Did he forget that she had an interest in the paper, that she was Kate Rideout.

Tinney intervened. Perhaps they had better discuss this point afterwards; meanwhile they were keeping Mr Mardew.

Mardew then said his piece. But with a certain amount of fumbling which disappointed Tinney.

The fact was that Mardew had prepared a statement with which to impress Ackroyd; he knew all about the trouble on the *Argus* board, but he had been advised that Ackroyd would win.

He had been angling for a financial editorship for the last three years. He considered most of the reigning financial editors completely out of date, ludicrously ignorant and narrow. He was especially contemptuous of the *Argus* man. He had however taken care not to contradict him too openly, only to suggest developments.

But having heard with great interest the argument between Kate and Ackroyd, he had decided to hedge. If the Hooper party won, Ackroyd's man would be out at once.

Meanwhile it was obviously dangerous to take sides. He must

play clever. Time enough to push his views when he had got a job and made a name. What he needed now was publicity. He would get nowhere without publicity.

14

Out in the street, Ackroyd burst out laughing, 'What do you think of that, Bob?'

'What's that, Eddy?'

'Old Kate – but she's always been like that. She used to blow up at Johnny too.'

'She's always felt that she wasn't getting enough consideration. All women do in any kind of authority. So do men, of course, but they don't imagine at once that they're being discriminated against because of their sex.'

There was a pause and Tinney said, 'At last we've got a clear line on Hooper – she's lost interest in that gentleman.'

'I'm not worrying about the twerp; but his gang on the board.'

'Now's the time to move, while Kate's out of it.'

Ackroyd said nothing to this, he liked to play certain tricks of the man in power – to keep silence when he might have been expected to show an opinion, to change the subject unexpectedly, as if his thoughts followed a course too deep for other people's logic. He exclaimed suddenly, 'That chap Mardew. There's another wangler.' The old man liked to use what he thought the latest slang. 'A fine specimen of the smart alec – trying to run with the hare and hunt with the hounds – I've no use for these wide boys, and what's more they're out of fashion. We're getting over the war – the last election was a sign. The people didn't really vote Tory – they voted against the wild men – the clever boys.' And so on. Ackroyd could always make a new case for an old policy.

There was a short pause. Then suddenly he burst out, 'She doesn't realize what's happening to us. I wonder if anyone does. All this hustle to be smart, to catch the eye. And why? The people don't want it – they were quite satisfied with what they were getting – good honest stuff. Who is it that's smashing up every decent standard? A minority – a tiny minority, of bum-suckers on the make. That's all they are, Bob – sucking up to the mob. And not just the mob either but the worst instincts of the mob. The dirtiest kind of bum.'

Tinney said, 'After all, our circulation isn't going down, not appreciably. It's only our costs have gone up.'

'This I.T.V. – it's the same thing. Give them filth. Give them sadistic violence –'

He was shouting so loudly that people turned to look. Tinney, startled by this outburst, a little alarmed by his old friend's extraordinary excitement, began to talk of mass education, the American influence, but Ackroyd only grew more excited. What was this civilization they boasted of? What was free about it if a few irresponsible millionaires on the grab could pour any dirt or lies they liked into the public ear and prevent any answer?

Tinney was still preoccupied with that word, 'Shop-window.' What a silly and a mean charge. He, Tinney, the great independent brain – the destroyer of vulgar illusions. To be called a show-off, a popular comedian. It was a piece of spite. But where did it come from? Did a lot of people think like that? Was it a popular delusion? And how did one put people right? How did one make them realize that in fact one did not care tuppence for their opinion? That one was a completely independent brain, aloof from the mob.

Ackroyd's chatter annoyed him. What a bore the old chap was. He had never been very clever, a good second-class was about his mark and now he was simply a senile ass.

'I'm going into the Theseum,' he said. 'Got to meet Pontoff about a broadcast we're doing.'

Ackroyd, to his annoyance, also turned into the club. He quickly dodged away – not, however, before his old friend had tackled a startled archdeacon about the universal degeneration of standards throughout the whole of so-called Christendom, the competition between all forms of publicity for the lowest appeal.

The room was crowded in that most crowded of clubs and a group formed, chiefly of younger members who have brought in so much frivolity, or what to the Theseum is frivolity, since the war. One youthful headmaster in green tweeds wanted to know if the Press had any influence, good or bad, except in shortening the price of a favourite horse or lengthening that of a favourite girl.

'Influence – of course it has influence – you can't take a daily dose of poison for years without being affected.'

68

'But surely,' a young man murmured. 'The good grey *Times* –'

'I don't think anyone can say that the *Argus* is not keeping its form.' This was from a member just elected, a young Fellow of All Saints, already marked down for extraordinary self-confidence and double-edged remarks.

'I *like* the *Argus*,' said the first speaker.

They were baiting the old man in the manner of dons in a college common room, politely, discreetly. Ackroyd perceived it and thought, 'So they think I'm an old fool.'

This was the judgement that he had dreaded for twenty years past so that his whole manner was designed to contradict it, his loose lounging walk, his wide gestures, his shouts, his slang, his bellowing laugh; above all, his opinions. He had backed every new movement, all the modern arts, he had tolerated everything unless he was sure that at least a large section of the young was against it. He was all against censorship, except, of course, for horror comics, violence and pornography; he was all for the teenager, except the Teddy boys and the bebop parties. He had, he felt, a truly youthful and lively mind. He could hold his own with the most brash young person.

But now something had broken down. And the polite chaff of these young men only infuriated him. What a miserable crew they were, without imagination, without values, without manners full of cheap conceit. All the worse for them if they had brains, and used them simply to play in with the scum who were pulling the whole nation down into the gutter.

'The *Argus*,' he bawled. 'Yes, I think it has done a good job. It stands for something that matters. And let me tell you it's going on that way –'

'Hear, hear,' said the young Fellow from All Saints, in a very grave, too grave tone. 'In these times of flux – to stand for –'

'Progress,' murmured the other.

'Under the law.'

'We have a record that can't be touched,' shouted the old man. 'I can tell you we aren't ashamed of the *Argus*.' His cheeks were red, he was beginning to look a little crazy. Bishop Mantoffle, an old friend, interposed his large body and took his arm.

'Excuse me, Eddy, but I wanted to ask you about something – shall we try the library.' He led the old man away. His something was a long tale about Church reunion. The *Argus* might be so helpful if it took a certain line.

But Ackroyd was restless and impatient. Reunion was a minor issue. What was the good of tinkering with the Church while the whole moral basis of the country was cracking up – while the young generation was going to the devil. No – not the devil. Nothing so dramatic. Just down the drain – with the sewage.

Mantoffle was not so pessimistic. No, the picture was not so black – there were some slight signs of grace. The censorship bill had received unexpected support from the people. Yes, even one of the miners' associations had been all for it. The tide might turn any day.

This was Mantoffle's common form; what he called 'qualified optimism.' It had got him a bishopric and he hoped it might take him even further, if he could keep in with the Press.

Ackroyd had always heartily agreed with him before. But now he broke out with an astounding remark, 'Humbuggery.'

Mantoffle stared at his old friend. He couldn't believe his ears. For this charge is one not allowed in the Establishment, especially not among Bishops. It's not fair; it's hitting below the belt. It can't be allowed, that is to say, if the game is to go on. What on earth, his eyes asked, had caused old Ackroyd to break away in this wild manner.

'Humbuggery,' Ackroyd bawled again, in a furious voice. 'And it's strangling the country – not to speak of your damned old Church.' He levered himself up on his long thin arms, for a moment he resembled an ancient grasshopper about to take flight; then, suddenly balancing on his legs, he plunged forward out of the room. Mantoffle was left in much distress.

'Poor old boy,' he shook his head. 'It's come – ah, well, no one can last for ever and he's had a long innings.'

15

Kate Rideout had listened to the men with a kind of disgusted horror. Their talk seemed to her like a child's patter, nonsense words. She was tired of Edward Ackroyd's slogans, of Tinney, with his tricks of argument. What was behind it all? Only two old men, older than she; Edward trying to make the world stand still. Tinney trying to dominate it. In Tinney's mind, he was the master, all others were foolish and naïve. And what was he in essence – a little man devoured by conceit and fear. Fear that he would be passed over, pushed aside, reduced to the common dimensions.

Thirty years ago she had had a brief affair with Tinney. It had been very brief for he had suddenly deserted her for a younger and prettier woman. His explanation was simply that he liked the other woman better.

This frankness had been meant to seem like a compliment to Kate. It set up the assumption, 'You and I are superior beings – we scorn the sentimentalities of the mob. We deal in truth and are not afraid of it.'

'We agreed to tell the truth to each other,' he had said.

'Yes, and the truth is that you have no feelings at all. You are as cold as a fish.'

Tinney had been amused by this charge; he remarked that the affair itself proved the opposite.

'Oh,' said Kate, 'you sleep with women all over the place. But only for your own amusement. What you call love is simply an itch. And, of course, you like to be admired.'

'Good heavens, what else should it be?'

'If you really don't know, I can't tell you.'

But she suspected that he did not want to know; he was afraid to know, because it would make nonsense of his logic, and spoil his peace, his self-satisfaction. He had arranged his life to avoid any kind of worry, to get the maximum of pleasure for himself with the least trouble, and to do that it was necessary to avoid any strong sympathies, any real affection, any real belief.

What was fearful to her was the coldness of these men; behind all their masks they did not care for anybody. Ackroyd cared for the *Argus*, but what was that. What was a newspaper – a collection of words, a commercial product. It seemed to her all at once a very dim and wavering object, a thing less real to her than her dressing-gown. Oh, to get home. But she must be careful. She must not be too eager. That might be fatal. Those doctors might take it for a sign that she must be kept longer. No one knew how their minds worked; least of all themselves. They were simply pretending to each other. That's why they jumped at any piece of nonsense – it sounded new, broad-minded, impressive.

Preedy could serve as pretext. He had suggested in his letter that she should attend a private service to avoid publicity. Apparently he gave such private services often. What she wanted above all was to get out of hospital, to get home. If she could tell Joanna, 'I have to go to this service – it might cure me,' Joanna would not dare to stand in the way. She would never take a responsibility like that. Neither would the doctors have her back, if she went to that quack. Of course, if they tried to get her back, she would fight them, she would call out, if necessary, to the people in the streets. She would risk a scandal, and let them make the best of it, from Joanna to Ackroyd.

She took care, however, to explain the matter to Joanna in a casual manner in the midst of a routine talk about bills, servants, family plans.

'By the by, I've got to see this man, what's his name – Preedy – at work. Apparently, I gave him a kind of promise – or he thinks so. Of course, I'm going to a private service. He's undertaken to keep it quiet. No publicity. And the last chance is on Friday next. It's at the Grand Palace. Some Australian family.'

'It's a bit soon, isn't it; are you sure you'll be all right?'

'Of course I'll be all right. You can take me in an ambulance if you like.'

'I'll see the doctors.'

'They'll say no, of course. But if they do, Preedy's going to raise the question.'

'Raise the question?'

'Yes, ask what right they have to keep me against my will. That's the real point, you see – he might make trouble – he's very suspicious already. He thinks there's a plot to keep me here.'

As Kate spoke of a plot she looked keenly at Joanna. But there was no sign of embarrassment.

16

Joanna, suddenly realizing that Preedy might make a convert of her mother, did not know exactly what to think about this situation. What did she really think of faith-healing, or Preedy? And again she found herself in confusion. She felt lost and frustrated, and after a bad night, she telephoned the *Argus*'s office for the Preedy dossier. There proved to be little in the file and the woman in charge of the information room, called for some reason the Bureau, seemed surprised by the inquiry.

'You mean that faith-healing man – we're not collecting anything about him now.'

'But weren't there a lot of complaints against him – there was someone who kept on phoning.'

'There've been several – but we didn't keep track. Do you want an address?'

'I just wanted to know what they were saying.'

'Well, I'll inquire.'

The woman was obviously surprised by this inquiry, and Joanna was now sorry she had made it. She hated even to seem to intrude on the affairs of the *Argus*. She felt that they were too complicated, too tricky; she dreaded to be accused of interfering, of pulling strings, earning hatred. The *Argus* seemed to her like a trap – if she got in there she would be caught in all kinds of tension and hatreds; she would never be free again.

The Bureau woman's voice was full of interest; she was certainly wondering why Miss Rideout wanted to know what was wrong with Preedy. Joanna felt as though the *Argus* had suddenly shot out a hook to pull her into the trap. She was angry with herself; still more so when on the next morning, coming in from shopping, she was accosted by a young man, just outside her door.

He tipped his hat, worn at a slightly rakish angle, and said, 'Miss Rideout? Fred Rodker. I believe you were asking for me.'

'Oh, yes,' Joanna recognized the name. Rodker was the name she had been trying to recollect. He was one of the original complainants against Preedy, and he had bombarded the *Argus* for weeks afterwards with letters saying that Preedy was a crook and ought to be in jail.

Such letters come every day to newspaper offices about people in the news. There are apparently thousands of people obsessed with the bitterest grievances, with murderous hatred. Their letters usually don't even reach the editor. But young Rodker sent newspaper cuttings, first about a case in a juvenile court where a girl of fifteen, Alice Rodker, pregnant by some unknown man, was cited as being beyond parental control, and then about a coroner's inquest on a two-year-old baby, Margaret Rodker, who had died of meningitis. No doctor had been called because the mother had belonged to a sect which rejected doctors and trusted only in God's direct healing. The jury had censured the minister concerned, a certain Jackman.

The cuttings were stuck on a sheet of foolscap and Rodker had typed under the first, 'Alice is my sister, and the real father of the baby was this man Preedy, he admits it,' and under the second, 'It was Preedy who persuaded my sister not to have a doctor for the poor kid. He wanted it to die. And got right away with it.'

Ackroyd had had the evidence checked with the two papers and it was found that it might possibly have some substance.

He spoke to her in a calm, matter-of-fact tone.

'I've been waiting for you. Look here.' He took an envelope out of his pocket. 'You read this – here's a proof you can't get over.'

Joanna reached out her hand. But the young man held on to the envelope. 'No, excuse me. I can't let 'em out of my sight. They're the original letters from Preedy himself.' Joanna hesitated. Finally she said that she was sorry but at the moment she was engaged. What was his address and she'd give him an appointment.

'Today?'

'If I can – I'll ring you.'

'I'm not on the phone.'

'Very well, call at six this evening.'

Rodker lifted his hat again an inch or two with the same abrupt gesture, as if he resented the ritual, and walked off.

Joanna was still regretting her new entanglement with the *Argus*, half an hour later, when Hooper rang up.

'Hullo, Joanna. Has that fellow Rodker been round?'

'Oh, it's you.' Joanna spoke gaily, in a cheerful tone. She had not seen him since the night of the *Post* party, and she was still highly irritated against him for his crude attempt upon her peace of mind. She regretted more than ever her call to the *Argus*, that it had brought him down upon her. Experience should have taught her by now that that organization was like a complex but highly active and sensitive nervous system. If you touched it anywhere, you set reflexes going through the whole.

'What did he tell you?'

74

'Nothing yet. He says he's bringing me some proofs about Preedy.'

'When and where?'

'Six o'clock – here.'

'All right. I'll be round. You can do the talking but I'll be there.'

'If you want to see him, why not have him to the office? He'd be very willing.'

'Because I don't want him to think I'm interested. He might shut up altogether if he knew who I was. It's got to be a chance meeting for me. But if you're still peeved, you needn't see me. Put him in that little back room – what do you call it? – the book room. And I'll come upon him by accident. Six, you said?'

'As you like. At six.'

Hooper arrived five minutes early. Joanna had decided to take him at his word, and to avoid him. But he came up the stairs on the heels of the young butler and walked into the room. He wanted to know what Rodker was like and what he had said to her.

17

Hooper had avoided Joanna since the *Post* party. Partly this was calculation. He had proof of the girl's interest in him. She had been furious with him, especially at that charge of coldness. He thought of her. 'The poor oaf, she's as simple as a cuckoo clock, I can have her when I want her.' But he had not been sure that he wanted her. In the last three days the whole situation on the *Argus* had changed. First of all, it had come to his ears that Ackroyd had proposed a trust for the *Argus* Company with five trustees; that's to say, himself, Tinney, Lady Rideout, Penfold, the economist, and an old lawyer called Sir James Gadd, who was trustee already for Sir John Rideout's grandchildren by his first marriage. Gadd himself had called Hooper with the news. Gadd was a very small man in the middle sixties, with a high bald head; dry, scholarly, an old-fashioned Liberal, like Ackroyd. But as representative of the Rideout grandchildren he had considered it his duty to keep an eye on the finances of the paper. He had, therefore, been inclined to the Hooper interest, and the

Hooper projects, and now he told Hooper of the plan in confidence, apparently as an encouragement. 'Of course,' he said, 'I don't go as far as you do. We'll have to keep the general features of the old *Argus*, but I do think we want a new editor.'

Hooper, taking this as a plain intimation that his course was clear, had promptly written to Ackroyd proposing a complete new *Argus*, with his friend Cleary for editor, and the managing editorship for himself. Ackroyd's answer was to accuse him of general disloyalty to the *Argus*, and to the present editor, whereupon Hooper had offered his resignation.

That had been two days before and Hooper had had no answer. At first this had elated him. He felt Napoleonic; indeed, he had let several of his friends know, including Cleary, that he was not taking chances, as it might seem to a careless observer, he had prepared his ground and struck at the right moment; the enemy was in dismay and confusion. But on the third day he had had a call from James Gadd asking him why he had 'rushed in like that,' and he added in his hectoring and peevish tone, 'I thought it was a well-established rule in newspaper as well as Cabinet circles, never resign.'

Hooper despised Gadd as a pettifogger, a mean mind in a mean body, but he knew him to be a shrewd man of affairs, and he was on the board. He was also in Ackroyd's confidence. All at once his bold move had seemed extraordinarily risky. He realized that he might actually lose his job and that this was something he had never expected. When, therefore, he rang up Joanna he was both alarmed and exasperated, and spoke to her with a careless rudeness that was meant to show his indifference to a creature that had joined in this conspiracy to ignore his value. What did it matter to him how this stupid, obstinate girl felt? She belonged to a class that was finished; her sensibilities were as foolish as silver forks on a desert island. They were in fact a weakness; they made her still more vulnerable, and her class still more defenceless.

When he arrived in Portland Place, he did not bother to offer his hand, he said only, 'Where's this man Rodker?'

'I expected him before this.'

'Though it doesn't matter what he's got against Preedy. What does Preedy's character matter if he can deliver the goods?'

'Do you really believe in Preedy?'

76

'What do you mean, believe? He's a first-class, spell-binder, he gets results, and spell-binders don't grow on trees.'

'That's not really believing in Preedy – in his message. What I wonder is if you believe in anything except, of course, getting on and getting your own way.'

'Oh, that stuff. People have been talking about me. Of course I want to get on – I want to do something to this bloody world – and I want to do it to the *Argus* first. As a start. And I do believe in something. I believe in freedom. Don't laugh. I not only believe in it, I want to do something about it. Before it's too late. Before there isn't any left. I know, of course, most people don't give a damn for it – you don't, old Ackroyd doesn't. He thinks he does, but he's dead. Tinney doesn't care for anything or anyone but himself, and ninety per cent of the people don't neither. They only want to get tickled in the right places and draw down their weekly pay. They don't even want responsibility. Have you read this article in the *News Cronk*, "Teenagers"? Not one of 'em wants any responsibility. Not one of 'em wants even to be a foreman. Too much worry. And too cocky. Separating 'em out from the mob. No, it's the one cry among the lot. Feed me, keep me comfortable but don't ask me to believe in anything, stand up for anything, defend anything. Oh, nice children. Na-a-ace children – so matey. One of 'em says he wants to make friends among the lowest. How sweet. Straight out of Dusty Evsky. Let everything go to slop. Up with the slop merchants. And you say hear, hear.'

'You can leave me out of it, please.'

'Certainly, if you like – I was a fool to bring you in, but I thought you had a mind of your own – I thought you were a real princess. I thought you had some guts – moral guts. But you're only another society Home Chatter. Another lambkin saying baa-baa – nice tender meat for any parlour Bolshy. All right, all right. I'm going.'

There was a knock at the door. Rodker had arrived. 'Show him up,' said Hooper at once. The man looked at Joanna but she did not contradict. She could not trust herself to speak. She was too angry with this cad, this brute.

Rodker was startled to see Hooper. He stopped in the doorway and demanded, 'Here, who's this?'

'I'm on the *Argus*,' said Hooper at once, 'I happened to be here and I thought you might like to tell me your story.'

'Is that all right, Miss Rideout?'

'I must leave it to you.'

Hooper glared at her and took out his wallet. 'Here, Rodker – my Press card.'

Rodker looked at the card and at Hooper. 'You're the chap who backed Preedy?'

'Well, I want to know about Preedy.'

'Does this mean you're going to show the bugger up at last?'

'I can't promise anything. What's the story?'

'Oh, I've got all you want to smash him.' He produced a large blue envelope and drew out a bundle of letters.

'There you are, letters from Preedy to my sister – a kid of fourteen at the time – and his confession, signed.'

Hooper was about to take the letters when Rodker, like a conjurer, stowed the envelope out of sight, produced some typewritten sheets, and handed them over. 'Certified copies.'

Hooper read a page and said, 'Well, they're love letters, of a kind. Quite an ordinary kind.'

'But the confession – the last one.'

Hooper read a letter saying that the writer acknowledged himself the father of the child, and that it had been a 'noble act,' on the recipient's part not to tell upon him in court. He would be 'extremely grateful to her', and could never forget the experience of her goodness, which would always be 'an inspiration to his soul'.

It was signed, Walter.

'Walter,' said Hooper.

'That's Preedy. It's all in his hand. Look.' Rodker held up several letters, like a fan of cards. 'There you are. An inspiration for his soul. And he never went near her again. Nor even offered to do anything for her. No compensation – though she wouldn't have taken it from him. Eternally grateful. If I sent those to the public prosecutor Mr Preedy would go to jail right off.'

'And how would your sister like that, having the whole thing brought up again?'

'I'm doing it for her – it's the only way to get her away from that bastard. You don't know her; she's always been a trouble to us; she killed her mother, and the last thing her mother asked me to do was to look after her, and here she is getting back to that bastard again.'

'Perhaps she likes him, and she's of full age, isn't she?'

'All I know is she's never out of trouble since he got hold of her. First there was that remand home, and she's walked out of two jobs since. As soon as Preedy comes hanging round out she goes.'

'Isn't that her own responsibility? And why did she come to the office to tell me she'd nothing against Preedy, if she needs protection?'

Young Rodker was disconcerted; his pink cheeks became pinker. He said at last, 'That's just a tale because she wants to keep out of the papers. She hates his guts. Why, what do you think, after he's ruined her life – and goes on after her all the time. She doesn't have a chance.'

'Are you on good terms with your sister? She says you stole those letters from her.'

'If I don't look after her nobody else will.'

'Well, you can settle it with her – I sent her a message to come on here.'

'That's all right by me. You can't get round those letters – to a kid of fourteen. That's what you've got to remember. And him twenty-eight.'

He began to read, adding now a certain scornful emphasis to such phrases as 'My little sweetheart', 'My darling girl', 'You are all I have in life', 'It it weren't for you, I'd have cut my throat long ago.'

Hooper was bored; and irritated that the girl was late. He had sent a staff car for her to pick her up at six when she left work. This was her own arrangement. But it was now nearly half past the hour. He looked with disgust at the young man, thinking, 'What a fool – what a bore this is. The letters are just the usual stuff.' Suddenly he interjected, 'Why do you call him a hypocrite?'

'Well, all that stuff about him loving her – and cutting his throat if she didn't love him.'

'Perhaps it was true – it sounds like it.'

'But – to a kid of fourteen.'

'It didn't kill her.'

Rodker stared in amazement. But he spoke coolly enough, 'No, it nearly did. When he left her like that – ruined.'

79

'I suppose they quarrelled.'

'Here, what's this line –'

'I'm not taking a line. I'm talking sense. Why dig up this thing after all these years?'

Joanna said suddenly, 'Why should Preedy be allowed to treat the girl like this?'

Hooper turned upon her as if she had stabbed him. In fact, he had been acutely aware all the time of her critical air.

'It's like this,' he said, with the elaborate patience of one speaking to a half-wit. 'Preedy and the girl had this little affair. It's all over. And no one knows whose fault it was. But it happens to be the sort of thing that stirs up all the cant and slop merchants to a lynching party. And it's damned unfair to bring it up against him now.'

'Not much use talking to you, is it? After I knew you were for Preedy. The *Argus* is all for Preedy. Think there's money in him. That's all that counts for you, the money. Well, I've been wasting my time; I ought to have gone to the Public Prosecutor right away.'

'Why are you so keen to ruin this man? You know he's left all that behind him; you know he's doing good work. Don't you see that the whole thing was finished years ago?'

'What do you mean, finished? Why should it be finished? It happened, didn't it? Why should it stop mattering just because he's got away with it for a few years? It ought to matter more. It's all wrong if no one does anything about it, and I'm not going to take it. The bugger has got to be shown up; it's a duty.'

He put the letters in his pocket and remarked, 'What I've got to do is beat the bastard up.'

'Then you'll go to jail for quite a time.'

'Yes, but I'll tell the story first – in court. They'll have to listen to me then.'

'I shouldn't bet on it.'

'Like that policeman they sacked and he went on breaking windows. They had to listen to him in the end.'

'Do you really want to ruin your life for a grievance?'

Rodker turned crimson and began to shout. 'For justice, I tell you. Justice. Why should anyone get away with a thing like that? There's a bloody sight too much of that already, getting away with things –' and he made for the door.

Hooper ran to hold the door. 'What's the trouble? Wait a minute.' He was really surprised at this foolish youth's indignation. He thought, 'There you are – cant, cant, cant. He's full of cant – I ought to have remembered that the whole lot of that class are simply robots – reflex actions. You touch the button, whatever it is – class – sex – and you get the squeak.'

But he was irritated with himself for forgetting these points; he did not want Preedy to go to jail and he saw that there was a real danger of it. Suddenly he had discovered how much he wanted to defend Preedy from these worms, these rats; and this was a keen pleasure to him. He perceived that his admiration for Preedy, his work for him, had been sincere and disinterested. Preedy, in short, was a man after his own heart. He had made a position for himself; he had become a power in the land, without help from anybody, and especially without support from the establishment.

For Hooper the establishment which he wanted to defend was also the enemy. It was because he loved it, indeed, that he hated it. He loved it for its dignity, its power, its romantic distinction, for all that it could do in giving him position and dignity and power; he hated it for its weakness, its slackness, its cant and meanness, its hatred of the original mind, of all that is enterprising and brave. Joanna said suddenly, 'I don't see why Preedy shouldn't go to jail; he behaved as badly as possible. A man who treats a child like that deserves to go to jail.'

'What do you mean, deserves?' said Hooper. 'What do we all deserve? It isn't what you deserve, it's what you are, and Preedy is a real person. I suppose that's why you hate him.'

'What is a real person? Do you mean someone without any feelings – who does everything simply from some kind of calculation?'

'Here, let me out,' said Rodker. 'I've had enough of this sort of talk.'

But the door opened against Hooper's back – the Rodker girl had arrived. As Hooper made way, she walked slowly into the room, staring at each in turn with a frown of suspicion.

She was extremely like her brother, but in a feminine edition, in fact, a very pretty girl of the type that charms from a magazine cover – large brown eyes, rosy lips, neat figure.

Her expression, however, was not charming; she was frowning, glaring; she thrust out her lower lip in a manner that would have been comic, if it had not been menacing.

18

This girl, Alice Rodker, who played so great a part in the Preedy affair, was very far from a floozy. She had, for one thing, much more education than Hooper gave her credit for. Hooper, son of a lorry driver, who worked his way through the grammar school to a varsity, had, like many of his type, a great contempt for the class from which he had sprung. He called it the prolies. He thought of a proly as a born slave and parasite, a creature who did not even wish to improve his lot, to learn, to advance in life, to take responsibility. The only ambition of a proly, in Hooper's view, was to be safe and fed, to have a home and a woman of his own, to have enough money for his beer, his cigarettes, his amusements. The furthest reach of his ambition might be to own a television set and a car, to see his wife well dressed, to get his child into a grammar school, to cut a dash before the neighbours. His politics were a mixture of fear, greed and envy. Give me peace and safety, a rising standard of living, and see that no one earns more. Down with the clever ones, the chaps who work too hard, who've got brains. Why should brains earn money? Put 'em all in the factory, like me, and teach 'em where they get off.

Of course, he did not own publicly to this belief. No one could put forward such ideas in daily journalism and expect to have them published. Liberal papers had to believe that human nature was getting better and better on account of education, the health service, more pay, better living; and conservative papers pretended to believe it. Any other creed would be defeatist, and also unpopular. It would cause discouragement and lose votes.

In private, like thousands of people in every class, Hooper expressed this view every day. It was one of the most powerful ideas of the time, repeated everywhere, by trade union leaders as well as cabinet ministers, but only in private – like many other powerful and influential ideas, like, for instance, that other idea, not so widely expressed, but even more deeply held, that the welfare state would inevitably lead to the destruction of liberty in Britain, and the destruction of liberty to final ruin and subjugation. This idea was usually only hinted at; the welfare state was, at the moment, too powerful a slogan, a slogan that had not only an inevitable attraction for the politician but also exerted a strong moral pressure on those others, the richer, more independent class, the professional men, ambitious and successful manufacturers, because of their feeling, inculcated for several generations at public schools and grammar schools, that they had a duty to the poor and the stupid. To be well-off carried a certain guilt, a certain shame.

Hooper, indeed, had spoken violently enough about the welfare state. He had always regretted it the next morning. He knew that for an ambitious young man, it was extremely rash even to hint a criticism of this popular juju.

But in refusing to be dominated by one idea, he had fallen under the rule of another. He did not subscribe to the welfare state; but he accepted the other idea of a working mass, already parasitic, without question. And that in spite of his own experience, his own ambitions, which had taken him from lodgings in a back slum to the board of the *Argus*.

His father had been a steady worker, but completely devoid of ambition; a man whose only interests were football, darts, his pub-friends. A sober decent fellow, not only without any general interests, but without curiosity. He had wished his only son to follow the same line; he had tried to take him from school at fourteen, to make him a car washer in a garage. For the elder Hooper, learning, the arts, were simply games, a kind of superior darts but superior in a bad, a pretentious way. The belief in that decent, sober, honest mind was unshakeable. Hooper had been saved by an energetic young schoolmaster and his own violent and suspicious temper. His father had forgiven him for his writing, but looked upon him as a weakling, a traitor to his class.

That was why Hooper looked upon the workers with contempt and fear as the enemies of every good thing in life; he saw them all in the light of that battle with his father.

Evidence that the working-class was as much broken up as any other class, that the classes were all in continual movement and interchange, that the movement was occurring every day, and that interchange was growing always more rapid, could not

83

modify that view; because it was a fundamental part of the man's creed, by which he lived. He could not understand the Rodkers, and especially Alice Rodker, because he did not want to do so. Yet they had a very similar history and came from the same class.

Their father, clerk in a woodyard, had been ambitious for them and urged them to learn. And though he had died when the girl was twelve, her mother had worked hard as a dressmaker to keep the home together. She also took in lodgers, of whom one, a friend of Preedy's, had first made him acquainted with the child at the public library. Then Preedy had met her again and begun that secret passionate friendship so exciting to them both.

To the poor mother it was incomprehensible when Alice, a straightforward, responsible child, began to lie and steal, to play truant from school. It was as if some devil had possessed her.

19

In fact, the child often did not know anything about it. She was living in a world so important, so enthralling, that it was the events of common life that seemed unreal. When her mother asked her, 'What did you do with the half-crown I left for the milkman?' she heard the question as from another kind of existence in another time, where strange creatures, blind to real life, to the real world where real people lived and suffered and agonized, fussed about half-crowns, a debt to a milkman.

She had forgotten all about that half-crown, taken three days before to pay her fare to a place where she might meet Preedy. She was then already pregnant, and the question, far more important to her, the question that debated itself in her mind night and day without result, was, 'Does he love me?' She had discovered that he had another woman, a grown woman at least forty years old, of the worst character. Yet, when she had challenged him, he had sworn that she was his only love, and implored her not to leave him. They would go away together, abroad, and hide till she was old enough to be married.

He had convinced her, and she had agreed to this flight; and then, within the week, he was back with his woman. And the same story was repeated. The story and the excuses – he had got drunk, he had despaired of his new life with her, he had been

84

caught by this woman whom, in fact, he hated. He was a miserable weak creature, and she alone could save him. This was agony to the girl. She had been brought up in religion, she felt responsibility; and what more enormous responsibility than this for another soul.

She had loved Preedy with all the headlong devotion of an adolescent girl who is still half a child; whose natural feelings are operating in a creature without balance; a character all in extremes, who has as yet no power of self-analysis; whose experience has not yet taught her to depreciate her inclinations.

And as for her pregnancy, how could she concern herself with a condition that would not come to effect for eight months? Eight months ahead in her mind was as far away as next century. She did not even try to imagine what life would be like in eight months. Her whole mind was filled with one overwhelming question, 'What am I to do about this man now? Does he love me? Should I run away with him? Is it true that he needs me? Will they put him in prison if I go away with him?'

And when Preedy himself three months later disappeared and her mother suddenly demanded to know if she were pregnant, she had answered in sullen anger that if she was pregnant it was her own business.

For it seemed to her no one else's business. What did anyone else know or understand of her fearful misery; or the wonderful joys that had preceded it? Who else had lain in Preedy's arms and felt his love, heard him speak it in that voice which could make her tremble and weep in happiness?

They thought of her as a silly, bad and deluded little girl, but they were fools. They didn't understand anything. It was no good talking to them. And so she would not talk.

She would not talk even when the magistrates bullied her. Let them do or say what they liked; they were a lot of old sour fools. They did not understand anything. They did not know Preedy or her; they had never been in love. They did not know how things happened to girls in love, or how girls felt. Not even the woman magistrate who talked to her in private. The woman was the worst – especially when she was pretending to be kind. The worst because she tried to make the whole thing seem like a silly mistake – the sort of thing a silly girl might do. But it had not been silly. She was not silly. She had done right to love Preedy even if he had deserted her. She couldn't have done anything else.

If people wanted to think the whole affair silly, let them. People were fools, her brother who wanted to shoot Preedy, he was a fool. She loved him, but she could not even talk to him about Preedy, because he was a fool.

20

The Rodker girl looked round the room from Joanna to Hooper, then at her brother who had stepped back. 'Where are my letters?' she said to him at once, in a furious tone. 'How dare you take my letters, private letters? I could put you in jail for that.'

'Your brother wants to send them to the Public Prosecutor,' said Hooper. 'He'd like to see Mr Preedy in jail.'

'So that's the idea, Fred, to drag me through all the dirt again.'

'Then why do you stay in the dirt, why do you go on seeing that swine?'

'Who says I see him? He sees me. And what business is that of yours? You give me those letters, now.'

'You can't stop it now,' Rodker said. 'I'm going to get that bugger.'

Alice walked up to him, planted herself before him and said, 'So you think you can push me about, and that's what you call justice. Put me in the courts, and let everybody know I'm a girl from a remand home.'

'It's the only way to get you out of his grip,' and he turned to Hooper and Joanna. 'That's the way he keeps hold of her. Tells her if the thing comes out, she'll have to go through it all again. He's ruining her whole life.'

'That's a lie, how do you know what he tells me? And what should I care? I don't care what he says, my life's my own, isn't it?'

'No, it isn't your own, he's got you where he wants you.'

Alice raised her hand and it seemed for a moment that she might strike her brother; but as he stepped back she dived the hand into his coat and pulled out the big blue envelope, then she

86

retreated backwards across the room, saying, 'I thought so, now you can go to hell.'

Rodker, startled, stood staring at her for a moment, then straightened his coat, brushing it down with his hands, and said in his cool way, 'What's the good of that? I've got copies, I'll send them all round. I'll send them to all those blasted fools that go to his tin-pot chapel, and the papers too.'

'That will be libel,' Hooper said.

'Of course it is, that's the idea. Get him in the courts, then he's finished.' He walked out of the room.

Alice turned to Hooper. 'Can he do that with the copies? Could he have me up in court?'

Suddenly the girl became panic-stricken. 'I've got to get home before him. Get me a taxi, quick. He's been at my desk. He must have got a key. I must get home and find out what he's taken.'

Joanna at once proposed to drive the girl home. Alice accepted eagerly, saying, 'That would be real nice of you, and stop at the first litter bin.'

21

The moment they entered the car she began to tear the letters into small fragments which she then stuffed back into the envelope. As soon as she had finished this operation, carried out with impatient violence, she began to look from the window and called out suddenly, 'Stop.' She jumped out and poured the contents of the envelope into a bin by a lamp-post. She then returned to her place, not having spoken another word. And Joanna felt a strong attraction to this young girl, an attraction and an interest so strong that she could not explain it to herself. She felt it even in the concentrated violence with which she had torn the letters, the energy of the movements as she jumped from the car and vigorously shook the envelope over the bin, frowning as if she were wrestling with an enemy. She was impressed by her silence now.

To Joanna, a girl like Alice, with her history, seduced at fourteen, sent to a remand home and still carrying that stigma, losing jobs because of it, and now apparently held by Preedy, by a kind of blackmail, had the fascination of the forty-niner to the respectable Victorian; of one outside the law meeting all hazards with nothing but his own courage, his own wits; of some wild creature fighting for its life in the jungle, to the sophisticated naturalist. She was fascinated by the idea of the girl's struggle, her sufferings, her courage. In that moment when Alice had raised her hand as if to strike, and then snatched the envelope, she had felt the thrill of the spectator outside a lion's cage, and also the humility of one who watches from safety. She wanted to express her sympathy but she did not know how to begin. How did one talk to a girl like this, with her completely different experience, her unexpected sensibilities and her sudden temper? For the first few minutes she drove in silence, then suddenly Alice turned to her.

'I've seen that chap Hooper's photo in the *Argus*. Is he your friend?'

'More or less.'

'Well, that's all right – I didn't want to make any trouble for him if he belonged to you; but you tell him to keep out of this. Don't let him put anything in the paper.'

'I haven't really any control over him,' Joanna said, 'but I think you can be sure he won't mention anything about this trouble of yours.'

'Yes, but he's all for Preedy, isn't he? He'd like to do my brother in.'

'I don't agree with him about Mr Preedy, who seems to have behaved very badly to you. Is he really bothering you now? That would be an absolute disgrace.'

'If you'll excuse me, all that's between Preedy and myself. That's what Fred won't understand. It's my own business. It's private. Well, wouldn't you want it private between you and your chap? Not that I'm saying that Preedy is my chap now – far from it. But that makes it all the more private.'

'I can understand that, but I do have some personal interest in the matter because Preedy wants to treat my mother, and I don't trust him.'

'You're too right – he'll murder her. What does he care, he murdered my kid, and he nearly murdered me. He doesn't care for anybody but himself and his old God, which is the same thing. It's not as though he even believes in that old God. He just wants to think he's saved; him saved! Well, all I can say is, he needs it.'

'That's very much what I think myself. But is it really true that he still pesters you, that he makes you lose your jobs? Have you got a job now?'

'I have but I don't know how long it'll last.'

'If ever you do want another job, I hope you'll ask me. I should like to help if I could.'

There was a long silence and Joanna was afraid that she'd given offence. She was casting about for some form of apology when the girl said, in a threatening voice, 'You'd better be careful – I might need it a lot. It's wonderful how people get to know about you, about that remand home.'

'But all that was years ago. Can people be so mean?'

'Can't they. Well, secretaries, you see, get to know a lot and they think I'm not the kind of person to know a lot – I know too much already, and if it isn't that, then it's because I can't stand them knowing. I was with a doctor last year and somehow he found out. Well, he was very nice about it, really nice, said it wouldn't make any difference to him, but it did – well of course, it did – me knowing what he knew. Why, you could tell it just by the way he said, "Good morning", or "Take dictation". You knew he was thinking how nice he was being to this nasty little bitch. So he was being nice, but one morning I just couldn't take it any longer. I said I wasn't feeling well, and I went home and never came back. Left him flat. So, of course, he said, "That's what comes of being nice to a creature like that."'

'I know exactly how you feel, I can't blame you. But who would be so mean as to give you away. Your brother seems to think it's Preedy, and he certainly sounds capable of it.'

But at this Alice suddenly lost her friendly loquacity. There was a long pause and then she said, on the same defiant note as before, 'I wouldn't know, and if I did, it's nothing to do with Fred, or anybody else.' And she said no more except to utter a brief thanks when Joanna put her down at her door.

22

It had been known for some time to the Pant's Road committee
that Preedy had been meeting Alice Rodker. Fred Rodker had
reported it. When they observed that Fred Rodker was working
with Syson, the committee began to be alarmed. The story was
having a very bad effect on the congregation. Preedy's success
at the Mission had brought in a great many of the middle and
upper-middle class, and such people always have a sense of
what is owed to an institution; they felt very strongly that
Preedy was letting the Mission down. But what had really
brought this agitation to a head was the refusal of the *Argus*
to continue the articles about the Mission. For even the most
respectable and conventional new members of the congregation
were genuine evangelists; they were the kind of people who,
having had a revelation, are eager to convert the world. They are
eager too, to feel themselves in the vanguard of the new gospel.
and that one *Argus* article had both assured them of their power
and promised them a triumph. To have such great opportunities
for the world's good cut off short by irresponsible and foolish
action in their Missioner was unendurable.

Some of the new members, indeed, who had attended services
elsewhere, who had been advocating healing for years, had
already proposed other prophets. They pointed out that there
were plenty to choose from. All the same, the old committee
members who had been with Preedy from the beginning, would
not hear of a change of minister, and were extremely cautious
about approaching Preedy himself in this delicate matter. His
moody arrogant temper was well known to them, but finally they
had deputed a certain Colonel Marris to make approaches to
him. Preedy had always been friendly with the Colonel, one of
his earliest converts, who had given all his savings to the Mission
fund; he was, in fact, Preedy's closest friend, if he could be said
to have any friends.

The Colonel had duly approached Preedy one evening while
both were sitting over the fire in the Mission house, a time when
Preedy was in his best, most relaxed frame of mind.

'We had another letter from that fellow Rodker this week.'

'So had I – he's always at it.'

'Yes, but this time he has a new story – that you've been visiting his sister.' Preedy looked at the Colonel for a moment and said, 'What then?'

'People were wondering if there's any truth in it.'

'That's my business. Yes, it's true.'

'Isn't that rather dangerous?'

'In what way, dangerous? The child's unhappy and lost and by my fault. What are you driving at, Marris? I didn't think you'd worry about the threats of a creature like young Rodker.'

'I'm not worried about his threats, but possible damage to the Mission. A lot of people feel the same way.'

'Yes, I know, some of them would like me out. In fact, I've half a mind to get out, to get out now. I don't like your new people in the Mission – a lot of parasites, vermin who feed on God's love and charity, like lice who suck a man's blood and never say thank you. They give nothing and ask for everything. That's why I want that child back in the Mission, because she has a soul, she knows what love means, she's given herself to love, she's lived with God. How many of that sort do you suppose we have in the Mission? Half a dozen?'

'I hope more than that.'

'You can hope, and here you are telling me it's dangerous to do God's work.'

'Yes, you're right and I'm wrong.'

Marris was ashamed and wondered at the ease with which he had been seduced by time-servers and tempted by the devil. He said no more, but next day Preedy called an emergency committee and gave in his resignation. He had done this twice before; at any kind of opposition or criticism he was apt to resign, but on this occasion he seemed to mean what he said and the committee were highly alarmed, especially as they now knew, through the secretary, Kerne, that Preedy had re-established relations with Lady Rideout. They hastily explained that they had no intention of finding fault, but Preedy did not withdraw his resignation, he simply walked out of the room.

He could not have brought himself to speak to these people. What enraged him was the idea that he had been spied on, that his relations with Alice Rodker were a matter of gossip to these vermin, where he perceived that they would not be understood.

Actually he himself did not altogether understand them. For instance, he had told himself often that she was now a hopeless case, hopelessly corrupted, and he could do her no good, that only harm could come of his seeing her again. But at certain times, especially when, as he put it to himself, the spirit had failed him, when he had had continued failure in his healing services, he had suddenly an irresistible desire to see her. Indeed, it seemed to him sometimes that he was led to her. For though he would say to himself, 'I shan't see her again, whatever happens, it's simply a waste of time,' he would find himself as if by accident, somewhere in her neighbourhood. He would go shopping perhaps, or to visit some outlying member of the congregation, without the least thought of Alice Rodker. Then he would look up at the name of a street and say, 'So that's where I am. I'm quite close to where Alice works and she'll be coming from her office between five and six,' and from that moment he would set himself to catch her on her way.

He would stand in some shop door until she came past, step out in her path and accuse her of trying to ruin the Mission.

And she would say, 'Why shouldn't I ruin your rotten Mission?'

'Because you're afraid to fight against God.'

'I don't believe in your old murdering God, as you know very well.'

'But God believes in you.'

'Get out of my way; why won't you leave me alone.'

'I daren't leave you alone while you're going to the devil – and simply from spite. You don't really want to be so foolish.'

She would try to brush past him saying, 'People are looking, there's been quite enough talk as it is. Do you want me to lose my job?'

'There's more important things in life than jobs,' and he would say, if she didn't want to talk in the street he would come to her flat. Was she alone that evening?

'You know very well I'm always alone on a Friday; Fred goes for his class, but I'm not going to have you there.' And, in fact, it was always on a Friday that Preedy found himself in her neighbourhood.

'I wonder you're not afraid. Fred's got his spies all round here.' And she would hurry away.

But Preedy would follow at her shoulder, asking her if she had forgotten that time of their love, a thing given by God, for a proof of his love for them and all men. When Preedy spoke of this time, and remembered it, he would tremble with excitement. He knew perfectly well that his love affair with this girl when she was not much more than a child had been full of deceit and cruelty, and pure lechery. But as he spoke of it now it seemed to him that he was merely leaving out all the unessential things, that the 'moments of ecstasy were the important truth. So too, he told himself that the girl herself was quite an ordinary young girl, not especially clever or good. And yet when he had spoken to Marris of her as an exceptional creature, a rare being who knew how to live in the very love of God, it seemed to him that he had spoken a deep truth. That here had been a miracle of grace, to prove that miracles could happen. And he pleaded with her. He spoke of his sin against her, in taking her so young, in deserting her afterwards. He would call himself criminal and say that she was the noblest soul he had ever known in her forgiveness. That was why it was such an agony to him that she had forsaken the truth; that she no longer believed.

Then he would speak of love of God, given by God, and their joy in that love which they had known in each other, and she, hurrying always faster, would throw over her shoulder, 'Go on, get it over. Why talk so much? You don't think it's doing any good, do you?'

But on the Friday evening after his resignation, when he accosted the girl, she turned upon him and said, 'You know they're all after you now. Why don't you stop?'

And when he began his usual explanation she said, 'You've picked a Friday again but Fred isn't at his class this Friday, he's gone to see that parson. You can come up if you like to take a chance.'

'Yes, I'll come up.'

'But suppose they come back early. I'm not promising they won't. Suppose they come and catch you; that'll spoil things a bit, won't it? Aren't you afraid for your wonderful racket?'

'Why should I be afraid?'

'They'll throw you out of your precious Mission.'

'I don't care for the Mission – I've just walked out of it. They wanted to stop me seeing you.'

The girl burst out laughing; she was flushed and excited and stared at him with a peculiar expression, which might have been either contempt or triumph.

'You mean you've chucked the Mission because of me?'

'I would if they tried to interfere in my private affairs.'

'And what are you going to live on now? What about that lovely big car you go about in, and all those women bringing you flowers and slopping over you? But of course you'll just start again – in real style this time, get in the really big money; nothing could stop a born crook like you.'

But she still kept staring at him with amused excitement. She seemed all the time to be struggling with laughter, and when they reached her flat, she made him sit on the sofa and planted herself opposite him. 'So it's because of Fred that you've chucked it up, Fred and me, or did they just throw you out? Yes, I'll bet they threw you out. Well, you needn't think I care, you had it coming to you, you're just a crook.'

'Do you remember that time when you came to me every night, when you used to climb out of your window in the dark and come through the streets, regular slums?'

Alice frowned at this reminder. 'You don't think I could forget it, do you?' she said shortly.

'It was in winter too, it was often freezing or raining. You used to come in quite frozen.'

'And you like to talk about it, that's what gets me – digging it all up again. I should have thought you'd want to forget what a brute you were, making a fool of a kid; that was pretty easy.'

'Night after night, and you used to come in shaking all over with cold and fright. Sometimes you were crying with fright.'

'That made you feel good.' Alice was flushed now with anger.

'Yes, it made me feel good – because you always did come in spite of everything.'

'If I didn't you'd go on the booze and say it was all my fault, a great oaf like you.'

'That only happened after I'd been waiting and you hadn't come. But even then you'd wanted to come. Remember that first time you didn't come. Some aunt was put to sleep with you and you couldn't get out.'

'After that you had me where you wanted me, in spite of those awful streets. I nearly died every time that dog barked, but when

94

I asked you to meet me somewhere else instead of me going to your room, you said it wouldn't work, it wouldn't be private enough – a lot of talk, you always had lots of talk. But the real truth was you'd got to have me frightened, creeping past that brute of a dog and climbing in your window.'

At this memory the girl's legs drew up and her chin went down – she shivered as if from a chill. Then she jumped up and went across the room as if to escape from the man's nearness.

'But you always came – you had to come.'

Alice turned sharply on him. 'Listen to you – and you wonder I hate your guts. What did you come here for?'

Preedy answered in the same meditative fashion, 'It was because of you, coming like that, that I was saved.'

'I like your God – a nice sort of God, to send me along to an oaf like you, a kid of fourteen.'

'Yes, and you didn't even look fourteen, you were really a child – all skin and bones – you didn't look twelve.' Preedy pulled out his pocket book and deliberately selected an envelope. From this he took a snapshot at which he looked for some moments with raised eyebrows – then suddenly laughed. 'No, not twelve. And what eyes – like a scared rabbit.'

'Oh, so you've got a picture of me.'

'Yes, you stole it for me from your mother. Don't you remember it?' He held it out to her. But she did not offer to take it. 'A scared rabbit. I always wondered if you'd dare again, but you always did dare, and I was always sure you would dare.'

'That's what pepped you up, didn't it? Especially when that brute of a dog caught me, when I got those bites – when I got really hurt, when I was crying and bleeding and you kept on laughing and kissing me and pulling off my clothes. You were roaring with laughter.'

'That first time the brute bit you and you screamed, I thought you'd run back, but you didn't run back. That was a wonderful thing, that you didn't run away then, that you had to come – I simply couldn't believe it. I was simply astonished,' and Preedy, gazing still at the photograph, opened his eyes in amazement.

'Not so wonderful for a kid of fourteen – and it wasn't because *you* were wonderful either. Anyone could have got hold of me that way, any dirty swine who was mean enough to make a fool of a silly little girl brought up with chapel people and stuffed up

95

with those Bible lies. Any dirty low brute could have had me who was a big enough hypocrite and liar.'

'Yes, he could, but you were happy to come, and this swine was saved.'

'Saved – as soon as they stopped me coming you went on the booze worse than ever – booze and women.'

'Yes, I was trying to forget you – I was trying to forget the God that sent you, but he was working in me all the time, and when the moment came he knocked me down like a stroke, like a bullet – I didn't know what had happened to me.'

'That was about the time I was up before the magistrates and they sent me to that home, your God did a nice job there.'

'The magistrates were fools; what do they know about anything real and true? When you came to me you were doing something big, something beyond their imagination, that's why you had that great happiness.'

Alice walked up to him and held out her hand, 'Show me,' and he gave her the photograph. She stood gazing at it with a frown.

'Yes – a silly little fool, a crazy fool. No one can be so crazy as a kid in a thing like that. And what a face – a hideous crazy kid.'

'Do you remember that night you were bitten – the last time – how you begged for me to take you away with me – you said you couldn't leave me again and why shouldn't we go on being happy together for always.'

Alice tore the photograph in half. Preedy gave a cry and snatched at it, but she jumped up and ran across the room, tearing the thing into small fragments which she scattered out of the window.

Preedy fell back on the sofa with a gesture of resignation.

'You hate her, do you – of course you do. She was a real person.'

Alice suddenly bounced down on the sofa beside the man. 'And that's your idea now, too – to see how much I can take.'

But Preedy did not even look at her. He gazed at the envelope still lying on his knee and then picked it up and looked at it as if he expected it to show the face of the photograph.

'You were so enormously happy,' he murmured, 'you couldn't believe such happiness was possible. It was a wonderful time for both of us,' and Preedy, after reflecting a moment, gave a long sigh. 'What a wonderful thing it was – a revelation.'

'I was a wonderful fool and you were a wonderful brute, making me get bitten so you could get a special kick out of it.'

'Why do you want to forget the truth, why do you want to turn it all into spitefulness and jealousy because I left you?'

'So I'm jealous,' said Alice, absolutely trembling with rage. She had no words to express her hatred of the man. Suddenly she turned her face to the window; she had recognized her brother's voice in the street. At last he'd come.

'Jealousy and vanity and spite,' Preedy said, 'that's why you tell lies to yourself, why you're ruining your life.' Alice stared at him for a moment. Suddenly she jumped up and caught his hand, 'Well, if you want it again come into the bedroom.'

'What do you mean?' Preedy was surprised.

She tugged at his hand, 'Come on, what are you afraid of? You say it was a wonderful time. You say God sent me to you. Why shouldn't he have sent you to me now? Am I too old for you?'

'He did send me, to save you, to save you from wasting your life.'

'Come into the bedroom then, what are you afraid of? I wasn't afraid of that dog. I wasn't afraid to spoil my whole life, but you're afraid of going to a girl's room for five minutes; someone might talk – and spoil your nice fat racket for good and all.'

This argument made no impression on Preedy, but he was struck by the girl's excited mood, a touch of hysterical excitement in her voice. The very strangeness of her suggestion impressed him. Obviously she was acting upon impulse, she had not reflected on what she was doing, and for him such sudden impulsive actions were always highly significant and important. As he liked to say so often in his sermons, 'God moves in a mysterious way.' He was used, too, to excited and hysterical people who said one thing and meant another, who showed a violent hostility to him and a moment later were kneeling at his feet. It was, he thought, precisely at such moments, when the mind was given up to impulse, when the will, the self-will, with all its prejudices, was overwhelmed by violent feeling, that God had his opportunity to seize again the direction of a soul.

And when in the bedroom, she began at once to make love to

him, saying, 'Now it's you who've come to me. This is going to be a wonderful time,' and while she unbuttoned him she burst out laughing and said, 'A revelation.'

The girl was playing the fool, but she had lost control of her temper, she had broken away from her resolution to stand apart. And at last the man was carried away by her excitement, a mutual excitement; it seemed to him that a way was opening out of their quarrel of words, their isolation, the only way back to that time when they had known a miracle together.

He was quite as excited as the girl when she pulled him down upon her, and it was perhaps true at that moment that Alice did not know any longer exactly what she wanted, that she was lost in a confusion of motives.

But a moment later she was pushing him away with loathing and saying, 'You beast, get off me,' and jumping from the bed, she looked down at him with malignant hatred. 'Now what are you going to do? Fred will be here in half a minute.'

Preedy stared at her for a moment and then he said, 'So all that was simply a piece of spite.'

'Yes, I led you up the path, didn't I? A nice fool you look now. You laughed at that kid, but who's laughing now?'

'That kid, as you call her, couldn't have done a trick like that; she couldn't have made *that* a spiteful act. It was a holy thing for her –'

Fred's voice was heard in the sitting-room, talking to some companion, but after a moment he was heard opening another door; he had gone into his own room to leave his hat and coat. Alice said to Preedy, 'Get under the bed.'

'Why, what for?'

'Because Fred will be back in a minute and I'm going to open the door.'

Preedy stared at the girl wondering if she was serious, and again a laugh, a kind of hysterical giggle, burst through her compressed lips.

'Go on, hurry up, you'll find lots of dust down there, and be careful of the po; it's a low bed too, you'll have to wriggle yourself right down on your face.'

'What sort of a silly trick is this?'

'Down you go and be quick about it, what's the good of arguing? There's nothing else to do, go on, crawl.'

Fred's voice was heard again in the sitting-room. Alice put her face within three inches of Preedy's and muttered furiously, 'You silly fool, get under the bed – it's the only way. Get under the bed and I'll make them take me out to supper. Be quick, I'm going to open the door now – I mean it.'

'So am I,' Preedy said, and reached for the door-handle. Alice caught his arm and muttered again, 'You can't go out, he'll kill me.'

'What would that matter after a trick like that? You're ashamed of the child you were, but that child couldn't have done a thing like this – a prostitute's trick – you've rotted your whole life with lies and spite.'

Alice hit him in the face with her fist, but he was already opening the door. And with the door half open he said to her, 'You're quite right, that child is dead. She doesn't exist any more. And I've nothing to do with a creature like you. You won't see me again.' He went into the sitting-room with blood on his lip.

Fred Rodker and Syson stared at him in silent astonishment.

'Excuse me,' Preedy said, 'I was calling on your sister,' and he made for the outer door.

Rodker, recovering himself, rushed to bar his way. 'Here, what have you been doing in her room?'

'You'd better ask her – kindly get out of my way.'

'You can't talk to me like that,' said Rodker, bridling like a cock.

But now Syson intervened. 'Oh, let him go, Fred. It's enough that we've caught him out, that he's given himself away so completely. I should think this ought to finish him as a prophet.'

Fred then drew out of the way and Preedy left the room.

In the bedroom Alice put her bleeding knuckles to her lips. She was trembling and fighting against tears. A great sob burst from her and suddenly she knelt by the bed. As a child she had prayed often, and especially during that agonizing time with Preedy, but she was surprised to find herself on her knees and told herself that she was not praying and did not know why she knelt. But she continued to kneel, though her body as well as her mind was full of rage; at last she said aloud, 'I hate your God, beast and murderer, and you're not going to get me again, never again.'

23

It was this incident that drew Syson into his first slander on Preedy. Syson had told Rodker already that he had no intention of making any inquiry into Preedy's private character. He was objecting only to his doctrine of faith-healing for everybody and for every disease. In fact, that interview with Hooper had surprised Syson, and made him realize the power of the opposition, and he had decided to be cautious. Besides the vicar had sent for him, on a private intimation from Clarry, and had warned him again not to get mixed up in a quarrel with the Pant's Road Mission, and especially not with an evangelist of Preedy's quality.

But he was very much concerned for the Rollwright child and he had come to Fred Rodker's to see the evidence of the case about Alice's baby. It seemed to him that if Preedy had already been responsible for a child's death, then he would be in a strong position for intervening between him and Mrs Rollwright. He might be able to convince her that the man was not to be trusted.

Even after the startling appearance of Preedy out of the girl's bedroom, he was inclined to be careful. His first contemptuous exclamation expressed his feelings. For him, anyone who professed the Christian religion as a minister, and committed a vulgar fornication was the lowest kind of hypocrite. A cheap indulgence like that was unforgivable. But though he expressed his feelings, he did not mean to carry the thing any further. And even when he had seen Rodker's cuttings, he still decided to take only private action with Mrs Rollwright.

It was Fred Rodker who reported to the chief members of the Pant's Road committee, and to Hooper, Joanna Rideout, the police – everyone he could think of who might be induced to take action against Preedy – that Preedy had actually been caught in his sister's bedroom, and that the Rev. T. H. Syson was witness to the fact.

The committee was so alarmed that it asked Preedy for an explanation. The request was put through Mrs Hartree verbally and in the most tactful form. It was not even known that Preedy still regarded himself as the Missioner, but he had returned to the Mission house and was holding services as usual. He told Mrs Hartree that he had no intention of explaining himself, neither would he agree to a court action. Mrs Hartree, strong supporter of Preedy as she was, made it plain that she expected him to take an action for slander. Allday asked Hooper's advice, and, to do Hooper justice, he at once pointed out the danger of a court action. It would almost certainly bring up all the old stories against Preedy, and possibly lead to a prosecution. Preedy might end in jail. But when Hooper saw Mrs Hartree he had second thoughts. The fact was that Hooper himself was in a desperate position. Ackroyd, to his final astonishment, had accepted his resignation, and his name had disappeared from the *Argus*. His famous column had simply stopped. This had been such a shock to Hooper that it had seemed to change his whole character; he had become loquacious; he talked in pubs. He still had his arrogant air, but it was an arrogance that was eager to support itself in speech. He had been seen with the most junior reporters, pointing out to them the extreme folly of the old gang on the *Argus*. 'It's their sacred cow – they'd rather see it die in the road than call in a vet.' He let it be understood that thousands of readers had abandoned the paper when his name was suppressed. 'Reader reaction is something they've never heard of.'

What, above all, had surprised Hooper was that the *Argus* editors had already hired a new columnist, a certain Walter Biggs. No one had ever heard of Walter Biggs before, but they had printed a paragraph, 'The readers of the *Argus* will be glad to hear that we have secured the services of Mr Walter Biggs, well known for his brilliant work on television, from Monday next.' It appeared, that is, that they were going to make Mr Walter Biggs's name in place of his. What's more, Hooper's fan mail had suddenly stopped, except for a few belated letters from remote parts. He laughed at this as merely another proof of the moronic quality of the general public. He said to himself, 'I always said they were a lot of sheep and now I know it.'

He even congratulated himself on this enforced rest; he said to himself, 'I've been overworking for a long time, and I didn't realize it.' In fact, he couldn't sleep and had violent indigestion. His eyes began to give trouble and he had neuralgia in the right cheek, causing a tic.

His doctor perfectly agreed with him that he needed a complete rest, and advised him to take a long holiday.

But when he went away for a holiday to Cannes both the indigestion and the tic got worse, and he came back to town after a week to take new advice. He was growing really alarmed about his health. It was at this moment that the Pant's Road committee consulted him, and he threw himself into the cause with all his old energy. He assured Mrs Hartree that Preedy would be in no danger from Rodker. Then he wrote a private note to Rodker affirming that copies of letters would not be accepted as evidence. 'All you'll accomplish by forcing an action for slander is to get yourself into jail for nothing.'

Hooper knew from Joanna that the original letters had been destroyed, and his letter did have a strong effect with Rodker, who answered that Syson would support him. Hooper at once demanded Syson's evidence and Rodker sent to Syson, who gave him a signed statement to the effect that, 'I shall certainly give evidence on your behalf if required, but you needn't be afraid, they wouldn't dare bring an action; they haven't got a leg to stand on.'

Syson naturally thought it disgraceful on the part of the committee and Hooper that they should try to cover up Preedy's scandalous conduct by threats against a poor clerk like Rodker, and he thought that the threat itself was pure bluff. Like most people, he had no idea of the law. He did not imagine for a moment that it could be illegal to tell the truth. As he said to Clarry, who was very much alarmed by the situation, she needn't be afraid, 'that gang is bluffing, it would be absolutely suicidal for Preedy to bring an action.' For then all the evidence about the old case, about Alice Rodker, and especially that case in the coroner's court, would come up again and the man would be absolutely ruined. 'The whole thing is simply a bluff and obviously Hooper is behind it; he's putting his money on Preedy and he's the last man to let him get into court. He's committed himself to the Preedy stunt and if I know newspaper men, he's not going to spoil the wicket at this stage of the game.'

Syson, in fact, had never known what he called 'a newspaper man' until he met Hooper, and he never understood Hooper. It was impossible for him to understand any newspaper man because he had already lumped together the whole journalist profession under the one idea of sensation-mongers, people who live on 'publicity'. In this conception, of course, he agreed with his whole class, including his father-in-law, Simpkins. Sir Harry, as it happened, had had some publicity recently in the popular Press, and especially in the *Argus*, after a B.B.C. broadcast about the atom; there had even been photographs. He had been at pains to explain that he had not sought this advertisement, for university colleagues had been looking askance at him ever since. Clarry had explained his misfortune in the parish, especially to the vicar, whom she privately regarded as the only real gentleman in the Pant's Road district. And the vicar quite understood her point. He, too, despised publicity and for his own part read *The Times*. Like the Sysons and the Simpkins, in short, he did not regard *The Times* as going in for publicity.

He considered, for instance, that if Fred Rodker was threatened with a libel action on account of his letters about Preedy, it was no more than he deserved for going in for publicity, and he thoroughly disapproved of Syson's action in making his statement in support of him; but he did not say so because he realized that Syson's sense of honour would oblige him to make such a statement, and he respected that sense of honour although he considered it injudicious of Syson to give way to it in this critical matter of the Pant's Road Mission and the *Argus*. From his point of view as a vicar, almost any kind of publicity was harmful; and he was even more alarmed by Syson's quarrel with Hooper than by his action against the Pant's Road Mission.

24

Syson himself heeded the vicar's warning enough not to write any further account of what he had seen or what he knew of Preedy's past. Unluckily, however, he did tell the whole story to a certain Mr Wills, who had, till then, been a faithful member of St Enoch's congregation. Syson knew that Wills had certain sympathies for Preedy, that he had been at Preedy's services, and this made him more eager to answer his questions about Preedy, and to show him what a crook the man was. He also made a quick casual remark to a young man in a greengrocer's shop who said something about the Mission House bills, that

Preedy's committee were also worried about his way of doing business, and this remark reached Mrs Hartree's ears about the same time as Syson's story to Wills. The trouble was that Wills was really alarmed and made inquiries from several members of the Pant's Road committee. Within forty-eight hours it had travelled all over the district. Hooper immediately went to his lawyer and they concocted a letter to Syson threatening an action for slander.

Hooper, of course, was bluffing. He did not conceive that Preedy would be fool enough to bring an action. What he wanted was to frighten Syson; as he said, with Syson's statement in his hand he had both Syson and Preedy where he wanted them.

One morning a few days later, when Syson was coming out of St Enoch's vestry, Preedy walked up to him and said, 'Mr Syson.'

'Yes.'

'I'd like a word with you about this story that's going round the district.' Two or three choirboys due for a practice in a quarter of an hour were standing waiting for the organist and they closed in now to speak to Syson, a general favourite with them as a war hero, and Preedy said, 'Could we go in for a moment?'

'I don't know why,' said Syson, 'I haven't really anything to say, except that the story you speak of is true.'

'Perhaps you don't know the truth,' said Preedy, with a gloomy and absent-minded air, 'and perhaps you don't want to hear it. If so that's an end of the matter, otherwise we'd better be in private.'

The boys were now crowding round the two men; they had realized that there was some kind of conflict and were as eager to watch it as a fight.

Syson hesitated a moment and then said he certainly wanted to hear the truth and turned into the vestry, where he sat down on the large box containing old hymn books. Preedy took his seat on the only chair. The room was small but extremely high, running up almost to the roof of the aisle. One side showed the naked organ pipes, the heavy pipes at the back of the organ, another was taken up with a cupboard holding vestments. Heaps of dusty hassocks were piled under the only window.

'I'm afraid,' said Syson, dryly, 'we're rather dusty here.'

'Your accommodation is better than mine,' Preedy said, 'you have the advantage of me there, but I think that's the only one.'

'About this story,' said Syson, impatient to challenge the man, 'are you denying what I saw with my own eyes at the Rodkers'?'

'I am saying that you don't know the truth, the real truth, of my relations with Alice Rodker or hers with me.'

'You mean that nothing of any importance took place in the bedroom?'

'I mean it was not at all what it seemed.'

'Do you deny that you ever had any physical relations, criminal relations, with the girl?'

'I certainly deny that I ever had what you call criminal relations with Alice Rodker.'

'She had a baby at fifteen – do you deny that? And it was by you.'

'Oh, by criminal you mean illegal? Do you really think that everything against the law is criminal? I've heard of parsons in your church who break the law; that's to say, who don't do what their bishop tells them.'

'Look, Mr Preedy, this whole thing has been started on your side. I don't want to go to law, but I had a letter from a lawyer last week threatening an action for slander on your behalf. I don't know if you meant that threat, but I suppose you realize that if the case came into court you would have to answer for seducing the girl at the age of fourteen – the whole story would come out.'

'You're calculating on that?'

'I'm not calculating on anything, I'm just pointing out what would happen – which you know quite well yourself.' The more Syson thought of it, the more disgusted he was at the man's impudence. It seemed to him that the whole of Preedy was impudence; he was simply a brazen crook, playing a confidence trick, bluffing for all he was worth. 'What I'm wondering is why you asked for this interview, you haven't a leg to stand on and you know very well that you couldn't afford to bring an action. I suppose that fellow Hooper is behind it. You're bluffing, Mr Preedy, but that cock won't fight this time.'

Preedy reflected for a moment, looking at Syson with an air of surprise, or rather through him, and said then, almost in a dreamy voice, 'I suppose you really don't care about the truth.'

Syson, more and more irritated against this man, answered sharply, 'That's what I'm trying to get at.'

'Do you realize, for instance, that a girl of fourteen is capable of devotion, is capable of giving her life for what she thinks is right?'

'What sort of a man were you to play upon a child's innocence and force of affection?'

'Yes, she was innocent – she knew no corruption. But you're not interested in the truth, only the usual cant, newspaper stuff about seduction and so on. Suppose I said that Alice Rodker was sent to me by God, you would think I was making up a clever lie.'

'I shouldn't call it a clever lie, Preedy.'

'No, you're not interested in the real truth.'

'The truth is all I care about. What on earth do you think I'm making all this trouble for, stirring up all this horrible mess?'

Preedy looked at Syson with a new expression – he had barely noticed him before. Then he exclaimed in surprise, 'You know, I believe you mean that.'

'Mean it, of course I mean it. Do you take me for a liar?' Syson had nearly said, 'That would be just like the liar you are.' But he had been surprised by Preedy's tone.

'Yes, I believe you do want the truth above everything, and that's why you're getting into all this trouble with your vicar and your wife. You know, Syson, you're like me – you're a man who *has* to have the truth – at all costs. We're the last people who ought to quarrel – we ought to be friends.'

But to Syson this was merely a rather too obvious attempt to flatter him out of his duty – to win him over. He smiled scornfully straight into Preedy's face and said, 'Did Hooper advise a court action?'

Preedy was disappointed and did not answer for a moment. Then he remarked, 'You're quarrelling with your church and I'm quarrelling with my own Mission. You think your vicar is simply a hypocrite and I think most of my committee are hypocrites. You're in trouble in your parish and I'm in trouble in mine.'

This unexpected offer of friendship struck Syson simply as a naïve attempt of Preedy's to avoid the action in court. He answered him coolly, 'You wanted to discuss this action; what surprises me is that you brought it at all, knowing what we know.'

Preedy gave a long sigh and dropped his eyes. He had, for the moment, forgotten about the slander action and his own motive for this meeting with Syson. He had not met Syson before and he was impressed by the man's forthrightness. Till that moment Syson had been a name to him, the name of a curate in the Established Church, and therefore, to his mind, a whiffler by nature, a dodger of any important issue. But he knew, of course, that Syson was at odds with his vicar; that was common gossip at Pant's Road, the Mission had been delighted to know of any trouble among the St Enoch's clergy; of any evidence that the Established Church was breaking up. His offer of friendship to the man was spontaneous; as he would have said to himself, 'God has sent me to him.'

'If you want to withdraw,' Syson said, 'I suppose it is still possible.'

'I did not mean to come to you today,' Preedy said, 'I was directed, and I am directed now to ask you why you are fighting the Pant's Road Mission, for I believe that your heart is with us, I believe you are a man who truly desires to know God who is truth and goodness and reconciliation.'

Syson turned quite pale at hearing these words; the blasphemy caused in him a physical disgust, he could not bear what he called the hypocrisy of the man. He said at last, 'I don't expect, Mr Preedy, we should agree about religion or the obligations of a Christian, but I think it is fair to warn you that the court action would be extremely dangerous to you. Have you forgotten those letters?'

Preedy seemed surprised. 'What letters do you mean?'

'Those letters you wrote to Alice Rodker, confessing that you were the father of her child.'

'I didn't know they existed, has she given them to you?'

'They will certainly appear in the evidence.'

Preedy seemed to reflect for a moment, and said at last, 'That, of course, alters the situation a good deal.'

'Entirely, the truth would come out at last.'

Preedy jumped up. 'Yes, or at least the facts.' He seemed to be looking, not at Syson, but through him. 'And that would be an entirely new situation. We might have the truth as well as the facts.' Before Syson could answer this he offered his hand and murmured, 'Thank you very much, I'm glad I came. It was upon impulse, I admit, seeing you at the vestry door – I thought it was an impulse, but now I know that it was intended, for both our good perhaps, to bring out the truth,' and he walked out, leaving Syson considerably surprised. He was still more surprised when, three days later, he was cited to answer a charge of slander in the courts. This letter did not come from the same lawyer as Hooper's. Preedy, it seemed, had picked a lawyer of his own.

25

When Alice Rodker was subpoenaed as witness for the defence in the Preedy-Syson case her first idea was to pay no attention. The Rodkers had been chapel people. The father's clerkship was a responsible post, but still not superior to that of a factory foreman. The mother was a small farmer's daughter. They had lived in a terrace of five-roomed houses occupied by petty tradesmen, by head clerks in the humble and rougher kinds of occupations, intensely respectable, intensely aware of their status, not ambitious of rising in life, but extremely afraid of sinking into what they thought of as the working-class, real proletariat. The father, a teetotaller, never visited a pub. He had an incredibly small acquaintance; no one who could be called a close friend. The family were on friendly but guarded terms with their neighbours on both sides; the friendliness was a protective measure against ill-feeling, so dangerous in a neighbourhood so close; but their real circle of acquaintance consisted only of fellow chapel people. That is to say, they were among the most exclusive and isolated people in the whole country, with none of the gregariousness of the real proletariat below, and no part in the social organization and social traditions of those upper classes in which visiting is a matter of course, and social relations a duty. Their attitude towards the Press and the law, towards authority, towards the whole established state of affairs, was that of people who stand aside, who say, 'You go on with your job of running the country, and we'll do our job as citizens, then we're quits.'

This did not mean that they took no interest in the outside

world. On the contrary, they were great newspaper readers. Each of the Rodker parents had taken a Sunday paper and spent most of the afternoon before evening chapel reading it. Their special interest was in crime, personal stories about prominent people, scandal generally. It was perhaps the very privateness, the isolation of their lives which gave them this intense interest in social gossip, their deep respectability and law-abidingness which made for them so fascinating the criminal and the sinner. They had their only contact with violent feelings and independent ruthlessness in these papers – their very secretiveness gave a thrill of horror to the violation of privacy, so essential to their own peace.

But Alice had a special reason for that horror. She had herself suffered that violation. First, at her appearance in the juvenile court as needing care and protection and being out of control of her mother; and secondly, two years later, when her baby had died and the coroner had held an inquest. In both cases she had felt a deep grievance. Her private affairs, the long, complicated agonies of her relations with Preedy and afterwards of her child's death, had been discussed by people who hadn't the faintest idea of her motives; who, it seemed to her, did not want to know how she felt or why she had done anything.

The magistrate's court, a woman of sixty and three men all in their fifties, had obviously looked upon her as an obstinate and self-willed young fool, a thoroughly difficult case; irresponsible, ungrateful, wrong-headed and vicious. Her refusal to give the name of the man in the case was looked upon simply as sulking and mulish rebellion.

Then in the coroner's court it was perfectly true that her baby might have been saved if a doctor had been called. It was true, too, that the Jackman Mission and Preedy, who had joined it, had forbidden her to have a doctor. They had made her believe that to call a doctor would show lack of faith in God. But her mother had always taken that view; she had been brought up among people who believed in that Mission. It was because she had belonged to it, that Preedy had joined when he was converted.

Perhaps it was true that Preedy had wanted that baby to die; a baby still unacknowledged by him, undeclared by her. But, if so, that was between themselves. She herself had chosen not to have a doctor, and if Preedy had urged her to that decision, it was still her own decision. The baby's death was between them, a private thing, the most private thing possible. She could not discuss it. But the coroner had insisted on asking her questions about it, on treating her like a fool; and then the Press had published the whole case as if it was a disgrace, as if she was some kind of criminal lunatic.

So when she got the subpoena for this new appearance in court she simply tore it up and threw it away; and when Fred, who had noticed the envelope with its official superscription, asked her about it, she would not answer him. Brother and sister had been on bad terms since the visit of Preedy to her room. When Fred had begun to abuse her for scandalous conduct she had answered that it was her own affair, and that she intended to look for a new flat; she would live alone in future and have peace from nosy parkers. This ultimatum alarmed Fred very much, not only because he loved his sister, but because she was extremely useful to him. She cooked his meals and mended his clothes – he needed her as much as any poor man needs a wife.

When he heard from Syson that Alice had been summoned as a witness and realized that that envelope had contained a subpoena, he was very much alarmed. He pointed out to her that if she did not attend the court she would be arrested.

'It's no good blaming me or Mr Syson, it's Preedy who brought the action. Nobody knows why he's been such a fool, perhaps he thought he could frighten us into making a settlement out of court. As it is, of course, the whole story about you is bound to come out. He'll be properly shown up.'

'They can't ask me about that old case when the magistrates had me up, or about the baby? That's all done with.'

'How do you mean, done with? Those are the most important points in this case, to show what Preedy really is.'

'You can't have people up twice for the same thing, every fool knows that, it's in the law.'

Fred pointed out carefully and patiently to his sister that she was not to be had up twice for anything; she was only being called as a witness. But in Alice's mind to be had up was the same thing as being examined in public. The witness-box for her was quite as bad as the dock. And now, perceiving at last that one way or another she was bound to be dragged into court if the case went on, she fell into a panic. She did not tell Fred of her intentions. With him she simply kept silence; she sent him to

Coventry. For the next few days she carried out all sorts of plans to stop the case. She had decided already that if she could not stop it she would simply run away from London. It would be easy to hide in the country.

Her first visit was to Joanna, because she might be expected to understand her objections to the witness-box; and also because she believed Joanna to have power over Hooper. She knew through Fred that Hooper was backing Preedy in the case.

She told Joanna, first of all that she would not appear in court, and that, if they arrested her, she would simply say nothing, that they could kill her if they liked but still she wouldn't say anything, 'So you can tell your friend Hooper he'd better settle the case.'

'But if you refuse to give evidence, Mr Preedy will win the case, and that's just what Mr Hooper wants.'

'Then you can tell Mr Syson to settle.'

Joanna was pleased by this development; she thought quite as badly of Preedy as did Syson, but she had suddenly entered into a new relation with Hooper. Ever since that evening in Hooper's flat after the *Post* party, she had been raging against him, but she knew quite well that her rage was founded in guilt. It had merely increased her anger that this was just the feeling he had tried to implant in her when she had fought him off. She knew it was a trick on his part and resented her own feeling of guilt; not only as a weakness on her part but as a calculation on his. He was taking advantage of her in a particularly mean way. Yet the feeling was still there; she felt that she had been unkind, ungenerous; she had made the touchy little man look silly and small. She had deeply hurt his vanity. Though she had seemed to avoid him since their meeting with the Rodkers, actually she had gone to every party where he might possibly be seen, and when she did encounter him, looking at him with that curiosity which had brought them together in the first place. It was as though she were asking herself, 'Is he the man?'

But she did not want to speak to him; her resentment was too great. And then one day she heard that he had lost his job with the *Argus* and she realized at once what a tremendous blow this dismissal would be to his self-regard. Immediately she felt within herself the accusation, 'Why was I so silly with the man?' and the conviction that she would make it up with him.

This spontaneous conviction amused her; she could not tell whether it was a surrender or simply good nature.

Three days later at a party for her set given by one of the débutantes of her year in celebration of her rather unexpected marriage, at twenty-nine, to a very rising conservative M.P., rich, good-looking and no older than herself, Hooper walked in after supper and actually danced with the hostess. Apparently he was a friend of the husband's, who cultivated the Press, and he had now become a friend of the house. Joanna had never seen him in such a mood of ease and gaiety, nor thought him capable of it. He danced badly but energetically, talking all the time, and afterwards, glass in hand, he chattered to anyone and everyone. His air was that of the amiable bachelor uncle among girls just out, though, in fact, he was little older than they, and most of them were married women with children already at school; women still technically young but already showing the first lines of disillusioned maturity. One could see already how later on they would take it; some with bitterness, some with patience, a few with humour. Meanwhile they had still a zest for pleasure. They danced hard but their faces showed their resolution to seize on this enjoyment; not one had the transported expression of a young girl, for whom dancing is an intoxication. They did not forget themselves and, from the beginning, there were many who preferred to sit and talk. Joanna was one of these. She loved dancing but she was too tall a partner for most men and she did not attract partners. If she were asked by a friend, she was embarrassed by the feeling that he was sacrificing himself, so she had always found dances more painful than pleasant. To-night she had met some old acquaintances not seen for years, but had discovered that the longer the interval since their last exchange of news, the less of interest there was to say, and it seemed to her that these rediscovered friends were even more bored with her than she with them. The young mothers wanted to talk with other young mothers, the spinsters wanted to talk with men. Hooper was a success with both; he was accepted as a privileged house friend. Those faintly bawdy remarks which were his staple to women at such a party were received with delighted smiles even by those who had married parsons or had been converted. There had been not a few of these during the powerful turn towards religion in the ten years since that Queen

Charlotte's Ball when they had come out, but the staidest, the most fanatical, accepted this bald and ravaged man in his genial mood as having the privileges of an uncle.

Genial as he was, his eyes seemed to avoid Joanna. Once she smiled at him and he seemed to notice her, but without the least change of expression.

She had placed herself in the corner of an ante-room opening from the buffet; Joanna loved corners where she could be out of the way of the crowd, and yet enjoy the sense of propinquity. Here she had been talking for some time with a young wife just home from Africa, where her husband was Chief Secretary. This woman, who carried already that confident and rather imperious air of a Governor's wife, talked children like the rest. Education was her problem, its enormous expense nowadays. A woman on Joanna's other side, wife of a shipowner, rich and smart, but obviously pleased to renew her acquaintance with the Service lady, remarked, laughing, 'But probably there won't be any public schools in another year or two.'

'That's what's so annoying,' said the first. 'One never knows where one is.'

'If you can say that one is anywhere.'

And for a moment the two talked politics, not party politics, but general politics, the politics common to such women; educated, accustomed to make conversation, but too deeply immersed in an active life of management and contrivance, in household and nursery, to have much time or interest for parliamentary news. And both of them agreed quite cheerfully that they had no great hopes for the future of Europe or indeed of America, of Western civilization generally. It would be destroyed, if not by war, by the steady erosion of the barbarian flood. For one thing, increase of population in Russia and the East would put those masses into an overwhelming superiority, and those masses would be hungry masses, growing hungrier every year.

Joanna, relieved that she need take no part any longer in conversation about children and schools, sat silent. This talk was too familiar to her to be interesting. Especially from Hooper she had heard it; she could see him across the room, orating with energy to the host and three or four people gathered about him, and she could bet by his expression and theirs that he was on the subject now; either that or the need for a revival of faith.

In her dreamy and reflective mood Joanna was ready to believe that these women were speaking the truth. No doubt, like Hooper, they meant it partly for provocation. They wanted to utter the worst in order to discount it, as savages propitiate an angry god by cutting and beating themselves. But wasn't it very likely, in good fact, that the world was going to the devil?

As her mind and feeling, unguarded and almost impersonal for the moment, calmly examined this terrifying pit into which civilization was sliding – all that she valued, all that made life worth living for her, courage, honesty, above all, common kindness between man and man – she was aware of a darker and deeper chasm beneath this gulf and, gazing curiously downwards, like an explorer committed to accept everything, she realized that beneath her despair of civilization lay another huge doubt – was life worth living? What was it for? What was all the trouble about? Why all this agony and anxiety and conflict?

Look at all these women at the height of their beauty and happiness, their children still too young to have ruined themselves. She supposed that every one of them this evening must be regarded as enjoying the luckiest good fortune. That was why they had been asked, so that the hostess could let them realize her own rather late triumph. As they danced with such determination, or walked about the room, most of them magnificently dressed, all belonging to an envied minority of cherished, well-bred, well-educated, well-cared-for families, what had they to look forward to, what was the sense of their lives? She remembered how her father had rushed off to his river at the news that the mayfly were out. Were these women any better, born in glory to live for a day in the sun, to find a mate, and die in producing a new generation of mayfly; that is to say, those who were successful in life, those that had not been gobbled up, too young to breed, by some fate or other.

This civilization of the social graces, the arts, without which, lonely as she was, she couldn't conceive herself to want to live, had gone out once before, overwhelmed by the barbarian horde. Tens of millions of people had lived for centuries like beasts among the ruins of the first empire, and died like beasts without leaving even a cry; probably without knowing even that a complaint might be justified. They were hardened to their fate, they didn't get much, but then they didn't expect it.

This civilization that she valued so much, was it not a kind of accident, and if it had its pleasures, were they not paid for by enormous miseries? How many people had any real happiness or security? It wasn't surprising that people took to religion but you had to be a special kind of person to believe in Heaven, and she wasn't that kind of person, she didn't even want to be that kind of person. But then, no doubt, if she had been born in the dark ages she would have believed, she would have been taught to believe. Were they right after all, who asserted that man was unfit to be free, who said, 'Keep the mass in slavery, religious or political, make them beasts again – sheep of some master hand, feed them well and let them die happy in a dream of bliss?' The trouble was, no doubt, to find the master; then to make him prevail against the other aspirants.

At this moment the shipowner's wife asked her if she were going to the Fielding party. She realized that both the women were amused at something, probably at her absent-mindedness.

'Or do parties bore you too much?'

'Good Heavens, no, I adore parties,' Joanna animated herself; it was necessary to show that she adored parties, why she did not know, but probably no one in the room would have cared to admit that he could be bored at a party. Since the war it was impossible to say that parties could be a bore, just as it had become eccentric or merely rude to be sceptical in religion. One could say that one had reservations, difficulties, but not that one did not believe. The necessity to enjoy parties was so urgent that she was obliged to dance with the shipowner husband, a short and fat man of fifty, who could not hide his alarm at the instruction and his misery during the performance. And Joanna perceived very easily that the two young mothers had been anxious to get rid of her, probably because they wished to establish an acquaintance of mutual advantage, with plenty of money on one side and social prestige on the other.

This realization and the embarrassment of the dance depressed her much more than the reflection that life, after all, at least civilized life, might be a complete fraud. She had perceived that possibility without any shock or even surprise as if perhaps her whole existence had prepared her for it.

Hooper left early, before one o'clock, but Joanna had managed to keep her eyes on him. She caught him in the hall as he came from the cloakroom and said resolutely, 'What I really want is a little peace before I go home.'

He stared at her with a very unamiable expression and said, 'Does that mean you want to come to my flat?'

But now this rudeness, his obvious intention to humiliate her, for some reason only amused her. Something inside her laughed at this man who was so eager to insult her, and she answered at once, 'Yes, it does; that's to say, if you'll have me.'

'Have you?' the man said. She did not answer this crude quip, but again she was amused, and also exhilarated. She felt that whether in spite or good humour, if he had any good humour, the man would fall. And this was what happened. Indeed, Hooper had made his first advances as soon as they entered the flat. He had treated her in a very careless manner, handling her much as he would have handled the commonest kind of whore, and with the deliberate intention of making her feel like one. But this treatment also had only served to increase her sense of elation, of confidence, of power. It made her feel that she was mistress of the situation; that it was she who was acting reasonably, with good nature and good sense, while he, rough and rude, deliberately putting on an act, played the victim's part. Not that she felt superiority to the man, only an affectionate sympathy for his touchy moods. So too, when she complimented him on his performance and perceived his self-satisfaction, she could have thrown her arms round his neck and kissed him, laughing at him as a mother laughs at her baby, who is flattered in his childish humours.

And now, all at once, just as she had hoped and expected, she could greet him happily and talk freely. Some barrier was down, some barrier of pride and guilt, and they were at ease together. She was able to accept the man's touchiness, his violent conceit and ambition, and to admire his strength of purpose, his strong will. However much she detested the very idea of Preedy, she could approve Hooper's energy on Preedy's behalf, and that was why she was glad to seize this chance of helping him.

26

She suggested to Alice that they should go to see Hooper together about the case.

But when she phoned, a voice she hardly recognized, an exhausted voice, answered, 'Well, what about it?' Hooper was still in bed. That morning, after a sleepless night, he had found himself so full of aches and pains, so full of disgust with the world, that he could not bring himself to get up.

'I thought you'd like to see her about the case. She's so against it.'

'I'm not interested in those lunatics – they can take what they get.'

'Couldn't you see her for a minute – she's upset. Poor boy, are you feeling very rotten?'

'Oh, come if you like.'

It was this last question which caused Hooper to give this invitation. He could not admit to his captive that he was feeling ill, still less that this feeling could depress his spirits. But he did not shave to receive his visitors, or change his old and filthy dressing-gown, he was too disgusted with the world.

'Well,' he said. He stood in front of the fireplace, examining his nails.

Joanna explained the situation – that Alice wanted to stop the case.

'She needn't acknowledge those letters.'

'No,' said Joanna. 'As they're only copies she needn't acknowledge anything – Syson only saw Preedy come out of her room.'

Hooper said nothing to this and Joanna looked anxiously at him – too anxiously, for he felt it and suddenly she received from him an angry glare. At that moment, Hooper felt for Joanna a flash of real hatred. This was not only because of her possible power – the power she did not use, her possible importance as a great shareholder in the *Argus* Press – but because of something in this new relation with the woman. His sensitive nerves detected in her sympathy a patience that deeply affronted him, especially since he so despised already the plain, gawky and ineffective creature, a failed woman if ever there was one, and no credit to her owner.

This anger and contempt at the moment was so intense that it made him impatient also with Alice, simply because Joanna had taken the girl up. He snapped at her, 'You don't want to give evidence?'

'No, and I won't tell them anything. You can tell Mr Syson.'

'It's no good telling Syson anything, he's the defendant – you want to talk to Preedy.'

'But surely,' Joanna said, 'Syson might settle out of court if he knew that Alice would deny everything.'

'I can't quite see her getting away with much in court – not if counsel know their business.'

'Can they bring up that old case – it was years ago?' Alice said.

'That's what they'll do if they have any sense.' And he added, 'A nice bit of stuff for the Sunday papers.'

'That's what's so unfair,' Joanna said, 'that Alice should be dragged into court and cross-examined about something that happened when she was little more than a child.'

'Yes, most unkind of people,' said Hooper. 'But how do you propose to stop it if the case comes on? And that's up to Miss Rodker.'

'What have I got to do with it?' Alice exclaimed.

'It's quite simple,' said Hooper. 'Go to Preedy and tell him if he goes on with the case you'll put him in jail. You can, can't you?'

'Of course she could,' said Joanna.

'The man is absolutely at your mercy,' Hooper said. 'You could ruin him at a word.'

'Preedy, I wouldn't go near him.'

'Then you can't complain if you make the Sunday papers.'

Alice burst out, 'Of course, he's doing it – Preedy. He would. Because I won't crawl to him, the swine.'

'He's bringing the action,' said Hooper, 'if that's what you mean – I'm telling you how to stop it.'

'Stop it,' Alice was suddenly enraged. She jumped up. 'If he wants to go to jail he can, that's all. Why should I worry? If they have me in court, if he goes on with the case, I *will* send him to jail. Tell him from me, if he goes on with the case, I'll send him to jail.'

She then rushed out of the room. Hooper turned to Joanna and said, 'So much for your Alice. I thought she was a vindictive little bitch at bottom.'

'Why my Alice?'

'You don't seem to have done much good with the sweetness policy.'

'Naturally she's upset – think of what she's gone through.'

'Where did you get that hat?'

'This hat? I've had it for ages. Why?'

'It makes you look more like a horse even than usual.'

Joanna coloured. She was startled and embarrassed by this new proof of the man's incessant will to hurt her, taking a still pettier form. She said at last. 'I'm not good at hats.'

'I know that – the question is what are you good at?'

'Have you got a pain?' said Joanna, with spirit.

'Why don't you pay someone to turn you out decently? You're rich enough.' He was trembling with hatred. And then, with a sudden inspiration, he went up to the woman, sat down on the arm of her chair and said, 'I'm sorry – but you don't realize how much I care for you – that's why I can't bear to see you going about like a dejected charwoman. Why do you try to look like a failure? Are you really so discouraged?'

His tone and look were convincing in their sincerity and Joanna, astonished by this tenderness, was suddenly moved. Her lips shook, her eyes filled. She smiled hastily and said, 'I'm sorry about the hat.'

'I must get you one,' and he embraced her warmly, closely.

It had all the appearance of an affectionate reconciliation, but Joanna went away happy because she had so nearly cried. This had surprised her very much, and she said to herself, 'Perhaps I really am fond of the man, if he can hurt me like that.'

Hooper too was happy. He told himself that he had got under that creature's skin at last and made her cry. And now he was full of energy and enterprise. He rang up Preedy and warned him of Alice's threat.

'I dare say,' Preedy said. 'She's capable of anything.'

'I think, you know, Syson would be quite ready to settle out of court – pay your costs at least.'

There was a long pause, then Preedy answered. 'That would be an admission of guilt on my part, and I'm not guilty.'

'But according to Alice Rodker she could put you in jail.'

'You can tell her from me that I'm not to be blackmailed,' and he rang off.

'I like that chap,' Hooper said to himself, warmed with the assurance, 'and I shouldn't wonder if he gets away with it too. What a nerve – what a bastard really.'

27

The Preedy-Syson slander case at once made headlines: a minister on one side, a parson on the other, a charge of immorality with a young girl, it had everything to stir the deepest, most primitive feelings. Those who hated the headlines, as Hooper pointed out, hated them simply because they did concern those powerful senses; those everlasting preoccupations. For the less Britons go to church, the more they are troubled by religious problems, moral issues. They are like refugees, whose cities have been bombed. All at once they reveal the fundamental needs of their souls – men who thought little of a comfortable home are seen painfully cobbling a shack of a few sticks and an old blanket to give themselves and their families a habitation in the wilderness of ruin. And for this shelter the desperate owner will fight to the death.

So atheists do battle for the ideal dignity of mathematics, and scientists war savagely among themselves about the moral responsibility of atomic physicists for the atom bomb. Rationalists rush from their holes at the very sight of a gaiter and positivist philosophers bark all night at the whisper of a loving couple in the back lane.

For among the displaced it's every man for himself – all neighbours are enemies and all possessions are a provocation to somebody. Both Preedy and Syson were used to occasional letters designed to rob them of any religious confidence they might profess, but now they had them by every mail and on a quite new note of malice. Some of the anonymous ones especially exhausted grammar in their rage and developed a kind of language, without stops or syntax, which was like the scream of epilepsy. And this was quite natural. For all those unhappy unstable souls who, if they had not believed in Preedy's message, would have found life unbelievable, Syson was worse than Judas; and all those who clung to the Church thought Preedy an impudent fraud, and more fearfully, a deadly peril to their faith. For that faith rested in their attachment to the Church, their profound feeling that it aimed at good things and did its best to make Christianity work and that no other institution could begin to take its place. But they realized too that it was always open to attack on logical grounds, if only because of scientific development in the last two thousand years. Preedy's attack had raised just such a question in an acute form: Did God really have power? Was he really the Almighty? In short, the problem of evil, a problem to which the proper answer was, as Clarry said, 'How do we know – it's beyond *our* understanding.'

Besides the scores of letters, there were also cuttings from papers, whole magazines, and books arguing for beliefs which belonged to neither.

Preedy's counsel opened with a general account of Preedy's life. He admitted the early wildness, described his conversion, his devoted service since, and the magnificent work of his Mission of Faith and Regeneration.

He then related Syson's charges, accusing his client of hypocrisy, making him unfit for his position as a Christian minister. The object of the slander was, in fact, to have him turned out of that position, and it had actually caused an agitation among certain members of the Pant's Road Mission to have the plaintiff deprived of that important post. The grounds for the charge seemed to be only that Mr Preedy paid occasional visits to an old friend, a woman whom he was anxious to bring back to his congregation. But behind it there was a long record of malicious persecution.

The first evidence for the plaintiff was given by Mr Wills and Mrs Hartree. They confirmed the slander and the attempt to make Preedy resign if he did not bring this action. Then the greengrocer, whose son was a member of the Mission, gave evidence that Syson had called Preedy a crook on the make. The greengrocer described himself as an agnostic who had disapproved of Preedy at first but had now formed the opinion that he had 'special powers'.

The next witness was Preedy himself. He said that 'hypocrite' was the worst thing that could be said about a man in his position.

He also showed that the slander had raised an opposition against him in his congregation; he had actually been asked to resign, he had been told he was unfit for his position.

In cross-examination he admitted that he had visited Alice Rodker and that he had gone to her bedroom.

'For what purpose?'

'I went as a friend at her invitation.'

'You say she asked you into her bedroom?'

'Yes.'

'And what happened in the room?'

'She proposed to have relations with me.'

'You say that this occurred at her instigation?'

'Yes.'

'How old is she?'

'Nineteen.'

'And you?'

'Thirty-three.'

'Do you say this girl so dominated you that you had to obey her?'

'No, I thought she was moved by a true impulse of affection.'

'And you gave way.'

'I thought it might be a means to bring her back to God's service.'

'Is this a usual method with you?'

'No.'

'You expected affection from her?'

'She has unusual powers of affection. She always had. She is very loyal.'

'And you valued her affection and loyalty?'

'It marked her out for me as one especially gifted to do God's work.'

'How long have you known Miss Rodker?'

'Five years – a little over.'

'So she was fourteen when you first knew her?'

'Fourteen and a half.'

'Did her family know then of this acquaintance?'

'No.'

'Was it then you commenced sexual relations with her?'

Preedy's counsel at once protested and a long argument followed.

Meanwhile Preedy stood in the box with an expression of perfect indifference. He might have been alone by himself in a field. This expression was habitual to him in certain moods, for instance, at committee meetings during any kind of argument.

He had been warned of the danger of bringing this action. He had been specially warned not to admit any previous relations with Alice Rodker. It had been explained to him that he could refuse to answer any questions on the point. Why then did he incur the whole revelation? He said, of course, that he had submitted himself to guidance, to God's will; and, in fact, he was convinced that in pursuing the truth at any cost he was doing God's will. But it is very likely that he felt the danger to himself as an even stronger attraction. In another life he might have been a test pilot, a racing motorist, an explorer, a climber of Himalayan peaks; or perhaps a cat burglar, safe-robber, or hold-up man. Danger and suffering do have a fascination for people of Preedy's type, who are set apart from the ordinary common judgements of the world by all sorts of reasons as well as religion. It has been argued that Oscar Wilde, for instance, was driven to his ruin by the same deep sense of contempt for the standards of the mob, perhaps even by desire to suffer, to be a martyr for the truth as he conceived it. And perhaps too, as it was suggested of Preedy, by some overwhelming appetite for the dramatic gesture.

Certainly Preedy hearing his counsel fighting his legal argument, felt complete indifference to the result.

The judge ruled finally that Preedy was not compelled to answer this question unless he chose.

Counsel then said, 'You hear his lordship's ruling. You needn't answer that question unless you choose.'

Preedy said at once that he would answer any question counsel chose to put to him.

Counsel then repeated his question, 'Did you have sexual relations with this child of fourteen?'

'Yes.'

'Did you realize it was a criminal act?'

'I was then a criminal in all kinds of evil – it was before my conversion.'

'Did she have a child?'

'Yes.'

'Your child?'

'Yes.'

'Did you own it?'

'No. I ran away – I deserted her.'

'And the juvenile court sent her to a remand home; but she didn't give you away.'

'Yes, she had wonderful loyalty and courage.'

'Which you took advantage of.'

'Yes, I relied on it.'

'But since then you say you have not molested her until this recent occasion in her flat?'

'No.'

'And you say that that was her fault?'

'I did not say so. I said she made the suggestion.'

'Did she invite you to her flat?'

'No.'

'Were you welcome there?'

'No.'

'Yet you say she invited you to her bedroom?'

'Yes.'

'Did she say anything like this, "I didn't ask you here. Will you go away and let me alone if I give you what you want"?'

Preedy's counsel protested against this question and the judge disallowed it.

'Have you caused her to lose jobs by telling employers this terrible story of her childhood?'

'Once I intervened to tell her employer, her first employer.'

'To have her at your mercy?'

'I wished her to come to the mission; I had work for her there. I was instructed to seek her.'

'Who instructed you to cause this young girl of seventeen to lose her first job, for which she had struggled so hard?'

'It was by God's command.'

'That she should be absolutely subservient to you?'

'No, to God – her duty was to serve God because he had marked her for his own.'

In re-examination Preedy explained his conviction that the child Alice had been sent to save his soul by the revelation of her unselfish love and that he attributed his salvation to her.

He was then allowed to stand down.

Two witnesses then gave evidence that Preedy had cured them, one of blindness, one of cancer. Both declared that the doctors had given them up.

As it was now nearly time for lunch, the court adjourned before hearing the defence.

28

This adjournment left Syson triumphant and Preedy's friends in despair. It seemed impossible that he should escape prosecution and imprisonment. Thus there was a perfect explosion of excited talk as soon as the judge left the court.

Most of the spectators stayed in their places for fear of losing them, but there was a large number in the courtyard who had not got places, waiting to hear first reports of the case. Most of these were enthusiasts for Preedy, but, as the case had already been headline news in the tabloids, there was a large group who had come only for the excitement. Syson's supporters were few – only three or four personal friends from the parish. Pant's Road followers at once grouped around committee members as they emerged. Dr Jinks, a fat red-faced man, had a small group of what might be called solid citizens, to whom he was describing Preedy's last admissions, repeating every few moments with great satisfaction, 'It's finished him, he's finished for good.' Allday, among some other committee members, was trying to avoid making any decision. Kerne, surrounded by a crowd of fifty or sixty young people, was declaring that Preedy had been trapped, that it was a wicked injustice to bring up a man's past after he had repented of it. Half a dozen other committee members standing discreetly aside, were discussing an immediate approach to Jackman. They were united in dislike of Jinks, who had joined the Mission only six months before, and they did not see why he should have the prestige of bringing in the new Missioner. As for Preedy, they had already assumed that he must go. At that moment, in fact, probably no member of the committee supposed for a moment that Preedy could carry on. Even Mrs Hartree, however regretfully, considered it hopeless to support him.

At this crisis Hooper was in his element; he hurried from group to group, giving to each what he considered its proper antidote. To Jinks and his officials he said that Syson's case was already lost and Preedy would certainly get heavy damages, 'This will put him in a very strong position with people like Allday.' To Allday's party he said the same thing except for the last sentence which went, 'This means that he can checkmate Jinks; if Jinks tries to bring in anyone else he could be run into court himself.'

To Kerne and his excited youngsters he said, 'Preedy has behaved himself magnificently; he's not been afraid to tell the truth, even though it lays him open to the most spiteful kind of attack. It's just because he's a good man that he's got himself into this position.' To a group of reporters he pointed out that Preedy's past had nothing to do with his present.

The little man was shaking with urgency and excitement. He was perpetually twiddling his papers, flourishing them in the air, stuffing them in his pockets and taking them out again. At especially exciting moments of an address he would stand on his toes as if to dominate the crowd by height. But as this was impossible, he would throw back his head so that at least he was enabled to look down his nose at them. And with it all he was obviously enjoying himself. Something in him responded to this crisis with delight. He was at the centre of events and though these were small events compared with some that he had dealt with in the *Argus*'s columns, they were making the headlines, they were having influence on people, and, he was telling himself already, they were going to have much more influence. Preedy was going to be a very big noise and Hooper was going to run Preedy.

To a party of bystanders who wandered in from the street, he explained that even if Preedy went to jail it wouldn't do him any harm, 'It will only make him more popular.'

'Good publicity,' said a young man, who was probably a reporter.

'Yes, publicity,' Hooper snapped, 'and why not? Why shouldn't people know the facts when they're all to the good?'

And to Joanna he pointed out, 'A case like this never does a spell-binder any harm, it makes him human to the mob; it makes him more exciting, especially to the women, and I believe Preedy knows it himself. I don't mean to say he's deliberately got himself into this jam for the publicity and the reactions but

I shouldn't be surprised if that was his real motive. Fellows like that, born spell-binders, have got a sort of instinct for stirring up the mob where it lives, and believe me, if Preedy goes to jug over a case like this, the mob is going to be stirred, millions of it.'

Joanna, in fact, was his principal target, for Joanna had turned definitely and violently against Preedy.

She had been seeing much of Alice and a friendship had grown up between the two. She was fascinated by this girl. She told herself she had never met anyone so completely honest and independent, so free of small vanities. And she was eager to fight her battles. But there was more in her hatred of Preedy than sympathy for her new friend. She was horrified by the man's ruthless cruelty. She had gazed at him in court, and asked herself, 'How could he dare to behave like that to a child – and how can he dare to admit it now? He doesn't care a pin.'

She felt an astonished horror as at a monster, a creature lacking in the essential feelings of a human being.

This horror filled her still, now among all these people. She felt it like a physical presence, an illness. She was like a person suffering from shock, and when Hooper had begun his first exoneration of Preedy, she cried out, like such a patient, whose nerves cannot bear any more.

Catching Hooper's sharp and disgusted glance, and aware that she was in no condition to argue, she then kept silent. She would have gone home if she had not been ashamed, but, in spite of her angry reaction, she found herself standing close to Hooper. After all, she had come with him; it would be rude as well as absurd, to go home and leave him. It might hurt the little man. Besides, her mother was now at home and though she felt that she ought to be with her, she knew too that her presence was only an irritation to the old woman. She ought to be there and her absence might be resented, but being there, she wouldn't know what to say in order not to offend.

She had fetched her from hospital at last, on the day before, but the effect had not been encouraging.

The time fixed had been ten o'clock and Joanna had arrived punctually, but she found her mother not yet dressed. The nurse was awaiting the visit of the specialist who had himself been awaiting the result of a test.

The old woman was angry and excited. 'They don't want me to go home,' she told Joanna. 'They want to keep me here for ever, to chop me about. If this goes on, of course, I shall soon be completely helpless, and they can do what they like with me. I suppose that's what they're after, any excuse to keep me here till my brain goes too.' The old woman, staring at her daughter, was wondering if Joanna also was in this plot. She thought, 'What they're afraid of at home is that I shall be such a nuisance to look after, that I shan't die soon enough.'

'But, Mother, Sir Shanklin is expected any moment now, and the result of this test may be important.'

'How can it be important. Every one of them has a different idea. Last week it was some kind of poisoning, then it was a virus infection; one of them thinks I've got a brain tumour, or something like that. Sir Shanklin thinks it's cancer of the spinal cord. Well, if it is, he can come and tell me at home, can't he? The truth is, they don't want me to go home; you don't want me to go home.'

Joanna, astonished, glanced at her mother and met a furious stare. 'But, Mother, you don't really think such a horrible thing.'

'It's not horrible at all – it's quite natural.' And in the end they had not waited for the specialist. In such a case, Joanna could be energetic and even formidable. She had appealed to the matron and pointed out that it might be extremely important for her mother to be at home, as she was now working herself into an hysterical condition that must be very bad for anyone with such a high blood pressure.

The matron had then telephoned to Sir Shanklin, who had satisfied himself with a warning that he could not undertake further tests in a private house without hospital facilities. But this ultimatum had merely served to excite Lady Rideout still more and Joanna had resolved to move her at once. She had been startled and dismayed to discover this violent nostalgia in her mother, to realize what terrors and suspicions underlay it.

She accused herself of wanting sympathy; how imperceptive she had been. As soon as they reached the room, she kissed her mother and said, 'How lovely, darling, to have you home again.'

But the old woman did not respond. She was looking about her with so vague and wild a stare, that for a moment Joanna had the terrified thought, 'It's another stroke.'

She touched her mother's hand, 'Can I do anything? Are you comfortable?' The hand was pulled away and Kate, looking impatiently at her daughter, shook her head and murmured, 'Thank you.'

29

In defence Syson's counsel claimed privilege on the ground that Mr Wills was a member of Syson's congregation – it was Syson's duty to prevent him from being misled. Syson, in examination, confirmed this statement. He had certainly thought it was his duty to warn Mr Wills and his parishioners generally against Preedy and his Mission.

From his first appearance in the box Syson alarmed his counsel by his impatient air. In this case, in fact, counsel on both sides, and solicitors, were holding their thumbs from the beginning. Such cases have the worst possible name among lawyers; that is to say, cases where parsons, priests and ministers are concerned are even more troublesome than those in which medical experts appear. Witnesses are capable of anything and no middle-aged barrister forgets the case where a medium in the box declared that she saw Christ present in court and Mr Justice McCardie, with great presence of mind said, 'Don't touch her.'

But in addition to this awkward fact, that the Syson-Preedy case was fundamentally a religious quarrel, there was a special difficulty that belongs to all slander cases, that the defendant invariably suffers from a violent grievance. He always thinks that he has been victimized.

The reason is perhaps that slander is so common. Nearly all gossip has some slander in it and probably no one goes through a day without hearing or giving cause for an action at law, so that the ordinary defendant always has the feeling, 'Why should I be chosen for this persecution? It's not fair.'

Certainly Syson felt like that, for the principal witness against him and the chief cause of action was one of his congregation and a former friend, Mr Wills. That was why, even in examination by his own counsel, he spoke with the air of a man whose time was being wasted and who really could not bother to weigh his words.

Cross-examined, he agreed at once that he had described Preedy as a hypocrite and a liar.

Counsel then asked, 'Did you wish to drive Mr Preedy and his Mission out of your parish?'

'I wished to warn members of my church against the Mission.'

'Because members of the church preferred it?'

'No, because it was teaching lies.'

'How did you describe it, as a racket?'

'Yes, I certainly did.'

'By racket, meaning swindle, fraud, run for profit?'

'Not exactly. Preedy may believe in it himself.'

'But you said he was teaching lies.'

'He might believe in the lies.'

'Do you really tell the court that that is what you meant by racket?'

'These people live in a fog.'

'Please answer my question.'

'Perhaps they think they have a right to deceive people.'

'I see – you say Preedy deliberately chooses to deceive.'

'No, exaggerate.'

'You say he tells lies – do you mean that?'

'He may think it right to do so.'

'Please answer my question.'

Syson coloured and said angrily, 'I'm trying to explain that he might think it right to express a confidence he didn't feel. I'm giving him the benefit of the doubt.'

'You still haven't answered my question.'

'But I'm answering——'

Here the judge intervened with some sharpness to tell Syson to answer Counsel's questions. What annoyed Syson was that he was not only trying to give the truth, but one favourable to Preedy. He was using, deliberately, a Christian charity towards the man. Like most people unused to legal procedure he did not understand the principle of examination. He thought it was meant to get truth directly and as much of it as possible. He had no idea of the complicated rules of advocacy. From the moment of the judge's rebuke he began to lose his temper.

Counsel then repeated his question and Syson answered, sharply, 'No.'

'And that's why you call the Mission a racket.'

'Yes, it promises what it can't perform.'

'Do you know that Mr Preedy has cured hundreds of people of grave diseases? We have had two witnesses who were cured when doctors had given them up.'

'Blindness is a common neurosis and everyone over sixty who has a pain thinks it's cancer.'

'Do you believe that miracles are impossible?'

'No.'

'Did you preach a sermon in recent weeks declaring it was unnecessary to believe the Bible stories of miracles?'

'Not all of them, for instance, the miracle of the loaves and fishes.'

'You choose what to believe?'

'The resurrection is necessary to believe for any Christian.'

'It's a matter of choice?'

'If you don't believe the resurrection you couldn't call yourself a Christian.'

'Please answer – is it a matter of choice?'

'Yes.'

'Who chooses?'

'It's the general opinion of modern churchmen that –'

'I asked who chooses? Did you choose for yourself?'

'Yes.'

'Why?'

'I just don't find some of the stories credible. And they aren't necessary either.

'You choose to believe that the Bible tells lies?'

'No – but not a factual truth.'

'You've just told us you couldn't believe in all the miracle stories.'

'One can accept them as religious truth.'

'Do you mean religious truth can involve telling factual lies?'

But it's unnecessary to give all the cross-examination; counsel had no difficulty in making Syson say that he did not believe in the Bible or the Articles, that he believed only what suited his personal fancy. And it is very doubtful if any Bishop would have done better in a witness box. He was then asked if he had signed the Articles in which he did not believe and if it was not hypocrisy to do so.

'So that you accuse Mr Preedy of hypocrisy although he does believe exactly as he professes?'

'I say he couldn't do miracles. It's blasphemous to imagine it of a man of his character.'

'You think Mr Preedy unfit to be a minister?'

'That's what I'm saying all the time.'

'You wanted to stop his work in your parish?'

'Everywhere and anywhere.'

Syson was now enraged and disgusted; he was only anxious to get away from this court and all its foolish prevaricating tricks. As for Preedy, it was already established that he was a man of the lowest character, actually a criminal. What was the good of all this talk?

This was why he grew so impatient at last and was easily led to declare that, yes, Preedy was a crook and he had wanted to drive him out of the parish and put an end to his mission.

30

Syson's evidence concluded that day's hearing, and Clarry was waiting to drive her husband home. She had suffered even more than he the agony of that cross-examination; no woman who loves likes to see her man made to look a fool in public. And she had felt his helpless anger in her own bones.

A hundred times she had said, during the hearing, 'But it's his own fault – didn't I warn him?' She was still exasperated with his obstinate folly, but seeing his pale grim face as he pushed through the staring bystanders towards the car, seeing that some of them were laughing at him, she was moved only to pity and thought anxiously, 'What shall I do to comfort him?' She jumped out to embrace him, and as they drove away she broke out furiously against 'those lawyers. What do they care for the truth or anything except money? Everything's arranged in their favour – to *stop* the truth.'

Syson kept silence. He was at first hardly aware of what his wife was talking about. He was like a man who has had an unexpected accident – shaken but restless, weak but full of confused agitation, and still not certain how much he has been hurt. He tells himself one moment that nothing has happened to him that matters – nothing to do any real damage, the next he feels that somewhere inside, out of sight in the depth of his body, he is quietly, painlessly bleeding to death.

Suddenly he broke in on Clarry, 'Do you mind if I smoke?' Clarry was delighted to see her husband light his pipe – it seemed to mean that he was ready to relax. A moment later, he gave a short appreciative laugh and said, 'They know their stuff, those fellows. All or none. That's Preedy's line too – the obvious line.'

'But how mean to ask you about the Articles. Everyone knows they're wildly out of date.'

'It's all in the game, my dear, logically I hadn't a leg to stand on.'

'What's logic got to do with it?'

Syson smoked for some moments in silence and then interjected, 'That's where the Romans have the start of us – you couldn't make a fool of an R.C. in the box – he swallows the lot, or says he does.'

'It's easy to say anything. But you couldn't be a Roman.'

'I'd have had to be born to it.'

'And the Romans don't really believe like that – not the educated ones.'

'Ah, my dear, but that's the point; they get the best of both worlds, and why not, if it's A.M.D.G.?'

Clarry was silent, not quite liking his papistical sentiment, and there was a long pause. Syson settled himself more comfortably and tamped his pipe with the end of a pencil.

'Anyhow,' said Clarry, at last, 'you've won – I never heard anything like Preedy's evidence.'

'Yes, he's done for. I said he was insane to bring the case at all. But fellows like that always do themselves in – they're so used to getting away with everything that they lose all sense of what's possible.'

31

On the second day of the case the only witnesses for the defence were Alice's first employer, to show that Preedy had disclosed her past to him, and Alice Rodker herself.

The defence did not propose to call Fred Rodker, to his great indignation, for his rage against Preedy convinced him that he would be a vital witness. It was just for this reason that Syson's counsel didn't trust him in the box. They agreed, too, that Preedy's old letters could not be used, since only copies were available and these might well be invalidated.

Alice was called because it was realized that the case for justification would turn largely on the girl's evidence. Also she was known to be greatly embittered against Preedy.

Alice, after being sworn, stood gazing at the front of the judge's desk, thus looking at nobody in court. Her expression was obstinate and defiant – her rather thick brows were drawn together in a frown, her lips compressed, her colour high.

She was aware, of course, that they were all looking at her. She was on show, like a prize pig or a freak. All these people were staring at her and thinking, 'That's Alice Rodker, Preedy's mistress. She was the wicked little girl who had carried on with a man at the age of fourteen – look at her, what does she feel now, what's going on in that vicious creature, what sort of a creature is she to do such things, and stand up there in the witness-box and brazen it out?'

She fixed her eyes on the judge's box and tried to forget them, these people who were staring at her. She felt a little dizzy and she had no idea what she was going to say. She knew that Preedy had agreed that those old charges were true, and she felt exceedingly bitter against him. Her one clear thought was, 'He's punishing me because I won't submit to him. He's making trouble for me all the time. He doesn't mind what he does to break me down. But I'll teach him – it's what that Hooper said, I can send him to jail if I like.'

She kissed the book in a kind of angry dream and heard the counsel ask her if she knew Preedy.

'Yes.'

'Did you admit him to your bedroom?'

'Yes.'

'And what happened there?'

'He told you.'

'I'm afraid you must tell us.'

She then gave appropriate answers to all his questions, saying that she had not wanted Preedy's visit and that he had had sexual relations with her. She gave these answers by a kind of reflex and in such a low voice that the judge was obliged to ask her several times to speak up. But now, when the counsel changed his note and asked how long she had known Preedy, she suddenly awoke from this somnambulism; she felt the man's change of intention.

'I don't know,' she said. 'Does it matter?'

This was a hostile answer, and the counsel felt it; everyone in the court felt it, and fixed their eyes curiously on the witness.

'Did you know him five years ago?'

'It may have been, I suppose so.'

'Were you a friend of his five years ago?'

'I don't know.'

'Do you mean you don't know if you knew him then?'

'I used to go and see him sometimes.'

'Would it be true to say that Preedy was your lover?'

'I used to see him.'

'You had a child, I believe?'

Alice was silent, and continued to stare at the judge's box. Some woman in the gallery uttered an hysterical giggle, and the ushers looked indignantly in that direction. In fact, there had already been a great deal of whispering and rustling in the galleries and the judge had looked several times towards them with a doubtful frown. It was obvious that there was a good deal of explosive material there, particularly a large group of the younger members from the Pant's Road congregation. To them the whole case was simply a scandalous attack on their hero. Especially they resented this bringing up against him of past sins.

Counsel repeated his question and Alice was seen to move her lips. The judge asked her to speak up, whereupon she turned scarlet and said in an unexpectedly loud voice, 'Yes, I had, and they sent me to a home.'

'Was that Preedy's child?'

Alice was silent and again the judge interposed. 'I'm afraid you will have to answer counsel's questions. You can be sure that we sympathize with you in your painful position, but it is absolutely necessary that we should know the facts.'

Counsel repeated his question, and Alice muttered something which was inaudible. She then stood silent, looking at the man as if she had never seen him before. She had suddenly an acute sense of that time when she had stood before the magistrates. She had never forgotten that time. There was always present at the back of her mind a vision of herself as a thin ugly child with a swollen belly, standing before the four magistrates in a bare room designed as a private sitting-room so that children should not feel alarmed by any appearance of a court. She fully understood this point and despised it. Did they think she would be taken in by such a piece of silliness? She was bitterly aware of her ugliness, of her face swollen with crying, of the absurd child's frock that looked still more absurd with that belly and those skinny legs. She felt as if her whole body was raw inside with the same misery of disgust at herself and everybody else.

They had begun by being kind, saying that no doubt she was sorry for deceiving her mother who loved her so much. But she asked herself why her mother had sent her to the court, why her mother had never understood or tried to understand anything about her and she remained silent.

'Do you realize how much pain and trouble you have given her?'

But she thought, 'How much pain and trouble she has given me,' and she couldn't speak.

'She's done everything possible for your welfare and happiness.'

Alice thought of her mother's appeals and complaints and tears over the last three months and looked still more sullen. She realized that no one in the world could begin to understand what had happened to her, except Preedy, but Preedy had deserted her. Though, when she was first pregnant he had understood how she felt and promised to run away with her, he had tortured her too by making her come to him, by his want of sympathy, by his laughter. She knew, of course, why he laughed – she could not explain it, but she knew it was an expression of his feeling for her. He would say, ' I wonder where you got it from,' and 'You're a tough one.'

And though she was anything but tough, she knew that he was admiring her.

No, even if he had not deserted her as soon as her mother had gone to the police, he would have been no good to her now; he had never been any good to her. He always left her to fight her own battles – that's what he liked, to see her struggling and suffering. He had needed her, and he had always treated her as one who needed nobody, certainly not him.

'We're trying to help you,' the woman magistrate had said.

She was a tall handsome woman with beautiful white hair, beautifully dressed, 'but if you go on behaving in this foolish way, if you simply refuse to help us, we'll be forced to decide without your help. We don't want to send you to a home, but it may be the only course open to us. You won't like that, you know – you won't be free there to do exactly what you like. I think you'll agree we've been very patient with you. If you simply won't speak to us, and won't tell us anything, you can't be surprised if you seem to us uncooperative and simply determined to have your own way at all costs.'

Alice stared at the woman with sulky hatred. She hated particularly the beautiful way her hair was dressed and blued by the hairdresser. She thought how much it had cost to make it look like that; a good deal more than it would have cost to give her a new frock, a frock that wouldn't make her look like a scarecrow.

So she was to be called foolish because she would not give Preedy's name, and wicked because she had loved him and let him use her, and gone to him when he needed her, as if she had enjoyed that painful experience, those nights of terror.

She wanted to spit at this handsome, expensive woman. She felt the whole self-confidence of the creature, her enormous certainty that she was wise and good, that she knew all about Alice, that she knew better what was good for Alice than Alice could possibly know for herself, and she would not speak to her, she could not have spoken to her if she'd tried. What was the good – you might as well talk to a wax image.

Now again there was a wall between her and these people who were judging her. The judge began to speak again. She heard him asking her if she were ill, if she would like to sit down for a time. He was being kind to her, like those magistrates, and suddenly she exclaimed loudly, 'I don't want to sit down. I'm not going to faint or anything.' And now she looked round at the crowd, glaring at them, defying them to overwhelm her, to make her need a chair.

The counsel repeated his question. 'I'm sorry, Miss Rodker, but I must have an answer. Was your child Preedy's child?'

Alice was silent.

'I'm afraid you must answer.'

Alice did not reply to this question, not because she was intimidated, but because she had not listened to it. She was staring at the gallery, as if to say, 'You've come here to see the show, but what do I care?' She felt such hatred of everybody in the court, in the world, that she did not even think of what she would say.

Again the counsel repeated his question, and she answered promptly, 'Just as you like.'

'I'm afraid it's not as I like, but as it happened. I must ask you again to answer my questions.'

The judge then again intervened with a warning and somebody at the back of the court among the spectators got up to make a protest.

All this time there was a certain amount of noise and disturbance during which Alice was understood to answer, 'Yes' to counsel's question.

The judge then threatened to clear the court and in the silence counsel asked, 'Do you mean that you will answer my questions or that Preedy was not the father of your child?'

'Yes, that's it.'

This lie was quite unpremeditated. It had come into Alice's head and jumped from her lips really in contempt and defiance. But the moment she had uttered this lie it seemed to her that lying was just what these people had asked for. It was the only proper answer to their attempt to tear out of her things that were the most private in her life.

'Are you suggesting that you had relations with other men besides Preedy?'

'The magistrates said I was as bad as I could be, a thoroughly vicious girl. Why don't you ask them?'

'Because they may have been wrong. That's why I'm asking you now.'

'They couldn't be wrong, could they?'

'Do you mean that Preedy was not the father of your child?'

'I say I was bad – I had lots of men all the time. That's why they sent me to a home.'

In summing up the judge pointed out that Preedy's conversion had taken place after his affair with the child Alice and there was no reason to doubt its sincerity. Dealing then with the question of malice and privilege, about privilege in the case of Mr Wills he was obviously doubtful, but he was quite definite that malice had been proved, not so much in the communication to Wills, as in the remarks to the greengrocer. The greengrocer's evidence, corroborated by Mrs Hartree, was definite for malice, and neither communication had any tincture of privilege. All the same, a great many people in court were surprised by the jury's verdict of guilty. The damages were fixed at five hundred pounds. Syson himself was so astonished and angered by the verdict that he jumped up in his place and said that he would not pay a farthing; that the whole case was a ramp, and so on. In fact, the man quite lost his head and made a very painful scene. The judge warned him to behave himself and when he repeated that he would not pay, committed him to the cells with a general warning that if he did not apologize to the court he'd stay there.

To this Syson answered, 'Just as you like, that's your business, but I shan't pay. The whole thing is absolutely iniquitous; it would be wrong to pay.'

32

Syson actually spent that night in the cells. He absolutely refused to see Clarry, sending out a message that she didn't understand what was involved. But on the next day some friends from the parish, including the vicar, persuaded him to apologize to the court and to agree to the sentence, on the grounds that by remaining in jail he would be deserting his work in the parish. In fact, after this one outburst, Syson seemed to be taking his misfortune very well. True, he had not understood then exactly the magnitude of that misfortune. To lose a case, especially a libel or slander case in the British courts is extremely expensive. And when Syson discovered that he would have to pay costs and damages together of more than three thousand pounds, he knew that he was bankrupt. His whole savings, kept for educating the children, amounted to less than a thousand.

He seemed at first little concerned by this situation, and not even to recognize it as a major disaster. This, of course, is also a familiar phenomenon to lawyers. People who rush into a slander case are always confident of winning and never seem to grasp the consequences of defeat, the enormous expense of paying the other side's costs as well as their own. And men financially ruined seldom accept the fact until they are actually thrown into the street. The gamblers go on gambling, the high livers go on giving parties, the inventors go on ordering new models of their perpetual motion machines until the bailiffs break in. They are like those wounded artillery horses that try to gallop after the guns with their entrails falling out. In a kind of automatism, they not only go on in their accustomed ways, they cling to them as if any others had become impossible.

Syson, having seen the account, did not even tell Clarry about it for another three days. And then to her horrified question what should they do, he answered only, 'Don't worry – we'll manage.'

Clarry, who hated to nag, was obliged to worry in silence.

Meanwhile Syson made himself busy in the parish, even busier than before. He resumed his visits to the pub, where he took his pint and his pipe in the public bar and discussed trade union affairs from a Christian point of view. The only change in the man that was generally noticed was a slight absent-mindedness. He was not quite so prompt in remembering people's names. His next sermon after the case, on the mystery of redemption, contained a very strong attack on rationalism and scientific materialism, and it gave great satisfaction. As for the Preedy Mission, he left that subject alone. When Fred Rodker broke some windows at Pant's Road chapel with the intention of getting arrested and once more bringing up his sister's case, it was Syson who persuaded him to go away before the Mission people were obliged to call the police.

What enraged Rodker was that the public Prosecutor had not taken action against Preedy. But Syson pointed out, reasonably enough, that Alice's own evidence had removed most of his offence and that further publicity was the last thing the girl wanted. At the moment, in fact, she had returned neither to her flat nor her job and nobody knew where she was.

33

Lady Rideout read accounts of the case but made only the comment that Preedy was worse than she had thought, and when Joanna explained that Alice, for this brute's sake, had told lies in her evidence, she said nothing and showed no interest. Yet she had fallen into an extraordinary excitement when, some days later, she discovered that Alice was actually in the house.

On the very evening the case ended, Joanna had had a telephone call from Alice, saying, 'You said you'd help me and I'm asking you; I told you it was dangerous.'

Joanna assured her that she had meant her offer of help and Alice, in the same resentful tone, warned her again, 'It's quite a lot of help. I'm at a call box now, and I don't know where to go. I'm not going back to Fred again, nor my job either; not if I starve.' Joanna had asked her where the call box was and told her to wait in a nearby teashop till she could come with the car. Before night she had found her a room in a hostel for girl students, run partly on a Rideout grant, and given her enough money to pay her way for the next month. Alice refused even to be known by her own name; she called herself Alice Rowe. She showed, however, no signs of distress, and, in fact, very little emotion of any kind. She treated Joanna with a kind of off-hand frankness, and did not say a word of thanks. Instead she repeated several times her warning, 'I told you to be careful of helping me; it's a real job.' Her last words were, 'You brought it on yourself.'

But Joanna did not want gratitude; she understood very well how much this girl resented an obligation, and she was glad to be able to help her on terms that did not create a sense of humiliation on one side and embarrassment on the other.

It had seemed easy for her to find Alice work, shorthand-typists were in demand everywhere, and Joanna had a large acquaintance among authors and women needing secretaries. The difficulty was to find a job that the girl would take. She wanted one where she could live in; she didn't want to be seen in the streets. At the hostel she scarcely left her room except for meals, and when Joanna proposed to take her for a drive into the country for the sake of fresh air she insisted on the car being closed. When Joanna suggested to her that it was impossible she would be recognized – there had been no photograph of her – she answered, 'You wouldn't believe how they get to know about you.' Yet apart from this obsession the girl seemed perfectly sensible and declared to Joanna with great force of conviction, 'There's nothing wrong with me, it's just you don't know what happens when you get into trouble. Well, it's been a surprise to me too.'

Joanna found the ideal job, with two old ladies writing

memoirs, in Teddington. But twenty-four hours after settling the girl in, she had a call again from a box, that she daren't go back, that the address was being watched by detectives. And Joanna finding the girl unshakeable in this idea had brought her back with her. She was to sleep in what had been a dressing-room, on the same floor.

But Lady Rideout's ears were sharp. She had wished to know who was Joanna's visitor, and had at once demanded to see her.

Joanna, for her part, was glad to see her mother take an interest in anything, especially in a matter that might give her a better idea of Preedy's character. Since her return from hospital the old lady had hardly spoken – with Joanna especially she was laconic. She had the manner of one absorbed in some course of difficult reasoning. In fact, Kate was not thinking at all, and she was far from apathetic – she was filled with an enormous resentment and urgency. But the resentment had no object, she could not find anyone to blame for her predicament, not even the doctors or Joanna. And though she felt every instant that something must be done, that time was slipping away, she did not know what to do.

Home had failed her – what she had expected from home, what support or encouragement, she did not know, but from the first minute of her return she had found it a traitor. It too had turned against her. Because she was ill and helpless it had become her enemy.

Here she was at home, at last, she was surrounded by home and it seemed like a prison, more fearful, more sinister even than that bare hospital room. The hospital had been impersonal, a mere place of detention; but here everything, every chair and table, the pictures, the rows of photographs on the mantelshelf, the books, the Italian brass bed with its half-tester and damask hangings, was like a separate jailer, saying, 'There you are again – we've got you.'

All these familiar things with their associations had suddenly become hostile. They had no longer any sympathetic relation with her. It was not only that they presented themselves all at once as shabby old furniture, faded photographs, portraits of the dead, which were simply waiting there to be transported to the bonfire or the junkshop when she should happen to die; but they were a burden and a nuisance. They did not give anything to her weakness, they made demands on it. They demanded attention. They said, 'You can't throw us away – you are responsible for us. See, I'm your dead husband's arm-chair – I'm the rug your dead mother gave you – I'm the cross-stitch chair Joanna stitched for you at school with so many pains. And where is that Joanna now – that child of twelve? She is gone even more completely than the rest. She is not merely dead, she doesn't exist even as the dead exist; she is the ghost of a memory.'

The room was like a graveyard, full of family tombs. And it had been waiting for her, to bury her in a tomb, a loneliness, a darkness, far more remote from the living world than the hospital.

Suddenly she turned to Joanna, 'Don't leave me.'

Joanna was startled, she coloured darkly and took her mother's hand. She recognized a cry for help. But it was the first time her mother had ever asked anything of her and she did not know how to respond. She pressed the hand and said, 'I was just going to call nurse – you know you are supposed to go to bed now.'

'Joanna, do you think I'm a fool?'

'Of course not, Mother.'

'Edward and Robbie have written me off.'

'Oh, no.'

'Darling, you can be honest with me.'

'I am being honest – you're much better already.'

'You don't need to build me up – I'm not afraid of the facts.'

But Joanna perceived that it was vital to build the old woman up. That cry had shocked her. It gave her a glimpse of her mother's loneliness, her desperation, that shocked her with pity.

She too cried out, urgently, convincingly, 'Darling, of course you aren't. But the facts are that you are better. Of course, these weeks in bed have left you feeling rather weak, but you'll soon get over that.'

The old woman dropped her hand, and gave a long sigh. For both of them it meant, 'So no one will tell me the truth.'

'Darling,' Joanna was blinking back tears, 'you know I wouldn't try to hide anything from you – you must believe that.'

There was a short silence, Joanna, exceedingly embarrassed at the scene, at feeling herself suddenly brought so close to this mother who had always been remote, sought for some form of affectionate consolation. But already the old woman had withdrawn. Her smile had once more erected a barrier, not that old transparent one which had always stood between them, but another far more impenetrable. Through that old barrier between mother and daughter, she had at least had a clear view, she had been able to construct for herself, by observation, a working model of her mother's mind, her wishes, her motives, her reactions. And so, though so much of the essential woman was still as mysterious as her real thoughts, her real motives, she had not been helpless in her dealings with her – she had sometimes been able to understand her actions, to please her.

But now there was a complete wall between, she had retreated into a realm so dark and mysterious that it was impossible even to imagine what was going on in her mind. She could only follow the rule, the formula as laid down for all desperately sick people, 'Keep up their courage. Tell them they're getting better.'

'You know, darling,' she said at last, 'you really do look so much better. You're quite different.'

The old woman looked up at her, straightened her back, and smiled broadly, candidly, as at the unconvincing efforts of a child. And at once she did look different, like the competent, forceful Kate Rideout of legend.

'That's all right,' she said, patting Joanna's hand as if to comfort her.

34

As soon as she saw the two young women, Kate recognized in Alice the hostile glance of the delinquent. She had met it often before in the court. But she was determined to have her confidence and set herself at once to be winning. 'My dear,' she held Alice's hand, 'what a terrible story, and how stupidly they treated you. That court – what were they thinking of.'

Joanna, knowing Alice's touchy moods and her mother's temper listened nervously to this unexpected opening. But it was surprisingly successful. As Kate sympathized, abusing that foolish court, Alice began to talk. They hadn't understood anything – they had just put her down as bad. But she hadn't been bad – only silly. A new Alice appeared – naïve, loquacious, with the believe-it-or-not of sixteen.

'What would you do,' she asked, 'if a man said he was done for if you didn't help him? Well, I didn't want to get into trouble and I didn't want to have him on my back either – I used to say "never again" and then when the time came and I knew he was waiting I couldn't bear it.'

She described the death of her child under Preedy's influence. 'He kept on saying, "It's just your obstinacy, you can believe if you want to, you know it like you know I'm me and you're you." That's why I say Preedy's sort of mad, telling me I'd got to believe. When my baby was dying and I wanted to call a doctor, he got so angry I thought, "He's mad. He thinks you can believe anything you like, even in that old murdering God of his."'

'So he came after you again?'

'He joined the Mission where we were and wanted me to join again – but I wouldn't go out.'

'Because of the neighbours – I know.'

'All the talk. So he used to come to the house and pray with me. It was Mr Jackman's mission, that was the chapel where we had gone. It was quite close, but when Preedy joined it he used to come and see us, me and Fred. Of course, Fred didn't know then he'd been anything to me – didn't even know we'd met before, and I wasn't telling. So he used to come and tell us how he'd been saved, in Hyde Park, and joined Mr Jackman. Well, I didn't go out – I knew what the neighbours were saying, and when Fred was at work at his office, Preedy'd come along and get after me to pray with him. And I did pray too; well, I was only a kid and what does a kid know, except what it's been taught? Mum and Dad had taught me to forgive them that do evil to you, and I had forgiven Preedy and it made me feel good. It made me feel it was the only thing I'd done for a long time, and I thought it was the same God that Preedy talked about. I didn't know any difference, and I didn't know how to believe. When my baby got ill and I wondered about getting the doctor he said that would be an insult to God, and he said, "You can believe if you want to," and I thought perhaps he had the answer. Well, I wanted something to believe, I was half mad myself, what with that court, and my mother dying because of me, and the baby being so ill. I thought the baby being ill was a judgement too and I'd better be careful with that old God, not to get across him any more. Why, I used to pray to believe, as if that was any

145

good. You believe or you don't believe, don't you? If you believe you know it all right.'

'Were you very attracted by the man? Of course he was so much older and quite good-looking too – very good-looking.'

'I just had to go along with him – well, he said my love could save him – he said God had sent me to save him – I was afraid to keep away.'

'I know, it's a very old story.'

'I hadn't any sense.'

'And you were a woman in feeling – a grown woman. What a mean trick nature plays on girls – it makes them women before they have any experience of life. And men like this Preedy know how to take advantage of it. The cunning devil.'

'I wouldn't say he was so wicked. I think he's just mad.'

'So much the worse – your half-cracked devil is the worst kind – so you still love him?'

'Me, no. I never did –'

'That's another mean trick nature plays on us – the first man – we never really get away from him, especially when it's a fellow like Preedy.'

'I say I never loved him – and I ought to know.'

'Why did you get him off in court by blackening your own character?'

Alice was now suspicious – she looked, frowning, at the old woman. She said at last, briefly, 'Perhaps he *wanted* it all to come out – in the headlines.'

'What, and go to jail –'

'I shouldn't wonder – then we'd be quits.'

'What do you mean, quits?'

'Me doing him in like that – and then I *should* have him on my back, shouldn't I?'

'You'd much better make it up with him – Preedy's your fate, my dear.'

'I'd sooner kill myself.'

'Tell me, did you make love to him first?'

'That's like the woman in that court –'

'Well, you were precocious – and mad about him.'

'It's a lie – I wasn't precocious – he hurt me – and I wasn't mad about him – I thought he needed me – it's what he said.'

'Well, don't be so cross – you were enjoying yourself – you'd got a man and a pretty unusual man, too. You knew he was different. You knew he was somebody. Tell me – I noticed how dark he is. Is he dark all over?'

'What are you getting at now?'

'As soon as I saw him I thought he might have Indian blood – and that would explain a good deal, wouldn't it? I've known a lot of Indian prophets. It's a thing they go in for – or if they aren't orientals they look like it, and that gives them the idea and then they believe it themselves. They think they have special powers.'

'Preedy didn't believe in anything –'

'He made you believe in him, my girl.'

'Once.'

'He ruined her life,' said Joanna, warmly.

'What nonsense,' Kate exploded. 'Look at her. How old are you – nineteen? How can anyone be ruined at nineteen. A thing like that could be a piece of luck – to make a girl into somebody – to give her a character.'

'But, Mother, she has to hide from him.'

'Why has she? Why does she? That's what I say. What a silly girl, dodging about like this, typing and footling when you might have a real life and do something that matters.'

Joanna, seeing Alice's fury, interposed. 'But, Mother, you say yourself Preedy is either a crook or a lunatic.'

'So he is but he's somebody. He's not the ordinary caterpillar in trousers you see about the streets. I say Alice was lucky – and now she's throwing it all away.'

The old woman, looking at these two children, strong, healthy, with tens of years of life before them, was carried away by contempt for their want of enterprise and imagination.

'My God, what silly stuff you talk. What's Alice going to do with herself at eight pounds a week – and here's Preedy, a flourishing prophet already – a real power and whatever you say rolling in money and glory – all the women mad about him.'

'He didn't even propose to marry her,' said Joanna.

'Of course not – that sort of creature never does. But so much the better – if Alice can't run him she can leave him.'

Joanna, gazing at her mother with a high flush on her cheek bones was thinking, 'All this is her illness,' and the old woman perfectly understood her thought, and understanding it, grew

147

still more irritated. Because she was ill no one listened to her. Now, when she was talking better sense than ever in her life before, when, illuminated by the tremendous experience of the last weeks, she had something worth saying and was not afraid to say it, everyone treated her as an idiot, whose words had to be excused. She was barred off – it was as though the world had already shut her in with those screens which, in hospital, are put round a dying person in the last agony.

'How do you know,' she exclaimed, 'that Preedy is not going to be a great man?'

'But, Mother –' Joanna opened her mouth to protest.

'Yes,' cried the old woman furiously. She waved her hand as if to abolish all this silly nonsense of youth, 'Really great – like that other one – what's his name – Krishnamurti.'

She had felt Joanna's alarm at the first mention of Indians. She knew that she was thinking, 'This is real insanity.' And now, for some reason. she deliberately spoke of Indians again. It was as if she said, 'Let them think what they like – if they want to make fools of themselves, why should I prevent them.'

'But Krishnamurti isn't a crook.'

'I'm not saying Preedy's not a crook – only that he's a remarkable man – that's obvious. And perhaps a very big man. Of course, it's all nonsense about his healing, but he might believe it himself. Look at the people, quite intelligent people, who believe in Christian Science – and if he believes it, you can't call him a crook.'

The old woman looked at them keenly for a moment and suddenly her expression changed, 'Oh, don't think he takes me in with his patter,' she exclaimed. 'Probably he is a crook – it's only because people believe in *him* that he gets away with it. But that would be enough, just to be the kind of man that people do believe in. I've known lots like that – it's a very queer thing – but what do we know about hypnotism even – about hypnotic power? Why, look at the way he fascinated you – you would have died for him – you'd still die for him.'

'Well, he'd like to kill me, I dare say.'

'And how do you know he isn't an Indian?'

All were relieved when the nurse came in and announced that it was Lady Rideout's bedtime.

It was on the next morning that Kate rang up Hooper direct

148

and asked him to arrange a visit for her to one of Preedy's private services. 'And he mustn't know about it – I know that kind of apostle. If he hears I'm to be there he'll have the photographers waiting – he'll say I'm a convert. I don't believe a word of his stuff but people will think I've fallen for it, and it won't be any good putting out a contradiction. Though, of course, if I do get well – that is, if this disease just stops by itself, as it often does, you know – he'll claim the credit.'

The old woman went on for a long time in this strain, about the trickery of quacks and faith-healers; and Hooper warmly agreed with everything. He promised above all that nobody but himself should know of this enterprise, especially not Joanna.

'She's a good girl,' Kate said, 'but she wouldn't understand – she'd think my brain was going. She's got no curiosity. She's no idea of how real newspaper people feel – people like you and me – about news, real news – and how right you were about Preedy. I said so from the beginning, didn't I?'

It was an appeal as from one old comrade to another. Hooper at once betrayed the old comrade to Joanna and Joanna agreed that he was right to do so – promises to a person so ill as her mother could be disregarded.

'But that let's you out,' he said. 'I'll make all the arrangements. You won't have any responsibility.'

'But you're not going to do it,' Joanna protested.

'Certainly I am. I promised – your idea is to do nothing.'

'But if Preedy gets hold of her she won't listen to the doctors.'

'We have to chance that – and Preedy may cure her – especially now, when she's in the mood. You want to do nothing – as usual.'

'It's so difficult.'

'Yes, sweetness is not enough, is it? You've got to take a chance.'

'Do you realize what you're asking me to do – it might kill her.'

'Yay, so I'm not asking–'

This conversation threw Joanna into an agony of indecision. There seemed to her no way out; she must make up her own mind and take all the risks. It was obvious that her mother in this strange state to which illness had brought her, in her re-action against the doctors, might easily be a victim to Preedy's technique. In that case she would very likely refuse to see any more doctors.

And on the other hand was it possible that Preedy might cure her? Joanna suddenly found in herself enormous doubts about doctors. She had been astonished by their helplessness in her mother's case. Above all by their inability to agree, even on a diagnosis. Could this very inability mean that her mother's illness was, partly, at least, due to some kind of neurosis. There was no doubt that she was not in a normal frame of mind. Nothing had been more astonishing than to see this strong and self-willed woman, highly intelligent and accustomed to rule, in a few weeks full of absurd obsessions; for instance, that there was a conspiracy to make a prisoner of her, and to keep her in hospital against her will.

Joanna was furious with Hooper. She said to herself, 'It's all very well for him to tell me I have no responsibility, but he has never loved anybody. He's completely insensitive. He doesn't even realize what a brute and a cad he is. As for his faith in Preedy, I don't believe he has any real faith in anything; and, of course, it would suit him down to the ground if mother did die and I got her shares. In fact, that's just what he's counting on. He thinks he can do what he likes with me, and if I had the shares he could do what he liked with the *Argus*. It's too simple.'

35

Syson understood his wife's feelings and even her difficulties; he forgave her, but he could not bear her presence or her chatter. She represented for him the whole force of the circumstances which had inflicted an agony of rage and self-contempt upon him. As he sat beside her, feeling her like a jailer, like a cunning mistress who had tied him up in a net of obligation everywhere yielding and everywhere unbreakable, he longed only to be alone. He wanted to think. He had been asking himself what would be his next move to destroy this crook Preedy, and to make people realize his wickedness. But all the time he was aware that there was some other problem to be dealt with, some other question that needed an answer.

He went suddenly to the vicarage and resigned his curacy.

This was both a relief and a surprise to Parsloe. But he felt it his duty, all the same, to point out how foolish and unnecessary it was, and to urge Syson to stay with him; at least not to take such decisive action on the spur of the moment.

'My dear chap,' he said, 'I know how you feel. But why take this desperate step? You've done fine work here, and I don't know where I'll find anyone to suit the parish so well – a parish so mixed as this. What's the real trouble? You needn't think this verdict is going to worry us – most people here are all on your side. Or is it because you don't like my line about Preedy? In that case, of course –'

'You've got to do what you think right,' Syson said.

'And so have you. I quite see that. But can't we carry on on those terms?'

Syson made no answer for a moment. Then he said, 'I've been reading Hutley about faith-healing. You know, the telepathic effects of prayer and undoubted miracles. All the same, you must consult the doctors.'

'It's a good book – it covers the ground pretty thoroughly.'

There was a short pause and then Syson muttered, 'I suppose so – but it's not very convincing.'

'What do you mean?'

'About those miracles.'

'Oh, that's as you look at it.'

But he was worried about this large, slow curate of his. He liked the man, though he considered him both stupid and obstinate, a bad combination in any church. He said at last, 'A man like Preedy can always get a start of us because he has a slogan – something quite simple that any fool can understand. But, as we know, things are not so simple.'

'No.'

The 'no' expressed a faint irony and the vicar, glad of any clue to the man's thoughts, said, 'They can't be so in the nature of things – I mean, things as they are.'

Syson said nothing to this. He was gazing at his toes while he slowly wagged one foot.

'You get all sorts in any church and they have all sorts of belief – from the most credulous.'

'Do you suppose Hutley believes his own stuff,' Syson said, 'or does he just want to hang on to his job?'

This startled Parsloe. He said cautiously, 'Do you know how I came into the Church?'

'From a college mission, wasn't it?'

'More or less. I helped at the mission – that was in the twenties. And of course, I was a good socialist, a bit of a prig, I dare say. Taught a class for the Fabians – it was down near the docks. Not a nice spot. But it seemed to me that the man who was doing the best work there was a parson – he happened to be a socialist too. And the reason he had a pull on me was simply that he had the Church behind him. I mean, the whole institution, with its tradition and ritual. You can call it glamour if you like. Anyhow, I learnt its value, and I took orders.'

There was another pause and then Syson wagged his toes again and said, 'I believe Archbishop Temple was a bit shaky about miracles.'

'I shouldn't think many of the bishops take them as matter of fact, should you?'

'Oh, I see your point – what is the word. You take 'em as religious facts – to give the right feeling.'

'And so they do – as we both know – and to give truth too, the larger truth.'

Syson said nothing to this and Parsloe went on, 'Take the resurrection – its symbolic truth is fundamental – "I am the resurrection and the life." These are good and true words for the individual. And for humanity, isn't it a fact that you can't kill Christ – he rises again for ever.'

Syson had listened to this with his usual rather dreamy expression, stretching out his long legs. He said now, after some moments' reflection, 'I see,' as if agreeing with some general statement about the weather. Then after another pause, he began to draw up his legs as if in preparation for departure.

Parsloe as usual, was slightly exasperated by this curate of his, so energetic when you wanted him to be reserved, so lethargic when you expected him to be interested. He said with emphasis, 'What shall I tell Mantoffle?'

Syson, instead of answering this, said, 'So your position is that miracles are bunk.'

'Good heavens, no. If you think that, you've completely misunderstood.'

'All the same, that would be a clear answer to Preedy.'

'Which unluckily we can't use.'

'No, I suppose not.'

'Do you think he does so much harm?'

'The Church thinks so, though it doesn't seem to care.'

'We're always getting these fellows – revivalists of one kind or another. And I doubt if they do much real harm. More good than harm anyhow. They stir people up – they make 'em realize there's something more in the world than just drawing down your pay and going to the pictures.'

Syson was again silent. He kept silence because he wanted to find some word which would make the man feel what a mean, cowardly creature he was. And yet he knew that this would not be fair, that Parsloe was not a coward or a mean-spirited person. He was doing what he thought to be the wise, the right thing, not only for his people at St Enoch's but for the Church as a whole.

It was this that so appalled and horrified Syson, the sense of this vast apathy. It was as though the whole organism, the whole immense creature, was lying fat and inert upon the steaming dung-heap of its past slowly dying, already rotting, and in its rottenness poisoning the air for anything young, healthy, that might be trying to draw a first breath of truth.

'I'm sorry,' he said at last. 'But I think I'd better go – I've thought it over for some time.'

This wasn't true. It was an impulse. But now he felt an enormous relief. He was sure that he had done the right thing. And it was not until he was in the street again and had turned automatically towards home, that he remembered his wife and children. The thought stopped him where he was, not because of his forgetfulness, but because he did not want to see them again. They were an interruption, something superfluous and unnecessary, unbearable in its foolish irrelevance.

And when he turned up at home, two hours later, after the children were out of the way, he was in an impatient mood. He spoke kindly, but too shortly. He explained his position, and proposed that Clarry should return for the time to her own home, until his future was more settled. He could not take any more pay from St Enoch's.

Clarry was so astonished by this unexpected crisis, so angry with the man who was treating her so cruelly, that she said little.

She was afraid of losing her temper. And for all her anger she perceived that Syson was hardly responsible. He spoke, as usual, confidently, as if he were proposing the most reasonable thing in the world, but when she offered objections such as the impossibility of simply imposing herself and the children on her parents at a day's notice, he did not answer at all, or said vaguely, 'I don't know what to do about the furniture.'

She said to herself, 'It's the shock of everything – I shan't say anything more today. I'll just wait.' But Syson left the house that afternoon and within a couple of hours she had an alarmed phone call from her mother asking what had happened, and saying that of course she could come home and bring the children home if she liked.

'And what does he mean about leaving the Church?'

'I don't know – he wants to resign his job here.'

'He said leaving. He hasn't lost his faith or anything?'

Lady Simpkins's tone expressed discreetly her amused scorn of people who lost their faith or anything. She liked Syson but she had always felt that parsons were rather comic, like eunuchs. They were wanting in some essential. And a parson who lost his faith was indeed ridiculous.

Clarry, who had had exactly the same feeling about parsons, recognized the note in her mother's voice and resented it. She answered sharply, 'Good heavens no, not Tom. It's only this wretched case has upset him. Vicar didn't like it as you can guess.'

'Well, my dear, you must know. We'll expect you on Saturday. Luckily we're clear for the next month.'

But it was true that Syson had spoken of leaving the Church. When Lady Simpkins had expressed surprise at his news that he was leaving the curacy, he had said, 'I don't really know if I ought to stay in the Church,' and at once he perceived that he could not do so. It was as if some long process of argument, that had been proceeding all by itself in his subconscious, had suddenly spoken through his lips. He had hung up at once, cutting off his mother-in-law in the middle of a sentence. He was not aware of this rudeness – he was startled by his own remark and wanted to consider it. After all, what did he believe in? What had happened to his belief? Was he like Parsloe, merely holding down a job because he thought it, on the whole, worth doing?

And as he strolled out of the telephone box, he shook his head. Parsloe was a good chap, no doubt, and doing good work, but he couldn't play that game. It might be a necessary game, as Parsloe believed, but it wasn't his game. He couldn't carry on with telling old ladies one thing and believing another, or rather not believing anything at all.

36

Kerne, the Mission secretary, telephoned Allday to say that someone connected with the *Argus* wanted to attend a private service incognito. 'And I'll bet it's for the old woman herself.'

'How do you know?'

'It was Hooper phoned. I know his voice – and Mr Preedy has been expecting him to arrange something all the week.'

'What's the next big private service?'

'For the Americans – the Clenches – not much chance there. Should I suggest the Marshalls? That's for the boy who went blind – and it might be a really striking case. We contacted the G.P. and he thinks it's quite likely a psychosis.'

'Yes, but Lady Rideout herself is a very thin chance – and some of the *Argus* people are out for our blood already.'

'I see.'

'All this is between ourselves.'

'Of course.'

So that Hooper, on that same afternoon, received two tickets for the Clench service, on the understanding that there would be no communication to the Press. He went at once to Kate, who did not even wish to tell Joanna. But Hooper insisted and went straight to the girl in her own room.

She said only, 'It's a pretty big responsibility.'

'Well, I'm taking it.'

'It won't do you any good if it makes her give up the doctors – it might kill her.'

'All right.'

'What do you mean, all right.' She flushed with rage. 'I can tell you it won't be all right for you if it does do her harm.'

'All right – I'm taking the chance. But I've not come here to talk nonsense. The thing's done – arranged. But I think you ought to go with her. Under protest, *if* you like. But she'll feel it if you simply wash your hands of her.'

'I'll do what I think right.'

'The trouble is you don't know what to think about anything. Suppose she's cured.'

Joanna said nothing to this. She was too angry. But in fact she perceived that she would have to take her mother to the service, not only in common kindness, but because she did not really know what to think. Preedy might be a crook but he had certainly made cures. And even if her mother were not cured, she might think she had been cured. Or she might blame her, Joanna, for preventing a cure by lack of sympathy.

So that it was Joanna who not only made the final arrangements to take her mother to the Clench service, but assured her that she highly approved of the plan. 'Preedy has done some wonderful cures.'

'Oh, I don't think much of him.'

'After all, it's not a question of his character – it's simply his special powers.'

'I'm just curious to see how he carries on – that's all – and apparently I needn't be seen.'

Kate was extremely anxious not to be recognized; now that she was committed, all her old scepticism had returned, and also her anxiety for her reputation as a hardheaded business woman.

'It's not that I believe in the man, but I've always thought he would have been a good feature for the *Argus*. Harry Hooper was right there.'

'So it's Harry again now,' Joanna thought, and felt new disgust for the man.

She quite agreed that the visit should be unobtrusive. She agreed that Kate, in the wheel-chair, should be taken to the Clenches' hotel, to a back door, and go up by the service lift. The chair could then stand in a private room until the service was ready to begin; and Joanna could wheel it in at the back of the congregation.

37

The Clenches had arranged for a private service in their hotel because the girl, Nona, would not attend a chapel service. She said that it would be hypocritical and useless. She knew by now that she was incurable and she was tired of cures. She had been dragged all round the world and put through every kind of agony, in hot springs and mud baths; with electric vibrations, injections, drugs, exercises; with hypnotism, gurus, and a Mexican who gave her snake poison; she was tired of it all and she wanted to die in peace. But she was patient as well as tired and when her parents confessed that they had invited Preedy to try his faith cure, as a very last resort, she gave way only with a sigh. But she insisted on a private service. A rationalist by conviction, she had a strong objection to faith-healing; and she knew that her attendance at any service would be represented as a conversion. Even in her extreme lassitude and resignation, she could not bear to seem like a traitor to her principles.

But of course it proved impossible to keep it completely secret. Nona was heiress to eight or ten millions, and everything that concerned her was news. What Preedy's choir members and the Clenches' close friends told their friends in strictest confidence was common gossip in Fleet Street within three days. A reporter lay in wait for Mrs Clench and was politely put off. That is to say, she told him a flat lie. She was an honest woman and hated the least appearance of insincerity, but faced with a choice – the chance of rescuing her only child from a slow, miserable death, and lying – she lied.

The reporter, having consulted some of the hotel staff and questioned some member of the Mission, put their evasions together and risked a paragraph in his gossip column. 'It is reported that the daughter of one of the biggest steel tycoons of the U.S.A. is to undergo treatment by the new faith-healer, Preedy, of the Pant's Road Mission. This is a considerable score for Mr Preedy, for the lady, educated as a scientist with a view to entering her father's business, has refused ever to consider such treatment before.'

This report, published on the actual morning of the service, was luckily noticed in time by Clench's secretary and kept from the girl.

But it reached Hooper – two of his friends on the *Argus* staff rang him up to make sure that he did see it. It struck him at once that Nona Clench was a very bad subject for Preedy.

He called Allday immediately, but was told that he was out. The secretary, Kerne, however, answered that Mr Preedy considered one case as good as another. 'He takes all cases.'

'Did he know that this Clench woman is being treated against her own convictions?'

'That I don't know. But quite possibly he didn't ask – he wouldn't be interested.'

The man's tone was perfectly neutral but that in itself, under the circumstances, had a cynical effect. 'In fact,' Hooper said, 'you and Allday are betting on a flop.'

'Not at all.'

Hooper rang off. He was now convinced that Allday had deliberately arranged for Kate to be discouraged. He was extremely angry and promised himself at once that he would get even with the man.

It was too late to forestall Joanna in Portland Place; the service was at nine, not to conflict with the public service at ten, and Joanna had already left with Kate. Hooper therefore made direct for the hotel and even then did not arrive till several minutes past the hour.

He had difficulty in getting admission; he had to send in his name for Joanna to be brought to the door, and then again there was delay before the doorkeeper allowed her to take him to Kate's chair, at the back, some yards from the door.

Luckily the service was late in starting; the Missioner himself had not arrived. In fact, there was already some nervousness among the choir members and the committee. There had been services before at which Preedy had not appeared at all; and even Colonel Marris admitted that he suffered, now and then, from 'moods'.

These moods were apt to come upon him most strongly at times when cures had been scarce. In the last week there had been very few cures and more trouble from Fred Rodker. Preedy had been exceedingly reserved and unapproachable for three days past.

The whole congregation was growing nervous when Hooper's entry caused heads to turn. As he spoke to Kate, though in a whisper, there were murmurs, and a loud shush from the Mission members in the front row.

But Kate answered in clear tones, 'You mean it's not a fair test?'

'Yes, a hopeless case,' Hooper whispered. But he was audible in the silence. There were more murmurs.

'Of course, you don't believe in this anyway,' Kate said sharply.

'I know he's cured some people – I've seen it.'

'Yes, but you think they're just neurotics who thought they were ill. You could cure them with potatoes in their pockets.'

Hooper thought, 'She's furious because she wanted to believe in Preedy. By Jove, Allday has a lot to answer for.' He hesitated a moment before answering, 'Preedy certainly has amazing powers, but he can't cure people against their will. He needs confidence, faith. And we know now that this Clench girl actually hates the whole scheme. It's her parents who insisted on it.'

Half the back row in front of Kate were now looking round. Kate glanced along the line and said, loudly, angrily, 'All right, take me away.' Hooper was surprised.

'Isn't it rather late – I only wanted you to realize the facts.'

But the old woman suddenly grew angry, 'Kindly do as I ask.'

Joanna, amid quite a clamour of disapproval, hastily wheeled the chair out through the side door.

'I'm not going to waste my time,' Kate said, but she added all at once to Hooper, 'Somebody let you down, did they?'

'I didn't know of the special difficulty of the case.'

'And you wanted a really sure thing.'

'I wanted a fair test.'

Kate said no more – she did not even look at Hooper again. What had annoyed her was his eagerness, his excitement. She knew, of course, that her sick bed was surrounded by intrigues. Ackroyd, who had been assuring her that she had ten years to live, had also been urging her again to make a trust of her Press shares, 'to take the burden off Joanna's shoulders', otherwise to secure his dominance.

And Hooper with his young men had made an issue of Preedy

and the religious column simply to shake the grip of the old gang on the Press.

It was an old story. She had seen it all her life, since her marriage. The only difference was that then she had been with the young men.

But now all at once, the very sight of Hooper playing this game, so eager to convert her to the Preedy side simply for his own ends, suddenly disquieted her. He was ready to see her victimized by this fanatic, perhaps betrayed to a miserable death, simply in order to make his career. Above all, there was no *truth* in him. He did not even care for the truth; he did not even want to know if Preedy had the power of healing; or if such a power were possible. He didn't want to know any truth. He was worse than Tinney, who did care about his own belief, even if it was blind and trivial. For Hooper life was a game like bridge or poker, you didn't want to be distracted by anything real, the events of real life, the way real people lived and suffered and struggled to find their way. All this was simply a nuisance to you. You kept yourself clear of it.

And Joanna, was she in with Hooper in this plot? She had been, they said, having an affair with Hooper. Mrs Mantoffle had spared another three minutes of her valuable time to telephone her warning of that entanglement. And Joanna had not been happy in her love affairs. Even if she were not in love with Hooper, she might well be anxious not to offend him. She would find excuses to support his schemes.

Did Ackroyd know of this affair when he again urged the trust? Probably. He had been very discreet about Joanna, as always. He had said only, 'She's young – it's really not fair to put so much on her.'

The deed of trust, drawn up by Ackroyd's lawyer, had been in Kate's safe for months, awaiting her signature and Joanna's. Ackroyd had insisted that the deed did not injure the girl's real interests; she would still get the income from her shares. What he obviously feared was that Joanna, whom he suspected to be completely under Hooper's thumb, would fight the deed. Hooper would be capable of suggesting that Kate had acted under pressure, that she was not fit to manage her own affairs. But now, as soon as Joanna had brought her back to her room, and Hooper had gone, she discussed it again.

'The idea is simply to take the responsibility of direction off your back.'

'Who would appoint the trustees – I suppose they would all be on the Ackroyd side.'

'And your father's side – he thought of the *Argus* as a trust – a public trust.'

'But it's losing circulation all the time – suppose it goes smash.'

'It's perfectly solvent – it lost some readers after the strike. But now it's pulling up again. Don't listen too much to friend Hooper. He is simply out for himself. He wants to get back on it as managing editor.'

'I don't think you're quite fair to him – he really does feel that the *Argus* could do more to –' She stopped, not quite knowing what Hooper wanted the *Argus* to do.

'He wants to turn into a tabloid,' Kate said, 'and that's impossible. The old readers will leave – and the new public he always talks of will simply go on with the existing tabloids.'

Joanna was silent. She reflected that her mother was probably right, but that she did not really care what happened to the *Argus*.

This question of the deed caused a sudden crystallization in her mind. She realized that in the last weeks since the renewal of her affair with Hooper, she had been living in a vagueness, a confusion of mind which was perhaps deliberate. She had known perfectly well why Hooper was so affectionate, so assiduous, but she had not gone further and asked herself how far she was prepared to pay the price.

And now it was with a dull surprise at her own weakness that she perceived how strong his hold was. He did not love her, of that she was sure, but she could not risk losing him. The very idea of this trust deed terrified her, simply because it might mean that he would leave her; and worse, that he would reveal his total selfishness and meanness, and that she would hate him. She realized now, in this affair, that she was capable of hate. She had been near it already. And she dreaded it.

'Of course,' Kate said, 'I'd consult you about the trustees.'

'I thought it was Father's idea that I was to have the shares.' Joanna turned deeply red. She was embarrassed whenever she talked about money with her mother.

'You still don't like the idea of a trust?'

'I'll have to think of it.'

'And consult Hooper.'

'That's not fair.'

'Of course he will fight the trust – he wants control – through you.'

'I know you hate him.'

'I don't hate him at all. I simply know him for a young man on the make. I don't blame him for being on the make. I was all for putting him on the board. He's a very clever fellow and could be very useful to us. But he's too big for his boots. He got a swelled head out of that best-seller.'

Joanna was silent. What could she say? Her mother was probably right about Hooper. She could not answer even, 'But I love him.' She didn't love him. She simply needed him. She had made the discovery that it was possible to need a man you did not love and who did not love you, need him so desperately that you could not face the least chance of losing him.

'Very well,' said her mother, 'I won't sign either – at least not yet. I'll tell Edward that I want to think it over.'

Joanna knew very well what an immense concession this was. And she tried to put off the guilt of her acceptance. 'But you must do what you think best for the paper.'

'The *Argus* is not everything,' Kate said. 'I don't suppose it will last for ever. Papers die like everything else. Nobody quite knows why. The experts don't agree there either.'

Joanna could say nothing to this. She felt the immense bitterness and despair behind the words, what vast changes were taking place in the old woman's world, behind the façade of this speech, but she could take no part in them. There were no means by which she could project herself over the enormous gulf that divided her from her mother; no words that could convey understanding or comfort.

38

Preedy's moodiness was well known to those close to him; to Colonel Marris, Allday, Mrs Hartree, Kerne. For Allday it was easily explained. Preedy was a strange, unusual person with an extraordinary gift, and could be expected to behave in an extraordinary way. Allday would have been indignant if anyone had accused him of thinking Preedy mad, but in fact this was near the truth.

Kerne did think him mad and did not say so only because he wanted to keep his job as secretary.

Marris, on the other hand, and Mrs Hartree, fervent and convinced believers in the whole Preedy doctrine, could not admit to themselves that Preedy might sometimes have doubts or fears about his own power. They discussed his moods merely as moods, and told each other that it was natural for him to be 'disappointed' or 'discouraged' when patients who averred their conversion, proved to be weak in faith, and failed to be cured.

Preedy, as usual in these private services, had left all the arrangements to them, and they had taken special pains. It was for them a gesture, perhaps unconscious, of encouragement, like the magic rituals designed to give strength to a hero in some critical test. By anxious selection of flowers, they were battling with Preedy's weakness, as Aaron and Hur held up Moses's hands. They fought the prophet's mood with silver candlesticks borrowed from the hotel kitchen, a fine Persian carpet spread before the altar, and a bridge table covered with a white cloth. Behind the table, on a velvet cloth, hung a large silver cross, hired from a jeweller.

The whole effort was very fine. The room was large, at the top of the immense building, with a south view across lower roofs to the Thames, so that the autumn sun, shining lemon yellow through thin cloud, made the altar candles seem like ghosts of flame.

A music stand served for reading desk, and the pulpit, brought from Pant's Road, the folding construction used by Preedy for open-air meetings, had been draped with brocade curtains.

Flowers stood everywhere, to give the impression of an Easter service. This had been one of Preedy's own ideas, thrown out at a time when his mood was confident, that as the Mission aimed at the resurrection of souls – souls first, bodies after – so every service should be like the service of Easter Sunday. And the faithful had firmly remembered it and acted upon it.

The choir sat at both sides. The space left between their two divisions and the first pews was occupied by some of Preedy's most faithful and dependable believers, brought from the Pant's

Road district by special coach, and promised an excellent lunch, all at the Clenches' expense. The edge of the rug marked the chancel. This open quadrangle was for the sick girl's couch, not to be brought in till the last moment, indeed until after the service had begun.

This was arranged at the girl's own request. She stipulated that she should be treated like a patient brought into an operating theatre; only after everything is prepared. And then she herself, if not anaesthetized, could assume the helpless indifference of one under an anaesthetic. But she had been waiting in a side room already for a quarter of an hour when Hooper caused the first disturbance of the congregation.

The second began when Mrs Clench appeared with an anxious face to confer with Marris; her daughter was getting impatient and restless. Everyone began to murmur; the passive part of the assembly had suddenly realized that something was wrong and proceeded to tell its neighbours.

There was at once quite a loud swell of talk and nobody said hush. Even the faithful of the choir realized that hushes would do no good; the gathering had lost its collective sense of propriety.

Marris, Allday and Mrs Hartree all reassured Mrs Clench; but they were extremely alarmed. For Preedy had, before this, failed entirely to appear at a service; on one occasion, he had vanished for three days together. The committee had not informed the police only because it feared a public scandal.

When he entered at last, nearly half an hour late, and the choir struck up, he did not, as usual, join with them. He stood staring at the congregation with an expression of angry contempt. And his first words were uttered in a tone of menace.

He was full of rage, not specially against the people in front of him, he was scarcely aware of them, but against the whole world of dull, dead souls, against all unbelievers with their dull, dead self-satisfied complacency which does not even want to perceive the unbounded majesty of God's world, in which they grovel and blink like mice under a floor.

39

Nona Clench was not brought in till the end of Preedy's first prayer. She too was late. At the end of the hymn she had suddenly decided that she would go in. It was only her mother's appeals and the promise that she would never again be asked to undergo such an ordeal, that persuaded her. When her mother and her nurse at last wheeled the couch into the chancel, she was still furious. Her cheeks were pink with rage, her lips compressed. She had rejected the Mission nurse, Sister Monica, and she had also refused to be dressed. Her attitude throughout had been, 'I will bear this folly for my parents' sake, but only if I am not asked to cooperate.'

Nona Clench was a highly intelligent young woman who had distinguished herself both at her women's college and at Oxford before the riding accident that made her a cripple. She had cooperated eagerly in all the first attempts to cure her; and it was only lately that she had given up hope.

As for the faith-cure, it was untrue, as Allday had been told, that having been a communist she was violently anti-Christian. The girl had been liberal like her family, and, like many American liberals in the thirties, had been very sympathetic to communism. That is to say, like many American liberals, she was fundamentally an anarchist, who believed in 'freedom', in an anarchist's mystical sense of the word, as a clue to all political problems. To fight against any kind of 'freedom' was to fight also against a principle which could bring peace and brotherhood to the world – not to speak of prosperity. That principle was a law of nature, that is to say, the will of 'God'; or, if you didn't believe in 'God', then it was an 'obvious truth', which is another name for natural law.

And communism, having murdered the Czar, denounced imperialism, and proposed the withering of the State, answered all these requirements. The surprising thing was not that many young liberals were sympathetic to communism, but that all did not join the party. Nona did not join because she was not a joiner. Fastidious, critical, she believed in the communist creed, but recoiled from the communists; from their self-assurance, and self-deception, their jargon, their lies.

How did she come, on this occasion, and so much to her own surprise, to be converted, and to suffer a 'miracle'? Her own account is as good as any. 'I didn't believe in faith-healing because I didn't believe in miracles. After all, I did science at college and I didn't see how you could depend on anything if miracles were possible. I mean, if steel could be changed into wood, or one drug turned into another. In fact, I used to say that if God could do a miracle then the world would simply become impossible. It would go out with a bang. God would be contradicting himself,' and so on. She had, in fact, the ordinary idea of an intelligent, well-educated modern girl who knows that atheism on the one hand and the omnipotent god on the other are equally impossible of credit; they simply lead to a nonsensical position and hypocrisy. She believed in God who was love, beauty, goodness; but not in the creator who permitted children to die in agony, although, if he chose, he could save them by a trifling miracle.

'And I was full of all this,' she said, 'when I was pushed into that room. I simply despised the whole affair. I was full of intellectual conceit – I had built a great wall of conceit and fear round myself – yes, fear, because I didn't want to believe in the real God, the God who does miracles. That's the truth. I was fighting against him that morning because I was so terrified of the truth. So that I would rather have stayed a cripple than be made to believe. You see,' she said, 'a miracle would ruin my whole belief – my own private belief – and that was the only thing I had in the world. It seemed to me that the world was simply too horrible, too cruel if there was a real God who could do miracles. Deep down I knew that in a world like that I should go mad. That's why I fought against God and against his Missioner. I was fighting for all I had left – my sanity – my power to forgive God for his cruel and filthy world. And I knew how to fight. Of course, all the service was very cleverly designed to upset my nerves, and get round my mind, to attack my feelings. All the music and the prayers. But I did not let them; I kept on saying to myself, "It's all nonsense, it's simply a racket, the old racket." Especially I was angry with the Missioner, because he had kept us waiting and because he spoke so contemptuously to us. "Who is he," I thought, "this crank, this fanatic, to keep me, Nona Clench, waiting all that time in my humiliating position, and then to talk to me and my friends as if we were inferior beings?"

'All through the service, I grew angrier and angrier with him. And I thought that if he touched me, I should scream, I should bite his hand. So when the moment came that he was to touch me, I had to grit my teeth to keep from screaming out, "Go away, don't you dare to touch me."

'I felt his hand before he touched me. My eyes were closed but I knew that it was coming close to my forehead; it was like something so hot or so cold that one does not know if it will burn or freeze, only that it will hurt.

'But when the hand actually touched my forehead and lay there, it was cool and hard, and it sent a kind of cold feeling right through me; I can't describe it; it was not a bit like electricity or the lightning shock people talk about; it was simply that I began to shiver and the shivering broke through everywhere. It was as if a lot of glass walls in my veins and nerves and brain and round my heart all began to shake and jump until they cracked and broke into powder. The Missioner's voice seemed to come from miles and miles away. And I knew that I had been living in a silly little world of my own conceit; that I had been fighting against a God who was simply beyond my imagination.

'When I heard the Missioner say, "Rise in the name of Jesus, rise and walk," I felt my legs bend and move. I felt as if some great power was lifting me and the next moment I was standing on my feet.'

This scene of the Clench miracle has been described since in various pamphlets which tend to grow more romantic and sensational than the last. According to the latest, only a year after the event, 'The young girl rose up as from the grave; a light of heavenly joy shone upon her face; and for a moment she stood with hands clasped and eyes raised upwards, in worship and thanksgiving. Her lips were seen to move but in silence. For this supreme moment of her life, she was alone with her Maker, her Redeemer.

'She was also, with the exception of the Missioner, the most composed, the most tranquil person in the whole room, crowded though it was with all the fashion and wealth of Britain. Even the most hardened were in tears; a Duchess famous for her luxuries

167

was heard to cry, "Let us praise God," and threw her precious jewels at the foot of the altar. Her example was followed on all sides; in a moment, the humble table, covered with a plain tea-cloth, was heaped with gold and jewels.

'Then suddenly the girl's clear voice was heard, calling all to prayer. And at once, sobs and cries were stilled, the whole gathering sank to their knees.'

This later account was an improvement on the first. There was no duchess in the first but merely a Lady A, who was, in fact, present. She was a knight's widow from Cardiff. She did not give her jewels to the altar, her jewels were glass; but she did offer the colonel a cheque. As for fashion and wealth, it was only true that he had a larger proportion of upper middle-class people among his followers than might have been expected from their comparative numbers in the population. But this is usually the case with a preacher who offers a simple and rational solution of any kind to the problem of evil. Perhaps because it is only the educated upper-class, and especially upper-class women, who have the time to feel the confusion of their existence and react against it.

As for the scene where Nona was raised from bed, what the congregation – who, all but the two front rows, had not been able even to glimpse her at all, as she lay flat on the low couch – now saw was a thin pale girl with long dark hair, dressed in a pink silk pyjama coat and blue and white striped trousers, supported by Preedy on one side, the nurse on the other. She was continually shaking back her hair, which tended to fall across her eyes, and laughing.

The odd point of the mixed suit of pyjamas has since been denied. The girl herself has declared it to be a monstrous lie invented to discredit the whole event. She says she has never had blue-striped pyjamas and she asks is it likely that she, so rich and cherished, should be wearing a suit of pyjamas that did not match.

But the truth is as stated, fifty people can testify to it. And it is odd that Miss Clench and the faith-healer Missioner should even try to deny it, because it is the best proof possible of a very important point in their case, that the girl herself never expected a cure. She had never imagined for a moment that she would be able, much less obliged, to get out of the bed, and reveal to the public the fact that her pyjamas, on that morning, did not match.

And as for 'sobs and cries' the congregation was remarkably calm. Preedy's own veterans were used to similar scenes, and knew his dislike of any hysterical display. They kept their places, with the choir, and waited for instructions. The ladies at the back of the room, of whom most were in fact ladies, were standing up to look, and were certainly moved; a good many of them did surreptitiously and carefully, having regard to make-up, dab their eyes or blow their noses; a good many cheeks were flushed and all were perfectly aware that something extraordinary, for some of them something decisive, had taken place.

But they were not people given to hysteria, to exclamation; they uttered here and there a few words expressing their feelings of wonder of pleasure. The greater part did not speak. The occasion, for them, was a great deal too big for ordinary flat words. When Preedy and the nurse called for prayer and the last hymn of thanksgiving, they did indeed pray and sing with fervour, but afterwards went away very quickly, as if to avoid talk.

The girl herself, after her few tottering steps, was led from the room, and put into her mother's bed. When the nurse proposed to wheel out her own couch, she was told to leave it where it was till the service was over.

This was usual. Empty stretchers, chairs, discarded crutches, were always left in evidence till the end of one of Preedy's services. They were better proof and reminder of the cures that had taken place even than the restored patients themselves, who on their feet suddenly appeared like everybody else and added nothing dramatic to the scene.

But the story put about by certain rationalist papers and hinted at in at least one medical paper – that the girl was not cured at all, that Preedy and the nurse simply lifted her out of bed, propped her on her feet and then carried her out of sight – is quite untrue. Nona Clench, though fearfully weak, was actually cured, and within a few days was able to walk quite well.

The case made news all over the world, simply because she herself was determined that it should. She was now a devoted Preedyite and at once promised to endow the Mission. There was to be a new church, with a large hostel attached for patients from a distance, and also a training institute for Mission evangelists.

40

The news of the Clench miracle did not reach Kate Rideout till the afternoon. But it had at once a surprising effect. She now took it into her head that Joanna had removed her from the service to get her away from Preedy; a charge at once true in fact and false in implication, so that Joanna had difficulty in denying it.

She insisted on calling up the Clenches; she wanted to speak to Nona Clench. But she was told that the girl had been ordered to rest.

The old woman was so excited that Joanna wanted to call the doctor, but she answered furiously, 'No more doctors for me. I've swallowed enough poison and nonsense.'

Several times she insisted on being taken out of bed, in the belief that she could walk, and though neither Joanna nor the nurse could see any improvement she insisted that, in fact, she had more strength in her legs. 'I've been giving way to the thing,' she said. 'It's those doctors telling me all the time that I'm ill – I mean really ill, and making me rest. Of course my muscles are wasted.'

What exasperated her above all was her failure to get in touch with Preedy himself. She made Joanna ring up the Mission at intervals of half an hour. Usually the number was engaged. When, at five, Joanna got through at last, she was told only that Mr Preedy was out and that no message could be taken. But Kate refused to accept this situation. She said to Joanna, 'You don't want to help,' and took the phone herself. Almost at once she got through, and looking triumphantly at her daughter, demanded to speak to Mr Preedy, Joanna heard the small whispering voice from the receiver, Mr Preedy could see no one, and messages were not to be taken.

'But this is Lady Rideout speaking – tell him Lady Rideout, of the Rideout Press.'

'Yes, but I'm afraid it's impossible.' The secretary's voice was bored as well as tired; it expressed very clearly the new fact that Lady Rideout's name had ceased to have any special importance at the Mission.

In fact, the Preedy boom had begun; that is to say, Preedy had made the evening papers, and it seemed that there had been something in Hooper's thesis that a large number of people were interested in his kind of message. The Mission had been overwhelmed with phone calls and reporters within a few hours of the Clench service.

It is not true, however, that the Clench case touched off a train of hysteria among society people resembling in its manifestations some of 'the effects of Buchmanism in the thirties, working on a class thoroughly discouraged and frightened by the war and slump'. There was certainly a crop of conversions but they were not hysterical, They occurred chiefly among people who could give reasons for their belief. It was not so much discouragement and fright that had prepared the way but simply the reaction which had been gathering weight among educated people for at least ten years past, against scientific materialism, against scientific cocksureness generally, and perhaps even against too much science everywhere. Neither were the real conversions at first very numerous. There was nothing like 'a wave'; the crowds which besieged the Pant's Road chapel at every service were mostly made up of the people who fill the streets for a society wedding, or stand for hours in the road outside the house where a film star has just become engaged or a murder has taken place; people whose imagination has been starved in the dullness of their own lives.

But many of those who were converted, like the Clenches, were people of influence and gave Preedy good service afterwards. Many too were young. It was especially among young people that Nona Clench's experience was understood. In fact, the first conversions were nearly all among friends of the Clenches, or the friends of their friends. It was in this way that Joanna was moved to join the Mission; or rather, was set upon a current which, in due course, carried her to Pant's Road.

She had gone to a party, two days after the service, where, hearing Hooper's name announced unexpectedly, and wanting to avoid him, she made for a back corner of the room. She had a special disgust of Hooper since the service, which had so enormously increased her difficulties with her mother.

She was still convinced that it was suicide for her to refuse the operation that Sir Shanklin advised, and though she had said to

Hooper, 'It's your responsibility,' she had found, of course, that this did not prevent her from feeling it herself. It seemed to her now that even in allowing her mother to return home from hospital she was guilty. For in hospital, she could have been kept quiet and docile with drugs, until the operation had been performed.

She had always failed as a daughter from the beginning, and now her return for so much love given to her without question might be to kill her mother, and from the same cause as always, from want of decision, want of courage to take a stand. The very idea was terrifying to her.

But, as in her corner, unconsciously holding half a glass of gin and French in the air like one who proposes a toast but actually to prevent its being spilt, she smiled on a friend, young Lady Milby, and uttered, with the usual affectation of interest and excitement the usual remarks and responses, she heard a man close to her elbow discussing the Clench affair. She knew the voice; it belonged to a retired diplomat, a friend of Ackroyd's and her mother's.

'Well, that's how it happened – and it was just as much a surprise to me as to Nona.'

'A miracle in fact,' said a man's voice, sarcastic and impatient.

'I really don't know what to call it,' said the other, 'I didn't think of trying to classify it.'

'I don't see why you should,' said a young woman.

'No, one didn't think of it like that – not at the time – it was so – well, unexpected – to anyone who knew Nona.'

The young woman remarked that, scientifically speaking, one ought to accept facts as they came. That was a scientist's job. This was apparently aimed at the other man who interjected, in the same ironic tone, 'A scientific miracle.'

'Well, something out of the common,' said the first man in the same tone of good-natured tolerance. 'It just happened and it's something that's rather, well, knocked me out. I'd heard about faith-healing, of course, as a possible treatment in suitable cases. But I'd never seen it in action – and –'

'Now, you believe that it can cure anything?'

'I don't know what to believe but –'

'You're not quite so dogmatic about the whole thing,' said the young woman with the same indignant note.

'No, I shouldn't like to take sides without knowing a good deal more.'

'At any rate, you think this man Preedy has extraordinary powers?'

'Well, I was there, you know – and that makes a difference.'

At this moment someone greeted the speaker and the party broke up. Joanna moved into a gap which placed her close to him; she meant to ask him about Nona Clench, about his whole experience at the service.

It had struck her, all at once, that she too had been dogmatic about faith-healing – she realized that she was rather like the objector in whom she heard an echo of Tinney, of half a dozen 'scientific' broadcasters. After all, what right had she to judge Preedy, she had never even seen his work.

Suddenly she changed her mind about speaking to the man. What had she to ask? He could only repeat what she had heard. She pushed, rather rudely and impatiently, towards the door and set out to walk home. And now all sorts of ideas half-recollected from old religious arguments became significant and lively in her mind. She knew that it was, nowadays, considered rather brash and shallow to call oneself an atheist. The thing was to be an agnostic, to say that one had an open mind. But had she an open mind? Wasn't she simply allowing herself to drift with the crowd, so despised by Hooper, the people whose whole set of ideas, whose whole conversation was a mere repetition of the fashionable phrases of the moment? Or was this the crowd? Was the religious revival simply a reaction against the Tinneys with their 'science'?

41

Lady Rideout's conversion provided only private gossip in Britain; no paper recorded it. It was news that a young American heiress had been healed by faith, but not that a rich old woman had joined the Preedy sect. Plenty of rich old women and many rich old men had joined all kinds of religious sects. One great newspaper proprietor believed in Yoga.

But in America, everything about Kate was news, not because she was rich, but because she was still titular head of the Rideout dynasty. As a tycoon of big business her ideas and activities were quite as important and interesting as those of any political leader.

So again British readers discovered from the American press the latest news about the split on the Rideout board and the battle of the tabloids.

'Religion is the latest stunt in the British tabloids and the former director, Hooper, always wanted to give the old liberal *Argus* the new look. Lady Rideout's conversion has put him on top and the general expectation is that the *Argus* will take up Prophet Preedy in a big way.'

This news, like so much American news about British affairs and British about American, was true in fact and slightly wrong in import.

It was not the Rideout conversion which put Hooper back on the *Argus*. Ackroyd, in fact, suddenly caused people to remember that he was an old hand in this kind of political game. He had been on the telephone to Hooper as soon as he heard of the Clench case, and made him an offer for a series of articles on the Preedy Mission, without waiting for any approval from the board and without even consulting the editor.

Hooper at once rang up Pant's Road, to receive the same routine answer – no messages, no interviews.

'But this is Hooper of the *Argus*.'

He called up Allday, who could make no promise, but gave him the addresses of Colonel Marris and Mrs Hartree. Within an hour he had established at least a moral claim on the Pant's Road Committee for preference in any newspaper contract.

It is a tribute to Hooper's sincerity – a plea offered by himself, but perhaps true at the time – that, during these first weeks of the Preedy boom, he was more concerned with the campaign for the Mission, than even with the struggle on the *Argus*'s board. He saw the enormous opportunity offered him and was determined to seize it. But he faced at once the problem which had already split Preedy's committee and hampered the Mission from the beginning; Preedy's own autocratic and difficult character. For instance, money was now pouring in but Preedy insisted on keeping all financial affairs in his own hands, and at once there had been trouble. Mr Clench, who gave five thousand pounds and promised more, had very definite views about the way it should be spent on organization and publicity. Preedy did not even acknowledge the cheque and he resented any inquiry into expenses as if his character were being attacked. He was always touchy about his character and continually referred to his past, saying, 'Of course, I understand crooks, I was a crook myself.' If anyone attempted to suggest that what he meant by crook was something not very wicked, that like so many religious mystics, like Augustine, St Francis, Bunyan, he wildly exaggerated his sinfulness, he answered fiercely that he was a great deal worse than a murderer; he had killed his mother with despair, he had counted on her death to get her money. The Clenches appealed to Allday as a practical man, and Allday, already snubbed by Preedy, appealed to Hooper. But Preedy answered only, 'I don't know what you've got to do with this business, Mr Hooper. You're getting the material for articles, and that's all I undertook for the *Argus*.'

'I'm interested just as the Colonel and Allday are interested because I'm with you – I believe in your work.'

'Allday doesn't believe in anything.'

'Well, I'm with the Colonel.'

'I doubt if you've any idea of what the Colonel means by belief. I see Allday is proposing you for the committee. What do you want to come on the committee for? It's only a nuisance to the Mission.'

'I want to help – and Allday thinks my experience on the Press –'

'Allday's ideas are usually bad – because he doesn't have any real faith.'

Hooper reflected on the advice of an experienced organizer, and saw that he had good cause to appreciate it. 'In choosing a revivalist, the rule is, stick to the ordinary rules of salesmanship. It's wiser to go for a good voice and a good appearance than what is called genius. A genius may get quicker results at first but you're lucky if he doesn't throw everything away by some piece of silly nonsense. Geniuses never have any discipline or common sense. You can't control them, and in any big campaign, you need the strictest control from the centre. It is the office work that gets the really valuable and lasting results. A second-rate man with a good office will beat a first-class man all the time, hands down.'

This was from Plattnower, probably the best of the professional organizers and propagandists. He had just raised thirty thousand pounds for a university college in the Midlands; he had handled Kleeno, and doubled its sale in a market thought to be saturated. He had been the brain behind two recent revivals in Wales and Scotland. But Preedy had refused to consider him; he would manage his own publicity and organize his own meetings. He was not yet persuaded even to tour. He had a plan for branch missions run by evangelists chosen and trained by himself.

Hooper argued that it was fatal to wait. Now was the time for the boldest possible action, while the Clench case was still in people's minds, and the Clenches were still news.

'And that won't last a week. It's a wonder the thing has lasted three days.'

'Your articles are appearing.'

'Articles are all right but personal appearances are better – and what we want is everything at once.'

But Preedy was in one of those moods, immediately after a service, when he hated to be badgered. He began to pull off the long cassock he affected.

'You weren't at the service today,' he said.

'No, I hadn't time – I heard it was packed.'

'Yes, with people who shouldn't have been there – just curiosity-mongers, reporters. And there were no cures.'

Hooper began to offer consolation. He had already discovered from Mission members, especially Allday, that Preedy was subject to 'moods' and required careful handling. He talked now with the tone of a nurse cajoling a difficult child. 'But you were wonderfully successful last week, and Nona Clench was a real miracle. It's not your fault if people fail in confidence – you can't blame yourself for their want of faith.'

'I do blame myself,' Preedy said in a gloomy and disgusted tone. 'It was entirely my fault.'

'But really, sir.'

'Do you think I don't know? In future, I'll have no reporters at the services. They make the atmosphere all wrong. We aren't a circus.'

He turned and walked into his study, a dark room at the side of the villa, looking out on a blank wall. Hooper, with the old habit of the reporter determined to get his man, followed him, saying in a deprecatory tone, 'But I've always thought you rather valued some publicity – that it brought patients to the services.'

Preedy said nothing to this. He had fallen back in his arm-chair, and now stretched out his long legs and gazed at the ceiling. He pretended to be alone because he wanted to be alone.

In his own words, he had lost touch, and he was obsessed as always by the fear that he could never get it again. For he did not know how to get it. Prayer, contemplation, reading, those exercises which he had designed for himself after the example of the Jesuits, none of them were certain means of renewal.

On the day before, at the morning service, he had been aware as soon as he entered the chapel that he had lost contact. A moment before power had possessed him with such force that his nerves quivered, he was hardly aware of what he was doing and submitted automatically to the woman who put on his surplice, like a child to a nurse; but suddenly as he entered and caught sight of a face in the back row, that of a young reporter who had interviewed him at the house, the thought jumped up in his brain, 'A good thing he chose this morning when I'm in this vein,' and instantly, his sense of power had gone. It was as though that thought had been a devil who jumped out of ambush to cut the nerves of his inspiration.

Not only was that sense of power which had vibrated in him completely lost, but his own vigour, his very will seemed to flow out of him through the broken connexion. He was drained of purpose as well as faith. As he stood at the altar, he knew that he should not go on with the service – he was unfit to act as God's vehicle, he ought to tell the congregation so and walk out. He had always refused to act unless assured of God's help and grace. But usually he had been aware of this want at least before enter-ing the chapel, he had been able to announce a postponement through the mouth of Allday or Marris; only once before had he been obliged to confess, actually from the chancel steps, that he was unfit to transmit the healing grace. And now when he thought, 'I must go – I can't insult God with a farce,' the reflec-tion had come to him also, 'But what about that reporter? What about the *Argus*? And just now when this great expansion of the work is being organized, wouldn't it be fatal to make them think I wasn't to be depended on – that I might fail at one of the big public meetings they talk of? Isn't it my duty to the Mission, to God's own work, to carry on? Perhaps too, in the service itself, connexion will be made, God will return to me.'

As he fixed his eyes on the ceiling, it seemed to him like a lid closed down upon him; its dirty cracked opacity was of one piece with the material barrier which had cut him off from the living God. He was a mere piece of flesh, of decaying sordid rubbish, as he lay in his chair, and his day's work had been an hypocrisy, an insult to God.

Hooper began again in the same cajoling tone, 'Of course, I understand that you don't want reporters to be seen. I'll take care that anyone from the *Argus* sits well at the back and keeps out of sight. No one will know they're there.'

'I'd know they were there – they affect me and that affects the congregation and the work.'

'Look, Preedy. I'll do the reporting myself – and you know I'm with you all the time.'

Preedy got up suddenly, 'All I know is you're with the *Argus* all the time – on a good stunt.'

Hooper lost his temper. He was, as always, enraged by this charge. 'What do you mean by stunt? If you mean I don't believe in your work, it's a damned lie and you ought to know it. The trouble is you think a newspaper man has got to be a sort of eunuch who's sold around the slave markets, to get whipped every time some old lecher can't raise a stand, and that's just the popular bull. I'd chuck my job tomorrow if anyone tried to push me around. I'd chuck it if the *Argus* went back again on you. I know a big thing when I see it – and I'm in this up to the neck. And why, because I am a newspaper man, because I know something about people and the way they tick, because I don't sit in a back room somewhere and whiffle ideas about ideas and what's wrong with the churches and why the British working man won't work except for pay. Let me tell you it's a damn good thing for you and the Mission too if I am a bloody journalist.' And then Hooper pulled himself up and said, 'I'm sorry – but all the same –'

'That's all right,' Preedy interrupted him. He had listened to the outburst with a bored and indifferent air. 'I've no quarrel with the papers – they're doing the Mission a lot of good. But no reporters, please, in the chapel.'

Hooper was not satisfied. For he had been struck by his own passion for the evangel. It seemed to him once more that he was a deeply sincere, a deeply religious man, so that his ambition on the *Argus* had been quite, or almost, eclipsed. For instance, he had been scarcely stirred by the news that Kate Rideout had refused Ackroyd's trust proposals.

It was Joanna herself who announced it, when she called him up one morning to tell him that her mother had arranged to be admitted to the Mission congregation, and she added, 'Are you ever in now?'

'Not very often – I'm pretty busy.'

'If you had a moment –'

Hooper, giving a little more of his attention, aware of a certain change in the girl's voice, said to himself, with impatience, 'So she's offering terms. But do I want her now? She might be a big nuisance. She's the very type.'

But he reflected that the girl had her interest in the paper – a respectable interest. And he said, 'Look, I'm up to the neck – I'm just off to Pant's Road this minute – a committee meeting, and it's important. I can't be late. But if you'd care to come along in the car.'

'I'd love it – shall I come round?'

'No, I'll call.'

But when, twenty minutes later, he came to Portland Place, he had new misgivings. He saw at once that the girl had taken unusual trouble to look well; she was almost smart. He had never seen her with so careful a make-up; she had even tried to improve her little eyes.

He felt not only his usual irritation against Joanna, because she had opposed him, but a certain scornful disgust at her weakness in surrender. She might, he felt, have shown a little more pride. He was even afraid of apologies, of some embarrassing approach. As he drove off he began to make conversation about the Mission, about Preedy, and the difficulty of managing him. 'He just puts cheques into his private account and no one knows what he does with it.'

'But he really does seem to have extraordinary powers.'

'You've joined up, have you?'

Joanna hesitated. Had she joined up, did she really believe? It seemed to her that she had passed only from a prejudice against Preedy into a strong but vague feeling that, after all, he might be a great, an extraordinary person; with mysterious powers. But this discovery had merely added to the violent confusion in her mind. She had changed that empty darkness in which she had felt like a creature imprisoned in nothingness, to a darkness full of mysterious shapes and noises whose meaning was incomprehensible.

And this darkness, this confusion of forms, was in herself as well as all round her. Till now she had at least known herself, been aware of herself as Joanna Rideout, a not very clever but well-meaning girl, lonely and not particularly happy, drifting without purpose through a world which neither made sense to her nor as it seemed, to itself. But now she had no longer a clear idea of herself. In the last week it seemed to her she had been half a dozen different people, sometimes a futile 'chatterer', Hooper's 'stickit deb', sometimes a coward dodging a plain duty, sometimes a creature torn half a dozen different ways, a split mind. She had had some terrifying minutes, in broad daylight, when, all at once, it seemed to her that she had no will at all. She had stood once for several minutes outside a shop window, because she was literally unable to decide whether to go in and buy a hat, or to walk away.

How ridiculous to buy a hat she would wear only to some party of chatterers, if she wore it at all; how stupid to go on walking down Bond Street, for no special reason, to Oxford Street where she had nothing to do, towards home where she would only be in the nurse's way and a perpetual cause of bitterness to her mother.

It was in a mood like this that she had entered a telephone booth and called Hooper. And now when she said to him, suddenly, 'Yes, I've come round – absolutely,' it was again an act of desperation, and she added, 'You know, my mother really is better. There's no doubt about it. She got up today and actually walked a few steps.' In fact, till that moment, Joanna had doubted her mother's improvement. The nurse and she had both thought it was simply an effort of will on the old woman's part. She had always been able to move her legs. On this occasion, she had tottered a yard between bed and chair.

But now, as she said, 'There's no doubt about it,' she felt committed, and she said with conviction, 'It's really like a miracle.'

'Why not?' said Hooper. 'Why shouldn't it be a miracle? What do we know about miracles. Fifty years ago wireless would have been a miracle – and the shock treatment at the asylums which cures so many of what used to be hopeless cases. Both electricity you notice,' and he began to talk about the connexion between electricity and the nature of the final power in the universe – electric impulses, light waves, telepathy. 'Telepathy is proved – there's no doubt about it. And that means that thoughts, ideas, feelings can pass through space.' Hooper had all ready a little speech about the phenomena of faith-healing, which he used to friends met in the club or to colleagues at the *Argus*'s offices. He was talking about faith-healing everywhere; he had now a great many suggestions all with a strong scientific flavour. He went on now about mental trauma. 'We know that the brain is a complex of electric currents – but no one knows what electricity is. Why shouldn't it have the same relation with mind and emotion as nerve with sensation – it is simply the physical aspect of mind. And Jeans said the world is more like a thought than a thing – a work of imagination.'

'I went to a service last Thursday,' Joanna murmured.

'Thursday – I can't remember if that was a good day.'

'It was a private service. A blind boy was cured completely. It was the most extraordinary thing I've ever seen.'

'Preedy is an extraordinary man.'

'Isn't he – that's what I do so feel – you are absolutely right.'

Her responses were either disconnected; or too eager, too enthusiastic, a reversion even exaggerated to that 'deb's delight' which he had resented at their first meeting. Hooper, after a pause, answered dryly that Preedy had been making extraordinary cures for some years past.

'Yes, of course – really extraordinary – it's the only word.'

Joanna threw a most eager interest into her voice but in fact she was merely echoing the man's last remark. She was not attending to his words at all, she was still astonished to find herself beside him; by the whole of the proceedings of the last two hours.

She had been exceedingly angry with Hooper, she had said that he was a brute and she never wanted to see him again. And then, apparently without the least premeditation, she had picked up the phone and made a complete surrender and apology. From that moment, she lived in that kind of dream when the victim knows that he is dreaming but can't stop. She had watched herself dress that morning and make herself up with the nervous excitement of a very young and very love-lorn girl going to an assignation, and though she had said half a dozen times, 'But I don't love him – it's impossible,' yet the dreamer had gone on preening in the glass, and trembling with nervousness.

And now, sitting beside Hooper, she was saying, 'The whole thing is insane –' but the dreamer who still had charge of her actions was enjoying an extraordinary sensation of peace, of contentment. She was like someone, who, after weeks of pain and terror, comes to in a hospital and is told that she is to have a major operation in ten minutes; and feels such relaxation that it is like a luxury, a unique bliss. Her fate is out of her hands, she has nothing more to worry about. And she realizes that it was the worry, the problem of what to do, that was killing her.

Her thoughts were not even greatly concerned with Hooper. She acknowledged to herself that she did not know the man; she did not know either why she disliked him or why he had such a fascination for her. And listening to him now, she had no curiosity, she gave no special attention to his words. The whole conversation seemed to her insignificant, it had no importance. No doubt he thought it important. He thought he was telling her what he believed, and expected her to be interested and gratified. So she gratified him by earnest remarks.

But she recognized the argument. She had heard it several times in the last week. It was going the rounds, even that quotation from the Astronomer Royal. For Mrs Mantoffle, giving her fortnightly five minutes to Kate, had said that the world is more like a thought than a thing, that thought was obviously some kind of electrical action and so pervaded space – that electricity was simply the ultimate power of the whole universe, so that a miracle might arise simply from the establishment of contact between the individual and the ultimate all-pervading power of God's will.

But now, when she said to Hooper, 'Absolutely,' 'Of course,' 'I do so agree,' she was not responding to his arguments, but to his presence. Her real attention was given to the point of her right elbow which was touching the man's upper arm. She was intensely aware of that contact, but whether it gave her pleasure or not she could not tell. She was only aware that she wanted it to go on.

Hooper turned to her, 'Have you heard a word?'

'Oh, yes.'

'What did I say last?'

And she found that she had no idea what he had said for several minutes past. Neither had she the least notion of what she herself had been thinking of; she seemed to have been completely mindless.

She opened her mouth to utter something about electricity as power, the only recollection she had. But Hooper began to laugh. He said nothing but he laughed in her face, a laugh which would have been wholly jeering if it had not also conveyed indulgence. Joanna, to her pleasure, felt neither embarrassed by her ignorance nor humiliated by the laugh. In this new extraordinary situation it appeared that all relations were different, inattention was a bond and jeers gave intense and mysterious pleasure.

Hooper had now turned in to the kerb and stopped. 'Here we are,' he said, and he stared at her, raising his eyelids and thus enlarging his prominent eyeballs in a glare such as children use when playing eye battles. And this too she enjoyed intensely, to be treated as a child, and mocked. It took from her at last all responsibility.

'And what are you going to do now,' he asked, 'while I'm at this committee?'

'I don't know.'

'I may be an hour – two hours.'

'I suppose I could wait.'

Hooper continued to stare for a moment, but then suddenly made an impatient face. 'If you want to be useful you could do something for me.'

'Of course.'

'But no – you'd muddle it. No, you'd better just wait.'

And he got out, banged the door and walked off with his usual swaggering, quick step, and looking after him, she thought, 'What a brute he is.' But she was pleased to find that she did not mind Hooper's being a brute. She did not want to be irritated any more against a man who knew his own mind and what to do in the world. She was enjoying already the bliss of total acceptance.

42

One result of Lady Rideout's cure was that she became exceedingly difficult to manage. In the old days she had been dominating, but always reasonable; it was possible to argue with her. Now she was still more imperious and allowed no contradiction whatever. She had declared against any great changes in the *Argus*, probably because Hooper was so strong for them and dared to urge them with her. In fact, he relied too much on their new relation since her conversion. But she did not thank him for her cure; she regarded him still as a young man on the make, and resented especially his influence with Joanna.

The reason Hooper was back on the *Argus* board was simply that, because of falling circulation, Ackroyd and the old gang had their backs to the wall. The board was now equally divided. One conference took a whole afternoon to discuss the question of girls on the front page. Hooper pointed out that the question was whether the *Argus* could survive at all. 'I'm all for your ideas,' he said, 'for putting over something that matters, but you don't need to put it over in a pill. What's the whole problem of publicity? Breaking the crust, getting through to the chap inside. It's the same with everything, shaving soap or sermons, religion or razors. People have been so pounded with words from childhood that they go about in an armour as thick as a tank. To get at the man inside you've got to crack that crust or creep in through the ventilators. And one ventilator is always sex.'

Tinney, who had till now voted always with Ackroyd and given advice only on scientific matters, suddenly took a strong line. He had objected violently to the commission for Hooper's articles on Preedy and now he picked a quarrel with Hooper. He seemed to have lost his sense of humour and grew almost as heated as Hooper himself. No doubt, he said, Mr Hooper knew all about sex, but if you got anywhere with sex, you stayed with sex.

Hooper interrupted him, 'Yay,' he said, 'we all know that story, but it just isn't true.'

'That last advertising campaign for Bingo soap with film stars in their baths sent up the sales of Bingo for two months and then they came down again.'

'Not right down, and Bingo was a thoroughly bad soap. Once you've got through, of course, it depends on the quality of what you bring in with you; but you've got to get in first; you've got to break that crust.'

When Tinney tried to continue the argument, Hooper, as usual, began to shout, dammit all, they'd only got to compare *The Times* of today with *The Times* of ten years ago. 'I'm not telling you anything new or extraordinary, and neither did I make the bloody world, or the bloody people in it. All I'm telling you is that the poor old *Argus* is about as out of date as the dodo and will soon be quite as extinct.'

Hooper annoyed Tinney but had little effect on Ackroyd, who had, as usual, made up his mind before the conference. He had given Hooper enough to keep him quiet for the moment and, meanwhile, he was determined either to organize the trust, or to retire. He was obliged to admit that he could not live much longer. His one object in life was to leave the *Argus* established on what he considered the only right lines and the old man felt that he might hope for support from Kate. She now said that she would agree to the trust provided that Tinney was not a trustee, and provided that Joanna agreed.

Gadd then paid a call on Hooper to explain his ideas, actually to do a deal. The little pettifogger suddenly disclosed his ambition to be a Press lord. It seemed that he had been talking to Press lords and two of them, whose names he did not disclose, were, he said, quite ready to put money into the *Argus* in exchange for a seat on the board of management.

'That's to say,' said Gadd, 'they're ready to back the *Argus* on the new line; in fact, they would want you as editor. In these circumstances you could count on me, but I shouldn't be really much good to you if the trust goes through unless I was on the board of trustees.'

Hooper made no promises; he wanted to know first who had made the offer of backing the *Argus*. Was it Thompson of the *Mercury* or Lord Wittenham of the *Dispatch*? And when Gadd would not answer, saying that the matter was confidential, he put the man off with a general statement that if he were made editor of the new *Argus* he would be very glad to work with Gadd.

Meanwhile Ackroyd paid a private visit to Joanna.

43

Ackroyd had ascertained already, by discreet inquiry, that Joanna spent most of her time at the Pant's Road Mission. He paid his surprise visit one morning at eleven o'clock and was received in a very casual manner by one of the new secretaries, a young woman in a uniform rather resembling that of a nurse without the cap; a very severe-looking young woman who obviously considered a lord, by that very fact, one of the heathen. She said she would find out where Rideout was at the moment and left him sitting in a bleak waiting-room for half an hour. Another young woman, equally severe, then appeared and directed him to the Hall, a new building, just erected on a vacant site near the chapel. He entered the large bare room which was being scrubbed out by six women. Chairs were piled against the wall, the windows were open, the whole place on a raw November morning could not have been more cold and dismal. All the scrub women were young, and none of them had the appearance of the professional char. But Ackroyd decided at last that the girl in the furthest corner scrubbing vigorously with her back towards him might be Joanna. He made his way round the edge of the floor and addressing the back of the girl's head said, 'Is that you, Joey?' The girl then came up to her knees, showing a flushed face, damp with steam, to which some wisps of hair were sticking, and proved, in fact, to be Joanna.

She greeted Ackroyd with a delighted smile and asked him if he had come to see the Mission, 'Because I'm afraid I won't be able to show you round till this job is over, and it will take us all day.'

Joanna was fond of Ackroyd. She had known him from babyhood and in his awkward way he had done his best to spoil her. She had felt for him that special affection of the niece for the generous uncle, where there is no obligation on the girl's side and all the benefits come from the other – an affection, therefore, quite free of any self-seeking, and enjoyed by both.

'No, my dear, I came just to see you. Is there anywhere we can talk?'

'Not just now I'm afraid; I'm awfully sorry, Uncle Eddy, but this is a rush job; there's a big meeting here tomorrow and we have to get the chairs back today.'

'I'm afraid it's rather urgent – in fact, it can't wait.'

'Well, tell me now; I could wipe you down a chair, or is it too cold?'

'As you know, we've been having a bit of a crisis on the *Argus*.'

'Poor old *Argus*,' and Joanna looked at the floor and dipped her scrubbing brush as if about to set to work again.

44

Joanna knew quite as well as Ackroyd about the crisis on the *Argus*; Hooper had talked of nothing else for the last fortnight. But the whole question had assumed a place very much in the background of her life. That life, for her, had changed profoundly since her mother's conversion; she was herself astonished at the change, she had not thought that it could be so different for the same person. For the Joanna that seemed so strange to Ackroyd, a scrub woman at the Mission, was to herself essentially the same person. She hoped she believed but she could not be sure of it. She had told Hooper she believed and as proof of it here she was, doing the humblest work for the Mission, placing herself absolutely at the disposal of Preedy, or rather, Preedy's staff, who obviously delighted in giving her the most unpleasant jobs. At least four of the six scrub women, indeed, were what the Mission regarded as girls in society. They boasted of their conversion and also of making them scrub floors as proof that at Pant's Road there was no distinction of persons.

It was the essential Joanna that scrubbed and enjoyed scrubbing, but what astonished her was this new existence. It was indeed Hooper who had suggested that she should work for the Mission, and she knew that he enjoyed even more than the Mission staff putting her to the humblest and dirtiest work. But now, although she detected very easily his purpose to humiliate her, to take it out of her, as he would have put it himself, she no longer felt that sense of toleration, of condescension to the man. She was too respectful of his character. She was enormously grateful to him for her mother's cure, for taking that line which had led to the conversion. She said to herself, 'Perhaps he's only a gambler, but he does things, he's not afraid to do things.' Hooper had for her the fascination of the leader, the one who unties knots, who breaks bonds, who sets free.

But what was most astonishing to her, in her new existence, was the change in Hooper himself. For the first fortnight he used to pass without seeming to notice her. Then one day he had shown her a new character. It was as though he sensed the change in her own feelings towards him. There had been a strange interview when he had come upon her mopping the bathroom in

Preedy's villa, still the Mission headquarters. While she had been mopping the lavatory bowl, he had taken his seat on the edge of the bath, and begun to chatter about *Argus* affairs and the campaign.

'I made a fool of myself last time,' he said, 'by trying to rush old Ackroyd; it's always stupid to resign. The fact is,' he said, 'I'm always apt to overcall my cards. It's not that I'm so conceited, it's simply that I get frightened. What happened that time was that I knew Tinney hated my guts and that old Ackroyd was quite ready to stab anyone in the back who threatened to push him off the *Argus*. It's such a dirty world; I've had some. You can't trust anybody,' and after a little reflection he added, 'I don't mean that everybody is a spiv. In fact, the funny thing is, when you think of it, that there are such a lot of quite decent people about; real unselfishness.' The little man opened his eyes as if in astonishment. 'Yes, I've had lots of kindness done to me by quite ordinary people who didn't expect anything back, at least I couldn't think of anything.'

'So there are some people you can trust,' said Joanna, beginning on the taps.

'Not a bit of it; those are just the people you can't trust. You never know what they'll do. They change their minds every day; they tell you a lot of lies out of pure kindness, or what they think is kindness; they go plotting and planning behind your back to push you around for what they think is your own good.'

He would chatter to her about anything and it was soon obvious to her that he enjoyed these new terms of confidence. Almost every time he came to the Mission he would seek her out, and often he would carry her off to his room. It became a custom that they should spend week-ends together in some country place. The liaison became so open that she began to avoid her old friends in town, especially those oldest friends who would feel aggrieved if she did not take them into her confidence; and she found it impossible to do so because she could feel in them already their surprise and pity. They looked upon her affair as an infatuation or possibly a despairing fling of the unwanted spinster, whereas she knew that she was happy, that she was enjoying a unique experience. How long it was to last she could not tell, and she did not care. She lived from day to day, a life almost without reflection, especially from the day when she realized her pregnancy. She was intensely happy, but with quite an unexpected kind of happiness. Her married friends had described to her in their first pregnancy their feelings of satisfaction that at last they were doing something that mattered, and she had been impressed by one who had talked of making life, in the sense of creation, but she found in herself no feeling like that. On the contrary, she had the sense of being acted upon, of being absorbed into a course of affairs over which she had no control. She was being carried along in a stream of physical existence which she could not change if she chose, and a great part of her happiness was just in the sense of belonging, of being managed. She did not need to think for herself, and she did not think; she was astonished by her own power of floating with the tide of events, of indifference to consequences. She would say to herself, 'This can't go on much longer. For one thing, he will be furious when he knows of my condition. It's absolutely certain that he'll leave me as soon as he does know.' And yet she accepted this certainty with complete apathy, a fatalist calm. She did not know that anybody could be so happy while calmly accepting the fact that her happiness could not last; that it might come to an end any day.

She took care not to give Hooper any suspicion of what had happened to her. She had undertaken to him that she would not become pregnant – all precautions had been in her hands, and she was not at all sure that she had been careless by accident. She had not been deliberately careless, but she had certainly accepted Hooper on several occasions when she had not been prepared, and rather than tell him to wait she had shown the eagerness that he expected.

She told herself that since it was her fault she would not expect him to marry her. The question could not arise and she was glad of it; she was afraid that on that point he might show in a bad light. Several times, indeed, he had taken the trouble to warn her that he was not a marrying man. 'I should be a fool to tie myself up; I've always had all the women I wanted, so why hang one of them round my neck.'

And Joanna had warmly agreed with him. She agreed with him in everything, even when his egotism made her laugh. And now there was no condescension in her laughter. She laughed because she was happy; because the whole spectacle of the world had taken on a new aspect to her.

45

The moment Joanna saw Ackroyd she thought, 'He wants to see me about the trust.' She had put the trust out of her mind for the last three months since her mother's return home, but she knew that it was very much in Ackroyd's mind and when he spoke of something important she perceived it could be nothing else. At lunch-time when the charwomen knocked off for half an hour to go to the canteen she faced Ackroyd across a corner table in the noisy room with the deepest apprehension. She did not know what she would do, and she had taken care not to think of it. She knew that Hooper did not want the trust, aimed directly at his policy. She suspected that her mother had now come round to Ackroyd's point of view.

'I dare say you know,' the old man said, 'that we're having trouble on the board. Of course, it's the same trouble that's affecting most of the newspapers nowadays, to get new readers without losing the old ones. Some people would like to turn the *Argus* into a tabloid, something on the lines of the *Mercury*, and of course that could be done, but it would lose all our old readers and it's not at all sure to get new ones. After all, if people want a tabloid they've got plenty to their hand.'

And so on. He said what she had often heard before, pulled out all the stops. He was for modernizing the *Argus* in certain respects – but he considered it a suicidal policy to vulgarize it on the lines of the *Mercury* – 'better let it go than prostitute it. We owe some loyalty to its readers – a special and important group. And it would be betraying all that the *Argus* stands for, all that your father stood for.'

And so on. Again she had heard all the arguments, and what she was asking herself was simply, could she go against her mother? For her, the question of the *Argus* itself had become quite unimportant; she did not even feel guilty about her lack of views on the subject. She did not care what happened to the *Argus*; she did not really believe it mattered. These famous liberal ideas of poor old Uncle Edward, what did they amount to? And when he told her that the *Argus* could be modernized without vulgarization, she was sure that he was thinking only of keeping his post and power as chairman of the board. Probably, indeed, Hooper was right; the only way to save the *Argus* was to vulgarize it, and she was longing that Hooper should have the opportunity. But could she deny her mother. And now Ackroyd began to talk about her mother.

'It's wonderful to see her so much better, and taking such an interest in the papers, but it's a bit alarming too. What do you feel? Isn't there a danger that she'll wear herself out? How long can we expect this burst of energy to last?'

Cautiously he let her see his doubts of her mother's cure, his belief that her sudden revival of energy was simply a last flash from the old woman's powerful will and high strung nerves. 'We have to think for the future,' he said, 'I can't go on for ever. In fact, a good many people think I've no right to be going on now. And there's only one way to secure sound management for the *Argus* – sound management on the lines of your father's idea for the paper, and that's some kind of trust. As you know, several papers, in fact, most of the more responsible papers, are under trustees, papers like *The Times*, the *Observer*, the *News Chronicle*. The only question is, is your mother prepared to hand over her rights? That's what I want to see you about. You know her mind better than anybody. What do you think? Do you think you could bring up the subject with her in the near future?'

He did not say to Joanna anything about her own rights, or the need of her agreement to any deed of trust. Obviously he had thought it more tactful, more diplomatic, to refer only to her mother's position. But Joanna felt already that if her mother wanted a trust, she would have to agree to it merely because she had been able to do so little for her mother, and this was something she could do for her. The very fact that her mother was so ill, that she might, after all, be dying, made it absolutely necessary that she should not thwart her.

And rather than let the thing hang upon her mind she told Ackroyd there and then that if her mother desired the trust she would certainly agree. 'It's really not right that I should interfere in any way with the *Argus*, because I don't know anything about it, and mother's given her whole life to the papers.'

She awaited then the reaction from Hooper with the sense of one who has committed a treachery; and when, two days later, as they met as usual at the small country hotel where they had been used to spend the week-ends, he suddenly attacked her, she answered, 'But I had to do it.'

'You had to do what?' And then she discovered that he was talking about her pregnancy. It appeared now that it was a matter of common gossip at the Mission. She had told nobody and Hooper was going upon nothing but the rumour, and his own suspicions.

'Did you do it on purpose?' he asked. And before she could answer, 'However, it's your own business; you promised to take care; it's nothing to do with me.'

'I quite realize that. I'm only sorry it should upset you so much.'

'Oh, I don't care,' Hooper said with emphasis, 'I just want to get the thing clear. Of course, if you like to get rid of it I dare say I could help. I can give you an address in Paris. And if you want a good excuse for going over I could work something; get you a commission to make some sort of report.'

He spoke coolly, as of a matter that concerned him very little. 'Of course, these meetings will have to stop. There's too much talk already. In another month you'll begin to show, and it would be simply impossible for me to go around with you.'

And again he asked her if she wouldn't have an abortion. 'It's quite easy nowadays, and quite safe, with this man in Paris anyhow. And really there isn't any alternative. You might work it if you were really a char or a typist, you could simply go off somewhere, put up a ring and call yourself a widow; but a girl in your position can't get out like that. You're too well known by too many people. You're news.'

And while he was speaking Joanna, for the first time, did consider the future; a future without Hooper and full of problems. It was the problems that suddenly appalled her, the organization of a new life under every kind of difficulty, the explanations, the false position.

From the bottom of her mind there floated up that question which seemed to live there, like a crocodile in a swamp. 'Was it worth while, was it worth the trouble?' How much easier and more sensible to do what Hooper suggested and avoid all the problems, all this enormous upheaval. A journey to Paris seemed not only rational, but even the right course. It would save her mother from a final distress with this hopeless daughter. It would take from her her own guilty sense that, if she had not willed this pregnancy, she had not done enough to avoid it; she had allowed herself to be carried along in the stream of events.

'You see,' said Hooper, looking at her keenly, as he followed her thoughts, 'it's no good being a sentimental fool. For one thing it would kill your mother. I tell you what, you can go over for the Mission to make a report on France as a possible field for evangelization. I can easily push it through the committee. They're eating out of my hand since the campaign started.'

But Joanna, to her own surprise, shook her head. She perceived that this was something she could not do. That course of events into which she had thrown herself was apparently stronger than any consideration of prudence, or even of kindness to her mother. She had done her duty to her mother about the trust, but here there was no question of duty, or even of sentiment. She belonged to a process, a movement of life, which seemed to be stronger than her will.

Hooper had jumped up in a rage; his face was suddenly flushed, 'So it is a game,' he said. 'Just what I thought. The old, old trick. I always thought you were up to something. So you were going to take all precautions, save me all the trouble and worry. My God, what sort of a fool do you take me for. Yes, I know, you'll put it about that I've let you down, the nasty little cad. You'll make my name stink. Don't you realize that I'd rather shoot myself than marry you? Don't you realize I've never cared about you, except as a week-end convenience, a comfort station? Really,' he said, 'I'm rather glad that it has happened this way. It's probably saved me a lot of trouble later on. It's cured me of a fancy I had that you were at least straight; that you wouldn't try to stab me in the back.'

Then he walked out of the room and a few minutes later he drove away. Joanna found that he had paid the bill for that night. He had also left an envelope containing a five-pound note on which he had scribbled the words, 'To get you home.'

It was a fine evening. It was their usual practice on such an evening to go for a walk on the downs before dinner. Hooper had the idea that these walks in the country air were good for his digestion and Joanna had always loved to walk. It was at such times that he had been most affectionate; he would take her arm and chatter for half an hour on end about his successes of the week; the sharp things he had said, the clever men he had outwitted, his brilliant schemes for the Preedy campaign and the *Argus*. Her duty had been simply to admire, to make the intelligent comment. And she had enjoyed nothing so much as these walks – not for the conversation, to which she barely listened, but simply for the touch, the weight of the man on her arm, the feeling that she was close to him and useful to him.

Now she put the note into her bag, put on her coat and went out for the walk alone. She followed the routine, like an automaton, and yet she was not unhappy. What she had expected to happen had happened. It had happened just as she had expected, even to his charge of treachery. Now that he had made it she could see that she had expected it; that he, being what he was, was bound to make it. She was not even sure that he had no right to do so. It was quite possible that she was guilty – or if not herself, this force that had taken possession of her, that had made her say so often when he had suddenly attacked her, 'Really I don't mind what happens,' as if not minding was the chief part of her pleasure.

46

[But Ackroyd still could not persuade Lady Rideout to sign the trust deed. He now suggested that Hooper should be made managing director, with a general mandate to produce a new layout and reorganize the staff. Lady Rideout agreed. Tinney resigned from the board.]

Hooper at once began the process of hiring and firing, of experimentation, which turned the *Argus* office, reputed to be among the easiest-going in Fleet Street, upside down. His new editor was Cleary, who had made the *Mercury* in its early days before he had quarrelled with the Thompson family about his powers. He did not object to their politics; in his view the editor's job was to represent any point of view that was put to him. What he objected to was any kind of interference with the make-up of the paper, or with his staff. He was getting old now; this was the reason he was available to the *Argus*, notoriously in a bad way and unlikely to do better while Ackroyd controlled the board. For the same reason Hooper hoped to find him amenable. But the old man proved to be as obstinate as ever, and even more touchy.

Thus, from the beginning Hooper was in difficulties with Cleary, especially as he could not explain that he himself had to please the board. For though, as managing editor, he had a seat and a vote on the *Argus* board, he was still obliged to get Ackroyd's support. When Ackroyd, for instance, protested against the photograph of a film star on the front page, and Hooper answered that he had understood the new policy was precisely to lighten up the front page with such pictures, the vote went against him; not, apparently, because of the photograph itself, but because of the paragraph belonging to it, which was held to be too much like a story for the Sunday press. And, in fact, Ackroyd was proved right; there were indignant letters from old subscribers.

Hooper had said often enough that the problem of reconciling the old *Argus* public to a new paper was tricky, but he had not realized till now how tricky it was, and it was no good for him to argue that risks had to be taken, that those subscribers must go, that quite probably circulation must suffer for the first weeks. The board were thoroughly frightened. They were suffering from that special panic which afflicts all newspaper owners, management boards, editors, confronted by a falling circulation and the enormous question, 'What shall we do to sell? What shall we do to be popular?' and everything they do brings only complaints, threats, and cancellations of subscriptions. They were discovering that those who approve of any change in a newspaper are the last to say so; either they do not trouble, or they do not care. Whereas those old, faithful supporters who have stuck to it through thick and thin will write at length at the smallest alteration, at a change in type, at the spacing of a headline, the spacing of a paragraph, or merely the tone of a new columnist; and they always write in furious indignation saying they will never 'read your rag again'.

When Hooper had been defeated on the board, he had to explain to Cleary why Cleary's plans for the new layout could not be carried out. Cleary, for all his reputation, was already out of date. His triumph with the *Mercury*, then a staggering beginner, was twenty years old. He conceived himself still as a pioneer in popular journalism, a regenerator of dying papers; but he was dealing with a different public, another generation than that which had savoured the old *Mercury*. He believed still that there was nothing like a good murder to sell the paper. Crime and sex were his great specifics and he was furiously impatient when

Hooper would not give them headlines on the front page; and when he was told that for the kind of public that the *Argus* wanted crime and sex were just as important as before but needed a different treatment, he threatened to resign. His reputation, he said, was at stake; he wasn't going to be connected with an anaemic rag like the *Argus* if it was going to collapse.

Hooper would smooth the old man down, telling him to keep his murder for the middle page and bide his time, a few weeks would be enough. 'The game is to change the paper without their knowing it; people don't keep old papers, thank goodness; in six months you can diddle away a layout that they've been used to for forty years and give them something completely new – make them like it too, so that they couldn't go back to the old one if they tried. But you've got to do it a paragraph at a time; a princess in a fur coat today going to a film première, and in six weeks you can have a model in a bathing dress, kissing an alderman.'

But Cleary was impatient and continued to demand complete authority over layout. It was his job, he said, what he was hired for.

What infuriated Hooper in this battle, with Ackroyd on one hand and Cleary on the other, was the waste of time and energy spent in management. For, at the same time, he was struggling with the immense problem of organization in the campaign.

It was true that he had delegated the advertising to the firm of Maule and Manward, and paid only occasional visits to Mission headquarters, but he was making all the big decisions. He had decided, for instance, on a grand meeting in the Albert Hall, and this was already being advertised. The response had been so great that some members of the Mission were already proposing a series of such monster meetings. The campaign, in fact, was going fast and had already reached that dimension when it had a momentum of its own. The great difficulty of direction was not that of driving it forward, but of steering it in a chosen course. Now Preedy himself was touring from one big city to another, holding services in each, and forty assistant missioners were permanently settled in big towns, picked to be centres of evangelization. Weekly congregations had reached half a million; tens of thousands attended evening services during the week, and Hooper had just started those meetings at factory gates which became one of the main sources for recruits.

It really seemed at that time that, as Hooper liked to put it, the tide had turned. He believed it himself; he could scarcely help believing it, living as he did at the centre of this enormous achievement. Though he gave more of his time to the *Argus*, his mind was almost totally preoccupied with the Mission. He spent, perhaps, less than an hour a day on the work of the organization, but he lived almost entirely in the peculiar atmosphere of a religious revival. Although it was not even every day that he went to the headquarters, sat on some committee, or talked with Allday or Marris, Kerne or Gomm, or Mrs Hartree, they seemed to him the most important, the most significant persons of his acquaintance. Their enthusiasm, their sense of purpose, their single-minded confidence, made everyone else seem vague and futile. It was difficult to have patience with old Cleary, fuming about his reputation and worrying about circulation, when one had just been with Marris, for whom nothing mattered but the salvation of a whole people, their real salvation from a life of confused fear and trivial ambition to the certainty of paradise..

But here again there was one great threat; greater than Cleary's to the *Argus*, as the Mission was greater than the *Argus*. Preedy, as the Mission grew in power and success, became always more arrogant and unpredictable. Several times already he had suddenly refused to take the service at an important meeting; giving as explanation only that he didn't feel like it. He was, of course, immensely overworked, but that was his own fault. All his friends, and Hooper especially, were anxious not to overwork him; they had reason to know his nervous exhaustion after a service of healing, the more successful the service the more exhausted he seemed. It was Preedy himself who proposed these long journeys, these immense meetings, one after another, often three or four in a week, and who then would suddenly telegraph for a deputy and hide himself away in his hotel. Often he disappeared altogether, leaving no address and no means of communication.

At headquarters people reminded each other that that had always been his practice, to take these short and sudden holidays. None of them said that in the old days such disappearances had often meant a visit to Alice Rodker, but everyone remembered it, and it was a standing fear among all his friends that a new scandal would break out any day and destroy all their work. When Preedy, due for a meeting at Manchester, did not turn up at the station where a deputation waited for him all the afternoon, there was something like panic, and at last those nearest to him did suggest Alice Rodker's name, where was she and what was she doing? Kerne went so far as to send a discreet inquiry to Fred Rodker but it appeared that Fred Rodker knew no more than anybody else.

It was then that Marris recollected a remark of Hooper's that Joanna Rideout had taken charge of the Rodker girl. He went to Hooper at once and put it to him, would Miss Rideout know where Alice Rodker was, and could she throw any light on Preedy's latest disappearance? To his surprise, Hooper returned a very vague answer. He did not think it was any good to apply to Miss Rideout, because if she knew she wouldn't tell.

'I thought she was a friend of yours,' the Colonel said.

'I suppose you could call her that, but she's a queer fish you know, a very hard case, and if she won't do a thing, why, she won't.'

The truth was that Hooper had already asked Joanna this question some time before. He knew very well that Joanna was keeping up with the Rodker girl and saw a great deal of her. It had struck him at once, at Preedy's first big failure, some weeks before, that Alice Rodker might be the cause. And at that time he had just begun to see Joanna again. He had come upon her by chance one day at Mission headquarters, where she was waiting in uniform, that is to say, in a large blue overcoat, to drive some delegate to a meeting in the suburbs. Headquarters, discovering that she possessed her own car and could drive, had promoted her from scrub woman to chauffeur. Hooper passed her in the hall and then upon an impulse turned back and asked her what she was doing. She answered that she was an official driver, 'and the overcoat is rather useful at present.'

And then she had added, 'But I shouldn't have said that – it's not your affair.'

'No, it's not my affair, you do agree to that.'

'Of course, I always did. I felt very guilty about it.'

He had walked away then, but he began to watch for her car and two days later, seeing it outside the Mission headquarters as he passed, he had gone in again to find her. 'So there you are,' he said. 'Do you ever take a week-end off?'

'No, but I should like to.'

'Very well, on Friday, as usual.'

And again they had spent Friday to Sunday, the pressman's week-end, together on the downs.

For that week-end Hooper had been dignified; he had talked of indifferent matters; her mother's health, affairs on the board and at the Mission, but no anecdotes about his victories, no talk about himself at all. He had even refrained from taking the girl's arm as they climbed. Above all he had made no reference to her pregnancy, now obvious enough when she was not wearing her big coat.

But on the next week-end he ceased to bother about his dignity. It did not seem to him necessary to care what Joanna thought of him. She was so obviously delighted at his return on any condition; she was so humble, so devoted, so uncritical, that once more he told of his triumphs, he bragged so enormously that once or twice he found himself apologizing. 'You'll think I'm getting a swelled head, but the fact is that most people are a lot of tram cars. They've got on the rails for a start, because that's all they're made for, and they don't want to get off because they wouldn't know what to do with themselves; they like the rails. Old Cleary, the great revolutionary, is just the same as the rest. He only knows one kind of revolution and he can't change a single move, or he doesn't know where he is; he's just another Ackroyd inside out.'

'Why shouldn't you tell me the truth,' Joanna said, 'I hate people who pose as being nobodies and everybody knows that they're anything but. It's really the worst kind of conceit; they want you to say, "How great this man is, because all he has done up to now is simply nothing to him."'

Hooper could not exactly agree with this view; he never agreed with Joanna. Not so much because it was his principle to keep her in her place, but because he was simply unable to do so. His impulse was always to find some small fault. It was a compulsion he sometimes recognized, and then he would make up for it with a kind word, so now he said, 'There's some truth in that, but I don't think it's true of me; I do tend to get a swelled head, it's my special danger, but it's a good idea of yours that modesty is often the worst kind of conceit.'

He was completely happy with Joanna; he returned always from his week-ends full of vigour and enterprise, for his brag was a kind of bet. When he had told her what a big man he was, he often had a moment of doubt. Some critic at the back of his mind would remind him of his difficulties, both on the *Argus* and in the campaign: a newspaper that was losing money; an evangelist who would go his own way in spite of the best advice. And then immediately he would affirm, 'Yes, but I've got to win; damn it all, I've got the ability, and nobody's going to keep me down.'

It was just because Joanna was a nobody who was merely devoted to him that he could not bear the idea of failure in her sight, and this was also the reason why he did not like to depend upon her for anything; why, when he had asked her where Alice Rodker was living, and what she was doing, and Joanna had answered that she had promised to keep the girl's secrets, he did not repeat the question. He was astonished and angry to be denied; he could not help a certain moodiness during the rest of that day. He knew that it would be mistaken for sulks. Joanna's anxious looks, her apologetic air, her too assiduous efforts to please, assured him of that. He was indeed still more irritated with the girl for supposing that he was capable of sulking over anything she might do; but he concealed the irritation as he struggled with his mood. He said to himself, 'After all, it's typical of the slave mentality, to make a juju of these confidential relations with other slaves. Joanna and Alice are a pair, pushed about by circumstances; that's why they've taken to each other in this queer way.'

Then Preedy was recognized one day by a patient in Hyde Park, as he was walking under the trees with a young, thin girl with pigtails. There was no doubt about his identity because the patient, a woman healed of a tumour, challenged him and he admitted it. But he showed also that he resented her inquiry and he at once walked off, taking the child by the arm and hurrying her away with him.

Naturally the committee were appalled by such a discovery, coming so soon after the revelations at the Syson case. Like a good many people they had been surprised that the Public Prosecutor had not taken action after that case. The fact that he had not done so was attributed by Mrs Hartree to prayer, though Hooper had pointed out that in an ordinary police action a young man guilty as Preedy had been guilty would, after the girl's confession of her bad character, probably be acquitted, or suffer merely a nominal sentence.

But it was felt that, if Preedy were involved in another affair of the same kind, there would be such violent prejudice against him that he would be very severely dealt with. In any case, it would be impossible for him to continue as Missioner. At two agitated meetings it was actually proposed that he should be got rid of at once and that Jackman should be asked to take the Albert Hall service. It was only by the most energetic lobbying that Hooper defeated the vote.

Then Preedy, the week before the Albert Hall service, walked into Pant's Road and began his preparations, locking himself up as he usually did before an important service to write his sermon. But at no time did he offer an explanation or apology for his absence, and when Hooper, using all the tact he possessed, spoke of the encounter in the park, and asked who his friend had been, he answered sharply, 'What friend do you mean?'

'I gather that you were with a girl, quite a young girl.'

'I suppose you mean Ada Rollwright, the daughter of Frances Rollwright at Pant's Road.'

'Ought I to remember the name?'

'I don't know, and I don't care; the child is ill, and I have been attending her.'

'At her mother's request?'

'Yes, and you can tell Mr Allday and the rest of the gang that they'd better mind their own business because they don't understand mine.'

This ended the conversation, but inquiries at Pant's Road showed that Mrs Rollwright and her daughter had left some months before, and no one knew their present address.

47

During the first three months after her conversion and healing Kate Rideout seemed to be stronger. She would totter a few steps to a chair, and she worked all day, especially at the Pant's Road campaign. As she said, 'Here is a discovery which is absolutely revolutionary – which could change the whole world, and nobody is paying any attention.'

She found even Hooper's advertising campaign too unenterprising. She was impatient with him for giving any time at all to his work at the *Argus* office. She was always calling him on the telephone with new ideas – aeroplanes sky-writing the message, 'Lift up your eyes to the Lord'; pavement-writing; cards to be stuck in hats; and loudspeaker vans.

It was she in fact who paid for the vans which went through London streets for a week before the Albert Hall meeting, giving first a fanfare of trumpets, then a verse from a hymn, then a short address and finally a prayer of thanksgiving.

But five days before the meeting, she had a fainting fit, and afterwards violent pains in her legs. She became very weak, and would not eat. That night she told the nurse to get Sir Shanklin, who came at once. The next morning she was taken to hospital and X-rayed. She was found to have cancer of the spinal cord. There was no hope of saving her life, but a fair chance of prolonging it for a few months. However, within twenty-four hours she began to sink – her heart was giving out, and she lay all that night almost in coma. Joanna sat by her bedside. She felt again that enormous guilt. She asked herself if she had known all the time that Preedy was a fraud, if she had accepted him only to please Hooper.

In the morning, the old woman suddenly rallied, and demanded her tea. Then at once she remarked, 'I believe I'm going now.'

Joanna took her hand and tried to speak. The old woman looked at her and seemed surprised by her distress. She thought, 'After all I believe she really does love me.'

'Don't be so upset,' she said, 'and don't blame yourself or anybody else. It was my own fault – I'm an old fool. Send for Willett – I'll have to make some new arrangements.'

Willett was the lawyer. The old woman was dead before he arrived, but, as he explained, there was nothing he could have done to make any great difference in the state of her affairs. They were in confusion, on account of large sums lately paid out for the Pant's Road campaign.

These sums, together with the settlement on Joanna three years before, and an additional settlement in trust on the grandchildren, were now liable to death duties, and, owing to the depreciation in the Press shares, and the probable impossibility of selling the country property at a fair price, it was not even certain that the estate was solvent. The old woman's own paper,

Woman's News, had been losing money for years and had a large debt on its account.

This news was kept strictly private; only Joanna, the *Argus* directors, and the editorial staff of *Woman's News* were told. It was realized at once that there would have to be a sale of Rideout Press shares. However, the market, with or without any exact information, at once marked the shares down, and they became unsaleable.

The crisis united the directors; Hooper was given a free hand, and the paper came out, at last, with the new front page. It was not as yet a very daring front page; it had a half-page headline about the Russian leaders, a leaded summary and comment, and in the other half-page a picture of a lady ballerina who had entertained the Russians, the account of a new murder, a women's strike at a jam factory and an elopement to Gretna Green.

But though changes had been designed for weeks, the actual production of the new *Argus* did not go at all smoothly. For Cleary as well as Hooper the paper which was actually to appear had a very different look from the numerous mock-ups of the last six weeks. Hooper found it dull and imitative, and he demanded full details of the front-page murder, and a picture. He criticized the reporting as flat, and said, 'After all, good reporting, good writing is just exactly what sells a paper.' He pointed out that this murder was likely to become a first-class sensation, especially at a time when the anti-hanging Bill was being debated, and five-sixths of the population were asking themselves, in secret, whether they preferred to be poisoned by their wives or stabbed by a teddy-boy, in preference to admitting that they were on the whole, unprogressive, old-fashioned, and perhaps even illiberal.

Cleary, who had brought in the reporter responsible, was vigorous in his defence, and extremely irritated by Hooper's telling him that he had missed the significance of this piece of news. 'It has everything,' Hooper said, 'sex, violence, blood, mystery. And it happened at night. No woman in any country ever goes out alone at night without the fear of being raped and murdered – knocked down from behind and cut to pieces with an axe. They don't talk about it even to each other – but that makes it all the worse – bottled up and corked down inside 'em. And what have we got, a piece of board-school prose about the body of a girl found in a lane with multiple injuries. Multiple injuries, my God

- what language. And you said you were getting in some cubs who could handle a story.'

'Goddam it,' Cleary bawled, 'how long have you been around a newspaper? And didn't we agree to keep everything short on the front page?'

'Yes, short, but short doesn't mean dead. Your murder is a bloody corpse –'

The end of it was that Hooper dashed off to the scene of the crime, fifty miles out, and wrote it up himself for the late issue. And not only the reporter but a sub-editor was very nearly sacked. Neither could Cleary protest when Hooper quoted his own principle at him. 'A reporter who doesn't know that his job is to get essential concrete details is no good and never will be any good. Sack him on the spot for his own sake and the paper's.' He bitterly resented any interference with his authority as editor. What in God's name, he asked, had Hooper to do with the make-up from day to day? If Hooper wanted to be editor, let him say so.

But he did not propose to resign because he suspected that Hooper might accept a resignation. And Hooper, exhausted by this crisis on top of all his other anxieties, would certainly have accepted it. He was ready to scream with rage at the smallest opposition. To Joanna that night, after the new *Argus* had finally been passed for press, he seemed like a lunatic. He had come straight to Portland Place at two in the morning. He had long possessed a key, given him by Kate Rideout herself, and he let himself in.

He was startled to find the hall full of flowers, wreaths and crosses. He had forgotten that the funeral was next day. For a moment, it struck him that this was not a suitable time to call on Joanna. In fact, he had not intended to call on her. He had not seen her since her mother's death and he was not sure if he wanted to see her. Her Rideout Press shares, if she was able to keep them, were of small value, even in voting power.

But on his way from the office, he had suddenly found the idea of his flat distasteful. He was fearfully tired but his brain was whirling with ideas, with memoranda, with anger against Cleary and that worthless reporter, with a sense of triumph, and still stronger anxiety. What was going to happen to the *Argus*? What would old readers say to the new look? It had been losing old readers fast, but gaining some new ones. And what about the banks? Would they lend any more money?

Suddenly he had turned his car and made north. He did not say to himself, 'After all, I could call on Joanna – it doesn't commit me to anything. I could ditch her just as easily next week – any time,' but this judgement had worked itself out at some lower level of consciousness. Neither did he ask himself why he preferred to see this girl to going home.

And as he stared at the flowers he thought again with impatience, 'What's it matter – I'm not proposing to go to bed with her, never again.'

He turned to the stairs, meaning to go to her room. But at the same moment, she appeared at the first half landing, in a dark dressing-gown. She came down slowly, looking at him with an anxious and inquiring expression. Without make-up she looked old and ugly; he thought with irritation, 'Why must she be such a gargoyle?'

'Is anything wrong?' she asked, stopping at three steps from the floor.

'No, I just dropped in.'

'You look fearfully tired – wouldn't you like a drink? Come into the back room. No, the dining-room would be better.'

'Why not the back room?' He made for the little back room. He knew there were comfortable chairs there, a couch where he had often lain with Joanna. The dining-room, cool and formal, had no couch.

But when he opened the door he saw the coffin there on its trestle. Even then he hesitated. It seemed that he had been reckoning on that couch for the last twenty minutes, ever since he had turned the car. Joanna touched his arm and murmured, 'You see.'

And at once, he was irritated by her assumption that it was impossible to converse with a woman in the same room where her mother was lying dead. It irritated him by the very fact that he understood her feelings. Why should it be impossible? Why should anything be made impossible by sentiment? Wasn't that just the kind of weakness, of feeble 'niceness' that was wrecking the country and civilization itself?

'Why not?' he said. 'I only want to talk to you. She wouldn't mind.'

Joanna at once switched on the light and waved him to a chair. 'I'll get you a drink.'

Hooper threw himself on the couch and put his hands behind his head. He did not look at the coffin but he was strongly aware of it and grew still more angry. It represented for him all that mysterious enemy that he was fighting, that might still destroy him and what was much more important, free civilization. The old liberal in her coffin seemed more formidable than in her life. It was death that gave its fearful weight to the dead hand. 'Nothing but good about the dead.' What a lie. Of a piece with all this English softness, sentiment, slop. He looked angrily at Joanna as she stood before him, the glass in her hand. How typical she was. So nice, so gentle, so conscience-ridden, ripe for the slaughter.

'Any more news of the will?' he said, for it would shock her to speak of the will in this room at this moment.

'It won't be read till after the funeral but it's obvious that there won't be much for anyone – if anything.'

'No, I suppose not. What will you do if you've nothing to live on?'

'I suppose I could get a job of some kind.'

'I doubt if they'd take you on in a shop.'

'You mean I'm not pretty enough.'

'Not for any of the better shops – and you can't type.'

'I could learn.'

'I believe you're rather enjoying the idea – becoming one with the workers.'

'I've enjoyed working at Pant's Road. There's so little I've done that was really useful.'

'No, you didn't even help to sink the old *Argus*.'

'Is it sunk?'

'It sank tonight – but not until it damn nearly killed me.'

'I suppose you've had an awful day.'

'You're telling me. The old hulk was full of crabs – there doesn't seem to be anything else in the sub-editor's room. Old shellbacks that have been chewing on Fowler for forty years.'

'What's Fowler?'

'An old shellback who chewed on English syntax for forty years and turned it into a coprolite.'

Joanna didn't ask what a coprolite was. She was, as usual,

giving very little attention to Hooper's talk – and tonight she was also but slightly interested in his mood. It was too familiar to her. What she noticed was his extreme paleness, the dark hammocks under his bloodshot eyes, his whole exhaustion. She said, 'You're all in – you ought to be in bed.'

'Is that an offer?'

'If you like.'

'Why don't you hit me?'

'What would be the good?'

'That's better – that's damned rude.'

'I didn't mean it to be.'

'Don't take it back, for God's sake. And don't leave me like that. I can't bear it.'

'Have another drink.'

'Since you fell for Preedy, you've been lurving everybody. You've simply come apart – you're nothing but lurve.'

'Shall I get you another drink?'

'Do you listen to a word I say?'

'I wish you weren't so tired – and the Albert Hall on Sunday.'

'You make me tired – how wouldn't I be tired – fighting that bloody gang of blimps and has-beens. And old Cleary who was supposed to be a live wire – but there aren't any more in England. The old mud heap is diminishing into slop – you can't make it stand up – not while it's still wet. And it always is wet – with tears for poor brother somebody.'

'I had a ring from Kerne about the list of patients for the Albert Hall.'

'Why did he ring you?'

'Because you were at the office and it had to be private. Preedy asked for the list and he wants to know how it was made up.'

'Oh, so he's on about that again. He would –'

From the very first Hooper had realized that the Albert Hall meeting must be a success, that is to say, there must be some cures. At ordinary services, it was not uncommon to have a blank day, or at any rate a day when, at the best, only one or two patients thought they felt better. But a blank day at the Albert Hall would be a disaster.

He had put it to the committee, pointing out that this was not an ordinary occasion. The crowds, the lights, would produce a special atmosphere which might be discouraging to patients. It was completely different from the ordinary Pant's Road services because it was unique. At Pant's Road a blank day would be succeeded by a successful day, but at the Albert Hall there would be no chance to retrieve a failure. He proposed, therefore, to cut out of the list for that day certain classes of patient which, as experience showed, were unlikely to benefit and might even make a disturbance. For instance, epileptics could be excluded.

Marris and Mrs Hartree had held out for the principle, first come, first served, without distinction. But Hooper had given an ultimatum – he would abandon the whole plan of an Albert Hall meeting if there were no selection of cases. And first Marris and then Preedy himself had so far come round to his view that they agreed to leave out the more difficult patients and instead give them special services at Pant's Road.

As Preedy had said, 'God's work would be enormously helped by a striking success at the Albert Hall, and it is only common sense to avoid the chance of failure.'

He had preached, for Mrs Hartree's benefit, at this time, a sermon on God's good reason which, though the real motive was known only to committee members present, had great effect. 'Christians,' he said, 'even the best of Christians, sometimes speak of common sense, of prudence, with contempt. They use the phrase, "a good business man", as if it were a reproach. As if it were better for a man's soul to be a reckless fool than to use his brains. But this is a folly, and more than folly, a wickedness, it is a crime against God, to despise reason. For it is God's own reason. God has given us reason for his own good end, for the safety and happiness of mankind. Religion itself requires reason, planning. Without thought, without organization, there could be no churches. The Christian life has two aspects, the duty of the free individual soul, standing naked and alone, to his God; and the duty of a man to his fellows. Neither can be discharged without reason. For it is by reason that we know ourselves, that we examine our own hearts and discover our own weakness, and it is by reason that mankind institutes the laws by which men in the mass can have the security to serve good ends, the Christian ends of peace and happiness. God is the God of truth, of reason as well as love; it is with reason that he teaches us to serve the cause of loving kindness.'

This sermon won over Mrs Hartree, and the committee had

finally approved a select list for the Albert Hall. Kerne and All-day, who were in charge of the selection, both had by now an almost intuitive knowledge of the kind of case most likely to respond to treatment. They knew that the delicate nervous girl might be, in fact, hopelessly critical and obstinate, the plump city man with his red face and confident careless air, making light of mysterious pains, a certain cure -- especially if he believed himself to have cancer.

Experience showed that a high proportion of cancer cases were favourable. As Kerne had remarked, most of these did not have cancer at all, but only a vague pain and big fear. And it was just such nervous and hysterical 'cancer' cases who, having been told by their own doctors that there was nothing wrong with them, were likely to come, in despair, to Pant's Road and demand treatment, because, 'It's no good going to the doctors – they don't understand my case.'

But there were two objections to accepting such cases for the big meetings. One was that cancer cures have no value as a spectacle, the other was Lady Rideout's case. It was realized that an inquest had been avoided only by the luck of her putting herself back into the doctor's hands at the last moment.

So the list of fifty, as finally made up, consisted chiefly of cripples, in a suitable mixture of ages, distributed among chairs and stretchers, and a few blind.

48

The next night, when Preedy's Albert Hall service of healing had already been advertised for a fortnight, Fred Rodker again broke all the windows of the Pant's Road chapel. But the committee refused to charge the young man and ordered new windows protected by wire mesh. Rodker then smashed a plate-glass window at the Health Ministry and was arrested. Pant's Road called an emergency committee meeting. It was now well known to all the members that Preedy visited the Rodker girl, and they were greatly alarmed by the idea of a public revelation. Dr Jinks criticized Preedy and suggested a protest. Jinks was a large subscriber, who had also valuable connexions with evangelical circles. He had written a popular book about miracles in the New

Testament and his name on the committee had brought visits from influential ministers. He was horrified by the idea of Preedy's sin, and by the possibility of further revelations which would damage the Mission and therefore his own credit. He wanted to make representations to Preedy.

Hooper answered that representations would be an insult to their Missioner. Surely they had confidence in a man whose wonderful work was so well known to them. 'The way to treat people like Rodker,' he said, 'is to pay no attention to them. It doesn't matter what he says or does or what's printed either, so long as we don't answer it. The public is used to grievance-mongers and despises 'em – they'll put him down for a crack-pot. If the Missioner is asked for a statement he can say that Rodker is referring to ancient history, that it is a private matter between himself and Miss Rodker, and that he has no fear of any inquiry.'

'What if they take him at his word?' Jinks demanded.

'He needn't answer – and the papers will drop the thing in a day or two – if they ever take it up.'

The rest of the committee were inclined to follow Hooper's advice. He had already a commanding position. Everyone recognized that his handling of the campaign had been a personal triumph. The 'Pant's Road Battle of Britain' was his idea, which is still quoted as a model in standard works on propaganda. Even if he did not invent the name, suggested first by a professional, he saw its value and adopted it against the strongest opposition from Ackroyd, Allday, and the Press generally. As he said, 'Of course it's shocking bad taste, but that's what we want – to give 'em a shock – to make 'em wake up. You've got to wake 'em up before you can make 'em listen. Of course, some of 'em are angry and are making a row. Of course, it's done us harm. But much more good. Because for one person that cares about taste or even knows what it is, there's about a thousand who are wondering how to care about anything – they don't even care very much about life. The early Christians hadn't much taste either – they were all for smashing those nice, domesticated Roman gods. But they won out – they gave people something to live for.'

49

Alice Rodker knew of her brother's action only when she saw it in the evening paper. It gave her a shock of horror and rage. She had not taken his threats seriously till this moment. She imagined her name again in the papers. Every Sunday she read in the *News of the World* and the *People*, about girls deceived, deserted, betrayed. She turned to them first, especially if there were pictures, 'Victim of the tragedy at Glasgow,' 'Found wandering', 'Mother at fourteen.' She would gaze for a long time at the photographs, as if by staring she could see what was really happening in this woman's soul. If she was suffering and how. If she had been in love. How she felt to find herself a public show. How she would feel in the street when people recognized her, when she saw them looking at her and knew that they were thinking, 'That's the girl who was had by those Teddy boys; that's the one who ran away with a married man of forty and told the magistrate she loved him still and wanted to go back to him.'

And now this. Preedy had been with her only two nights ago. Was that to come out and all the other visits. She felt as if she was to be rolled in filth; and suddenly running to her bedroom snatched up an aspirin bottle. But the very act, the very power to kill herself, enraged her against those who were making her life impossible. Why should she die? Why should she lose everything, why should she lose the very memory of her love because of these fools and brutes?

She put on her shoes and ran out to a telephone booth. Perhaps Joanna had enough influence with that man Hooper and he could stop the papers printing Fred's story.

The message was given to Joanna as she was dressing for supper with Hooper.

Tonight she knew that he was in a critical mood, that some new change had taken place in a relation that changed every day, always tense, nervous, wary, and that it was favourable to her. He was critical but strongly aware of her; he had squeezed her arm as she came from her room, hard enough to bruise it. And she had learnt that this was a punishment inflicted on the slave for an injury to the master's pride of independence. He was attracted or at least excited, and he satisfied both his passion and his pride by hurting her. But he was hers for the evening, she would be a woman to him and he was her man.

So that she was annoyed when the phone rang and she answered Alice Rodker that, no, she could not see her that evening, she had an engagement.

'Who is it?' Hooper said. He had followed her to the box under the stairs. He was in that respect like a tyrannical husband. He treated all her affairs as his, and often said when she pleaded some engagement, 'You can't go – I want you at Pant's Road,' or 'That's just a waste of time. You've better things to do than that.'

Joanna covered the receiver with her hand. 'It's the Rodker girl.'

'Is it indeed? What's she want?'

'To see me about her brother.'

'What, now?'

'Yes, this evening.'

'Here or there? Better go to her. Find out where she is.'

'But is there time?'

'My God, what are you worrying about? To hell with everything else. Don't you realize how important this is – either way? Whether she's going to help or whether she's turning against us. Tell her you'll be round at once. I'll drive you.'

'But, Harry –'

'Harry be damned. Hurry up, hurry up – what are you thinking of.'

And as he drove her west he instructed her on handling the Rodker girl. 'She already thinks you've got special influence. It's the name. If she wants to stop the brother talking, you can promise that the *Argus* won't repeat anything – if she's got some new hate about Preedy and is backing the brother, find out why and what her plans are.'

And at the door he had taken her wrist and jerked it and said, 'Look here – do you realize this is something that really matters? Or are you sulking?'

'Of course I know it's important.'

'If this chap gets loose at the Albert Hall he could smash our friend – and the whole show.'

Joanna, on the verge of saying, in her sulky mood, 'I know –

I'm not a fool,' checked herself and put on a tone of surprise. 'Do you really think he's so dangerous?'

'My God, yes. When are you going to realize that Preedy is a big risk?'

'I'll do what I can – where shall I find you?'

'It's no good me waiting. I'll go on home – you can get a taxi.'

'You don't want me to come in?'

Hooper hesitated and she knew exactly what was in his mind. Would it sound too encouraging if he said yes. But the very hesitation showed that he wanted her. She said quickly, 'I'll phone my report.'

'Yes, or come up if it's not too late.'

'Right, I won't stay if you're busy,' and as she went into the house she gave a little snort of laughter. She could still feel the bruise on her forearm, she knew what would happen at the flat. She already enjoyed that time when, languid and satisfied, he would lie on her arm and chatter about his plans, his battles with Ackroyd and Cleary, the new appointments on the *Argus*, forgetting her so completely that if, when her arm was numbed she tried to move it, he would start as if bitten and say, 'What's wrong now – can't you keep quiet for two minutes? Do let's have a little peace for once.'

She knocked at the door of Alice's room, and had suddenly to change her expression, to assume a less gay, less triumphant air, when she heard her step.

'Oh, you've come.'

'I was as quick as I could manage – I'm so sorry for this worry. What a nuisance for you.'

'It could be a nuisance for you too – and that chap of yours.' This in a threatening tone.

'What do you mean?'

'You know, the newspaper chap. He's working for Preedy, isn't he. And if Fred brings everything up, it will finish Preedy.'

'Do you really think so? It's such an old story now.'

The two women looked at each other, Joanna was asking herself what the threat meant, what was going on in this mind so different from hers. For her Alice was a primitive creature, elementary in all her ideas and impulses. And Alice, frowning at Joanna's lovely mink coat, was asking herself, 'Can I trust this lady, full of all sorts of fancy tricks and tied up with all the

things that happen in newspapers, with government and politics
– not only that, but with a man who writes in them?'

'It's not such an old story,' she said.

'You mean he's been seeing you?'

'I didn't mean anything. I suppose you'll go and tell your chap everything I say.'

'I can promise you anything you say will be kept strictly private. The whole idea is to avoid publicity. Mr Hooper believes in Mr Preedy's Mission and so do I. He's doing quite wonderful work.'

'Killing people.'

'You're fond of Mr Preedy, aren't you? You don't want to ruin him?'

'I don't want anything in the papers. How would you like it if they put you in the papers – you and your chap? Do you let him have you? I bet he does. Do you love him? Well, you asked me so why shouldn't I ask you? All right, you're not going to tell but how would you like it all in the papers? With your picture. And people all over looking at you and saying, "That's the bitch that's been turning it up" – how would you like that?'

Alice had become very red and was talking in a harsh voice. 'Disgusting,' she said, mimicking a lady-like tone. 'Oh, how horrible they are – those horrid crea-tures – going to bed with horrid nas-ty men.'

'That's nonsense,' said Joanna, flushing. 'I don't think like that. It's disgusting to think like that.'

'But you put it in your papers like that.'

'They're not my papers. You don't understand.'

'Does he have you – your chap?'

'That's my own business.'

'Well it's my own business too – and what I think of Preedy and what I did with Preedy and what he does with me and whether I love him or hate him – it's all, all, my own business and I'm not going to have it changed into dirt and lies in the papers.'

'I tell you it won't be if I can help it. That's why I've come, to know what we can do.'

'Fred's going to the meeting with a loudspeaker. He's got some other chap to help.'

'But it's all so old – and if he tells lies, he can be contradicted.'

214

The two women looked at each other again. At last Alice said, 'You swear there won't be anything come out?'

'I tell you that's the whole idea.'

'Well, he's been seeing me every week – I can't stop him. And Fred knows – he's never caught him – but he knows.'

'You are fond of him then?'

'Never mind what I am. I hate him coming. I never want to see him again. But that doesn't stop him. He's mad. He's got God on the brain, and he thinks he's damned. He is damned – he's a damned nuisance.'

'But couldn't you warn him about your brother?'

'Warn him. That makes him worse. He's mad, I tell you. He needs a keeper. Why, look at the murders he's doing all the time.'

'The only other thing would be to stop your brother at the Albert Hall – catch him before he interferes. If anyone could only point him out before he started.'

'You'd put someone on to him.'

'After all, it's only to save him from trouble – he'll end in jail if he goes on.'

'He'd never forgive me.'

'He needn't know – and it's for his own good.' Alice sat, red and fuming. She was full of rage against Preedy, against her brother, against all the world. She said at last, 'He ought to be in jail – that's where he ought to be. I told him to let me alone. What business is it of his what I do. It's my own life. I could throw myself out of the window if I liked and what's that to him – or Preedy – or the papers either. And if they give him the option I won't pay. I've got the money. But I won't pay. I said he could go to jail and I'll let him go. And if they give him fourteen days, he won't be able to do the Albert Hall.'

'Is it safe to count on his going to jail at all?'

'I'm not going to put a detective on him – it's hard enough not to pay his fine. And if you go on at me, I'll put myself in the river and then it will all come out. And let it. If I'll be dead, they can print all the dirt they like. I'm fed up, I'm fed up with the whole lot of you, dirty snoopers and murderers.'

She was screaming, and made a gesture as if to fly at Joanna, then suddenly began to sob. Joanna began to soothe her, 'Don't, don't – it will be all right.'

The girl, gasping, trying to catch her hysteria, turned on her and shouted, 'What did you come here for? You're just having me on like all the rest – all the other dirty spivs working their dirty rackets. I know your sort – you'll tell on me to that chap of yours just to sweeten him up so he'll come down with a few diamonds – you'd sell me for a cuddle.'

Joanna jumped up in a fury, 'That's enough – good-bye.'

But the girl seized her by the front of her coat.

'I've told you, you tell me – he has you?'

'Yes, of course he does. Why not, what of it? Go and tell if you like.'

And to her surprise, the girl suddenly fell against her and began to sob.

Joanna, who had not cried from childhood, was shocked. She stroked her and murmured, 'Don't do that – it's all right. I shan't tell on you.' She drew her to the couch, and made her sit. But she still clung to Joanna.

'I knew you were nice,' she said, 'I thought you were nice first time I saw you, with that chap. I thought he was giving you a bad time too – and you were hating it like me. It's awful to have to do with a beast. You can't get on and you can't get off.'

'I know – I know.'

'Bossing you about – sending you here to worm it out of me. And why, why? But you like it, do you? He's got you.'

And Joanna, to her own surprise, as if this question had found its own answer in a reaction deeper than her mind, answered, 'Yes, he's got me.'

'You love him?'

'I don't know – sometimes.'

'That's what it is – and then you hate him. You wish he was dead – you wish you'd never seen him. He has you and you do it to spite him and make him feel like dirt and then you feel like dirt and what does he care. He's up in the air again as soon as his thing is flat. He's the great man – he's the great big name and if you spat in his face he'd only laugh at you. He'd only say, poor kid, what does she know – that's what she's for but of course you mustn't tell her. She's got to take it, so what. Or she don't get nothing at all.'

'Preedy treated you very badly.'

'I never said so.' She jerked away from Joanna. For a moment she seemed about to fly out again.

'What do you mean then?' Joanna said, irritated on her side.

'I said he was mad – it's this God stuff. But you believe in him now, I mean, Preedy's God.'

'Yes, but still I think he treated you cruelly.'

Alice, as suddenly placated, said in a gloomy, disgusted tone, 'I was just a kid. I thought he needed me – yes, I asked for it.'

'But now – if he wants you why doesn't he marry you?'

'He's all against prophets getting married. Does your chap mean to marry you?'

'I don't think so – I don't know if I want to marry him.'

'He hasn't got you so much as Preedy's got me.'

'He's got me a good deal.'

'Did he send you along today to do the job for him?'

'He said I ought to come.'

'I thought so – when you told me to hold on. Well, I've done something for you. You can tell him you found out about the Albert Hall plan. You didn't, I told you, but you can say you found out.'

'I won't say a word about Preedy coming still.'

'No –' Alice stared at her suspiciously. 'That's a promise, isn't it? I'm trusting you.'

'And I'm trusting you.'

'Yes, but what would you care if it came out about you and him?'

'I'd care a lot.'

'Well, I've got to trust you.'

'It's a bargain.'

'Mind you, I don't expect a lot. What can you do with a fellow like Preedy? But I expect you have your troubles too.'

'What can I do about Preedy?'

'Stop him coming. Keep it out of the papers. Even if Fred talks – don't let them print it. And you can tell your chap we're friends and I won't do anything to upset his little game if he lets me alone and keeps me out of the papers.'

'I'll do what I can.' Joanna got up.

'Yes. He's waiting and you're just longing to go. But I'm trusting you.'

'I won't tell a word.'

The girl put forward her face, frowning, as if to say, 'You can

217

take it or leave it.' Joanna kissed her and she put her arms round
her and held her. 'I'm trusting you – as a real friend.'

'Yes, we're friends.'

'I'm trusting you.'

These were the last words. And Joanna was glad to escape to
the street. She was exhausted. She did not know whether to laugh
at this naïve creature who contradicted herself every moment, or
to admire her. Was she a friend? How could she be friends with
anyone so different? And yet this evening, the meeting was un-
forgettable. Alice had done something to her – it was as though
she had torn down barriers and veils. And she was still in her
mind – her looks, her tone of voice, were still vivid to Joanna's
feeling, the girl was lodged in her mind. Like something hard and
definite, not to be melted away into social adjustment.

She had to walk half a mile for a taxi, but she was glad to be
alone with herself in the streets, to let her pulses grow quieter.

Suddenly at the corner of the main road, in a house window
opposite a street lamp, a poster jumped to her eye. It was one of
the big red, white and blue posters advertising the Albert Hall
meeting, which the campaign committee had distributed to
householders all over London. And underneath the great headlines, 'Battle of Britain Mission of Healing. The Rev. W.
Preedy,' there were three lines of smaller print giving addresses to
which patients could apply for admission to the special service,
particulars of the volunteers who would drive the sick to and
from the Albert Hall. And underneath in bold black type, the
signature, 'Harry Hooper, Chairman of the Campaign Committee.'

The self-display, and back-slapping appeal of the 'Harry' as
usual moved Joanna to disgust; but the disgust instantly produced a reaction. How small to be offended, to think of Hooper in
his great and important task as vulgar.

'He's got to use the popular touch,' she thought. 'And he's got
to advertise himself – he's got to keep his name before the public
or he won't be able to do anything. And he really is trying to do
something important. Something he really believes in. Yes,' she
answered herself as she waved for a taxi, 'and I believe in it too.
I believe – I believe –'

Hooper received her with particular indifference, probably
because he wanted her.

Having opened the door to her, he said, 'Oh, it's you – you could have phoned.' And then, 'Sit down a moment – I've got to finish this article.'

He considered her interview with the Rodker girl unsatisfactory. She should have found out more particulars – for instance, if Preedy was still seeing her. But he would soon put a stop to the loudspeaker business. Then he pretended that she had come to make love. 'Oh well, I know what you want – let's get it over.'

As she went to bed that night, she thought, 'I really am in love with him – sometimes. I shouldn't like to be his wife –' and then she reflected a moment and thought, 'But he would never marry me – he wants to be free.' She felt again a deep fear. She realized that she could not bear to lose Hooper, or at least, the life that he had taught her. At the idea of being without him, she seemed to be falling, falling, once more into that gulf of boredom and frustration in which she had hung suspended for so long.

50

Fred Rodker, brought into court next day, stated that his action was meant to expose a crook who ought to be put in jail before he brought off this Albert Hall show which was a bit too much even for a religious swindle.

Stipendiaries are used to hearing the wildest tales in court and Rodker's impassioned speech was listened to with business-like patience. The magistrate's expression as he leaned back in his chair said plainly, 'Perhaps there is something in all this, it's not very likely, but you never know.'

But when Rodker, asked why he had broken the Ministry of Health windows, began to talk about Preedy's relations with his sister, 'And he goes on pestering her,' the magistrate checked him and asked a policeman if he knew anything about the case. The policeman answered that he had seen the sister who was of full age and said she had no complaint to make against anyone and it was her brother who was making all the trouble out of jealousy.

Rodker agreed that the sister was of full age, and when he tried to get back to his charges against Preedy, he was sharply checked. He received a sentence of fourteen days or a fine of five pounds which was paid in a few minutes.

The *Argus* did not report the case. Some of the other papers had a paragraph, but they were cautious, and the general impression was encouraged that the young man was cracked.

In fact, this protest of Rodker's seemed like a failure. But the Pant's Road Mission and Preedy's name were mentioned, and it was also revealed, discreetly, that Rodker was complaining of an actual situation, that Preedy was visiting the girl. And two papers had a note that the Albert Hall meeting referred to was due on the next Sunday evening.

51

Preedy had addressed his sermon not only to the Pant's Road congregation but to himself, and it convinced him. The point he made to Marris afterwards was that the Albert Hall occasion was unique, and that the selected list would be used only there. All patients would be received at Pant's Road.

But it happened that the day before the Albert Hall when Preedy, Allday and Kerne were going to the office in the morning, they were accosted by a woman, limping on a stick, who had been refused by Kerne for the Albert Hall list. She appealed direct to Preedy, 'Why won't you have me? I'm just what you need. I'm ready to testify; and I know how to do it.'

'What do you mean, testify?'

'Why, to be cured.'

'How so – cured? How do you know – what's wrong with you?' She indicated Kerne with an inclination of her head. 'I told him I'd do anything he wanted. I could be on a stretcher and I've got some medical knowledge – I know all the symptoms.'

Preedy was surprised, 'Do you mean you offered to act the part of a cripple?'

'I am a cripple. Can't you see? Polio. My right leg's in an iron. But I can walk a little without the iron. I could get up from the stretcher and walk like the man in the Bible.'

'But that would be a fraud. Do you really think we could allow such a thing?'

'You need some cures so I'm offering you one. Think of the effect. And I know how to do it. I've done it twice before and both times it's been a big sensation.'

Allday said abruptly, 'Do you get paid for the job?'

'Paid – what are you thinking of? I couldn't take money for doing the Lord's work. I'm not like the parsons. I'm a believer – God will provide and He does provide. It's because I believe I try to help his work.'

'You can't help his work by acting a lie,' said Allday.

'Why, the first time I did it, up north, it was in all the local papers and filled the church for weeks. I should think I brought a hundred souls back to God – and it isn't a lie neither. God did make me walk on that leg. Why, I used to be in a chair all the time but Mr Leather gave me faith-healing and I got up and walked – it was a miracle.'

'All the same, it would be a lie if you did it again.'

The woman became abusive and told Preedy that she was a better Christian than he was – a common enough charge from her kind.

Suddenly Preedy turned upon her and shouted, 'Get out – get out,' and made a gesture so alarming that the poor creature started back and nearly fell. He then turned round and made off. The other two had to run to catch up with him. He was still in a fury.

'There's a foul thing.'

'I had my suspicions,' said Kerne, 'that's why I wouldn't accept her for the Albert Hall list.'

'Your list seems to me a fake.'

Allday and Kerne were thunderstruck. After a moment Allday said, 'You agreed there had to be some selection.'

'Yes, some faking. I never liked it.'

'But surely this very case shows how necessary it is to take some precautions. If that woman had been admitted we should be wide open to a charge of fraud.'

'You have no right to refuse her – we have no right to refuse anybody. Yes, I know I approved the selection – and preached about God's reason – God forgive me. What do we stand for? What do we believe in? That God has to be protected from fools and crooks – what sort of God is that?'

'But at the Albert Hall,' Allday muttered, 'as a special –'

'At the Albert Hall. What is the Albert Hall? We're all so afraid of a failure there. We're so afraid that already we've made sure of a failure. We've made a fake and a lie of it. I won't have your list, Kerne. If you use it, I won't go to the Albert Hall. I'll hold a service in the street outside, for all comers.'

They'd reached the door of the office. Kerne and Allday halted there to turn in, but Preedy walked on. And they did not dare to follow. But neither did they tell anyone else on the committee, much less Hooper, of his rebellion. They hoped that he would come back from his walk, as often, in a calmer, more reasonable state of mind.

But on the contrary, he did not come back at all that day. And on the next, the actual morning of the Albert Hall meeting, he telephoned to the committee from some unknown address to say that he would not appear unless the list was thrown open to all comers. Names must be taken in order from the register and he would deal with the first fifty.

52

Preedy's first and last Albert Hall meeting, so much advertised, was a failure, almost from the beginning. It began indeed in such elation and fervour that probably no one of the 8,000 people present was not affected. But from the moment of Preedy's own appearance this tension of excited hope began to leak away. Preedy repeated the prayers in an absent-minded manner, as if he were performing a task, and his first short address was chiefly an attack on unbelief, an attack which appeared to be aimed at most of the audience. His text was, 'Whom have ye come out to see', and he suggested that most of the people in the hall had come there merely from curiosity. They didn't believe, and they didn't want to believe; they didn't want to change their ways, and those whose ways were most self-indulgent, most removed from any kind of faith, were least ready to change them.

But the most serious failure was in the healing. There were no spectacular cures whatever; nobody was made to get up and walk; no blind person was given back his sight. Men who arrived limping on to the platform returned limping. Half a dozen people declared themselves cured of various diseases, one man of cancer, another of rheumatism, a third of an ulcer, but they showed no difference, and the audience was obviously sceptical. The last hymn was sung only by the massed choirs, very few of the audience joined in; most were already leaving.

Hooper and the committee had already written their report of an immense success which was duly sent to the papers, posted on the mission chapels and meeting halls, and hung in the windows of sympathizers throughout the country. Actually, there was consternation, and Hooper called a committee meeting that same evening to discuss the disaster. Again the committee showed its deep division between those who supported Preedy whatever happened and those who were always doubtful of his fitness to be at the head of such a campaign. His supporters now declared first of all that the meeting had been a success, and then that it had suffered from certain disadvantages which were not Preedy's fault. The afternoon had been wet, which kept some people away. Then certain evangelists who had been expected to carry placards on the pavement outside had been driven in by the rain. Also it was complained that anti-mission pamphlets had been distributed in unprecedented numbers, not only to the audience as they walked in, but in the streets at bus stops, both before and after the meeting. And one of these, so Marris claimed, had done special damage. It consisted of a single sheet, once folded, with the title, 'All or None' and it purported to be put out by the Truth Society.

For the most part this had put forward the usual rationalist arguments against miraculous intervention in the chain of causation, already proved by scientific inquiry to be completely determined. All this was common form and had been said so often that it could have no effect on anyone of religious intuition; but there was one damaging clause – this, according to Marris, was sufficient to explain most of the failure of enthusiasm at the meeting. The writer declared that Preedy was accustomed to select his cases for public appearance, in order to get spectacular cures. 'For instance, wheel-chair cases, or stretcher cases, in which the patient or victim actually gets up and walks off the stage will always be preferred to those suffering from internal complaints whose cure, or pretended cure, makes no impression on an audience. It should be noticed that his policy is quite different from Mr Preedy's private practice and his actual statement of faith. He claims to accept all cases – with a consequence that has already been commented on by a coroner's jury, and may well bring him into court again on a similar charge.'

This leaflet was obviously libel, and some of Preedy's more devoted supporters were eager to bring an action at once. They were especially irritated, since selection had not been practised at the meeting, and it was precisely because it had not been that the healing itself, as a show, had been a fiasco.

It was agreed to inquire who had put out this leaflet, but two or three members of the committee were ready to assure them that the author was Syson and that the Rational Truth Society was simply another name for this malcontent.

53

It was quite true that Syson had written the pamphlet, which in the next weeks was distributed outside all Preedy's branch chapels, and at the mother church itself. From the very first it did Preedy immense damage and raised the question everywhere, 'Why doesn't he bring a libel action?' When the news was passed round that Syson was the author of the libel, people began to feel that prejudice against him which was shown so vividly in the violent scenes before and after his trial at Bow Street. He had got the reputation of vindictiveness, and that is an unpopular vice.

In fact, Syson had much less to do with the second attack on Preedy than Tinney. It was Tinney who had suggested the leaflet and had raised the funds for printing and distribution, for at this time Tinney absolutely controlled the Rational Truth Society. In the last few months since his resignation from the *Argus*'s board, he had taken charge of the Society and reorganized it with enthusiastic support from a millionaire chemical manufacturer, a lapsed Irish Catholic and notorious fanatic, who had for years subsidized various rationalist enterprises. But Tinney's new enthusiasm was a surprise to most people who knew him. As an old-fashioned Victorian radical he had always stood for scientific determinism but he had never shown any violent bias against the Church; he had treated it as moribund, and spoken of it with the good-natured cynicism of a man who regards nine-tenths of humanity as fools. But his closest friends knew that in the last year or two he had been seriously alarmed about what he called the religious reaction. He had come back from a tour in the United States very deeply impressed by the revival there. He assured his friends with astonishment that more than half the population in the States attended some church or other, 'It's an eye-opener,' he said, 'of the real state of affairs. If we don't look out the same thing will happen here, and we shall be back where we were a hundred years ago; in fact, we shall be a good deal worse off because this new reaction knows what it's up against. It's taken our measure and it's organized for attack. It's got big business behind it, big business and the government; all the governments, and it's out for blood. Already it's demanding every kind of censorship. That Horror Comics Bill was a warning. Look at the support they got there; there was scarcely any opposition at all. Of course, they picked their point of attack. They jumped at a chance to get at mama and papa. They worked up a scare about juvenile delinquency, which is always first-class news in the papers, and they roped in some of these psychiatrists to talk about sadism. You can get psychiatrists to say anything, most of them are batty on their own account. And don't forget the Censorship Bill which stopped the papers from getting full reports of court cases, which actually cut them down more than had ever been attempted under old Gladstone. That went through so easily that nobody even noticed it. And now they're waiting for the next big move; in ten years we shan't have any more freedom to write or print the truth than they have in Russia or any of these new national republics. So far as I can see nobody will care one damn. The fact is that nobody cares for the truth any more. I don't know whether it's because of the discovery that the big lie always wins or simply that everybody's got too comfortable. I've never known a time when people were so little interested in anything that matters. They don't care for politics, not real politics; they don't care for truth, they don't care for anything except peace and a good pay packet.'

For the first time in his life he became a bore, a monomaniac, on this subject of the return of superstition, the rise of new oppressors of the truth, the end of freedom; and people said of him that he was growing senile. But Tinney was not senile, he was simply frightened. He had had such a shock that he had ceased to bother about manners or his public appearance; he ceased to strike attitudes. He felt there was no time to waste on trifles; he had to save the world. Old men are like old mountains. As they wear down and lose their softer parts they show the hard core underneath, often in an unexpected form. So now, cynical Tinney, who had loved to be regarded among scientists as an accomplished man of the world, and among men of the world as a scientist, who had thoroughly enjoyed shocking the public with some mischievous jibe, suddenly appeared as a fanatical mono-maniac, of a type belonging to the late eighties. He was still fighting the battle that his father had fought for the Darwinites; he was still raging against old Wilberforce.

When he had found that the Rational Truth Society consisted of thirty or forty subscribers, all over sixty, and an unpaid secretary of seventy-three whose office was a desk in his own back room, Tinney put money into it, and a few younger recruits. Thanks to his appearances on television and the B.B.C. he was still a big name among the crowd who knew nothing about science and less about politics or religion. A television interview about the new Victorianism brought him a good deal of support among science students, especially in the north; in fact, it came most strongly just from those parts of the country where the evangelical churches still had power and authority. Also he revived the Society magazine and looked for contributors. This was how he met Syson. He wanted an article from him about the slander case and the faith-healing missions, and went to seek him out. He found that he had resigned his curacy and left the Pant's Road district on his bankruptcy. His wife and children had gone home to her parents, and even his oldest friends at St Enoch's did not know his address. But Tinney was as persistent on the trail as any monomaniac. He went to the police who, in a couple of hours, found out from a local chemist who had sent Syson some medicine to an address off the Tottenham Court Road. And here Tinney found him, still wearing a dog-collar, though otherwise very un-clerically attired in tweed coat and corduroy trousers, taking what he described as a refresher course at the British Museum. That is to say, the man was reading theology, philosophy, church history, the largest books on the largest subjects. He was lodging with three university students and Tinney, at his very first visit, was involved with the whole party and half a dozen visitors, students also, in a discussion about the meaning of life.

Apparently a student had lately committed suicide. Tinney had not heard of the case; one of those that happen every year in which coroners and their juries, having discovered that the deceased had not been disappointed in love, had no debts and no troubles at home, had not failed in an examination, and was far from friendless, fall into extreme perplexity and produce riders like, 'No adequate reason has appeared for this tragic act.' One of the students present, a fair youth in spectacles, had known this boy of nineteen, and he said that what had bothered him was simply the question of what life is for.

'I saw him only the night before and he was talking about it the whole time. He asked me if I could see any sense in it.'

'And what did you tell him?' asked one of the girls, a dark young woman with a pony-tail.

'All I could say was I knew what I wanted to do with it.'

'Research into what-is-it,' said the girl. 'That wasn't much good to him.'

Here Syson took his curly bulldog pipe out of his mouth to remark very gravely that research might be a very good answer – it depended on the spirit in which it was done.

Tinney who, as a mark of respect, had been given the only arm-chair, sat looking round with an intelligent and interested expression. Actually he was divided between a powerful impulse to laugh and a raging impatience. The whole scene, the shabby little room, blue with smoke, with its cracked ceiling, dirty wallpaper and rickety fragments of furniture, the gathering of young people with their intensely solemn faces, Syson smoking over them with his air of concentrated reflection, seemed to him a subject for farce, and the conversation even too ludicrous for farce.

At Syson's grave interventions from the kitchen chair he twitched with fidgets which had to be passed off in a hasty scratch at his nose, neck or ankle. He found him even more exasperating than he had expected. He thought to himself, 'The man is a far bigger fool than I took him for. He must be thirty-five at least and he goes to read theology and God knows what rubbish at the Museum. Look at him now, pontificating with these children. It's a hundred to one he'll turn out an impossible ass.'

But afterwards, rather to his surprise, he had found Syson quite easy to manage. He had at once agreed to write the leaflet;

he would even have signed it. He began on a draft there and then.

He seemed hardly to reflect on what he was doing, eager to get this unimportant matter over in order to talk to Tinney about his own works. For instance, Tinney had once written in a symposium called *The Faith of the Scientist*, 'All proofs of the existence and omnipresence of God make him also like air, shall we say, hot air.'

He had long forgotten his passage and now when Syson brought it up for discussion, he felt such irritation that he exclaimed contemptuously, 'I've written about a lot of things,' and seeing Syson's surprise passed it off with a laugh as if he had made a joke. But Syson persisted in his questions, and it was only when he showed his impatience very plainly that he brought the man back to the point; that is, the leaflet.

But it was done at last; he carried the draft away in his pocket.

People were surprised by the irresponsibility with which Tinney urged Syson to this disastrous act. But they did not realize how willing Syson was to be implicated and they forgot that Tinney had been in jail himself as an objector in 1917, and that he had always been ready to encourage rebels against the Establishment. In 1926, for instance, it was Tinney who had urged the hunger marchers to besiege the Town Halls and it was by his advice that Pooley had led a march through Tinney's home village and violently opposed a police order to evacuate the cottage hospital where he had camped his men; for which he went to jail for six months. But that was thirty years ago and for a long time now people had thought of Tinney as a distinguished old gentleman and popular broadcaster who was not to be taken quite seriously.

They had forgotten the essential fanatic and anarchist inside the urbane public speaker. It is fair to say that Tinney warned Syson that he was laying himself open to an action for criminal libel and possible imprisonment. This was Tinney's own defence when he was charged with entrapping the man, but he forgot to say that he had given the warning after Syson had drafted the libel.

Whether he had realized, with his pretty shrewd knowledge of men, that Syson, having committed himself to any act, however dangerous, was not the man to withdraw from it because of such

228

a warning, cannot be known. He probably didn't know it himself. He had never bothered to know his own mind. His whole interest was turned outwards upon the world which he despised so much and for whose welfare he agonized.

54

There's no doubt that this leaflet by Syson distributed outside Preedy's forty new mission centres did immense damage. It frightened the committee so much that the Jinks party at last passed a resolution to invite Jackman to take over the Mission in Preedy's place. This was done in Hooper's absence; he was far too busy to attend committee meetings, but as soon as he heard of it he called the members together again and pointed out that what they proposed to do was now impossible. 'For the public,' he said, 'Preedy is the Mission and the Mission is Preedy. We have had his face on the posters for the last six months and now we have to keep it there. It's the face that does more than half the cures.'

Jinks got up and made an angry speech pointing out what fools they would look in case of another scandal about Preedy. 'You don't seem to realize,' he said, 'how far we're out on the limb, and what a rotten limb it is; or what a frightful crash we'll have when it breaks off. Because there's no doubt it's going to break off. It's cracking already. We've had fair warning. People are asking already, all over the country, why we're taking this libel lying down, and naturally they give themselves the answer that we're afraid; there must be something in it. And it's pretty obvious that they're right. There's a lot in it, and as far as I'm concerned, it's the last straw. We simply can't afford to carry on with Preedy.'

Jinks had very strong support and it was obvious that if the matter went to the vote he would carry the committee again. But Hooper was determined that it should not come to a vote. He proposed to adjourn the meeting for that day while they obtained an explanation from Preedy. He himself, he promised, would see Preedy at once and put the question to him.

He had, however, no intention of approaching Preedy. He'd tried that already without the least effect. It was obvious, in fact, that Preedy quite realized his strength. When he received notice of the committee's vote, he answered only to Hooper by wire from Liverpool, 'Why do we need the committee? Tell them they're sacked.'

He paid absolutely no attention to Hooper. In fact, he took every occasion to show his contempt of Hooper, who took a great deal of care to avoid meeting him. To say that Hooper had come to hate Preedy would be mild. He loathed the man with an obsessive disgust that kept him awake at night. For, even more than Jinks and his party, he realized the danger of the position. Another scandal about Preedy would not only ruin the Mission, but himself. He had now identified himself so closely with it that he dared not let it fail; not only that, but he committed the *Argus*, in which the Mission progress was reported day by day. [Moreover, the *Argus* had to have money, and he was certain that Laney, the Anglo-American financier, a friend of the Clenches, who was fascinated by the Mission but wavering about endowing it, would tide the *Argus* over this difficult time once he made up his mind to back the Mission.] And now Hooper's interest in the *Argus* was more than professional. Since his marriage to Joanna he had begun, not only to talk, but to think of the *Argus* as personal property.

He was fond, in fact, of giving the impression that he had married Joanna so suddenly and unexpectedly simply as a move to secure the *Argus*. This was the pretext offered to Joanna herself when he proposed. The couple were spending one of their usual week-ends on the Downs and Joanna had suddenly announced that it must be the last. 'I'm getting too big,' she said. 'People are beginning to look, even when I wear my biggest coat.'

Hooper asked where she was going and how long she proposed to stay and the girl answered cheerfully that she would go as far as she could and stay probably a year – a year at the very least.

Hooper cried out at this, 'A year; why a year?'

'I can't appear in England with a new-born baby. That is, if I appear in England at all. It might be better to start again altogether. I'll call myself a widow of course and wear a ring, but nobody in England will accept a story like that, even in a year; five years would be the minimum.'

What had astonished Hooper was the calm way in which Joanna announced this programme. She seemed to have no thought for him at all; she did not utter a single word of regret at breaking off their relation, so long and so intimate. He was not only astonished and wounded, he was shocked. For a moment he had the impulse to tell her what he thought of her and to leave her there and then. He thought, 'After all, she's just another light-weight; a creature without the first idea of loyalty; without any real feelings at all; a complete egotist, heartless and selfish.'

But he did not say it because, looking at the girl's face, even in his amazement and anger, he saw that she was not thinking of him at all.

And this realization shook him so deeply that something cracked in his idea of things. For a moment he was aware of a realm beyond from which blew a wind so cold that it made him freeze. He had a glimpse of a solitude like that of an arctic waste where man is alone, not only physically, but spiritually, where he does not belong at all, where his existence is simply an anomaly.

He had already had inklings of a novel loneliness. His success of the last few months had given him enormous happiness. He had enjoyed popular success before at the time of his best-seller, but this new triumph was of quite another order. For the first time he was a power; people deferred to him as to a man of weight. When he walked into a room the atmosphere was changed. Even those who had not heard him announced or seen his entry knew of it and looked round to see what had happened. All this gave him intense pleasure. Even to see heads turn in the street as he passed was something he looked forward to, and when people did not look he was amused within himself. He thought with indulgence, 'What do they know?'

But already he had discovered that though people deferred they did not admire. Secretaries, mission organizers, editors, brought their problems to him and expected him to solve them, they took it as a matter of course that he would solve them. It was extraordinary how quickly they had acknowledged his leader-ship, and how quickly too they took it as a matter of course that he should lead. It would have been foolish for him to point out to them the brilliance of his ideas, because they expected him to have brilliant ideas.

It was only to Joanna, in those stolen week-ends, that he could explain why he had done this or that; and how he had saved some blind fool from making a still bigger fool of himself than he was born. He had been sure of Joanna's sympathy; he had been sure, too, of her interest in the subtleties of his analysis of any situation.

He had known for some time that he would miss her but he had not realized till that moment how much. He had never dreamt that she would not miss him. This was a shock that cracked some essential defence of the man's soul, that all Joanna's interest, her affectionate sympathy, might be a mere pretence, that the girl was simply another traitor, cleverer than the rest.

Joanna at that moment was not thinking of Hooper. She was preoccupied by the enormous problems of her own decision. She hated to face them. She had put off for as long as possible any kind of decision. She had made it now, only because she was compelled to do so, by the fear of scandal, not for herself, but for the child. She was not obsessed by her pregnancy. At the moment she was angry with herself for incurring it, for taking the least risk of it. She was exasperated by all the trouble it was causing her, but being committed to it, she found she was committed to a whole course of action, of which she could not even see the end. For instance, having had the baby, she must see that it had a fair chance, that it did not start life under some public stigma. That was a duty which she dared not avoid for her own sake as well as the child's. It was absolutely necessary that the child should as far as possible be like anybody else's child and have a normal upbringing. That was why she would be compelled to stage a lie, to pretend to be a widow, to commit herself to a false position, which would itself be a perpetual nuisance to her.

As for the suddenness of her announcement, she had merely said what had been on her mind for weeks as something that would have to be done some time. It had always been obvious that she would have to go abroad to have the child; as obvious to Hooper as herself. His exclamation had startled her almost as much as it startled himself, but, looking at him in surprise, she thought only, 'What a funny little man he is; why is he so surprised?'

When she began to explain why she had to go soon, Hooper changed the subject. He began again to talk about his difficulties with Preedy, 'The trouble is that he's got too big for his boots. Of course, you may say that it's all my fault. I've made him what he is; I've made him a national figure, and that's true. But it was a risk I had to take and I'm not afraid of it. If Preedy thinks he's going to come it over me he's very much mistaken. All the same, it's a tricky problem. What we've got to realize is that Preedy believes in himself. He has this extraordinary power, whatever it is; he's not the ordinary type of man and he knows it very well,' and so on.

It was not till the next morning that he proposed in these terms, 'Has it ever struck you that we might get married; I mean that although the Rideout shares are shaky, it's quite a possible proposition. It would strengthen my position on the *Argus* too. It's not perhaps a very romantic point of view, but then we aren't romantic people, and that's another point, we wouldn't be expecting too much,' and he had gone on for some time in the same vein. They could each afford their own car.

Joanna was ready to accept him as soon as he spoke; she would have accepted him even if she had not cared for him, simply because he provided the way out of her worst difficulties. Marriage to Hooper would at once produce a normal situation, not only for her, but for their child. It was an admirable solution to all her problems.

But she did care for him very much and this sudden unexpected proof of how much he needed her moved her almost to tears. She did not answer him, but took his hand, and her flushed cheeks, her uncertain smile expressed so naïve a gratitude and affection that Hooper himself was moved in an extraordinary manner. For that moment it seemed to him that he was in love with this plain awkward girl. He had not known the feeling before and it astonished him. He could not actually say to Joanna, 'I love you,' but he found himself behaving in a manner which must, he felt, reveal the fact. For he wanted to show affection; he was anxious to make the girl happy, to see her happy, even if she did not thank him for it. He was, of course, sure of her gratitude, but he recognized in himself the unselfishness of his intention and it pleased him to think of it. In fact, during this week-end Hooper enjoyed an extraordinary happiness, something he had never known before.

It did, of course, occur to him that exactly what he had foreseen had come about. Joanna had caught him, and it was very likely that she'd caught him by a trick. But now he contemplated this possibility without rancour; he reflected that if it were true, it was only another proof of Joanna's love for him. 'A woman's trick,' he thought, 'but what could she do?' He felt an immense indulgence towards women because Joanna was a woman.

They were married at once by special licence at a Register Office, on the excuse that both were too busy for a wedding. Joanna moved into Hooper's flat with as little ceremony as if she had been a week-end visitor, and their happiness endured, even increased. For Hooper, indeed, it was like one of those week-ends continued for every day; he was able to report to Joanna every evening instead of only at the week-end, and when, during the day, he had said or done anything unusually clever, he was not in fear of forgetting it before he could relate it to her. He was intensely happy, but he did not confess it. He still talked of his marriage as a stroke of policy. It was all the more exasperating to him to find himself in danger from an irresponsible lunatic like Preedy, but the danger was urgent and he set to work at once to meet it.

55

He judged that the first point of attack should be Syson and he obtained Syson's address through the Rational Truth Society. Syson was out at his arrival; according to the landlady he was at the reading-room, but he would come in to supper. And Hooper, impatient, walked round to the Museum at closing-time to see if he could meet the man on his way. He was lucky; he came upon Syson in the street with two companions. All carried notebooks under their arms and looked at Hooper with that air belonging to all students and researchers; of those who are interrupted in highly important affairs by some trivial encounter. Hooper had been surprised by this new phase in Syson. He had not imagined him as a man who took any interest in books.

He said impatiently, 'Hullo, Syson, I've been looking for you all day.'

'Very well, here I am,' said Syson.

His two companions had stopped also and were looking at Hooper with the same disinterested curiosity.

'It had better be between ourselves,' Hooper said.

'Oh, it's about that leaflet, is it? My friends here know all about that.'

Hooper, irritated, answered promptly, 'Very well, then, if you don't mind having witnesses present. Are you admitting you wrote the leaflet about Preedy?'

'Certainly.'

'Do you realize it's criminal libel? Preedy could put you in jail tomorrow.'

'I dare say, but I notice he's in no hurry.'

'No, because he doesn't want to drag you through the courts again. It wasn't his fault that he was forced into court the last time.'

'If he wants to bring an action I've no objection.'

'Do you want to go to jail?'

'I shouldn't mind. It would be in a good cause.'

'Very well, you've had your warning,' and Hooper walked off.

But he could not accept this defeat. On the next day, by collusion with the landlady, he was able to find Syson alone, and made a different appeal. He brought with him the record of the case in the coroner's court and it showed that Preedy's name had not even been mentioned.

'I'm not thinking so much about what the man has done, as what he is doing now,' Syson said, and he began to talk about Rollwright, the parishioner who had complained to him months ago that his wife refused to summon a doctor for their daughter. Preedy was attending the child.

'I tried to intervene with the mother,' Syson said, 'but it was no good. She left her husband months ago and took the child away to an address in Pimlico, to a sister's, who has the same faith.'

Hooper realized at once that this Rollwright child must be the one seen with Preedy in the park. He agreed therefore with Syson that if the child were really ill, Mrs Rollwright should be encouraged to see a doctor.

'If you know the address,' he said, 'I should like to see the woman. As a member of Preedy's committee and a friend of his I might have some influence.'

'But if you're a Preedyite how do you propose to call in a doctor; isn't that all against your principles?'

This talk of principles irritated Hooper so much that he had to be careful of the tone in which he replied. Certainly he had principles, but he had some common sense. He thought to himself of Syson, remembering those notebooks, 'Here's another of these hair-splitters.' But he began to talk in a very reasonable manner about the application of principles in special cases.

'Certainly I believe that faith can cure anything, literally anything; but first the faith must be established, and one of the means, strangely enough, by which faith can be reached, is through a doctor's opinion, and even doctor's treatment; that is to say, treatment that would be worthless without faith can be completely effective if faith is present.'

'Faith in the doctor,' said Syson, 'this is a new line of yours.'

'No, faith in God, by means of the doctor.'

'What I wonder,' Syson said, 'is if you believe a single word of it; in fact, of anything.'

But Hooper did not trouble to argue this point. He looked very grave and allowed it to appear that the matter was too serious for argument. In fact, the argument was of no interest to him; he had invented his explanation only at that moment.

All he wanted was Rollwright's address, and that Syson wouldn't give him. At that moment Syson was already planning with the father to get the girl, Ada, back again. She went every day to a small private school close to her aunt's lodging and the plan was simply for the father to intercept her in his car and take her home with him. He was quite confident that once he had control of her she would want to stay with him. But as Syson was on visiting terms with his wife, Rollwright had asked him to be present when he intercepted the girl, so that he could go at once and explain the situation to the wife. He was very fond of her and did not want her to suffer any anxiety. His main object was simply to have a doctor's report on the child, who had been spitting blood. Armed with the report he was sure that he could persuade his wife to allow treatment.

As he could make no headway with Syson, Hooper found out Rollwright's address through the Vicar and went to see him. Rollwright, finding him highly sympathetic, told him of the plan. Hooper engaged, on his part, that Preedy would not interfere. He suggested too that a doctor should be present in Rollwright's flat ready to make the examination at once, and that Rollwright should put in a claim for legal custody.

Hooper already had visions of headlines, 'Child Kidnapped', 'Pimlico Kidnapping Case', and he wouldn't have got mixed up

in the affair on his own account. The only reason he was in it at
all was because of his attempt to keep Preedy's name out of it;
but Syson made that impossible. From the beginning of the Rollwright affair Syson behaved like a lunatic, as Hooper put it. He
did everything possible to get himself into jail; he began to show
that obsession which caused a good many people, including his
own wife, to doubt his sanity.

56

When Syson had made his petition in bankruptcy and given up
his curacy and his flat at Pant's Road, it had been understood that
he would join Clarry at her home in Cambridgeshire. Though
the Simpkins, like most people, could not help finding Syson's
proceedings generally both exasperating and comical, they were
very sympathetic, and had asked him to stay as long as he liked
until he could decide on his course of action. They took the view
that if he was not actually mad, he was at least very odd, and
needed therefore special consideration. They were not only
highly civilized, but they had that scientific tradition which they
liked to think of as humanist. This meant that, while Sir Harry
and Lady Simpkins were both convinced that what they called
the supernatural was a mere piece of nonsense, they still went to
church on occasions and did not at all resent Clarry's convinced
faith. In fact, it was a private joke among them that Clarry was
politically highly conservative. For the Simpkins it was hardly
possible for a conservative to be a Christian. Sir Harry had been a
great League of Nations man and Lady Simpkins was on all those
committees and societies that seek to abolish bitterness and racial
feeling. Both husband and wife gave large sums to charity and
took severe views of luxurious living. The buying of a new car
after the war had troubled the family councils for months, for
both husband and wife felt guilty about buying a new car at all,
while German children and refugees needed help.

Sir Harry liked to call himself a scientific humanist, with a
vague idea that he thus combined his confidence in scientific fact
with humane principles. In fact, he was still essentially a Quaker,
like his parents; a Quaker who didn't believe in anything but the
Quaker ethic.

In such an atmosphere Clarry was completely happy. She loved her home and she had always hated London, especially the mean suburbs about Pant's Road. She had never complained; she had done her duty as a good wife and a good Christian. But to get back into the country was like an escape from a prison sentence. Never before had she so much appreciated the services at the village church, the church she always thought of as her own church. Brownhill church is not much valued by antiquarians; it dates from 1300, but it is little more than a stone barn, not even a big barn. It is one of the smallest in the county and since it lost its spire by a storm in the 1850s it is not even a landmark. But, on account of its insignificance, it has escaped restoration; its floor is still in flags and its windows are still a mixture of everything from early English to late Jacobean. It has even a sash window to its minuscule vestry and a chimney resembling that of a greenhouse. Inside it has been whitewashed, which still further increases its resemblance to a barn.

But only to enter it gave Clarry an extraordinary peace, a deep appeasement to her spirit. The prayers and hymns had here quite a different sound and meaning for her, as the commonplaces spoken by a beloved person are different from the same platitudes in the mouth of a stranger.

The first morning service at Brownhill on her return home had the effect of revelation to her; she was astonished to find how quickly and easily she had lost the sense of refreshment and renewal that they had brought to her before her marriage and exile; how the same prayers, the same readings at St Enoch's had not only failed to mean anything important for her, but had actually hidden from her the meaning of the church service as a religious experience.

At Brownhill she did not so much hear as feel the words and they moved in her as a sense of new life, like the transfusion which flows into the half-collapsed veins of someone who has been bleeding to death. The Eucharist taken at the chancel rail at Brownhill, a rickety fence of plain wooden bars, constructed on the same principle as a local hen-house door, was for her less a solemn rite than an expression of her joyful gratitude; her allegiance. Here she made her homecoming complete, surrounded by the people she had known from childhood; people as simple as their church, for whom the regular Sunday service was as much

238

part of the week's routine as milking or carting, whose very limitation of interests was a mark of their deep preoccupation with immediate domestic affair. Fields, cottages, people, cows, even tractors were at one in an existence which was simply the larger aspect of family life where everything and every person is part of a remembered and continuing story, full of personal interest and significance for all the rest. And the little church with its hump back and absurd stump of spire, where this village family had prayed for the last six hundred years, had in it for Clarry so intense a feeling of their patient, reasonable, undemanding souls that the very discomfort of her narrow seat was delightful to her. Not because it made her back ache but because it was a Brownhill pew that thrust its clumsy top-piece into her bones.

She was longing to have her husband beside her again in Brownhill church, where they had sat so often during their engagement. She was convinced that here he would find the strength and consolation he needed; he would get things in proportion again and forget his material worries; his humiliation.

She did not, indeed, realize the force of this hope and how much she depended on it until Syson's weekly letter failed to arrive one Monday morning. She had not pressed her husband when he excused himself from coming home to Brownhill with her; he had the excuse of a great deal of business still to be done in town, and she realized that under his reasonable air he was deeply preoccupied. Now she discovered how deep her anxiety had been, for her first idea was that he must have killed himself. She perceived that this fear had always been in her mind; that she had been aware for months, since the trial and perhaps before, of something profoundly disturbed in the man, and she had always known of a certain desperation in his nature. The same quality that had made him a good night pilot, that had projected him so suddenly and unexpectedly into the Church, that had made so energetic and unconventional a curate, could also carry him to suicide. For him every problem of life was a challenge to be defied. He was essentially a fighting man.

She was terrified but she did not panic; she took the first train to town, one of those eastern locals which wanders through the flats from one little brick station to another as if the tameness of the country had affected the powers of its own engine, so that the steam worked at half pressure and the wheels turned as leisurely

239

as the empty churn, rolled by a yawning porter, along a platform not much bigger than a milk float. She had loved these trundling journeys across the fields, so perfectly in accord with the heavy farmlands, where a labourer in the plough who tried to hurry would leave his boots behind. But now it was an agony; every moment she imagined herself just too late.

She took a taxi to save time, and went to him at once, but it was eight o'clock in the evening and she found him with a party of students in his room, who gazed at her in surprise and embarrassment. Syson himself was equally embarrassed and surprised. He gave her a hasty embrace, presented her briefly as his wife and sat her in a corner arm-chair, the only arm-chair, with a cup of coffee in her lap, then immediately turned to the company and said, ' I am so sorry, where had we got to?'

He was apologizing to a man in the opposite corner, sitting on a cushion on the floor, in whom she recognized Tinney. He was looking at her with his little sharp eyes full of cynical amusement; obviously he understood her feelings and was enjoying them, and now, catching her eye upon him, he smiled and made a little bow.

She had met the man at her father's; he had a great reputation with the Simpkins, who looked with indulgence on his public activities as the pastimes of a great scientist. But Clarry had always detested him. She felt in him the deep enmity to everything she valued in life. She was used to see him smile at the least reference to religion or the Church.

He was smiling now with the same tolerant scorn, but the subject was not, as she had expected from that smile, religion.

The student who took up the discussion made a long complicated statement about the electronic brain.

Apparently there had been a report in the paper of the claim of some eminent neurologist that science was at last approaching a solution of the problem of thought. It appeared to be simply electronic reactions at the nerve ends.

'You mean,' Syson said, 'that pretty soon we shall be able to make an electronic brain that really thinks?'

A girl with a pony-tail remarked, 'But that's a purely mechanist view.'

'Why not?' said the other. 'Any other brings in the idea of a mind working on its own.'

An older man, sitting on a chair, the only other chair, close to

Syson, remarked that, after all, the body didn't work on its own either. 'Isn't the whole trouble,' he said, 'this habit of verbal analysis? We treat a butterfly as an independent creature, but nobody supposes it works out its own metamorphoses. The whole development from the egg is completely mysterious. We can only call it a process which takes place according to some mysterious law; we think we know all about the human embryo, just because its development is confined within the womb. Actually it is just as mysterious. The same is true of the acorn that grows into an oak tree. All we really know is that at a certain point of development inorganic materials become organic and produce what we call life – and another life produces mind, just as the acorn produces the tree, the leaves and the seed.'

'We can make life already, in a test-tube.'

'No, you can't, you never make anything in a test-tube. No one invents an element – they find it. What you do is, you put certain ingredients together under certain conditions, and life makes its appearance. Life was there already. And, about its developments, all we can say is that they are characteristic; they are what we call natural. We know that an emotion is part of the natural order, we find it in animals; mother love, nobody tries to deny it. Why should they then try to deny the existence of mind against all the evidence of our senses just because its working is mysterious?'

'In fact,' said Tinney, 'everything is a mystery, like the problem of evil, at least to a bishop.'

This was recognized as a joke and several people laughed. But there was a note of politeness in the laugh. It was obvious that the students who laughed did so out of respect to the old man, and they returned at once to serious discussion.

'You could take that view,' said the girl, 'and still be a mechanist. You've only got to say that the mind is a tool of the body.'

The man in the chair remarked that no doubt a behaviourist would say that.

Clarry, from her corner, was listening with angry disgust. How could Tom have got into this company of hobbledehoys, with their childish nonsense? Could he really be taking them seriously? She had resolved from the beginning not to speak. She realized that she was an intruder; that even Syson was embarrassed by her presence. But Tinney's remark about the problem of evil and the laughter that greeted it suddenly enraged her. She had been watching Tinney with the fascination of hatred and fear; she said to herself, 'How typical of him to sit on the floor, among the students.' She remembered how on his visits to her home he had always made himself one with any young men present. His attitude had been always, 'I belong to youth; I understand youth, because I myself am always young in mind.' And she thought of him as a man without a heart, wholly intellectual; a man incapable of understanding the realities of affection and its anxieties.

Now to her own surprise she broke out, 'But nobody can believe in behaviourism.'

This produced at once a silence so deep that Syson could be heard sucking at his pipe. Some of the students gazed at Clarry with discreet wonder; most avoided looking at her, but with the same motive; they did not want to show their pity for the poor thing.

'Ah, yes,' said Tinney, 'that word again. You pinch the doll in the stomach and it says, "papa".' He gave a loud laugh and looked at Syson, as if to invite him to laugh also; and Syson duly smiled.

No one else laughed, all the young people looked still more grave; they were puzzled by the old man's intervention. After a moment a voice from the back asked, in an apologetic tone, 'But how could a mind exist by itself?'

'Nothing can exist by itself,' said the man in the chair, and seemed about to expound, but the girl with the pony-tail interrupted, 'I suppose you mean you can't find it in dissection; but you don't find life either by dissection, you stop it.'

'That's all very well,' said the other. 'But if you believe in the mind, you might as well believe in the soul.'

'The best leather,' said Tinney, and uttered another loud laugh, and then immediately changed his voice to one of the gravest conviction. 'All this is very interesting, but it's really off the point. What we were discussing was the new censorship, the new attitude towards research; that's the fundamental thing, this concerted attack from all sides on free speech, free thought, free publication, everything that has been gained in the last hundred years,' and he went on to describe what he called the tacit conspiracy of the churches and the Press everywhere to crush the new freedom. He spoke of the case against Heinemann over the novel and quoted the counsel's question to the jury, 'Is this a book you'd give to your daughters of twenty-five to read?' 'You notice,' he said, 'that he didn't say sons, he said daughters; he was appealing to purely Victorian prejudice, sex prejudice, and he got his verdict. But what is really ominous is that there wasn't a single objection to this piece of rank reaction; not even a comment. None of these women's freedom societies let out a peep.'

A woman student said that counsel's job was to put the case for the Crown to the best of his ability.

'Quite so – and he got his verdict,' said Tinney.

'You don't think there ought to be any censorship?' the young woman asked, and at once everybody began to discuss this point.

After her one explosion, Clarry sat silent. She could not understand why Tinney had seemed to agree with her, but she realized that he was not really interested in the point. He simply wanted to get back to his own subject, his old fixed idea about the dangers of censorship, and on this point Clarry knew herself confused. She had been all for the Bill putting down the horror comics, though her husband had been against it. She knew too that on his political side Tinney was sincere; he had gone to jail as a pacifist; no doubt he would go to jail again, if it were necessary, for free speech and free publication. But she gave him no merit, even for his sincerities. It seemed to her he used them only for corruption, to destroy loyalty, to undermine faith. 'See him now,' she thought, 'giving up time that must be valuable to so eminent a man to come here among poor and unknown students simply in order to pervert them.' She looked at her husband sitting by the table with his arms crossed, his nose in the air and his black eyes fixed on Tinney's face with a look of intense concentration, and thought again, 'What has happened to him? It's a kind of illness. What does he want with these people, with their silly ideas and silly talk? He knows what's true – he knows what's really important to do in the world, what it needs so terribly – no, he's ill. I must get him away. Unless I get him away soon, it will be too late,' and she asked herself anxiously how she would accomplish this task. Should she try to charm him, saying nothing about his failure to write?

Syson had been passionately in love with her; he could still be moved to passionate excitement if she chose. But in the weeks during his obsession with Preedy and the trial, he had been pre-occupied so that her occasional attempts to give him physical relief and distraction had not been successful. He had responded with the patient tolerance of one who does his duty, and she had felt that her affectionate impulse was simply an added nuisance and burden to him.

Yet, when the company had gone and at last they were alone together, she frankly made love to him. She said how she had missed him and longed for him all these months, and when again he had responded kindly but dutifully, she had suddenly lost her self-control; she began to cry and clung to him, asking him why he hated her. 'You know I'm not blaming you for anything that's happened; it's not your fault, how could it be, and why should it make any difference to us? We were so happy always; what has happened to make any real difference?'

And Syson could not tell her what had happened; he could not explain to her that all this talk about happiness and their marriage seemed so unimportant to him that he couldn't even give thought to it. He wondered even if this word hatred which she had suddenly produced were not true. Certainly there was no one in the world whom he less wanted to see. Just because he had loved her; because he was under the deepest obligation to her; because she was good and loyal, he found her presence, her very sympathy, intolerable. How could he answer her questions when he didn't know the answers himself? And as for sympathy, why should she sympathize with a man who was treating her so badly and could not help it?

He assured her that he loved her and for a long time tried to console her, holding her in his arms, kissing her, stroking her hair, and he knew that she did not believe a word of it. He knew that all his consolations, his assurances, simply increased the difference and the embarrassment that stood between them.

When, next day, she begged him to come to Brownhill, if only for the week-end, and see the children, he was bound to agree and to pretend that there was nothing he would like better.

Again Clarry was tactful, loving. She did not speak of anything that had happened.

Syson, using all his power to be kind, so far succeeded with the woman, anxious as she was to be reassured, that on the way home from church on Sunday, where he had seemed as attentive and as reverent as herself, she suddenly found herself speaking of Tinney. She had for the moment, in her hopefulness, forgotten her tact.

'I'd no idea,' she said, 'that you knew him. Of course, I know he's quite famous, but surely he's always been rather unreliable. I was wondering what those boys thought of him, and how seriously they were taking him.'

Syson was silent, he knew what a horror Clarry had of Tinney; and that she was shocked to find him on terms of friendship with the old man. He had felt her eyes on him, that evening at the discussion, and knew that she dreaded Tinney's influence.

The fact was that Tinney no longer had any influence on Syson; he had very quickly perceived that Tinney was merely a propagandist. For instance, on that very question of behaviourism, he had dodged the issue because, as he had pointed out to Syson, for some reason behaviourism was a joke. And when Syson had said, 'I suppose your position is really behaviourist,' he had answered, 'Logically, yes, I suppose so. But what is logic? Words mean what you like. If you want them to mean anything special, you pay 'em extra, overtime.' And then he had given again his loud, harsh laugh.

'It's just the word you don't like,' Syson had said.

Syson knew that Tinney was afraid that he, Syson, would commit himself to this unpopular and unfashionable view and so spoil his value for his propaganda.

'Oh, yes, it's a bad word; it's not a word you can use in polite society. Scientific humanism is the proper cry just now. It's beginning to stink a little, but it still passes with a good rich sauce,' and again the laugh.

Syson was already writing, at Tinney's suggestion, a series of articles in his magazine, and Tinney was anxious that he should use the right words and avoid the unpopular ones. His remark that 'scientific humanism' already stank a little was simply his way of pretending impartiality; his laugh was really a proof that he was seriously concerned.

By Syson did not care to tell Clarry that he no longer had any confidence in Tinney. He discovered all at once that he would have felt that like a treachery. For with all his arrogance, his malice, his prejudice, the old man had spent his life fighting for the free mind. He really believed in freedom. He did not practise truth or sincerity but he would have died for the right and power to look for truth.

'He can't really believe,' Clarry said, 'that people are just machines. He must have some feelings; machines don't feel, do they?'

'Some of them are remarkably sensitive,' Syson said. 'They can see further and calculate better than any human being.'

And he had gone on to give the whole mechanist position, to show that it was quite easy and, indeed, highly logical to believe that God was a figment, and man simply a complicated kind of mechanism. As for altruism, goodness, you could account for that very easily as a product of pure selfishness. It was just the most selfish parents who took the most trouble to bring up their children to be dutiful and good. It paid them to do so. So too it paid a society to teach and support Christian goodness, the herd loyalty.

At first Clarry protested, but anyone could say such things. Did he really believe them?

And she looked at him in terror, and he knew how much he was making her suffer. But he could not stop. He was full of a cold anger against all that Clarry stood for, against her tenderness, her sympathy, her faith in love. He had felt that faith, that hope in her during the service in Brownhill church. The touch of her shoulder as they knelt together had seemed to communicate the very thrill of her hope, and it had passed through him like an electric current, so that the particles of doubt, of questioning, the scores of moments when he had wondered, 'Do I believe?' or 'Do I believe this or that?' suddenly rushed together into a solid mass – a cold, heavy, metallic weight, at the very centre of his feeling. And now it was because of this weight, pressing down on his heart and brain that he was obliged to torture Clarry, to treat her as his enemy.

'But Tom, why tell me all this? You know you don't believe a word of it.'

'But I do,' he said coolly, 'that's the point.'

'Oh, no – you only say so because you're angry with me.'

'It's nothing to do with you – it's simply the truth. I don't like it any more than you do – it means of course that I can't go on in the Church. But truth is truth. You have to face it – no man can live a lie.'

Clarry's misery, her white pinched face, only increased the anger in him. Why must he make her suffer like this – why couldn't she reconcile herself to this necessity, that truth must be faced?

For now he knew that he did not, could not, believe any more. As soon as he had spoken the words to Clarry, he recognized that his old faith was impossible, and that he had known it for a long time. It had simply fled away, leaving a great vacancy, a darkness, which was filled with this new cold weight of revulsion against all that had belonged to that faith, even its beauty, its grace, its love, its hope, above all its hope. That was its biggest fraud and lie.

The Simpkins seemed to him all at once, not merely triflers playing at life and varnishing over their real cowardice, their refusal to face truth with all this refinement of feeling; they, quite as much as Tinney, even more than Tinney, were escapists and dodgers. All this talk of freedom, what did it mean except that they didn't want to make up their minds and were afraid to crush evil, even where they recognized it; the fearful evil of ignorance and wish-fulfilment. They were the people who refused to hang a murderer, not because the murderer might suffer a special pain, but because they could not bear to take the responsibility of judging him. They would rather that a man should rot in jail for twenty years, than carry that burden for a minute; it might spoil their appetite, at least for a day, it might lay them open to a charge of brutality. And Tinney wanted freedom for every kind of perversion and every kind of poison, however corrupt, because he himself wanted to publish sedition, because it suited his arrogance to hate all government, all authority.

So the world lived in this confusion of lies, ignorance and spite, and men like Preedy were permitted to do murder with impunity.

57

Suddenly he could no longer bear Clarry's presence, or the atmosphere of this place. He could not even bear to wait for luncheon, but as soon as he reached the house walked out of the back door and made for the station; and as soon as he had reached London, went direct to Rollwright and discussed the kidnapping. It seemed that from this time, from some sudden change that had taken place in the man during his visit to Brownhill, he was determined to get himself into jail. He had become like one of those grievance mongers who feel that by inflicting injury on themselves they take an obscure revenge on the world.

He pointed out to Rollwright that when the mother knew where Ada was she would almost certainly come and take her back again. She was hopelessly under Preedy's influence. Syson's new plan was to take the girl to some place in the country where she was not likely to be traced. Rollwright was nervous of this suggestion; he did not want to frighten the child or worry his wife, but Syson's answer was always that the child's life was at stake, and by mere force of character, that is, of persistence, he persuaded the man.

The kidnapping itself proved easier than either expected. Rollwright parked his car by the kerb at a place where Ada passed to and from school. She duly appeared on her way home, with satchel, in uniform, walking with two companions, and Rollwright put his head out of the car window to call her. The child, startled to see her father, of whom she had been very fond, at once went to kiss him, and he offered to drive her home. In the same mood of pleasure and excitement at seeing him she eagerly accepted, and he drove at once towards the agreed hiding-place in Kent. He told her the reason – that he had not been allowed to see her for so long, that it wasn't fair that her mother should keep her from him – and to his immense relief the child made no scene, offered no objection. She asked only that he should let her mother know at once what has happened to her. At once, because if she did not come back at the expected time her mother would be terribly alarmed. When he did not reply, she was obviously tense and frightened.

From the beginning of the adventure everyone was struck by this child's dignity and good sense. But those who have dealt with children even younger than twelve in such circumstances are always struck in the same way, with their poise of mind and body. Apparently what is considered appropriate for children is a kind of convention or formula – because they are children they are expected to be irresponsible. However that may be, Ada Rollwright obviously understood the situation immediately and used a considerable intelligence to deal with it. Of course, she was assisted by a complete lack of self-consciousness or pride. Since she was actually a child, she did to have not think what people would think of her; she was able to be completely herself.

Syson and Rollwright had chosen a seaside bungalow at Brinsea. They had had a good deal of difficulty in choosing a place. They had not dared to take lodgings where they would be under observation by a landlady, and they had picked this bungalow at least because Brinsea at this season was almost deserted. It was, of course, if possible, a worse choice than lodgings. The very fact that the place was empty of visitors made their party conspicuous to the few permanent residents, and when the newspapers published a photograph of the child next morning, the police knew her whereabouts within a couple of hours. But as it was not certain that the father did not have every right to take the child away, they merely notified Mrs Rollwright where she was to be found.

Meanwhile, as soon as they arrived at the bungalow where Syson had lit fires, got in some supplies and was waiting, Rollwright explained to the child that he was arranging a visit to a clinic in the county town. Ada answered at once by asking if her mother had been told of the arrangement. As soon as she arrived, she had opened her satchel and produced a piece of sewing; she was hemming a cotton skirt. She explained that she had to produce it for a school examination at the end of that week, and from that time she almost always had this work in her hand; but again, what seemed to her father and Syson a childish disproportion of sense, a lack of appreciation of what was at stake, was much more likely the ordinary tactics of much older women in the same predicament. This work was always her excuse for not answering questions, or seeming not to notice what was going on. And now, when Rollwright sat down and reasoned with her, she simply continued to sew.

Rollwright asked her first if she had had any more attacks of blood-spitting. She shook her head. 'And how's your cough been?'

'Better.'

'You understand that I'm not proposing that you should have any treatment; all we want is for the doctor to examine your chest and perhaps to take a photograph. Surely you wouldn't mind that?'

The child took a few stitches and answered at last, 'I wouldn't mind, but I think Mummy would mind. I'd rather you asked her first.'

'But don't you want to be well, to be able to play games?'

'I think I am better, a little.'

'At any rate, it can't do you any harm, can it, to let a doctor see you?'

The child reflected on this for at least ten stitches before she answered. 'I don't know, but Mummy thinks it would.'

'But don't you trust me at all? You know I love you.'

'Yes, I do know. I'm sorry, but it's rather difficult.'

It sounded as if she was going to weep, but she pulled herself together, got up and went out of the room.

Syson had known the Rollwrights during his whole time at Pant's Road. He counted Mrs Rollwright among his favourite parishioners. She stood out among them for intelligence and a certain grace of mind, rare in the neighbourhood. He could understand very well her husband's adoration of her, the unusually strong affection that bound the family together. The sudden defection of Frances Rollwright to Preedy astonished and shocked him. How could so intelligent and well-educated a woman accept Preedyism. The obvious cause had been the first illness of the daughter, so passionately loved, but it did not explain why she had chosen Preedy's advice rather than a doctor's.

58

Mrs Rollwright had come to Preedy at one of those times when he knew that he was carrying out his services simply as routine, when he found himself the prisoner of a time-table, the time-table against which he had often revolted. At such times he had various expedients to recover what he called his power. There were certain books and chapters of the Bible that he would read; he would pray and meditate since, as he knew from experience, all those arguments which he was accustomed to offer to others were useless to him. They became merely words without meaning. Even that final argument, so convincing to his closest disciples, that if God had not the power to abolish the frightful evil, cruelty and injustice of the world, he was not God at all, seemed to him then nothing but a piece of special pleading. It could not overcome the enormous despair in his soul; it had no more effect against that monstrous terror than wind against a rock; it seemed at these moments that all his structure of faith, his preachings, his prayers, were nothing but words, wind, on which he managed to float over that despair, that he himself was no different from the crowds in the street, those crowds of lost and bewildered souls which made the streets of any great town so terrifyingly repulsive to him; that he differed from them only in one thing, that they were more stoic in their senseless damnation.

Such times came upon him unexpectedly, at any moment, even in the middle of a service, even while actually laying his hands upon some sick person and telling him that if he had faith he was healed. It was immediately after such a service that Mrs Rollwright came to him and asked him to treat her daughter. He had asked her if she were a member of his Mission and she had said no, she was Church of England; she belonged to St Enoch's.

'But when I asked the vicar about a healing service for Ada he said that she must have a doctor's report. So then I came to hear you preach and I saw you were right; I saw it was true what you said, that it is blasphemy to ask for a doctor to do God's work for him, that the Church really denies God; it has no faith any more.'

Preedy had had many converts like Mrs Rollwright; he was not at all surprised that highly intelligent people should come to him. He understood very well the workings of Mrs Rollwright's mind, that it was entirely at the mercy of her feelings. For her this only daughter was all that mattered in life and she was terrified at the thought of losing her; so terrified that she could not bear even the idea of a doctor's report. Her very intelligence made her dread the diagnosis. The child was losing weight, had a fever and cough and had recently spat blood; it was obvious that she was consumptive; it was obvious what the doctor's report would be. But the mother would not allow herself to know it; she was completely the prisoner of her terror and her love. So her mind had eagerly grasped at Preedy's message and built up for herself from his arguments a logical case against the doctors and her own church.

And Preedy, in his own black mood of despair, listened to her in silence, and thought, 'Shall I tell her to go away? Shall I tell

251

her that all these arguments mean nothing whatever; they're just a lot of words to plaster over her fear?' But mere despair, as usual, prevented him. What was the good of words, of speech from one human wretch to another? What could he do for her, who could do nothing for himself?

And then she had called in the daughter, Ada. She had left the girl at the door until she could be sure that he would receive her. And at the mere sight of mother and child together he had felt again that mysterious movement of feeling which he called power. From the love on one side completely selfless, from the trust of the child, something flashed into him; something like those discoveries made by the pure contact of sense – a glimpse of the sea, of a ripe field, a scent from the ground, the noise of rain – known a thousand times before, which yet bring a shock of recognition; and in a moment he had again an absolute conviction, the absolute certainty of God's presence in the world, of God's meaning and intention for humanity. He did not need to ask for assurance; it was there, as real and certain as sea or ground, and immediately he asked himself, how could he be defeated, how could a thing so potent and universal be set aside except merely by ignorance, by lack of faith, by that evil mood which had just now fallen upon his own mind and made him think, if only for a day, that it was useless even to hope.

Since then he had gone often to the Rollwrights, and when Rollwright had tried to insist on a doctor's examination for his daughter, it was Preedy who had advised Mrs Rollwright to take flight. For if he had allowed a doctor to see Ada he would have felt that he himself was committing a blasphemy. It was through this mother and child, especially the child, that God had sent him reassurance. He felt it like a challenge to his own faith. For he himself was often anxious for the child. When she had fever and Mrs Rollwright kept her in bed, he would reassure her by saying there was a great deal of 'flu about, for everybody was having colds this year, and in these words he reassured himself. Somehow it had become understood between Mrs Rollwright and himself that Ada should no longer be weighed because it was quite unnecessary.

And it was the enormous success of the campaign that had made the Rollwrights more and more necessary to Preedy.

Now Preedy and Mrs Rollwright were in the sitting-room

before Syson could reach the door. Rollwright was sitting with Ada in the window seat. He had been talking to the child all that morning about her summer holidays at the sea, and how she had enjoyed swimming in years before. Last year she had been feverish and unable to bathe. Rollwright did not say, 'Unless you allow yourself to be cured you won't be able to enjoy swimming again,' but that was his intention, and Ada fully understood him. She had just disconcerted him by the remark, 'But perhaps I shall always have fever at the seaside,' when Preedy and Mrs Rollwright came into the room. He jumped up and placed himself between Ada and the door, but Ada did not at once run to her mother. It was Mrs Rollwright who went to her.

'You can't take her,' said Rollwright, 'I won't allow it; do you want to kill her?'

'That's the question we have to ask of you,' said Preedy.

'Please, please,' said Mrs Rollwright, 'do think what you're saying,' and she took Ada's hand with anxious sympathy.

'I don't mind,' Ada said. 'After all, Mother, I do know about it.' She picked up her sewing again.

Syson attacked Preedy impatiently, 'What do you mean by saying that Rollwright will be responsible? You know perfectly well what's wrong with her; she has an ordinary T.B. and she will certainly die unless it's treated; and its murder not to treat her. T.B. nowadays is a perfectly curable disease.'

Mrs Rollwright cried out again in protest and Ada put down her work and remarked, 'Shall I go out for a while until you've talked it over? I'll go to the beach. It seems such a waste not to go when I didn't expect to come.' This silenced the party for the moment. Mrs Rollwright fetched her child's coat and muffler; husband and wife fussed round her, each trying to show the most solicitude, but at last she was allowed to go to the shore, undertaking only to keep in sight from the window.

As soon as the door closed behind her Rollwright demanded an examination. 'I shall not let her go until she has had one; I called a doctor last night and he'll be here any moment.'

Syson's comment was that he had a perfect right to keep the child as long as he liked; that is to say, until Mrs Rollwright had a legal order giving custody.

'What are you talking about?' said Mrs Rollwright. 'It's nothing to do with the law; we're not separated. The only question is what will help Ada, and it won't help her if we quarrel. It has done her enough harm already that we can't agree,' and turning to her husband she took his arm and said, 'How could you keep her away from me against her will?'

And obviously this argument had great force with the man. He made a gesture as if to throw up his hands, as if to ask, 'What can a fellow do?' and then turned on Preedy. 'All I'm asking for is the examination; a doctor's examination. What harm can that do according to your views? He will merely look at the child's chest and tell us what he thinks.' He turned to his wife and said, 'Frances, are you going to refuse me that?'

Mrs Rollwright hesitated and at once Preedy intervened, 'I leave it to you, Mrs Rollwright; you are the only person here except myself who has the least idea of what's at stake. They say this examination means nothing; why then do they want it? Why do they call in a doctor at all? The very fact of calling him in shows a complete want of faith, or any understanding of it.' At this moment the doctor drove up and Rollwright cried, 'There he is now, thank God,' and ran to the door. Preedy turned again to Mrs Rollwright, 'You and I,' he said, 'know what Ada is to us, and what she is in herself, her complete faith, her complete lack of fear or anxiety for herself. Are we going to let her believe that she is simply a kind of mechanism to be tinkered by these quacks? Are we going to cut her off from the faith that alone can save her, body and soul?'

At this Syson lost his temper and began to shout, if Preedy continued to interfere he would throw him out of the room. Preedy said in a tone of disgust, 'I might ask what you're doing here,' and then turning to Frances Rollwright, 'I'm not going to fight with this man over a question so terribly important for you and for Ada. He knows nothing of either of you, nothing of the truth that we know so well. I leave Ada in your own hands; I don't want to see this doctor; I don't like doctors. When you want me, when you have decided whether Ada is to live or die, you can call me.'

He went out of the house then and turned towards the shore; as usual in this mood, he wanted to be by himself. He could not bear the contact and voices and looks of people, and at this time of year the beach at Brinsea, pebbly and broken by groynes, was deserted.

Preedy had felt during the campaign the loss of power never renewed – the impact of mere demand and expectation. Most people took for granted that he would cure them by something in himself. They touched him and stole objects – handkerchiefs, and so on – which he had touched. They thought the process mechanical like magic. Then without faith they would be cured. He would see them lying expectant, watching him with greedy eyes. He could often tell by their looks which were to be healed. That nervous stare is a mark, a sullen glare another – the expectant and the hostile who show hostility, but who, all the same, have come to him. In a word, hysterics, neurotics. They too need cure – their desire is real and deep enough – they need him. But it is their faith in him that cures them. And why do they believe in him? Because of the campaign, the build-up, the posters, the face on the hoardings. You might say that it is Hooper that has healed them. He, Preedy, is a piece of magic to them. They treated him like a dynamo, a machine, and he found himself acting like one, performing movements as automatic, repetitive and meaningless as those of a robot.

And afterwards he would feel not only exhausted physically but defiled, a humbug and fraud, and the gratitude of the healed, when they gave it, closed down about him like that invisible wall which cuts off the liar from the world.

Ada Rollwright, with her complete trust, her affection, her lack of fear, had something deeper than faith that can be expressed. She was always at home in the world, when she played, argued, grew indignant with her prep, or was noisy and violent at her birthday party. She questioned nothing and had the clearest sense of what she ought to do even when she did not do it. Preedy was always aware of her presence, but at first he didn't like her. She wouldn't come to services – she was spoilt – and yet he always felt her serious mind at work. She was at once attracted and repelled by him. Once she asked, 'Why do we live if we die?'

And he said, 'If we know how to live we don't die.'

'But everyone dies.'

'Only in the body.'

'Oh, that's just what you say.'

Her mother interrupted, 'Ada knows that death is not the end.'

'Well,' said Ada, 'it's the end of me, I mean as I am now, myself – and I shan't like that much.'

Mrs Rollwright said that she knew very well that Heaven was happier than any life on earth. Ada answered, 'But I don't know, and you don't want me to die, I notice,' producing an embarrassment that she herself became aware of. For after a moment she said in a tone of apology, 'Well, I expect you're right, only it's a funny idea.'

Preedy had forgotten that Ada was on the beach, and seeing her, he stopped. His first impulse was to avoid her as well as everybody else. She had not seen him. She was standing, balanced on a pile towards one end of a groyne, well beyond the water's edge and, to judge by the slope of the beach, beyond her depth. As the man watched, she took a cautious step along the top of the groyne, with the obvious intention of reaching the last pile, of which only a few inches showed above the tide.

It was this step, at once cautious and defiant of peril, like that of a tightrope walker, that made Preedy call her. Not that he was afraid for her; she could swim very well, but it conveyed to him something of the child's nature that suddenly made him need her.

She started, stood for a moment teetering on one leg, with swinging arms, and then with a quick turn, recovered her balance and came, stepping quickly but delicately, with a smile of pleasure in her own skill, to land.

'You might have fallen in,' said Preedy seriously.

'But I didn't. Where are you going?'

'Just for a walk.'

She turned to walk beside him and he put his hand on her shoulder as if to steady himself on the pebbles, but actually for the contact, not of affection, but of something more mysterious, of something belonging to Ada, as herself, that came to him only fitfully and by unexpected ways.

He was fond of the child but not easy in her company, for he had never discovered what she thought of him. There was no relation of understanding between them. She had come with her mother to mission services, but had, he felt, no religious feeling. Often when he called he found her with friends of her own age and he was struck then by her noisiness. She seemed to be always the noisiest, the roughest and rudest, and he felt in this a rebelling against the grown-up world, her mother and himself.

And yet it was somewhere in this rebellious independence that resided the sense she could give him of a faith far deeper than his own, a confidence that did not even know itself to be questioned. And at this time his own was so much at question that he did not dare look into or call upon it.

During this slow progress neither had spoken. Preedy was aware of Ada only as a frustration – like a prayer that had failed to give any sense of God's presence. And Ada, content like a child to do her duty as a support, picked her steps over the pebbles and kept silence because she had nothing to say.

But now she stopped suddenly and said, 'There they are – they're calling.'

In fact, a car had stopped on the road above and Mrs Rollwright was calling from its window.

'I expect that's the doctor,' said Ada, but Preedy was holding her shoulder firmly and did not move, so she stood where she was.

Mrs Rollwright had now got out of the car and came down rapidly across the shore, beckoning urgently, but Preedy still did not move. He obliged the woman to walk right up to him across the pebbles.

Mrs Rollwright spoke first to her daughter, 'Could you come now Ada, we want you at the house.'

'Is it the doctor?' Ada said.

'Do you mean to allow the examination?' Preedy asked.

Mrs Rollwright turned to him nervously, 'It's only for poor Ned's sake; it's so hard for him; can it really do any harm? We needn't pay any attention to the doctor; we know what doctors are.'

'You know what I think,' said Preedy, 'it's no good saying it again. Only you must understand that you're taking the responsibility for Ada.'

Mrs Rollwright, still more agitated, touched the man's sleeve as if in an extremity of appeal, then took her hand away again, as if afraid of offending. 'But can it do any harm if we don't mind it? After all, Ned is anxious too. He wants to keep her with him; he says he has a right.'

The doctor himself, impatient at this delay, had now got out of the car, and was picking his way across the shore. He was a tubby man and plainly resented the whole situation. From several yards away he called sharply, 'What have you decided? I can't wait now.'

Mrs Rollwright turned to him and said, 'We're so sorry, Doctor, we'll come back to the house at once.'

'But what about the clinic? There'll have to be an X-ray, and I must arrange that now.' He looked round for response, but nobody answered; and taking this silence for consent he pulled out his notebook, 'I'll phone at once from the post office and they may fit her in this morning. I won't be able to be there, but I'll send the particulars. What's the name? Rollwright?' He scribbled in his notebook, 'With a W, I suppose?' and then looking up, 'Christian name?'

'Ada.'

'Ada Rollwright, aged twelve, all right, take her back to the house and I'll be there in ten minutes.' He put up his notebook and went away.

Mrs Rollwright looked again towards Preedy with an anxious frightened glance of appeal, but Preedy had already turned his back and was walking towards the sea. She hesitated a moment as if wondering whether to follow him, but the man's whole air, the flat stiff back and even step expressed so strongly his complete rejection of her and all her works that she did not dare. She took Ada's hand and made for the bungalow.

When Preedy turned away from Mrs Rollwright he had already ceased to think of her and her problems. What had struck him with unexpected force were the doctor's words as he pronounced Ada's name. They fell into the blankness of his desolation like a flash of lightning illuminating its whole landscape in vivid black and white.

Very early in the first agitation of the Mission committee about Preedy and Ada Rollwright, a certain disciple, Brank, had remarked to Preedy, 'It's the same initials.'

Brank was a man of fifty or so, a bachelor, who had spent years on a plantation in the East. He had studied Yoga and Hinduism, astrology and the great pyramid, and called himself a mystic. He was writing a book about revelations and was exploring the Bible for what he called signs. So the letters of the first words of a certain psalm, added together, gave the date of the next war, which would also be the last, Armageddon, the end of the material world.

Preedy despised all such practices and had preached against them, calling them Shamanism. He found Brank a bore and a nuisance and also regarded him as a danger. He brought the Mission's faith itself into contempt.

So he had answered him sharply and roughly, 'What do you mean?'

'Alice Rodker – Ada Rollwright. And Alice saved you before. As you say, she was chosen by God.'

'I didn't say that she was chosen – she had no idea of doing God's work. She simply brought me the sense of God's love at work in the world.'

'She was sent, and perhaps this child too – can you believe it's an accident that she should have the same initials – a ten thousand to one chance?'

Preedy had said impatiently that such coincidences were common and in any case, Ada Rollwright had no importance for him and took little interest in the Mission.

'It is a sign,' Brank had answered, 'for us to read – you will know what it means when the time comes.'

Preedy, irritated, had said no more. The whole rigmarole of signs and hidden meanings offended his idea of God's majesty and truth.

But now, as the doctor spoke the name, he remembered. Brank's words came to him with a force of shock which broke the whole fabric of that solid construction which was his idea of things – the construction which, at that moment, stood over him like a prison or a convent cell.

He was suddenly in a different world; the walls had gone and the darkness was no longer an enclosed, stifling dark of the grave, but an enormous night in which darkness was not the absence of light but the presence of things unseen – of a whole world of being not known or realized before. He stood looking out to the sea, with its small waves extending away in parallel till they shaded into an horizon like etched glass. But he saw it only with his eyes, without recognition. All his senses were turned inwards; he was gazing into this immensity of his vision, straining his eyes to distinguish some form, listening for an intelligible sound.

And now the forms began to appear, shapes darker than the dark, that made the surrounding darkness seem transparent like a sky. These shapes, so rapidly building, like clouds, were those of his earliest childhood, of old stories, terrifying, mysterious, of murderous kings, savage prophets, a turmoil of cruelty and war. And over all the presence of Jehovah, like the whole night itself, a tension of primordial being, the very force of things, the divine will, the living person, the furious judge, the king of kings – and what kings, soaked in treachery and blood – who gave the sign to and tested Abraham with the demand that he should cut the throat of his only son as an offering. And Abraham was loyal; he proved himself. And Isaac lived.

Was this world today any different from that one of the Old Testament? Was there any less hatred, cruelty? What was the formula for a leader, a hero, a tribal chief? To teach hatred, to arm the murderer, to lie and plot, to despise all faith and practise treachery.

And what were the people, the mass? Were they any wiser, better, than the tribes of Israel – any less greedy and self-seeking, less brainless and noisy, less animal and cunning in dependence, less cruel in power, less responsible for themselves or anyone else? Haters of truth, adoring the flatterer, bumsucking equally to the demagogue and the tyrant, vermin meaner than the foxes or weasels, because they knew the evil they did and loved it for the kick it gave to their malice and their lust.

The miracle of history was that any goodness, any truth, had ever appeared on earth – how, in this everlasting war between the few good and the enormous mass of evil, the smallest remnant of the faithful survived. How did they know their leader and maintain their faith? By revelation only. By the sudden showing forth of his power, his grandeur, by the word out of the air, the voice heard at night in the sleepy soul unguarded and released from selfish fear, by the touch of kindness, the glance of a passer-by in the street, the mere glimpse of a face made beautiful by a momentary affection. By things unlooked for and unexpected arriving without order or preparation. By portents and signs.

Now Preedy remembered Brank's look when he had said, 'A man like Hooper thinks all this is silly, but perhaps Hooper is too clever to see anything but his own cleverness.' And Brank's look, the glance of that simple man now revealed to him his own blind presumption. Here was a sign of the plainest kind given to him personally. Saved by one childish messenger, he was to be retrieved by another. A sign made threefold sure by an actual signature – by a repetition of letters which was by itself beyond expectation or plan.

Conviction broke upon Preedy with such force that he turned and made for the bungalow so fast that he stumbled on the shingle. He was panic-struck with fear that he would be too late, that he had already failed his test, that Ada Rollwright would die.

59

In the inquest on Ada Rollwright, six weeks later, the Brinsea doctor's evidence put the parents in a very bad light. He had warned them that any delay in treating the case might be fatal, that she was much more dangerously affected than they realized.

The mother explained her religious objection to treatment and Preedy gave an account of his intervention, and added that it was Ada herself who had suggested waiting, 'to see if I have any more temperatures.'

The coroner gave his usual verdict, deploring the superstitious blindness of the mother and the disastrous teaching of the so-called Mission of Faith and Regeneration.

The evidence made clear what had happened at the bungalow. The doctor, impatient and cocksure, had announced that Ada's lungs were in worse case than he had expected, but he would await the X-ray for a final report. Then he had gone and Rollwright said, 'That decides it –' But Mrs Rollwright hastily covered Ada's narrow chest – that chest with its pearl white livid skin stretched tightly over the rabbit ribs, which filled her with terror and a desperation that was also defiance – she was not going to submit to Ada's being ill. It was impossible even to think of such senseless cruelty to a child. This chest, much more than the doctor's warning, remained in her feeling as she listened to her husband's voice, 'That decides it.' She thought, 'Why should it decide? Of course the X-ray people will agree with the doctor that the child is in danger. They know it won't matter if they're wrong; no one will blame them for saying Ada is ill when she isn't – no one will know – they'll claim they cured her. She's nothing to them either way.'

It was because Mrs Rollwright was a very intelligent well-educated woman that she was not ready to accept doctors as infallible even when they claimed to be certain. She knew how their claims were based simply on public ignorance of facts, on the naïve readiness to believe anything that called itself science.

She was especially repelled by this doctor, so impatient, so sure that he alone could be right, that anyone who did not agree with his scientific view of things must be a fool. Why should he despise them and a man like Preedy for believing that the world might not after all be quite such a madhouse of cruelty and suffering as he chose to assume. Yet she was shaken, for again intelligence told her that if the doctors could deceive themselves, so could she.

All she had said therefore to her husband's, 'That decides it,' was, 'But why – it hasn't really changed anything.'

And then Preedy had walked in and given his warning. God had sent him a sign that he dared not put aside.

Rollwright had told him to get out – he was talking rubbish, and the two men began to shout.

It was then that Ada herself had said, 'Why not wait a week? That won't make any difference.'

In the end Rollwright had agreed, because the only alternative was to carry Ada off by force and that was impossible. His last word was that if his wife did not keep this understanding he would go to law and demand custody of Ada.

60

When Syson appeared on the charge of criminal libel, Preedy's counsel opposed bail. He reminded the court that this was a second offence and much graver than the last. But to the counsel's annoyance, a gentleman arose in the body of the court and said that he had come from Mr Preedy himself to say that he had no objection to bail. Preedy's counsel then conferred with this person, and withdrew his objection. Bail was allowed and Syson left the court.

To Syson's surprise Clarry had sat in court throughout the proceedings and was waiting for him with her father when he came out. They were the last people he wanted to see. For the last half-hour during the proceedings for bail he had been asking himself how he could best continue his attack on Preedy. He still had plenty of his leaflets; but they were stored with Rollwright who might not want to let him have them after this libel action. But he reflected, 'At this time of day Rollwright will be at business, and I can go in by the garden gate and take them.' He was actually deciding how he could break in to Rollwright's house if the garden door was not open when he saw Clarry and Sir Henry.

They had also seen him. Sir Henry stepped up and shook hands, and Clarry, after a moment's hesitation, kissed him carefully on the cheek.

Syson thought, 'The good wife doing her duty,' and he felt sorry for the woman. He was also amused by that dutiful kiss and Clarry's resolute air. Sir Henry, his large red face shining with good humour and good living, had anxious and watchful eyes. He spoke with the quick deference of one who deals with lunatics. 'We brought the car, we thought you might like to come straight away to Brownhill and get a real holiday.'

Syson did not speak. He wanted to be polite to these well-meaning people but he could not think of what to say. He could not concentrate his mind on their affairs. They seemed so far off from him that he didn't know how to speak to them; he knew it was impossible to make himself understood. But when they had brought him to the car he drew back and said, 'What about a cup of tea?' They both hastily and warmly agreed. When they reached the tea shop Sir Henry suddenly recollected that he must park the car. Probably he had received a glance from Clarry, or perhaps he was merely exercising the Simpkins tact. Husband and wife went in together to the little eating house. At this time, nearly four o'clock, it was already crowded and hot with the steam of tea. It had that indefinable smell of a crowded eating house, compounded, not only of food and humanity, tobacco smoke and wet umbrellas, but of disinfectants and deodorants sprinkled on floors and seeping in from the kitchen. It seemed in its congestion of atmosphere and people a piece of concentrated domesticity in form so stuffy and citified as to become monstrous and malignant, like a cancer cell in some helpless, innocent, well-meaning heart; the analogue, on the domestic side, of a tube train in the rush hour, with all its crowded loneliness of business life.

At first sight there were no seats empty anywhere, but then a woman got up in a far corner, and Clarry made her way to it.

There was a seat also at the next table, and as Syson followed Clarry, a young man at this table suddenly got up, said without preamble, 'I could move over,' and took the departing woman's place, leaving his seat for Syson. When Syson forgot to thank him, Clarry turned and did so in a tone full of protest against her husband's bad manners. But Syson had not heard the man's remark or understood his intention; he was asking himself why he had come to this horrible place, why he was wasting his time. 'I can't even think,' he brooded. And sitting down mechanically, he gazed at a woman opposite sitting next to Clarry, a big pale woman of fifty or so with an exhausted face. She looked at Syson with large blue eyes, as expressionless as those of a dead fish, and then said across the table to a young woman on his right hand, 'The rush hour again – I don't know how we do it. We said we wouldn't, never again – and here we are.' She tittered and put a handkerchief to her lips. 'Right in for it.'

'We shouldn't have stopped for tea,' said the other.

'Oh, I couldn't go on without tea.'

This conversation to Syson was as if some poison were being dripped slowly into a wound in his flesh. He had not known of a wound, he had felt only apathy towards everyone and everything. Even his plan for getting the leaflets and continuing his campaign against Preedy did not give him either pleasure or excitement. He did not expect to have any success with that enterprise; it was simply something to be done.

Now he shrank away from these women. He felt horror for them, for all this crowd of tired, sweating people, jammed together in their own foul air like cattle in a truck being carried helplessly to slaughter. He felt horror because he felt his own likeness to them. He was one of this mass, a kind of silly beast, being made a fool of, being pushed about in a crowd, without dignity, without sense, without purpose. And the image of Rollwright's garden door came into his mind. Was it usually open? If not, how did it open?

Clarry had gone to order tea. She would not wait to be attended to, but in her usual energetic, impatient manner, marched to the counter. The waitress protested but came, and with a sulky scowl took the order.

Syson looked at his watch and began to get up. He wanted to escape from this place, from the noise and the stink, especially from the people. It was the people he could not bear, with their chatter, their dull, stupid, confused, senseless existence.

'Where are you going?' Clarry said, surprised and impatient.

'I've got an appointment.'

'An appointment?' Clarry was surprised. 'But you didn't even know you were getting bail.'

Syson didn't answer, and Clarry, after gazing at him in perplexity for some moments said, 'Are you still angry with me? I wish you'd tell me what I've done.'

'You haven't done anything; you've been very good.'

'Then why can't we start again? We used to be so happy. I simply don't understand what has happened to you.' Her lips began to tremble and Syson was afraid she would cry, but she controlled herself, feeling his anxiety, and said, 'Why not come to us for a time at least, and let us try again?'

But Syson was thinking how she had said she didn't understand what had happened and he knew that was true. Nothing would make her understand. For her he was a lunatic who had thrown away a good job, a respectable job, and all his happiness, for nothing. But what was the good of trying to explain anything to her if she didn't understand why he had not been able to remain in the Church? His experience of the last year had taken him so far from her that he could not explain his simplest feelings.

'Can't you even speak to me?' Clarry said, and now she was growing impatient. The man might be mad but, at least, he could use common politeness. 'Do you want to keep up this ridiculous quarrel? It isn't even a real quarrel. I never made it and I never wanted it to go on.'

Syson was thinking of his leaflet, he was thinking that he should have made it much stronger. If it was libellous anyhow, why hadn't he said right out that he regarded Preedy as a murderer – a deliberate murderer.

'At least,' Clarry said, 'you can come to Brownhill for a few days and take a real rest. I won't speak to you, you needn't even see me if you don't want to.'

'It's very kind of you, but you see I've got this appointment. I've made other arrangements.'

And suddenly Clarry was disgusted with this unreasonable brute; she had done all she could with him. It wasn't only that he'd behaved like a lunatic without the slightest regard for herself or the children, of whom he had pretended to be so fond, he had done wickedness, he had provoked all the trouble in Pant's Road exactly as the Vicar had warned. She had done her duty by him but really she would be glad of a final break. 'I am sorry,' she said, 'that I butted in today if you didn't want me. I had hoped you would be reasonable.'

'I've got – an appointment.'

'But you wanted to see me.' The younger of the two women next to them gazed openly from one to the other, but, catching Clarry's eye, let her eyes drop wearily to her plate.

'Yes,' said Syson, 'but I'm in rather a hurry.'

'Papa will take you to wherever it is in the car, and then we can go back to Brownhill, at least till the case comes on.'

'I'm afraid I can't come now.'

'But what have you got to do?'

Syson made no answer. The women began to talk again. The young one said, 'The shops are too awful nowadays; you can't get anything done.'

'There's too many people in the world,' said the fat one.

'But why didn't we come earlier? You always say, "We'll come early."'

And this conversation again made Syson feel a fearful oppression, as if an enormous weight was slowly crushing down on him, and he repeated, 'I've got to go.'

Clarry flushed suddenly and exclaimed, 'You're not going back to Pant's Road, are you? You're not going to see those people again? That man Rollwright or Rodker.'

The women broke off their languid exchange; they had heard the note of anger in Clarry's voice, but this time they didn't look, they realized that these strangers were quarrelling and they didn't want to intrude.

Clarry dropped her voice and leant forward, but this too was a social gesture, her natural Simpkins indifference to what the mob might think combined with her frustrated irritation with her husband to make her impatient. For her, Syson was not only a bad husband and a bad father, but a dangerous and even a wicked man. He had turned against the Church, which, alone in the world, was trying to make some peace and to preserve some goodness; a church that was fighting against every kind of hostility as well as indifference. Clarry, for all her stout looks and Simpkins obstinate courage, had a secret fear that the forces of evil, and especially the force of unreason, were winning, that the whole of civilization was going crash, especially that Simpkins civilization which seemed to her the most precious and, in fact, the only real civilization, that of highly cultivated people who loved truth and practised all the Christian virtues, at least among themselves, people who were essentially Christian in ethic, but essentially agnostic in faith. For Clarry was still a Simpkins, though she had taken to the Church; that is to say, she was still deeply suspicious of religious enthusiasm, and hated the fanatic. Hated indeed everybody and everything unreasonable. She had taken to religion as Sir Henry supported the Royal Society, as something that did good in the world, something she deeply believed in, but her idea of God was probably not much different from his idea of the President of the Royal Society. And it was because her fundamental belief in what she meant by goodness, in reason, in charity between man and man, was outraged, that at last she lost her temper with Syson.

'But how can you go on like this? Just spreading hatred. It doesn't even do Preedy any harm; it never does those lunatics any harm to abuse them, it's just what they like. People who hate just revel in being hated. Don't you even see how right Vicar was when he warned you?'

Syson was hardly listening. He knew that he could not explain himself to Clarry, and he was only anxious to escape. He looked at his watch and saw, to his surprise, that it was a quarter to five.

It had struck him suddenly that if he didn't get to the Rollwrights before five o'clock, Rollwright might well be returning from business, and then he would be prevented from getting his leaflets.

He was on his feet before he realized that he had not answered Clarry. He turned to her then and muttered again, 'I'm sorry, I've got to go.'

'Does this mean you don't want to see me again?' And he answered at once, 'It isn't any good, things are different. I've got to go on and you couldn't bear it. It would be bad for the children.'

All this was not what he wanted to say; it was not the real reason why he couldn't bear Clarry's presence or even to look at her. It was because she was an interruption to what was happening to him, to his thoughts and feelings. She had nothing now to do with him and his life, any more than any of these people in the restaurant, even less, for they didn't even think they knew him and she did. Preedy was closer to him, if Preedy sat before him now he would have something to say. He and Preedy lived in the same world and to Clarry that world simply didn't exist. It wasn't only that she thought it a world of lunatics, but she had no imagination whatever of the people who lived in it any more than of people who lived on Mars or Venus.

'I don't see how we can go on.' He turned round then and went out. He had just enough money for a taxi to Pant's Road, and jumped into the first he saw.

He was now in a panic. It was ten minutes to five and he was perfectly sure that if Rollwright had reached home he would not get those leaflets. And it seemed to him absolutely necessary that he should get them. Some fragment of reasonable machinery still languidly operating in the obscurest corner of his brain, was asking him why he wanted these leaflets, why, in fact, he was so eager to continue this campaign against Preedy. But he paid no more attention to it than if it had been speaking to someone else. He himself knew that he must have those leaflets, there was no other course open to him.

It was with extraordinary relief, a sense even of gratitude, that when he got to Rollwright's house and walked through the side door to the garden, he found a sitting-room door ajar and the unopened parcel of leaflets still where he had seen it last, in a drawer of the desk. In two minutes he was back in the road with the whole parcel, and going at once to the public lavatory and paying his penny for a W.C., broke the parcel open and distributed the leaflets, a thousand in number, among his various pockets, into the lining of his coat and under his shirt. From there he made straight to the Mission House, took up his stand at the gate, and began to hand out the leaflets to everyone that passed in or out of the villa. These were pretty numerous because, apart from the usual stream of callers seeking consultation with the Missioner, committee members were apt to call on Monday and Tuesday for informal discussion of points that might be raised at the weekly committee meetings on Wednesday afternoon. These informal meetings, in fact, were often more important than the actual committee, for it was here that the different pressure groups formed alliances and made their bargains.

61

Allday received his leaflet with a polite smile and said a few words of regret about the case, for which, in fact, he had always been sorry. He considered that men of God should never go to law because it only made them unpopular and damaged their prestige. And when he went in, he was upset to hear Kerne saying they ought to telephone for the police. 'You don't really want another scandal,' he said, 'Those police court proceedings did us a lot of harm.'

'That lunatic could do us a lot more harm if he makes trouble for us now with this big meeting due on Wednesday – at any rate we can't have him here then – we're going to have enough trouble as it is with this resolution at the committee.'

'About the Liverpool Mission?'

'No, about the healing of children.' Kerne, maliciously amused to see Allday's surprise, went on, 'You didn't know of that one? It's by Gillson. Not to admit any children for treatment under the age of eighteen; at least not without a doctor's certificate.'

'But that's impossible – the Missioner can never accept that.'

'That's the idea.' Kerne, as the easiest way of showing his contempt and hatred of the business man, then turned his back and walked off.

Kerne knew very well of Allday's secret attempt to limit Preedy's scope. He himself had always approved them, and actually hoped that Preedy would be curbed. All the same, he did not want Syson to make trouble. He hated any kind of noisy trouble, and when, next day, Syson, looking only a little dirtier, a little more unshaved, was once more at the gate, he telephoned a warning to Hooper.

Hooper thanked him warmly for the message. He fully realized how critical Wednesday's committee meeting was going to be, for Laney was going to attend, and Laney had definitely decided not to back Preedy unless he accepted the ruling that no case should be treated without a doctor's certificate. At the same time he had not yet decided to back the *Argus*. It seemed to Hooper that the two things hung together. That is to say, Laney was not going to back the *Argus* unless he could have Preedy where he wanted him, and that was why Hooper had finally made up his mind that Preedy must go.

As he said to Joanna, 'It's a pity, because what we wanted was a simple message – something absolutely clear. That's what gets 'em. Look at Christian Science. Laney is an old woman like Ackroyd. This cry about the babies has frightened the pants off them. It's just another angle on the general softness. The whole West is soft, rotten. They think what they've got is Christian feeling, but what it really is is the slop disease. Let's not take any responsibility for anything, not annoy anyone, especially not the crooks. They could be dangerous.'

Hooper was very angry, but also frightened. Things had been going badly with him since the Rideout bankruptcy. His debts were running up, and if the *Argus* failed, he would be faced by the extraordinary and unexpected question of how he was going to live. He had no other income except for a few royalties from his book and occasional articles. It appeared that Joanna's income would never be more than a couple of hundred a year, and he began to be pestered by duns.

Duns, to a proud man, are both infuriating and alarming. They alarm him because they reveal to him that his pride is not secure. He can be humiliated in spite of himself. So that this committee meeting at Pant's Road began to take on great importance for Hooper. However, he was really not much afraid of his power either to force Preedy to be, as he put it, sensible, or to resign. If the worst came to the worst he would throw Preedy out. The really important thing was to save the Mission as a running organization. It would be quite easy to find another Missioner.

It was through Joanna that he realized Alice's possible use at this juncture. 'She is back at her brother's flat, but she phoned me from work. She's at Dr Gale's surgery. She is very upset,' Joanna told him, 'about Syson. She thinks he was quite right to try to save that child. You know she lost her own baby in the same way. She asked me whether I thought she ought to give evidence for Syson. She seemed quite ready to offer herself as a witness, but I said of course her evidence wouldn't be accepted.'

'Why wouldn't it be accepted?'

'It wasn't that really, it was only that I knew you wouldn't want Preedy discredited. I knew what a very high opinion you had of him.'

Hooper looked at his wife, and wondered how she would take his change of mind about Preedy. He said, at last, 'Preedy did a fine job, the question is if he's going to ruin everything now by being obstinate.'

'Is it about money again?'

'No, it's about these children. Another Rodker case now could ruin the Mission.'

'I thought you said that was one of the risks we had to take.'

'Oh, I know Preedy is a God for you, but after all, he does make mistakes.'

Joanna was startled. When she looked up at her husband she met his eyes fixed upon her with that contemptuous, irritable expression which meant that she had hurt him. She did not know where she had hurt him, but she kept silent. She knew that he was worried about money and she suspected he had some deeper cause for his touchy and erratic temper. In fact, she was aware of some crisis in the man. He was both extraordinarily irritable with her and much more affectionate. He had suddenly taken to coming home early. He would sit with her the whole evening, and, though he was infinitely quarrelsome, it was obvious that he wanted her company. He would complain to her that he was tired. He seemed to be asking all the time for sympathy, even while he rejected it. He was certainly much more amorous, much more brutal and careless in handling her. She was often profoundly disgusted with him and sometimes very angry. And often she wondered that she bore with his whims, his rudeness, and his deliberate violence, which was obviously intended to humiliate. And perhaps all that restrained her was the sense that he was in a touchy and unpredictable mood.

It did occur to her that he was annoyed to find that this plain wife he had acquired was also poor, but she did not allow this feeling to weigh with her because she despised it. She did not want to despise her husband.

When Hooper asked her to send for Alice she demanded at once, 'Is it about Syson? You'll have to be careful about Syson. She's got that Rollwright child on her mind all the time.'

'So have I – that's the trouble. We've got to make Preedy see sense about children.'

'You can't set Alice at Preedy.'

Hooper did not answer this. He said only, 'Are you going to send for her or shall I go and see her?'

And then at once, seeing Joanna's opposition in her mouth, he said, 'All right, you can stand out, I'll see her myself.' And before she could speak he went out and caught a taxi.

He found that Alice was at Dr Gale's, and he sent in a note asking her to see him about the Syson case.

Alice detested Hooper as a newspaper man, but also she knew that he was Preedy's friend and since the Rollwright child's death she had felt a kind of desperation. She hated Preedy, but she knew that he was not responsible for her baby's death or the Rollwright child's. She knew that on this matter of religion he was mad. Perhaps he was mad all through. But this did not entitle him to be a murderer. And when she thought that, she was quite sure that she must help Syson, to stop him from murdering more children. Grown-ups could take care of themselves, most of them were mad too, but children had to be protected. At the same time, she did not want to join Preedy's enemies, she found it impossible to go to Syson and offer her help. Twice she had written to him and torn the letter up. She had written to Preedy and warned him, 'to let the Rollwright girl alone, you know very well that Mrs Rollwright is just the same kind of fool as I was when you strung me along.' And this letter had brought Preedy to the flat. But she had been on the watch for him; she looked out at every caller through the letter-box, and when she saw him at last she had refused to open the door. Apparently he had known she was at home, probably he had recognized her step as she came to the door. He had gone on ringing for an hour, pressing the bell for ten minutes at a time. At the end he had been shouting through the letter-box; he had said he would kill her, and she had been terrified, terrified he would break in the door. She had called him mad before, but now, as he shouted his threats, she felt his madness; she felt that he had completely lost control of himself. He had gone away at last only because some of the other tenants on the top landing complained to the janitor, who came up and threatened to send for the police.

And now, seeing Hooper's note, she felt all her old distrust of the man, but saw that he was the only person whose advice she would listen to. He was a friend of Preedy's, but he was not a mad man. She didn't want to see him, or even to speak to him, but he was the only way out of the misery of her indecision, so she went to him in the corridor, and asked him what he wanted. She had not meant to say these words in so rude a tone, but they were spoken before she had decided what to say.

'You had my note!' Hooper said. 'It's about Preedy and the Rollwright case.'

'Yes, I know. You're trying to get Preedy into trouble.'

'Not at all. I'm trying to keep him out of trouble.'

'I don't believe a word of it.'

'That's all right, I know you've got it in for me, and I wouldn't bother with you if I wasn't worried about Preedy. I happen to like Preedy and I don't want to see him go smash. And you know as well as I do how difficult it is to make him do the sensible thing. All I want, and all anybody wants, from him, is an understanding not to accept children as patients, at least without a doctor's certificate. You know what happened in the Rollwright case. Preedy was very lucky to escape a manslaughter charge.'

'What's all this got to do with me?'

'You have a lot of influence with Preedy, he has that case of yours on the brain. Besides, you have all the facts. I'm not asking you to bring up the case again, I'm the last man to want any publicity now, but, if you could see the Pant's Road Committee tomorrow morning, you would make them realize the very dangerous position Preedy is in.'

'I don't see why I should do your dirty work.'

Hooper suddenly lost his temper with the girl, and said, 'I'm not taking that, even from a piece like you,' and walked out. But half an hour later he had a phone call from Joanna, who said that Alice was with her and she was ready to do what he had asked, 'whatever that is. What did you ask her? She won't tell me, but it's obviously upset her. She's been flying off the handle about the Press and that's always a bad sign. You'll have to be careful what you say to her.'

But, in fact, when Hooper called next morning to take the girl to Pant's Road, she was perfectly amenable. She scarcely spoke to him and offered no explanation for her change of mind, but listened without protest to his instructions.

273

62

This critical meeting at the Pant's Road headquarters on Wednesday morning was disorderly from the beginning. The fact was that the split in the Mission committee had spread itself through the whole congregation. Probably the split had always existed between those who accepted completely Preedy's claim to heal all diseases, and those who merely believed that it did no harm for him to try. Probably at least two-thirds of his followers at any time had no sound faith at all. But they belonged to that enormous majority whose religious belief is essentially something between a bet and a prayer. They take a chance in the desperate hope of some boon, they declare their confidence in the hope that it will be justified. As the billiards player, after he has made his shot, moves his cue through the air in the direction which he wishes the ball to take, so they say, 'God will cure me,' in the hope that the very statement will bring a cure. It is sympathetic magic that they invoke. But there is a clear distinction between the billiards player who knows exactly how to make his shot, and the one who relies on some luck; and when the latter is challenged, he will either admit that his waving of cues has no importance, or he will try to maintain that it has real value. He will say that it trains the eye and the muscle, that it is a kind of rehearsal of the better shot he is going to make next time; the last thing he will admit is that it is an instinctive reflex action, inherited from magic-making ancestors.

So when the issue of healing either all comers or only selected cases was put to the mission, Preedy's disciples split into those who admitted to themselves that their faith was limited by reason, and those who were determined to justify it on any grounds. And, of these, the second party was much the more bitter because it had so much more to lose; because it found itself in a fog, and could not admit the fog. To be befogged is to be lost, and people who are lost go mad. The extraordinary violence of some of the Pant's Road disciples at that time, which once more got Pant's Road into the papers, and received such unfavourable comment, even from evangelical circles, was due, not to any special barbarism in that suburb, but simply to the strength of that faith that Preedy had inspired. For it is quite certain that Preedy had given to hundreds about Pant's Road and thousands in the Kingdom a guiding string in the black fog of their lives. Through him, for the first time in their bewildered existence, they had walked confidently forward in the certainty, or near certainty, of knowing, not only where they were going, but actually what kind of a world surrounded them. And these people, even the stupidest of them, perceived at once that any attempt to limit Preedy's promise to them cut that string, and left them once more lost and bewildered in the fog.

Their violence was that of people fighting, not merely for their lives, but for their reason.

As for the precautions of the different pressure groups of Allday's party or Mrs Hartree's party, of Jinks and what can be called the Hooper party, to keep their intrigues private, they were as futile as such efforts usually are. Everything was known to everybody in the congregation; the only result of discretion and secrecy had been to mix a lot of rumour with the truth and add a political thickness to the deepening religious fog. That was why, long before ten o'clock, the Mission House was in a state of siege. Fifty or sixty people of all ages were standing in the road or crowding in the front garden. Thus the policeman sent for by Kerne to make sure that Syson didn't make trouble was now useful to guard the door against Preedy's supporters, anxious to attack the Allday party, or alternatively to defend them.

Syson had been there from eight o'clock in the morning, silently distributing his leaflets. He looked like a tramp. And there was something in his mechanical air while he walked from group to group and, without looking in any face, handed out his leaflets, that made people stare after him. A good many of these said afterwards that they had expected some violent action from him, that he looked dangerous. But no one gave any warning and if Syson looked like a criminal it was probably on account of his three days' beard, and the apathy of his expression. An unshaven chin brings out the criminal in any set of features. And apathy, that kind of desperate apathy which goes with a general lack of hope or settled purpose, is common in very sick people and idiots, as well as criminals. In fact, nobody really expected any violence from this dejected-looking and ruined man.

Most of the recipients of his leaflets crushed them up as soon as they recognized their purport and threw them on the ground. But this made no difference to the distributor; he continued his mechanical march like a robot wound up and set only for this action.

Hooper arrived at ten punctually with Laney and Alice. He had not meant that Laney should attend a meeting that was likely to be violent, but Laney himself had insisted on coming.

Laney was, just as usual, dressed in a black suit cut in the style of 1910 when, as a young American visitor, he had ordered his first clothes in Savile Row. His linen was white with the faintest possible black line, simply to distinguish it from the ordinary business shirt of New York. He was dressed, in fact, as plainly and unobtrusively as possible, and yet, as he walked with Hooper from his car to the Mission House, he received more attention than if he had come with a band. He had lived to see the fashion of 1910 return as the latest thing, as the highest dandyism, and the Pant's Road suburbanites gazed on him with amazement as he was promptly admitted to the Mission House with Hooper and Alice.

There, the meeting had already started, that is to say, although it was not yet ten, discussion had started. The little back room was crowded with at least twenty people. Three were perched on the sideboard, half a dozen more were seated on the floor. Preedy had pushed the table to one side and seated himself upon it with an instinctive will to dominate the room; in this he had been completely successful, till that time. In fact, most of the gathering was with him, for it was the Preedyites who, because they were more violent, more desperate, had managed to push themselves in to this private meeting. Kerne had found half a dozen already in possession when he arrived at nine; they had come in through a back window, by way of a neighbour's garden. These six, all young, had constituted themselves bodyguard for Preedy, but they kept quiet at first and did not intervene while Jinks' ally, Gillson, spoke about the question of doctors' certificates. Gillson was a little man with a red face, streaked like a pippin, and a singularly white bald head. He was an aggressive little man, a grocer, from the High Road, who had made his own way and now owned four shops. He was a man with the instinct of management, a born organizer, who would stop in the street to see a council workman lop a tree. But on this occasion he began very tactfully with compliments to Preedy, 'Our Missioner, who has done such marvellous work for the sick and lost souls, and it is just because of that, of his great success, that enemies of all kinds have raised this scandal, and, as we know, all this talk about children being sacrificed is simply a lot of lies. All the same, I think it would be worth our while to take some note of what the coroner said in the case last month about consulting with a doctor before treatment. I don't mean for a moment to cast any doubt on our Missioner's powers of healing.' Preedy interrupted here from the table to say, 'That's just what you are doing, but not on my power, on God's power.'

Here Allday interjected that after all it was not safe to dogmatize about God's methods of exercising his power. And, in fact, Allday was about to make what Preedy called his 'Allday speech'. But Preedy interrupted again. 'We all know your position, Mr Allday, on the fence.'

'As a fellow committee man –' Gillson exclaimed, jumping up in defence of Allday.

'I suppose,' said Preedy, 'that this is a rehearsal for the committee this afternoon, but there's not going to be a meeting, or a committee either. I dismiss the committee.'

This brought the five committee men present, including even old Mrs Hartree, to their feet, and Hooper was heard to say something about the constitution. But the Preedyites broke into clapping; they were getting more and more excited and one of them ran down the corridor to shout the news to the crowd outside, above the roar of their hymn-singing, that the Missioner had got rid of the Gillson gang and sacked the committee. This brought cheers from the crowd, obviously almost to a man extreme Preedyites. Preedy himself cut short the demonstration in the parlour simply by raising his hand and telling everybody to sit down and keep quiet. Surprisingly enough, even Gillson obeyed this order. In fact, the silence in the room testified again to the extraordinary power of the man and certainly established his dominance for that time. He put his hand round his knee, nursing his leg in the attitude of a man very much at ease and said, 'This thing is not going to be decided by soft soap or cant, or political tricks. It is God's business and it is blasphemy to lie in God's face. Mr Gillson has just told us it's all lies about children dying. It isn't all lies, some children have died. There is someone here now

277

to tell us about it, about one child that died. Someone who accuses me of murder, murder of my own child.' At this, one of the Preedyites jumped up and exclaimed that they knew all about that case, that the charge was a lie, and brought for blackmail. He turned then towards Hooper and Alice and said, 'We know who's got it up too. It's a newspaper ramp to smash our Missioner.'

Hooper opened his mouth to speak when Alice jumped up and said, 'Don't believe him, he doesn't know what he's talking about.' The girl was very much excited, and for a moment nobody understood what she meant or who she was referring to. It was Gillson who asked sharply, 'Who doesn't know what he's talking about?'

'That man there,' she said, pointing at Preedy, 'when he says he's a murderer. Perhaps he is a murderer, but if he is he doesn't know it. He doesn't know anything straight. He doesn't really believe anything either, he just tries. He's a fraud.'

Two or three of the Preedyites jumped up together and Alice got involved in an argument with one of them, Gomm, but suddenly stopped, shook her head as if to say, 'It's no good talking,' and sat down. For some moments now ten or twelve people were all speaking together, most of them on their feet, and, in the middle of this turmoil, Preedy got down from the table and began to talk very earnestly to some of the young people in the corner.

Nobody paid much attention to this proceeding of Preedy's. For the moment the meeting had broken up into separate groups. The committee members, now joined by Hooper, were in conference by the door affirming to each other that they would not accept their dismissal. Hooper pointed out to them that they could probably take legal proceedings against Preedy on the grounds that the financial arrangements of the Mission were in the hands of a treasurer appointed by the committee. He saw very clearly that, in dismissing the committee, Preedy had put himself hopelessly in the wrong. Even Mrs Hartree had now turned against Preedy. For the first time she agreed with Hooper that it was not safe to trust him to act with complete wisdom in the conduct of Mission affairs.

It was in the middle of this that Syson walked in. For a moment nobody noticed him. Then Darley, one of the Preedyites, a young man with red hair, was heard to call, 'Throw him out.'

'Yes,' said Syson, 'send for the police, throw me out. It will make a nice story for the papers.'

This brought everyone's attention and for a moment there was silence. Then Darley said, 'That's blackmail, and we've had enough of it.'

'My business is with Preedy,' said Syson.

'Not here,' said Darley, 'I don't know how you got in, and you can get out now.' Two or three of the young people had actually laid hold of Syson to push him out of the room, when Preedy called out to them to stop. 'He's my guest, Darley,' he said, 'I asked Mr Syson to come in whenever he liked. After all, what he's got to say really matters. He's not one of your committee men, canting and wangling. He's interested in the truth and nothing but the truth.' And, going to Syson, he shook hands and asked him to sit down. 'I take it,' he said, 'the question between us is only what sort of a God we believe in. You say that God cannot do a miracle, even of mercy, that he has no power at all in the world to cure all its miseries and cruelties, its fearful injustice.'

It was the hymns that had seemed to have a provocative effect on Syson, especially when some of the choir who had got together near the gate, with an old bald man, one of the tenors, standing on the wall to conduct, struck up *Eternal Father, Strong to Save*.

At the very first verse he stopped distributing his leaflets and began to shout some protest or other. This was not heard. There were now at least a hundred of the congregation gathered in the road, both Preedyites and Alldayites, and they were singing against each other, making so much noise that a crowd of watchers was gathering, an attentive and respectful but shy and distant crowd, as at all such evangelical demonstrations in Britain. It stood twenty yards off in a large circle.

When this hymn was over, Syson's voice was heard shouting that God didn't save, and he was hustled, but more or less by accident, because the congregation pressed in to see what was going on. The policeman then came down to rescue him and brought him into the front garden, when he made a sudden dart and ran in through the front door.

Syson had not intended this action, which is possibly why the policeman had not anticipated it. He acted purely on impulse, impelled by the same mysterious obstinacy which had kept him for three days at the Pant's Road gate and hardly allowed him to eat or sleep. He scarcely, any more, felt rancour against the Mission and Preedy himself; he was not more disgusted with them than with everything in the world. For him, the world had lost all sense. It was a piece of incomprehensible nonsense, where imbeciles like the Preedyites were no more imbecile than the lawyers who had ruined him or his wife who thought it did not matter if he went on preaching a lie. What good were lies to him? He had tried to live on them, and they had starved him. He was like a man who had been living on dirt and now he was dead; his brain was dead and his body was working like a piece of rusty machinery that goes on turning over because it has lost its brake and is simply out of control. It was this machine that now rolled him into the villa and into the back room where he could hear Preedy's voice among the babble of conversation.

He did not see Preedy and when he was seized by the young men amid cries of 'Throw him out,' he simply stood and waited to be thrown out. He did not bother to speak or even to look at these young people; they were fools and he was dead. He allowed them to push him towards the door and when Preedy shouted, 'Let him alone,' he stood where he was until Preedy came up to him, shook his hand, and asked him to sit down.

When Preedy sat down before him and began to talk about religion, saying as before that the only difference between them was the kind of God they believed in, Syson paid no attention to the argument, he knew it all before, but he fixed his eyes on Preedy's face and thought of what Alice had said, 'He can't help it, he's got it wrong somewhere,' and he thought, 'Yes, he's got to believe all this. It would be better for me if I could have gone on believing my own nonsense. I can see now what a difference it makes. It's not just between lies and truth, it's between life and death. He's alive and I'm dead.' But while he was thinking this, he heard the rusty machinery move at the right place, as Preedy finished his speech, and he heard his own voice. 'What I say is, if your God can do such things, if he can do miracles, why doesn't he do them? Why doesn't he stop all the misery and injustice?'

'Come, Mr Syson,' said Preedy, 'you ought to know the answer to that one. I take it you read some theology. You know that, without freedom of moral choice, there can be neither good nor evil in man. If God did not permit man to do evil he could neither do nor know goodness, he could not know God, which is the greatest happiness, an achievement of man's soul. It is because of man's wickedness that evil is done in the world, and to cure that wickedness there is still God's miracle of grace offered freely to us all.'

And again the machine answered. 'Yes, but what about disease, what about the accident that maims a child for life? What about bad luck? That is not due to any evil will. God could stop all that evil if he liked and still leave man free to know good and evil.'

'There is no such thing as bad luck. "But everything and all our fates are from the Lord."'

'Then you agree that God allows all this misery? I say that a God who does that would be a devil.'

'If you're going to speak blasphemy,' said Preedy, 'we won't get any further.'

And at this point, Syson's brain suddenly moved and he perceived that Preedy was afraid, and promptly he said, 'Yes, you don't like that because you know he is a devil, your God.' And as soon as he said these words, he began to abuse the man, saying that anyone who served the devil was himself a devil, but a mean dirty little devil. Darley and the other Preedyites, very naturally, couldn't take this and made a rush at the man.

Their indignation was very reasonable because, of course, this was quite untrue; in fact, Syson knew that it was a lie. He knew that in the sphere where Preedy operated, this foggy element, it was impossible to say how much he served God, and how much he served the devil.

It was said afterwards that Syson had been provoked into this attack on Preedy and, of course, the Preedyites all said that Syson's action was disgraceful. But, according to the book Syson later wrote in prison, *A Sure and Certain Faith*, he was at this time what he calls, 'the devil's prisoner, so tied up in anger and fear that I was not really responsible for my actions. I hated Preedy, of course. But why? Because those posters of his, those preachings, had shown me that my faith was a muddle of wish-fulfilment and time-serving. He challenged me to state my case and I couldn't do it. I could only fall back on vague statements like "It's all a mystery – the thing is too big for human intelligence." And I knew all the time that if I used arguments like that I'd no right to any reasonable faith at all. You could defend any faith in those terms. Hitlerism, communism. But I believed, or rather I wanted to believe, in a God of love and truth who hated cruelty and injustice, who sought to abolish every kind of evil. Yet here was a man who told me that God could abolish any evil at will, and I was not allowed to believe him. I had to ask the doctors first if God would be any good in this case. That was the ruling of the Church, all the Churches. And I saw at that moment that the Churches did not really believe in this power of God to do miracles. I saw it but dared not admit it. I thought that if I lost my faith in the God that could do miracles I should not believe in him at all – I should lose him altogether and life would not be worth living any more.

'And, in fact, when one day, I realized that I had lost that faith, I did not really want to live any more. I did not want anything from life, neither family happiness, nor even my freedom. I was angry when, that first time, I was saved from jail. I had wished to stay in jail for as long as the courts would keep me there. And that was not because I hated the courts and the law but because I hated life. I longed for the prison which would guard me from life, which would make my existence a mere imitation, a shadow show of life, like that of figures in a clock who do the same things every time the clock strikes, who are simply bits of a machine. I knew, of course, that most people live just such puppet lives, but I had believed that I was free, a free soul serving freely the truth that alone gives freedom.

'But now it seemed to me that I was also a puppet. I was angry with my own vicar because he did not believe with me in the God who could do miracles. I thought him a time-server and a hypocrite and hated him for a puppet. I thought that the whole world was made of puppets. I believe in the people who say, "There is no freedom – there is no God. We are all simply robots, machines, pushed about by mechanical forces." And I could not bear it. I thought if that is true then I don't want to be made a fool of. If I am a machine let me live the life of a machine.

'So I was angry when they deprived me of jail and I set to work to get back into jail. I don't mean that I said to myself, "I will force them to put me back into jail." I didn't propose any course of action to myself. I had become a puppet pulled about on strings and perhaps it pleased me to give way to the pull of the strings, to behave like a puppet. Perhaps it was because they would not make a puppet of me, in jail, that I wilfully played the puppet out of jail.

'And so I made them send me to jail again. It was my pleasure to be a prisoner because I knew myself a puppet. I saw it was a pleasure but it was the pleasure of the man who hates the whole world, a pleasure like that of a beaten slave who tears open his wounds again and again in revenge upon his slavery.

'But God saved me in the very nick. For I was not taken at once from the court. There was a crowd of people waiting to see me come out and some of these people were very violent against me. So the police planned to take me away by another door, and took me back to a small waiting-room or lodge, and sent for another car in which I could be moved.

'But while we were waiting for this car, a note for me was brought by the constable who was guarding me. He read the note first, explaining that this was now the rule, and then handed it to me.

'It was a letter from a woman, a follower of Preedy, whose child had died. She wrote to say that she had changed her mind about Preedy and wanted to thank me for my efforts to save the child. But she wanted me also to forgive Preedy because he had not meant to do evil. "I know now," she wrote, "that you were right, and God could not save my poor child. But still you were wrong too for he can do miracles. He has done one with me, for he has given me forgiveness and peace. I am all alone in the world now, for my husband has left me, and once I wanted to die. But now I am glad to be alive to remember that happiness when I had my child and to thank God for all the love in the world."

'I remembered this woman very well, and how she had loved her child. And when I read her letter, I was suddenly moved to understand the thing that had stood before my eyes all my life, as wide as the world, as high as the sky, the thing I had repeated a thousand times in prayers and in sermons, without understanding, the miracle of God's love in the world.

'And so I found my truth where I had left it, and I wanted to go out and tell the people. It seemed to me that the truth was so great, so obvious that I had only to speak it and all should know that great joy, all should be free.

'But when I got up and made to leave the lodge, the policeman at the door jumped up and caught my arm and said, "Hullo, where are you off to?" Then I remembered myself and that though I was made free, yet I was a prisoner. This made me laugh, and then the constable at the door of the building called out that they were ready for me. So I went out.'

However, it does explain Syson's proceedings that morning at Pant's Road. It seems quite certain that he was out for trouble and what happened essentially, allowing for some rather confused evidence in court, was that, when Preedy tried to rescue him from the two enthusiastic Preedyites, he hit Preedy in the face and called him various names, including devil, and was then arrested by the policeman.

This scene, as you might expect, was decisive in Preedy's favour. The committee members expressed their horror at this assault on the Missioner, and they truly were profoundly shocked. Even Gillson perceived all at once that Preedy, for him, was a special kind of person, in fact, so far as Gillson was capable of a true religious feeling, a holy man. Hooper and Laney both congratulated him on his escape from any serious injury, and though they did not actually join afterwards in the public demonstration of thanksgiving, they stood by and did not get into their car and drive away until the attention of the gathering was attracted in another direction by Preedy himself mounting the wall to give an address.

When Hooper telephoned Allday that afternoon to know the result of the committee meeting, he heard that the committee had not met. 'I don't see how we could have met in the circumstances,' Allday said, and his voice expressed a kind of shocked surprise that Hooper should have imagined such a thing.

Hooper immediately telephoned the news to Laney, pointing out that, although Preedy had won this round, it was not decisive. Legally he was in a hopeless position and Gillson would certainly go to the courts for an injunction as soon as feelings in Pant's Road had quietened down. But Laney himself had already heard the news and he answered in his polite and formal manner that he had decided not to support the Mission. 'Mr Preedy,' he said, 'is not going to listen to reason, and he's bound to run into big trouble before long.'

'But, Mr Laney, I understood you to say that it was the Mission that interested you as a going concern and a name; it will still be a name when Preedy is thrown out, and he will be thrown out.

As you say, he's done for himself already. In fact, from a publicity point of view it might do the Mission a lot of good when Preedy is thrown out. It makes all the better proposition now.'

But Laney had obviously made up his mind. He answered that he quite agreed with Mr Hooper, Pant's Road was a big name, and a big name was important, it was what he was looking for. But he'd had some experience in these things and a name wasn't enough. You had to have the name, but you had to have the enterprise too, and he didn't fancy the Mission without Preedy.

'There's at least a dozen men who would take over the Mission tomorrow on our terms, and if they aren't names now we could make them into names in a week, and it wouldn't cost as much as starting with a new mission.'

Laney answered that he was sorry but he had already written to the Pant's Road secretary withdrawing his offer.

It was, perhaps, as Hooper bitterly complained, American of Laney, that, when he dropped his idea of backing the Mission, he abandoned the whole project and cut his losses. On the same day he sold his block of shares in the Rideout Press to a syndicate which turned out to be Gadd, Cleary and Ellis, a carpet manufacturer from the North who wanted to become a power in the Press. Hooper and Fleet Street were confident that they would lose their money and that the *Argus* was done for. But the carpet manufacturer proved to have a plan. He had an interest also in a northern paper called the *Morning Sentinel* and three days later it was announced that it would be amalgamated with the *Argus*. This gave the *Argus* another three hundred thousand subscribers among a conservative population accustomed to an old-fashioned paper with which they were already bored, who were enabled thus to change their newspaper and take in a more exciting sheet without losing the self-respect belonging to thoroughly sound old-fashioned supporters of the old-fashioned *Sentinel*.

Meanwhile there were great economies in the working of the two papers together. Several of the *Sentinel*'s staff came in to the *Argus* office. Its editor took Hooper's place, and its foreign editor became deputy editor in London. It appeared that Cleary had warned Ellis against Hooper as a dangerous intriguer. Ellis, in any case a conservative northerner, accepted the make-up of the *Argus* as he found it because he had become used to it in the last six months, but he wasn't going to have any more changes.

[Next day in the Magistrates' court Syson was bound over to keep the peace.

Preedy did not return to the Pant's Road Mission. There were rumours that he was ill, and Jackman, at the committee's invitation, took the services.

Hooper with some difficulty found a new job, as an editor on *The Dispatch*, one of Lord Wittenham's papers. He started work on it the day that his daughter was born.]

63

When the criminal libel case against Syson was resumed, it had to be adjourned again because Preedy did not appear. Nevertheless it was featured on the front page of the *Leader*, together with full accounts of the former slander action.

There was a photograph of the Rodker girl, snapped as she came from work. Hooper saw again the thin oval face, the large startled eyes. Obviously the girl had had time to realize what was happening to her; she had been frightened. She had refused a statement, but the reporter described her minutely. He gave her address where she lived with her brother – and her place of work, where she was secretary to a Doctor Gale.

The brother Rodker made a confused statement, with references to his evidence in the first Preedy case, and in his own window-breaking case when he had declared that he had caught Preedy with his sister, and that she had had a child by him.

The morning papers left no doubt about the popular appeal of the case.

There were sixteen reporters round the front door of the Shaftesbury flats that evening. Alice Rodker saw them as soon as she turned the corner, and guessed at once what they were there for. But while she hesitated, they recognized her and came running. She was surrounded before she could escape. She looked round at the ring and obviously she was terrified. One of the men took off his hat and said, 'It's all right, Miss – don't be frightened.'

But she could not speak. A camera man held up his reflector and took a flash. His face showed his satisfaction as he glanced at the subject; he had caught that look of terror just in time, before it disappeared.

A young man tried again. 'We don't want to bother you, Miss, it's simply about that article in the *Leader*. Your brother's statement. We thought you'd like to say what you think.'

The girl flushed. She had lost her temper. She began to say that they had no right – what business was it of theirs – he had told a lot of lies –

The men crowded round. Nothing could have suited them better than this outpouring.

Suddenly Fred Rodker came pushing through the crowd and seized his sister's arm. He too was furious. 'Let her alone,' he bawled. 'Get out –' He dragged at the girl, who shook off his arm and turned again on the crowd. But it was only to abuse them, to say they were cowards and brutes. Two more cameras flashed; Fred tried again to drag the angry girl away. 'What do you think you're doing – talking to 'em. Let it alone.'

She struggled with him furiously. She was now hysterical and incoherent. But suddenly she broke away and ran towards the flats. The whole train pursued; reporters, sightseers, at least sixty people pushed through the doorway and climbed the stairs. Startled children flattened themselves against the walls; astonished tenants opened their doors and gazed.

The girl, winning the race, banged the door behind her. It was only after ten minutes that she opened to Fred; and some of the reporters had by that time gone away. But at least a dozen remained on the landing for another hour. In the morning there were nine waiting for the girl to go to work.

Fred came out with her, rushed her downstairs and put her in a taxi; the cameras however got a good shot of the couple diving into the taxi, a shot which to any unbiased observer said, 'Here are guilty fugitives.'

There were seven more reporters with two cameras waiting outside Dr Gale's surgery. Fred pushed her through. But three, one woman and two men, had had the same idea – they came as patients. Alice was no sooner in her office than a young woman came in to ask for an appointment. And then immediately began to talk sympathetically about the Preedy affair. How difficult for her. But surely Preedy had done her, Miss Rodker, a great wrong. Alice asked her if she was a journalist and she frowned and said, 'Free-lance,' and began a story of her difficulties. She was only just beginning and it was so hard to start. This was her big chance, and Miss Rodker could do so much for her. After all, what was the good of trying to hide things. It wasn't any good – if she refused to make a statement people would think the worst. Besides the thing would be written up anyway – and the Press didn't like people who refused to help. You couldn't expect it.

'You mean they'll invent things?'

'Oh no, but they'll give it all an angle – you know how it's done.'

'I'm sorry – I can't say anything. It wouldn't be fair.'

'Are you still in love with Preedy?'

'Please go away.'

'Can I say you're not prepared to give Preedy away?'

'No, no, no –' the girl seemed about to cry and then jumped up and told the woman to go or she would go.

'Excuse me but I think you're being stupid.'

'I can't help that.'

'It's not as though a statement can do you any harm. You needn't look at the papers yourself.' She was indignant and a little scornful. Her tone asked why this silly creature could not put up with a trifling inconvenience.

The doctor's bell rang for the next patient. Alice rushed into the corridor and found it crowded, but with journalists, sightseers. At the flats that night there were forty cars waiting, and a crowd of more than a hundred to see her making her way to the door. Again Fred came out to take her arm. He was still more excited. He kept shouting at the crowd, 'What do you want – can't you leave her alone? She hasn't done you any harm.'

Again there were reporters on the stairs. The woman of the morning had had a column in the *Evening Post*. She described Alice's nervous terror, her fear of saying anything against Preedy. The picture was of a young girl bewitched by a villain and still in his power.

The sightseers were on the landing also and the two other tenants whose doors were on that landing had complained to the janitor; he was waiting to tell the Rodkers that if this went on, they would have to find a room somewhere else.

'No, I know.' The man was apologetic, 'But people can't get to their own doors – the children can't get to sleep. It's not my fault either,' and he made a gesture meaning, 'It's just the way things are.'

'You can't throw us out,' Fred said. 'It's a wicked shame.'

The same evening Dr Gale was on the phone. He was sorry but he could not employ Miss Rodker any more. It was not a question of her character but simply the crowds at the consulting rooms. He couldn't get on with his work. He was sure she would agree that the situation was impossible. He would pay her a month's wages in *lieu* of notice.

Fred threatened an action; he would appeal to the health authorities; he would write to the papers. And he insisted that Alice should refuse the notice.

Alice asked him how they could afford a taxi every morning to take her to work. He answered that he had his Post Office money; and he was not going to be done down. He ordered the taxi again for the next morning.

But in the morning Alice had disappeared. She had apparently walked out very early before six when the janitor came on duty. For he had not seen her go. And the first reporter, Prince of the *Dispatch*, had not arrived till ten past six. He was much disappointed to hear that the quarry had escaped. 'I had a hunch she might bolt for it,' he said sadly. 'It's just what I expected. That's why I came early – I ought to have stayed all night. My wife told me I was a fool to come away last evening.' The poor young man, fresh from a country job, newly married, a clean-living young Briton, was in despair. He had had his great idea and failed to profit by it. Now he had to face his wife and confess that she had been wiser.

Fred Rodker went to the police; then he telephoned Hooper at the *Dispatch* office, but was answered as usual by a secretary that Hooper was out.

64

The attack on Preedy in the Press came as a surprise to the Pant's Road committee. The immediate result was to frighten the Allday-Hartree faction out of their proposal to invite Preedy to return and to make them resolve to continue with Jackman. Allday had called a general meeting for that morning, and had a speech all ready in Preedy's favour. But now he changed it to a sorrowful explanation of why it was impossible for them as

Christians to have any dealings with a man so unbalanced. 'I do not say he is a man given to evil – I deny the charge of hypocrisy brought against him in the Press – I believe him to be more sinned against than sinning. But it is impossible to deny the sin – and it is a terrible sin to ruin a child.' This address was received with nods of approval. Allday was much surprised when Marris got up at once and declared that they were playing a mean and contemptible game. What had Preedy done to make them change their minds? If he had sinned, it had been years ago, and they had known about it for months. They had known about it when they made their decision. All that had happened since was this attack in the Press. Were they going to run away from their convictions because of a Press stunt aimed only at the lowest instincts of the mob?

Mrs Hartree jumped up to declare that Preedy was a bad man. And what they had to consider was the Mission itself – that is to say, God's work. It seemed to her that the fall in the congregation was not due to any deficiency in Mr Jackman – it was the consequence of their own differences on committee. It was a scandal that they couldn't agree. But clearly the fault was not with Mr Allday or herself. They had tried their hardest for agreement – and so on, ending with the charge that the whole of their troubles arose from the two or three members who were determined to get their own way, even to the ruin of God's work. At this moment Gomm jumped up, and began to wave his arms and shout. Kerne got up also and tried to speak; Mrs Hartree, purple in the face, raised her voice to a scream, and Allday began to beat the table with his mallet.

When this had no effect, he got up and at once the whole committee except Marris got on their feet – some to support Mrs Hartree, and others Gomm. It turned out that Gomm had more supporters for Preedy than anyone expected; he had in fact been lobbying to very good effect. Suddenly he and his whole group walked out of the door. Marris then, after a little hesitation, rose from the table and followed them. There was so much noise by this time that no one heard exactly what Gomm said but it was clear that he wanted Preedy back.

Allday then collected the remaining committee members together, and they agreed to keep to their decision. Preedy would not be admitted again. He then advised his followers to go home and not to make any further statements, public or private, to members of the congregation. If they were left to themselves, they would soon disperse and he was prepared to bet that most of them would come down on the Jackman side. It was, in fact, a good thing that Gomm and especially Marris had gone and carried off the trouble-makers, because now the congregation was for the first time in months a united body.

But the meeting continued for another two hours and at the end had split into three more factions, one that wanted to abandon the Mission altogether, another that wanted Preedy back but under firm guarantees; a third that wanted neither Jackman nor Preedy, but 'a really keen young man, preferably married, with a real gift. We could advertise in the church papers and put a new all-electric kitchen into the church house.'

One member stood out against this. She was employed in the gas company and she wanted an all-gas kitchen; and being opposed went from that to a general attack on the whole project for a married man. Why not have a woman? This caused a new split. Two or three feminists deserted the Jackman group and joined the advocate of gas in a new party, pledged to a woman preacher and leader, who was prepared to take over the Mission house with the single improvement of a modern gas stove and two gas fires.

65

Gomm's party, when he left the Pant's Road Mission, numbered thirty-three all told. The difficulty was to find Preedy. He had disappeared from the lodging in Pant's Road, and was said to be somewhere in London. He had left no address for letters, and his last words to his landlady had been, 'If anyone comes to look for me here tell them I'm called to my work.'

On the Sunday, Joanna had a telephone call from him, asking her for Alice Rodker's address. She, thinking quickly, decided that he was the last person who should have it, and said that she didn't know.

'So you're not going to tell me. But you can give her this message from me – if she tells any more lies to the papers, I'll write to them myself.'

'What lies did she tell?'

'That I didn't seduce her – that I told a lot of lies.'

'Do you want to go to jail?'

But the man rang off. When Joanna told this story to Hooper, he remarked only, 'You were right there – he wants to go to jail. It's the big gesture – the only way he can get out in style.'

'Do you think he's that kind of person?'.

'Everyone is that kind of person – but most of 'em haven't the guts and imagination to act up to it.'

66

Turner, the chief reporter on the *Dispatch*, was annoyed with his young men. Lord Wittenham was interesting himself in the case, but the reporters had lost touch with the girl Rodker. She was obviously a first-class story; her photographs especially had been an enormous success. She took well; that is to say, she was not only pretty, with a good bust and a neat waist but her face was highly expressive; her feelings showed. Above all she looked very young, much younger than her age. All her pictures had had exciting character; the first, with the enormous terrified eyes, and the half-open mouth, like that of some animal which is at once frightened out of its senses, and ready to bite, had been acclaimed by experts.

Both Preedy and Alice Rodker had disappeared completely. Turner was exceedingly angry, and with some reason. 'Didn't I tell you they'd probably do a bolt for it?' he said to young Prince, who had been given the assignment. 'You fell down on the job, didn't you? All right – you can go. Or you'll go if you don't find Preedy in time for the first edition tomorrow.'

And this method worked. The young man, just promoted from a small Midland paper, didn't mean to lose his chance in London. After a frantic seven-hour search, visits to Preedy's lodging, to police stations, to chapels, to Jackman, to Kerne, to various members of the Pant's Road committee, he had the luck, in approaching Colonel Marris's flat, to see the Colonel coming out with a small suitcase in his hand.

Prince was a good reporter, intelligent and curious. He not only noticed detail and remembered it, but he could piece details together and draw conclusions. He remembered that Marris was a Preedy supporter, and he had noticed a case very like the one in his hand, a cheap green canvas one with patched leather binding, in the hall of Preedy's lodging. He guessed that the Colonel might be taking clothes or supplies to Preedy and followed him.

This was easy. Marris was quite unsuspicious. He travelled by bus to Waterloo and from Waterloo to Paddington, and then walked to a lodging house in a back street within a hundred yards of the station, one of those Paddington streets which are, more clearly than any others in town, long past caring even to look respectable.

Marris descended the steps into the area and knocked at the basement door, and Prince, peering over the railings, saw that his luck had turned. The face he saw when the door was opened was not Preedy's, but that of a young woman. And even in the bad light, he thought he recognized Alice Rodker.

He hesitated a moment. Should he send for a photographer? But he decided at once that it was too dangerous to go away even for a moment. He knocked at the door. To his surprise, it was opened at once by a man he did not know, an old man, bald and shaky.

'What do you want? Oh, you're a reporter. He's not here – come and look if you like.' And he opened the door on a large bare room with a stone floor and blackened ceiling, still little changed from its original state as kitchen. The grate and stove survived in its alcove; a heavy deal table, with a thick white top, like a butcher's slab, stood under the barred windows. It had probably been the original furnishing of the place, too heavy to move. Beyond this were two small chambers, once scullery and larder, now kitchen and bedroom. The bedroom contained a wooden couch, one chair, some shelves with hooks and a new suitcase.

Colonel Marris was in the first room. He greeted Prince with a warm handshake and apologized for not being able to help him. 'Mr Preedy has gone.'

'Do you know where?'

'No.'

'And Miss Rodker?'

'Miss Rodker?' with an air of surprise.

293

'I saw her at the door.'

'I don't think, do you know, you ought to bother Miss Rodker any more.' The old man suddenly grew angry. 'Why can't you leave the girl alone? Do you want to drive her mad? But I suppose you'd be quite delighted if she killed herself like that poor creature the other day. Hounded to death.'

The young man apologized. 'Of course not, sir, I'm sorry for her. But you know how it is, the public are interested – and one way or another they'll get the story. Better for her to talk now to me – just tell me quietly how she feels – than leave the thing to be turned into a stunt by some of the others. It's the best thing for her, sir, really it is.'

But the old man told him to go. 'It's no good your staying here. You can't see her and if you did, she wouldn't tell you anything.'

'She is here then?'

'Will you kindly get out or shall I send for a policeman?'

'I'm extremely sorry, sir – of course I'll go if you insist. But I think you'll find it's not in the best interests of Miss Rodker or Mr Preedy either.'

Prince then went upstairs, hired a small boy for sixpence to fetch him a taxi, and when the taxi arrived, sent by it a note to the *Dispatch* office asking for reinforcements to come to Murden Street.

67

It is true that Marris did not know where Preedy was, but he could guess very easily. For there was one piece of luggage missing from the lodging, which he had known to be in Preedy's possession; the only piece that he had brought away from Pant's Road. That was the folding pulpit which he used for his open-air preaching. Preedy had started already to carry out his intention, as explained to the committee, of taking the true and only God to the people.

As Hooper had said so shrewdly, it was probably necessary for the man both to break with his closest friends and go back on the stump. 'He needed new juice in his batteries.'

And Preedy, who had never forgotten that phrase, who had

referred to it often, graphically or scornfully, used it that afternoon, for the first time, in his address.

'A great man, as they think of great men nowadays, a man of power, a man who boasts that he thinks for millions, and blows their minds here and there like gnats on the evening breeze – this great powerful man said to me, "You preachers preach to yourselves. You preach God because you are devils. You preach the life of sacrifice because you need the kick of suffering. You take to Christ as drunkards take to drink, because your batteries are flat, and without juice you're dead."

'And when he said this he thought that he was destroying me – he thought that he was showing me to myself as a worthless person, a fraud, a madman, a self-deceived fool who could not even face the truth about himself.'

These words, shouted in Preedy's big voice, had already caught the ears of bystanders. Passers-by, even city men with rolled umbrellas, had stopped; listeners to other speakers deserted them or stood hovering between Preedy and the next two gatherings. There was already a crowd of thirty or more in front of Preedy and seeing it increase so rapidly, he exulted in his inspiration. He perceived now that God had put that opening into his mouth, and he elaborated it.

'What do you say, friends?' He paused, raised his arms in appeal and bawled aloud, 'What do you think of these words by a great man, a clever man, a teacher and leader of the people – a man with power over millions of homes, millions of parents with children at their knees eager to learn from them the truth of the world. Yes, a man responsible before God for millions of souls. Do you think it is true that Christ is the lord of devils and madmen who fly to him for peace as the lost and forsaken fly to drink and drugs for a moment of forgetfulness?

'Here is a man who hates and fears God, whose religion is money and power, who sacrifices Christ every day of his life, or begs others to do so, do you think he spoke truth when he called the ministers of Christ lunatics, sinners, evil-hearted men, fornicators and adulterers, driven to preach God out of terror and guilt, out of the wickedness of their souls?'

A voice from the back of the crowd shouted 'Yes,' and at once other voices joined in, 'That chap knew something.'

Preedy, as if astonished by these interrupters, threw back his head and hands and stood gazing. Someone at the back laughed.

Preedy let his hands fall. 'Yes, you say yes. And of course you're quite right. That man who spoke to me so, that clever man who said that men fly to God because they are devils, why, of course he was right. For who can save the guilty but Christ, who can purge the filthy mind, the defiled body, but he who is all cleanness, all purity? Who can take away the fear of death, but he who gives life, the life so rich, so proud, that death is but the shadow of its glory?

'I say that clever man, that great man, was right. He was righter even than he knew. It is not only the ministers and preachers of the world who are guilty, who carry in their hearts a fearful emptiness, a fearful question.

'Ask of yourselves. Ask of your own hearts. What do you find there of happiness, of security? You are well today, in good health? At least able to go about the world, to see, to hear, to enjoy food, to work. How long will that last? Till tomorrow? Till tonight? And now you have your jobs, wives and children whom you love. They are waiting for you now. How long will they be there to wait for you? How long will your happiness last? Do you think you are sure of your happiness – and what would you do if you lost it? Would you pity yourselves? Would you curse God? But why? What right would you have? Did you make this happiness? Did you invent this love? What have you done to deserve it, to deserve your health, your pay, your loves? What have you given for them? What have you done to earn them? Look in your souls and ask. Would you dare tell any man what you find there? Would you dare whisper it even to those who love you, to whisper it even in the dark – those secret thoughts, those secret desires, the cowardice and the lies, the tricks and the meanness, the selfishness and the greed? Would you even admit them to yourselves? Would you dare to tell the truth in your own mind? Would you not rather find the speck in your brother's eye than the cataract in your own? Of course you would. Everybody would. And that is why that man of power, that great and clever man was so eager to prove to me that the ministers of God are really men of the devil, men so wicked that they need God and cling to him as drowning men cling to a raft.

'He was right, why should he not be right? He is a clever man.

He has read all the books, he has studied logic. He can prove anything, he can make words do his every will. For him, they fly like birds, they dance like girls, they sing like angels, they wound like guns, they cure like the wisest doctors, they kill like the subtlest poison, sinking day by day into the secret places of the soul, creeping through vein and nerve, till a man is changed into a drivelling beast, a raving maniac.

'But see, the words take their revenge. The great man, the clever man, has swallowed his own poison. He has said to himself, "All men are sinners except myself – all men deceive themselves except me. I am too clever."'

The sky clouded over, swiftly, darkly. 'My brothers, men are prisoners of darkness in cells expecting execution – condemned cells. They interpret the world by its noises – jail noises – and react in their various ways, resigned, frightened, angry, sullen, defiant, or full of some crazy hope of escape, a reprieve, a revolution, a thunderbolt to split the wall, the end of the world or the beginning of the millenium.

'To each of them the world is simply a condemned cell where he is locked up alone. He knows his fellow prisoners only as distant and mysterious cries. All the affairs of the world come to him as the disconnected noises of a jail, incomprehensible, terrifying. He is lucky if he can distract himself with books or catching flies, call himself a philosopher for being callous and resigned, shut his ears to the screams from the torture chambers with their ingenious machinery for breaking bones and nerve. But most hear little else and carry on as best they can, because they must – some with bluster and defiance, some with –'

The inky cloud had blown over and suddenly the sun broke through. Preedy abruptly abandoned his argument and changed his tone and gestures. 'But God sends his light upon the world.' He raised his face to the sky and threw up his right hand, 'Like the sun that pierces the very earth. See the trees are standing bare and as if dead. To themselves they are dead. But the sun will not allow them to die. He sends his light to their roots, and there, unknown to the bare branches, the sap is rising, the life they deny is rising through their cells.

'So life rises in the souls of men, whether they would or not. And so the light of grace drives the sap through dead words and brings them to life, to a new harvest of beauty and at last the seed.

So some men by grace realize their living power and their death. But the clever men refuse the light because they are afraid – they live in a tent of words, they weave over their heads a roof of logic, with strong beams of science, and tiles of self-sufficiency, corrugated glass and concrete spite, so that they can live in the warm dark with the rats and the bugs.

'Why then did that great man, that powerful man come to me and say, "I know you – you are one who believes in God because of your need?" Because he himself was afraid, because he himself was in need. Because he was terrified of the light that would show him his mean little soul, the need that would make him cry out for forgiveness.'

A shadow slowly deepened over the group; a new cloud was coming up. A sudden cold gust blew from the Park. A drop of rain fell. It mildly disconcerted the preacher. He stopped and looked up. Someone laughed. But Preedy at once recovered himself. He raised his voice, he began to shout, to wave his arms.

'What was the meaning of that great man's words – the real meaning – when he said that the ministers of God were evil men –'

'What about Preedy?' a voice shouted.

The preacher stopped, and then smiled. He leant forward and folded his arms on the shelf of his platform.

'Yes, I am Preedy. Didn't I tell you that man was right? He said that I had to cling to God because of the wickedness I had done, because of the fearful guilt on my soul. And I said he was right. Of course he was right, my friends –'

Big drops of rain were falling fast, but no one had left – some, running from the communist meetings further along, had even stopped at Preedy's. Collars and umbrellas were going up, but for the moment the group was held.

'My friends,' he repeated, 'you have heard talk, often enough, of Christ the Saviour, and thought little of it. Just words – words. Too often repeated. But you see here a man who knows what they mean. Who has been saved from fearful crime, from the foulest wickedness, from jail, from misery, from the lowest pit.'

The rain suddenly thickened into a downpour, and the crowd began to melt. Preedy began to shout at the top of his voice, 'Let me tell you what I did –'

But already the whole gathering has run off except for three figures at the back. He recognizes Marris, Gomm and Alice Rodker.

Alice Rodker and Marris are standing by the kerb. He asks her, 'What are you doing here?'

'We brought your coat.' She held up the macintosh.

'Miss Rodker has come to join us,' said the Colonel.

'And sell us to the papers,' said Preedy.

'No, it's because of the way the papers have treated you that she's come back.'

'I told them it wasn't your fault,' the girl said. 'But they made it seem as if I was trying to let you off.'

Prince came up with a taxi and Preedy began to get in. Suddenly he stopped and looked at the sky. 'There's the sun again –'

'I'm afraid that's only a gleam.' Marris took one arm and the girl the other to help him into the car. The rain was growing more violent. He submitted to them. But as Prince was modestly following the Colonel, he noticed him and shouted, 'Who are you? A reporter?'

'Excuse me, Mr Preedy –'

'Go away – I've had enough of your people.'

The Colonel intervened. 'This gentleman has been very helpful – I think perhaps it would do no harm – in the changed situation.'

'What changed situation. It's not changed a whit. It's the same as ever it was –'

'May I state that Miss Rodker has rejoined you?'

'No, I know nothing about Rodker. She must make her own statement – take your foot out of the door.'

He pulled the door to with a crash, and Prince had just time to withdraw his foot and hand. Preedy was shouting at the driver, 'Go on, go on. What are you waiting for?' and the Colonel, fearful that Preedy would become uncontrollable in his excitement, nodded to the man. The taxi shot forward.

'Who's rejoined what?' Preedy said. He was sitting in the back seat next to Gomm. Rodker and the Colonel sat opposite.

'So – what are you doing here?'

'I brought your coat,' the girl repeated, knitting her thick brows.

The Colonel, alarmed, said hastily, 'Miss Rodker wants to come back to us.'

'Oh, does she?' But he could not hide his satisfaction. His mouth and cheeks set in a formidable look; he was once more the master.

'Have you told Jackman?'

'No, I've told no one at the Mission. I just thought I'd like to come back.'

'This is the Mission – and it's not a question of what people like. But what they ought to do.'

'All right, I thought I ought to.'

'I'm glad you admit that.'

She was silent, and looking at the frowning face, the thick lips, he recognized that obstinacy that had so often driven him mad. 'If you don't believe that,' he said, 'I don't know what you're doing here. You can go back where you came from.'

'She wants to look after you,' Marris said. 'And I think we ought all to be grateful to her. It is an act of great courage.'

'I don't need to be looked after.'

The girl made a visible effort and said, frowning, 'I was wrong. It wasn't your fault – I see that now and I'm sorry –'

'It's a bit late.'

'I'm sorry.'

'What about those lies you told – lies were printed and read by thousands of people.'

'I know – I'm sorry.' Tears suddenly showed in the girl's eyes and Marris intervened.

'She's come back.'

'Why did she go? To fight against the truth? – why did she sell herself?'

For a long time there was silence, broken only by an occasional sniff by Rodker. She was struggling with her breakdown. At last she took out a handkerchief and blew her nose.

'Joining with liars and crooks to fight against the truth – to ruin the Mission.'

'You've no right,' the girl flushed and glared. 'I'm not – I didn't –' she gave a sob, and at once recovered herself. She went on furiously. 'Why shouldn't I think – you were wrong – after what happened. That's all I said. I didn't print anything. I didn't know anything would be printed.'

'Miss Rodker was taken advantage of,' said Marris.

Preedy looked at him for a moment in surprise, and sank back in his seat. 'Yes, she was a tool – the instrument.' He gave his sudden laugh. 'The deadliest of weapons – the jawbone of an ass.'

'I may be a fool,' said the girl in a sulky voice, 'but I'm not a liar and don't you call me one. I won't bear it.'

'What about my taking you from your home.'

'That wasn't me – it was put in – it was lies. It's all been lies – everybody has been making up lies.'

'And so you want to come back to the Mission.'

'Yes – I ought never to have gone away. I lost my temper.'

'Better late than never,' said Preedy. And Marris, catching the girl's eye made a signal of approval and congratulation, a slight movement of hand and eyes, meaning, 'So that's all right – leave it there.'

But receiving in return a suspicious glance and a frown he began at once to talk about the disastrous state of affairs at Pant's Road; the congregation down to fifty and that remnant split into three sections.

He hoped to draw Preedy into this congenial subject, to direct him from his simmering anger against Rodker. But Preedy, lying back in his corner with arms crossed, seemed gloomy and silent. He made only one remark before the taxi drew up at the lodging house door.

'The sun again – I daresay that was the only heavy shower we're going to have today.' His voice rose as if he were going to laugh. All three looked at him in apprehension. But he did not laugh. He seemed to hold his breath for a moment, then gave a faint sigh, then looking from the window, he did laugh, 'Yes, just in time for the camera. Cover your face, Rodker.'

And in fact, among half a dozen persons standing at the door, there were two camera men. As the party descended from the taxi their bulbs flashed. Preedy and Marris paid no attention, but Rodker put her hands over her face.

68

Lord Wittenham decided, on seeing Prince's report, that this was front-page news – it had a perfect combination of love and religion, with a pretty girl and a parson, or almost a parson, which always takes. For the parson, the minister, still carries some of the mysterious aura belonging to a worker of magic; in the popular feelings he is still a man set apart, not merely by his pretensions to a special goodness, but by his powers. His private life is even more interesting than that of a duke. Lord Wittenham sent for Turner to find out how they were following it up.

Two *Dispatch* reporters were already sitting in Murden Street with the others, hoping to catch someone from the garrison, going in or out. But when Lord Wittenham was told of this, he answered that that was not good enough and he wanted that story or he'd know the reason why. Turner then remembered that Hooper had known Preedy and went to him. Couldn't he give one of his men a message to Preedy?

'I doubt if that would do any good.'

'This is important, the Guvnor has been in the office and he sent for me about it and he's in a sacking mood.' He looked at Hooper for a moment through his little steel spectacles and said, 'You haven't any personal objections?'

'What to?'

'You were a friend of Preedy's weren't you?'

'Certainly not. I'd get this story now if I could. I'd go myself.'

'That's a good idea. It would do you a lot of good with the Guvnor if you did get through. It's just the sort of thing he likes, an editor getting out for news. He'd probably ask you to dinner.'

Hooper fully understood this already and suddenly he said, 'Tell him he'll get the story. I'll get it now.'

Turner stared at him again and asked, 'Do you really mean that, because it might be just the thing to please him.'

'Yes, tell him I'll get the story, it's in the bag.'

'It's got to be a real story, you understand. You've got to be able to say that you've seen the man and talked with him.'

'Certainly, that's what I mean.'

At the moment Hooper had no idea how he was going to get to Preedy. He was startled by his own brashness in promising a story. Once more he had bet his life, and this had the usual exhilarating effect. It was perhaps the chief reason why Hooper was a newspaper man, because he liked to bet his life and to feel his courage respond.

When he made the promise he had not even thought of any means by which he could approach Preedy. As he went out, his first idea was to go to Marris. The Colonel was a sensible man and would see how useless it was to dodge the Press. But then he had a better idea. Joanna had been seeing Alice within the last week. She had kept up that mysterious friendship. Why shouldn't Joanna call on Alice and take him with her? If she got in he could get in. All that was needed was to get the door open, and he tapped on the window and told the man to stop at the next telephone box.

Joanna was at home, by good luck, but when he explained Alice's situation and said, 'You ought to go and see the girl,' she answered at once, vaguely, 'Why? If they're not letting anybody in.'

'You seem to have a good influence on her and she's getting herself into an impossible position.'

'You know she's always hated publicity.'

'She's got the publicity already, all that matters now is how it's going to be handled. But you're the only person who could make her understand that.'

'Why are you so keen all at once that I should interfere? You know I couldn't talk if she told me anything, it would be in confidence.'

'Look here, are you going to be at home now?'

'Yes, why?'

Hooper rang off and drove straight home. He found Joanna playing with Patty, with that patient amusement, that air of resignation habitual to her when she was doing anything with the child. It was as though she was amused by her own absorption in the baby, an affection so irrational and so certain to be disappointed. Her very smile discounted in advance all the happiness she might get from her maternal love.

And she had obviously been meditating on Hooper's message because she said at once when he came in, 'I suppose the *Dispatch* wants a story?'

'Yes, Wittenham himself has been on about it and they've got to have one.'

'Can't the sub-editors make one up?'

Hooper was always angered by such remarks from Joanna. He said once more briefly and sharply, 'We don't do things like that on the *Dispatch*. Wittenham won't have it and he's quite right. Readers can always smell what you call the made-up story and they don't like it.'

303

'But are you really asking me to go to Alice and interview her for the paper?'

'It would be a good thing for Alice if you could, but I'm not asking you. I know you wouldn't do it, not to save my life.'

Joanna knew at once by this remark and especially by his tone of disgust that he was about to make some such demand on her and would be furious if she refused. He was already angry, working up a grievance before he had reason for it. And this amused her as much as it annoyed her. She tickled Patty, who waved her legs and smiled briefly at the ceiling, and said, 'Would it really help Alice if I saw her? What ought she to know?'

'That it's always better to tell the whole story.'

'Do you really believe that?'

'Look here, Joanna, I've promised a story and I've got to get it. I will get it too. But it would be better for all parties if Alice saw you first. She trusts you and she'll talk to you. But what's the good – you've made up your mind. All right – all right –' as if Joanna had spoken, 'I know all about it – and I haven't any more time to waste.' He made for the door, but not very fast, and it was this deliberation which really made Joanna keep silence. She was amused by the man's methods as a bully, but more annoyed by their clumsiness. She let him go.

All the same, while he was still opening the door, she was impelled to say, 'But you haven't even told me what you want me to do.'

And she thought of her quarrel with Hooper when he had left her for weeks and seemed ready to leave her for ever, when she had realized the man's morbid pride.

She had said to herself then, 'He made a fool of himself and that's so humiliating for any man, especially with his woman,' and after all she had liked him all the better for a weakness which seemed to confirm her importance to him. But she hadn't forgotten her misery in those weeks while he was punishing her for seeing his weakness. And it was a sharp recollection of that misery, a sharp fear, that made her call out now.

Hooper merely threw over his shoulder, 'You know damn well,' and slammed the door. He was, she perceived with surprise, really angry – he wasn't just trying to frighten her. Even that little moment of opposition had enraged him and she saw at once that the thing was important for him. She rushed to the door as it was slammed in her face and pulled it open again, an effort requiring some force, for Hooper was still holding the handle outside and seemed inclined for a moment to do battle for the door. 'Oh, what an *ass* the man is,' Joanna thought, ready to laugh in his face. 'Really, what a baby –'

And, face to face with him, her lips were smiling, but with the expression of a little girl who has done wrong and knows it, a mischievous, appealing smile.

'What have I done?' she said. 'Oh, what have I done? I'd no idea – really – what is it about Alice? I wasn't really listening. Is it something important?'

Half an hour later Joanna and Hooper were on their way to Murden Street. Hooper had expected a crowd at the house but he was astonished when he saw the street. A crowd queued as if for church, a long train, four deep, of quiet, decent-looking people of both sexes, but mostly young, and gazed at all that could be seen from a distance, the upper windows of 19. Sometimes, as if differing about which windows in the long row actually belonged to No. 19, they were seen discussing the matter, pointing. And when the policeman came their way they would ask him, and he would obligingly indicate the right windows. Then they would fix their eyes on these windows and keep looking, in case of losing them again.

But as, in the progress of two miles an hour, they approached, they would begin to bend sideways, peering towards the basements. Their faces grew taut with the expression of those who know that a great, a unique moment is approaching and that they must concentrate their powers of attention – the same faces, in fact, that can be seen among pilgrims visiting a shrine, as they are shepherded towards the reliquary.

At the actual spot there was a certain amount of disorder. Everyone wanted to stare down the basement at once, to extract from it the last ounce of meaning, of thrill, and some of the pilgrims, having seized the railings and craned their necks, simply could not tear themselves away. They were like creatures in a trance, mesmerized. It was one policeman's sole job to clear these railings, and it was a difficult and unpleasant job. The crowd, patient enough before, now grew rebellious; that is to say, certain members of the crowd, the more emotional, the more moved, or perhaps those who had not got so much reaction as they expected

305

and wished to stay for more, became exceedingly tricky to handle. Indeed, it was dangerous, strictly speaking, to handle them at all. One woman in a tattered fur coat, an old woman, who had clung for at least three minutes and was causing a block, being tapped on the shoulder by the policeman, at once turned on him and began to scream abuse. Don't he dare touch her. What right had he to pull people about?

And she had a good deal of support from others. There was already plenty of resentment both in the queue waiting and in those who had been moved on and were now dispersing. Why shouldn't they go where they liked and look where they liked? It was a free country, wasn't it?

But the majority were patient, good-natured and neutral. They didn't mind being pushed about, so long as they got their two minutes of thrill. They laughed at the old woman who made a fuss. She was obviously one of those crack-pots who always want their own way, who have a thing about liberty.

Even this patient majority found one cause of complaint and repeatedly brought it to the attention of the policeman. When, coming near the steps, they saw that the steps themselves, and the whole narrow basement area between the coal hole under the steps and the dustbin opposite, was crowded with watchers, their good-humoured expressions changed. They fussed and grew indignant. Who were these favoured persons? What were the police up to? Had they heard about equality before the law – not on your life. There was dirty work here, bribery, snobbery, privilege.

When Hooper and Joanna were admitted at once, and the policeman actually opened the gate for them to pick their way down the steps among the seated congregation, there were cries for a long way down the line. One man, a dark young man in pince-nez, broke into the road and came running. He was furiously excited, 'Who are those you're letting in? I've been waiting an hour. I'll report you to Scotland Yard. It's a scandal.'

'Press,' said the policeman, shortly.

'Oh, Press.' The young man collapsed at once, and returned to his place. He was not so much abashed as satisfied. He explained to his neighbours and they nodded. They too were appeased. The little rebellion died as it had started, in waves all down the line; the indignation, the shouts, diminished as the news was passed along, 'The Press.'

In fact, there were a good many in the basement who were not Pressmen. Hooper, making a way for Joanna, putting his foot cautiously between one of the *Dispatch* reporters and a photographer, sharing a single step, recognized on the top step as he turned to give a hand to Joanna, Gomm and young Darley sitting together, and greeted them with a nod and a smile, to which neither responded. Darley indeed looked both startled and angry.

Hooper, leaning over the photographers, explained himself. 'My wife knows the girl. She's hoping to get her away. She called her up. If only we can get in – you can get Marris, can't you.'

Darley at once jumped up, eager to be helpful. And he was certainly useful, first in getting the Hoopers through the mass below and the crowded passage beyond, and then at the door of the flat. He had an understanding with Marris and began by scribbling a note on a scrap of paper and pushing it through the letter slit in the door. He then put his fingers through the slit and rattled the flap beyond in a regular rhythm which sounded like code.

'Morse,' said Hooper.

'Yes, Morse.'

'A good idea.'

'We had to make some arrangement. They were rattling the letter box all the time; and we've cut off the bell.'

As Joanna stood at the door, Hooper pressed close to her and she realized that he intended to come in with her, and also that this question whether he intended to come in or not had been deliberately avoided by both of them. The understanding was that Joanna would try to persuade Alice, for her own sake, to give a statement for the Press, and she had assumed, or tried to assume, that this arrangement meant that she would go in alone.

Now she perceived her cowardice in avoiding this vital point. She was shocked at herself and said to Hooper, 'They won't want you to come in with me.'

'We'll see,' said Hooper, and his look defied her. 'After all, that's my affair.'

Joanna hesitated. She was determined that Hooper should not use her as a stalking horse, but she tried to pick some phrase that would not rouse his temper, and before she could hit on a suitable form of words, the door was opened six inches on a chain. The Colonel's face appeared in the crack and he asked her what she wanted. Then recognizing her he said, 'I am sorry, Mrs Hooper, but we're not letting anyone in. The Missioner gave strict orders not to admit the Press and he doesn't wish to make any statement.'

'I came to see Miss Rodker,' Joanna said.

'My wife is a friend of Miss Rodker's,' Hooper said.

At the same moment Alice's voice was heard. The Colonel looked round and then cautiously unchained the door. Alice pushed eagerly past him and drew Joanna into the room. She embraced her warmly, she was pretty in her pleasure. 'Oh, I was praying you'd come, but I didn't like to ask you. It didn't seem fair to bring you into all this trouble.'

They were interrupted by an argument between Hooper and the Colonel. As Hooper had pushed in behind Joanna, the Colonel hastily shut the door on his chest, and looked inquiringly at Joanna, as if to say, 'Did you mean to bring him in?'

'It's all right, Colonel, I came with my wife. You needn't pay any attention to me, and I may be of some use to the Missioner, but it's entirely up to him if he sees me.'

The Colonel still held the door and now he looked again at Joanna, and Joanna nodded her head to him.

'You're answering for him?' the Colonel said.

'Oh, I suppose so.'

The Colonel, with a very reluctant air, then opened the door another inch or two to allow Hooper to pass. Gomm and Darley followed in behind and the Colonel immediately closed the door.

Alice scarcely seemed to notice the man; she was too excited by this visit from her friend. She was still holding her hand like a child her mother's. 'You do understand, don't you?' she said.

'Wouldn't you like to get away now? You could come away with me at once. We can't talk here.'

'Oh, but I can't leave, not less Mr Preedy comes too. And he's not well.'

'I see. But surely you could leave him for a moment. You must hate all this fuss.'

'I can't help that, I came to be with Mr Preedy and to look after him.'

'You feel it a duty,' Hooper said, 'or did the Missioner send for you?'

The girl, startled, looked at Hooper for a moment and said, 'I suppose you want that for the paper.'

'Well, you know, if you take my advice, you'll let the papers know where you stand. It will save you a lot of trouble in the end.'

The girl stared a moment, frowned angrily, and then jerked her shoulder. 'Oh, I don't care what they say. They'll say it anyhow.'

Marris, hovering uneasily about the group, said suddenly in a low voice, 'I think the Missioner is asking for you.'

The girl made an exclamation and disappeared through one of the doors at the inner and darker end of the room. As the door closed behind her, Joanna turned on Hooper. She was relieved by Alice's last remark, which seemed to make her less guilty.

She said to Hooper, 'Won't that do? After all, you've had an interview, you've got a story.' Hooper did not answer and Joanna said, 'You can fill it in with description, the scene and the people here and the atmosphere. How the poor girl looked and spoke.'

But she saw that Hooper did not like even this small amount of chaff. He was still in his obstinate mood. Marris and Gomm closed in. Marris said in his tentative manner, 'I didn't understand, Mr Hooper, that you came as a representative of the Press. I didn't even understand that you intended to come in.'

'I'm not going to give away anything private,' Hooper said. 'I'll go out now if you like.'

'It's a bit too late,' Gomm said.

'Perhaps you had better go,' Marris said.

'Very well,' said Hooper, but making no move towards the door. 'But I wonder why you are so keen to hide the facts of this case. Why you are so frightened of the truth. I know, of course, that a lot of people nowadays are all against the truth – they want a censorship – in the Spanish or Eirish style – they would like to shut up the free Press altogether. And just push out propaganda to the people, any sort of lie that suits them.'

Hooper spoke with conviction and, in fact, he did feel that he was in the right. Perhaps he knew also that he had to feel it, but he certainly convinced himself.

'I don't see,' said the Colonel, in his grave way, 'that this justifies you coming into a private house.'

'If you knew what was good for you, you'd be very glad of the chance of giving an account, a true account, of the situation from your point of view. If you refuse any statement, of course, that's your own affair. You have a perfect right to do so. But you won't have a right to complain of the stories that get printed. You know there will be stories. Anyone has a right to give an account of what he's seen in the street, of what he knows about the affairs of the Mission, yes, and of Mr Preedy too, and can put any interpretation he chooses on the whole affair. I suppose you don't want to stop that, to stop every sort of liberty and free comment in this country. But if you don't want to stop it, the right answer is to give the right account. You can be sure I'll give it. All this stuff about the wicked Press is so much cant, or worse.'

'Worse,' muttered Marris.

'Yes, by people who have reason to fear the truth – the facts – who've got something to hide, who –'

Loud shouts from the back of the room, a sudden cry and the sound of a fall, stopped him in mid-sentence. Marris and Gomm ran towards the door. Hooper, after a moment's hesitation, followed them. The shouts, the blow and the fall had come from Preedy's room. But when Marris pulled at the door, it proved to be locked.

69

Preedy had not, in fact, called Rodker. That was an invention of the Colonel's to get the girl away from the dangerous presence of Hooper. Preedy, walking about his little crowded room in a fever of anger and despair, had forgotten about Rodker, and when she had come into the room, stared at her as if he had never seen her before.

'What do you want here?'

'*You* wanted *me*.'

He turned his back on her and began to stride about.

'Have you taken off your shoes?' she said. 'They were soaking.'

'No.' But he sat down on the bed and held up a foot. He had remembered that this young woman, whose desertion and treachery had done him so much injury, was now repentant. She had returned to the fold and taken him again for her master.

'You told my congregation that I was a fraud and a crook. Are you going to let that stand?'

'No, and I didn't say those things.'

'You said I had no right to preach.'

'No, I didn't – you know I didn't.' She struggled with the boot and her tears at the same moment; her anger with the stubborn boot distorted her face and made the tears jump. She said grimly, 'You're as bad as the papers.'

'Come,' said Preedy, suddenly moved by this creature's distress. Perhaps he remembered that he had loved her once, loved her as a woman, as herself. 'Come – don't get excited. I'm not blaming you – you lost your head, and you know that temper is not your strong point.'

The boot came away at last and she felt the sock. 'You're soaking – you ought to change everything.'

'You meant I was a fraud – or at least that I was a fool.'

'I know what a doctor would say – have you any dry things here?'

'Doctors, doctors – I should have thought you'd had enough of the doctors.'

But he allowed her to peel off socks, trousers. He was exhausted and he enjoyed this mothering, by a woman who was now completely his in body and soul.

'That was your trouble,' he said, 'you had the Hooper disease. You had no faith. You didn't believe in God.'

'Have you any pyjamas here?'

'You denied God,' he said, angrily, arguing not with her, but with the everlasting enemy, the shadowy devil of frivolity. And as she tried to pull off his shirt, he held down his arms, fighting against the world that had tried to make a puppet of him, to mouth its grey meaningless phrases.

'You hated God,' he said, 'because he was God – because he made you feel small – because of his majesty and glory.'

'You know I never did,' she muttered, struggling to pull off the shirt. 'I believed all the time.'

He stared at the sullen, flushed face, the swollen eyelids, the small bulging forehead that expressed so much obstinacy, and again he perceived the woman. He remembered her obstinacy, even in love, even in passion; it was, in fact, more than half true that it was she who had seduced him, who had insisted on being taken, who had defied him not to take her, who had put him into such a position that he could not tell whether the act had been more his or hers. And he remembered the long bitter battle before she had submitted to bring the child to him; he remembered again that day when she had sat with Hooper and seemed to approve Hooper's argument.

'The love of God,' he said, 'England, home and beauty. The God of the tabloids – the God that made his temple of an archbishop and his archbishop of a temple. The vain little God in a cage – you give him sugar and he'll sing to you.'

She tugged at the shirt and said, 'Do you want to be ill again?'

'That was your God,' he said, letting his arm rise. The shirt came off with the vest, he sat naked with his hollow hairy chest, his thin arms. 'You whored after a lie.'

He stared at her while she brought the pyjama jacket and held it out for him to put on.

'The God that never does anything – never upsets anyone – lets the sick die – and the liars flourish – the God who shudders at the very idea of a miracle. So unscientific.'

'Do you want to catch your death?'

'That's as God wills – my God – and your God.'

'Put it on and talk afterwards.'

'And your God. Your God now. He is your God –'

She tried to put his hand in the sleeve but he held it stiff and stared into her face. He was suspicious, he recognized that sullen obstinate look. 'My God – the real God – the God who judges, who punishes, who saves – the kind of the world – the omnipotent – you believe in him now.'

She was silent, her thick under-lip stuck out. Preedy, jerking at her grip, shouted, 'Are you playing with me – do you believe or don't you?'

'Afterwards –'

'What did you come here for – to make a fool of me – to spit your lies in my face? Let go of me.'

'You can't sit there naked.'

'Let go of me.' He was yelling now in his rage, and suddenly he struck her in the face, hurling her across the room against the wall, where she fell. She was up again in a moment and back at the bed, but he shouted at her, 'Go away – get out – whore – bitch.'

It was at this moment that Marris and Gomm came bursting in. They stared with amazement at Preedy naked by the bed, abusing the girl, and the girl's flushed face. Blood was running

312

from her nose and her left cheek was swelling so that the left eye had almost disappeared.

'What is it?' Gomm said, fussing. 'What's happened?'

'Nothing. He didn't want to go to bed.' She brushed past them into the other room. Joanna gave an exclamation, Hooper took her arm. 'My poor girl – what did he do to you?'

She was excited. 'I just don't believe like he does – why should I?'

'Why should you indeed. And he hit you.'

'It's not as though I want to interfere with him believing anything he likes.'

'You must come away at once – come home with us,' Joanna said.

'But I came to look after him. I've got to look after him – no one else is doing it. And he's really ill.'

'It's not even safe for you to stay here,' Hooper said.

'Oh, I can manage. He's like that. He won't kill me.'

She looked at the pair with a new expression, a new realization came into her face, that is to say on the undamaged side. 'You needn't worry about me,' she said, 'I'm all right. I can make it. I've got straight again and I can take anything.'

There was a tinkle of broken glass and at once the flash of a bulb startled them. Hooper jumped and looked round, to see a camera and reflector thrust between the curtains of the window.

'Oh, no,' Joanna cried and Hooper turned to the girl,' I didn't arrange that,' he said, and Joanna was going to apologize. Only an apology seemed unnecessary to her, it was too trivial in the circumstances. She had behaved too badly for any apology. She had not believed herself capable of such treachery and yet she was not altogether surprised at it. She had, after all, no confidence in herself any more than in anyone or anything. It was stupid to trust anyone or anything.

'I am so sorry, Alice,' she began.

But the girl interrupted, 'It's all right, I don't mind. Let him shoot. I don't care now. You'd better go and print it all. I don't care for anything you say – or anything you do.'

She tossed her head at them, with the universal gesture of the person who defies the world, the glance of a free soul.

The camera flashed again. She turned and marched back into Preedy's room.

'And that's that,' said Hooper. 'Come on, dear – we can't do anything here.' He took Joanna's arm and urged her towards the door. He looked at his watch. He had time to get the story down. But he wanted plenty of time. What a wonderful story. Please God that reporter with the camera was a *Dispatch* man. What a shot if it came off, if it showed that fearful eye, the bleeding and swollen lips and the poise of the head. Wonderful, wonderful. My God, human nature was a wonderful thing. You couldn't beat it. A little floozy like that out of some slum, or worse, some evangelical terrace, and she throws off phrases like that, 'Now I'm straight –' what was it? It's not too easy to make these things up. You think you can – but you can't.

They were pushing through the crowd in the passage; outside a photographer, recognizing Hooper, held up his camera. He was grinning and Hooper shouted at him, 'Come along now.' He didn't recognize the fellow; possibly he was a free-lance man. But the *Dispatch* must have first option on that snap.

He saw it in the paper – the swollen black eye, the blood stain from nostrils to chin. And even if it was a failure as a snap, what an easy job for the retouchers to black out an eye and put a black line down the chin. Which eye was it – let's see.

The man was pushing through. The crowd of disgusted Pressmen seemed unwilling to give him way. But Hooper waited, he wasn't going to let the fellow out of his sight.

Joanna said suddenly, 'But it won't be any good. You couldn't show her with that awful eye.'

This was overheard by half a dozen men standing or sitting on the steps. They stared at Joanna with the amused faces of professionals before the naïveté of an amateur.

'What do you mean?' Hooper flushed with irritation; he hated this public indignity. 'We have the facts – facts don't lie.'

'Of course they can lie. If you pick them out in bits. And they're a lie if you use that picture – a wicked, cruel lie against that poor man.'

The photographer had pushed through at last. He gazed with surprise at Joanna's flushed face, at the mysterious quarrel.

But Hooper said at once, '*Dispatch*?'

'No, free-lance. But I got two good shots then – she was right in the bullseye.'

'I may want those shots. I'm *Dispatch*. We'll go round now at once.'

'Sorry. Can't wait. Take 'em now – or never. This is a scoop. And I'd get fifty at an agency.'

'Did you deliberately break the window?' Joanna asked.

He laughed. 'Not exactly. It got broken. People pushing. But I took the chance of getting my camera snatched.'

'Come,' said Hooper. 'I'll take it – fifty –'

'I didn't say fifty to you. Sorry. But the agency would give me a rake off on reprints.'

'Damn it, what do you want?'

Hooper was thoroughly upset by this extraordinary rudeness in Joanna. What abominable manners to speak to her husband like that in public, possibly before some of his own employees. She was impossible. Why did he put up with her? But at this moment Gomm and Darley came hurtling out of the door. Darley seemed crazy with rage; he was shouting, 'Where is the bugger – it's you is it?' He rushed at the photographer and snatched at the camera; there was a violent struggle. Hooper tried to pull the boy away; Darley suddenly struck Hooper in the neck, knocking his hat off. 'He broke the window,' Darley was screaming. 'It's a police case.'

'Don't knock *him* about,' Gomm said. 'He's only the stooge. This is the man you want. This is the boss who sells the dirt – and sells men for dirt.'

He was perhaps even more enraged than Darley, but he kept his head. He spoke loudly and clearly – to be heard not only by every man in the basement area but by the staring crowd above. 'Mr Hooper – look at him – the millionaire who sucks the public bum – the dirtiest man on earth.'

Hooper after his moment's anger, recovered himself. He saw at once how to handle these angry boys.

'My dear chap,' he said. 'If you think that, you don't know much about the British public or the newspaper business either. All they want is the facts and they have a certain reasonable suspicion of people who want to hide the truth. As for bums, I am, it's quite true, a servant of the public – I study their pleasure – but their pleasure is the truth.'

'And what do they get?'

But Hooper was pushing Joanna up the steps, followed by the

315

photographer. The *Dispatch* man at the railings had already brought a car. They climbed in and drove away.

The photographer, still much ruffled, examined his camera. 'The silly swine – what did he think he was playing at.'

Hooper was suddenly tired and disgusted. He wished he hadn't to ride with this fellow. He looked at Joanna, dreaded another attack from her. He said, 'That young Darley – I don't know why he should take that line. But I suppose you would agree with him.'

Joanna was reflecting. She gave a slow sigh, then turned to him. 'No, I'm sorry – I'd forgotten Lord Wittenham – you can't really help yourself.'

For a moment he asked himself if he could take another line. If, for instance, he could describe the girl Rodker as really the stronger party; as a person of remarkable character who had come back to Preedy simply because it seemed to be the right thing to do and to whom that black eye was of no importance whatever. Who had perhaps even originally been more seducer than seduced. Though, of course, he could not exonerate Preedy. He could emphasize Preedy's cruel, or at least thoughtless and irresponsible action in allowing a girl of that age and that reckless character to sacrifice herself. It could be interesting.

But no, he could hear the reporters in the Press telling the tale of the photograph of the year, suppressed by The Professor.

And after all, wouldn't they be right? What did the *Dispatch* readers want, a piece of psychological analysis? A complicated story of mixed motives leaving them to make out their own judgements? It was crazy even to imagine it.

No, there was only one story here – the poor little girl seduced and ruined by a parson who then proceeds to murder her baby, who has such power over her still that he recalls her to his side and beats her up as a reward. And the poor little victim, besotted with love or terror, takes it. One could suggest perhaps that she likes being beaten; always a popular line. Really, whatever Joanna might think, there was no choice. And a good thing too. Yes, the story of the year.

MORE ABOUT PENGUINS, PELICANS
AND PUFFINS

For further information about books available from Penguins please write to Dept EP, Penguin Books Ltd, Harmondsworth, Middlesex UB7 0DA.

In the U.S.A.: For a complete list of books available from Penguins in the United States write to Dept DG, Penguin Books, 299 Murray Hill Parkway, East Rutherford, New Jersey 07073.

In Canada: For a complete list of books available from Penguins in Canada write to Penguin Books Canada Ltd, 2801 John Street, Markham, Ontario L3R 1B4.

In Australia: For a complete list of books available from Penguins in Australia write to the Marketing Department, Penguin Books Australia Ltd, P.O. Box 257, Ringwood, Victoria 3134.

In New Zealand: For a complete list of books available from Penguins in New Zealand write to the Marketing Department, Penguin Books (N.Z.) Ltd, Private Bag, Takapuna, Auckland 9.

In India: For a complete list of books available from Penguins in India write to Penguin Overseas Ltd, 706 Eros Apartments, 56 Nehru Place, New Delhi 110019.

Joyce Cary

MISTER JOHNSON

'Mister Johnson is a young clerk who turns his life into a romance, he is a poet who creates for himself a glorious destiny . . .'

A temporary clerk, still on probation, Mister Johnson has been in Fada, Nigeria, for six months and is already much in debt. Undaunted, he entertains on the grandest scale, with drums and smuggled gin. Not only that, he intends to pay a small fortune for a wife . . .

'Cary's insight into the springs of human feeling and action is so penetrating and so revealing that I do really believe that he is in the very next rank to the greatest of them all . . . What makes him a life-enhancer is the overwhelming sense the reader gets from him that the universe, for all its horrors and inexplicabilities, makes sense – obvious and glorious sense' – Bernard Levin in *The Times*

'A beautifully written, absorbing story which, I trust, will serve to bring many new readers to this magnificent novelist' – Howard Spring in the *Sunday Times*

MIDSUMMER NIGHT MADNESS
Sean O'Faolain

'One salutes, in these stories, an immense creative humour as broad in speech as Joyce's gloom' – Graham Greene

Alight with a young man's idealism in *Midsummer Night Madness* (stories about the Troubles), or turning his ripening genius to the Irish character and Catholicism in *A Purse of Coppers* and *Theresa* – Sean O'Faolain's prose is by turns lyrical, exuberant, austere, and his stories, the cream of Irish writing this century.

'He is the founding father – after James Joyce and together with Frank O'Connor – of the great and thriving Irish short story tradition' – Susan Hill

NO COUNTRY FOR YOUNG MEN
Julia O'Faolain

The Irish Civil War of the 1920s has left its mark on four generations of the O'Malleys and the Clanceys – above all on Sister Judith Clancy, a half-mad seventy-five-year-old nun. Dwelling on her experiences during the Troubles, she has withdrawn into a kaleidoscopic world of half-remembered visions. A recurrent nightmare haunts her, something dark and dangerous, a buried trauma that is slowly reshaping in her scattered mind . . .

'Skilfully spun and splendidly readable, it is illuminated by a seriousness that is refreshing to encounter . . . gripping and moving and very apt as Ireland's troubles continue into the '80s' – William Trevor

'One of the very best books of its kind that it has ever been my pain and pleasure to read' – Robert Nye

'A marvellous novel' – John Braine